EYEWITNESS

Eugene M. Koon

WESTBOW·
PRESS
A DIVISION OF THOMAS NELSON
& ZONDERVAN

WestBow Press books may be ordered through booksellers or by contacting:

WestBow Press
A Division of Thomas Nelson & Zondervan
1663 Liberty Drive
Bloomington, IN 47403
www.westbowpress.com
1 (866) 928-1240

ISBN: 978-1-4908-6037-4 (sc)
ISBN: 978-1-4908-6038-1 (hc)
ISBN: 978-1-4908-6036-7 (e)

Library of Congress Control Number: 2014920480

Printed in the United States of America.

WestBow Press rev. date: 1/19/2015

PROLOGUE

"Get out of my way!" Lucifer snarled as he waved his hand in a dismissive gesture toward the two guardian angels at the threshold of Heaven. "I have important business with your Lord, and I do not wish to be detained." The guards stood fast, spears crossed, no words spoken, restraining Satan and his band of demons. Satan brought his faces inches from the guard trying to break their will. He knew, however, no one would enter without permission from God.

"Must I ring the doorbell in order to gain admittance to meet with your Master?" spoke the Prince of Darkness in a sarcastic, irreverent tone. When the guards did not move, he began pacing, snarling, and wringing his hands.

Satan changed tactics as he tried tempting them to abandon their post and join him. "I can put you in a greater position than gatekeeper." He stood facing them, his eyes shifting between the unmovable guards. "Oh come now, don't tell me you've never thought about doing something that might be looked upon as evil. Everybody has thought about this kind of thing at one point or another, even the angels of heaven. Do you think you are better than the rest of your righteous comrades? Why you are nothing more than. . ."

Thunder crashed, silencing Satan for a moment. The sound reminded Lucifer the Almighty God is omnipresent and will not allow irreverence in the kingdom.

"Oh, what does His Majesty want now?" He threw back his head and sighed. "I tell you this; he is always on my back about everything I do. He even screams at me for the things I don't do. Satan, why did you do this? Satan, why did you do that? It gets so frustrating and really monotonous day after day after day, for centuries without end!" The demons behind him bellowed with laughter at the wild gestures and mocking voice. Satan turned and shot them a fierce look and they scattered looking for a place to hide.

No matter how he tried to manipulate the guards, he would not be allowed to enter. Patience, at this moment was not a virtue Satan possessed. His eyes constantly looked toward a building appearing brighter than the sun. His frustration continued to build.

"Look, it's just over there, only a few feet from here. Let me go over there and just wait outside the door. I'm sure he wouldn't mind if I did that. In fact, he would be grateful if I were to be there quicker so he may be rid of me sooner. Don't you think your Master would be grateful to you for your initiative? Why, he might even reward you and promote you for your efforts. I only wish he would make a decision to let me have this audience or not."

The powerful guards remained solid as statues.

Deafening thunder once again roared throughout the kingdom. The display of holy power even caused the mighty Satan to tremble, if ever so slightly. To those inside the gates of heaven it brought joy and praise with voices raised to honor their Creator. Outside heaven, Satan's demons covered their ears and fell to their knees in terror, fear, and reverence. Only Satan continued standing in front of the guards.

"Is he going to allow me to pass this day or what? I do have other pressing engagements on my schedule." Satan's voice sounded exasperated. "It is imperative I have this audience with your Master this day. I must insist he allow me to enter the Kingdom and go before his throne immediately. I have my petitions to be heard. If I am not allowed entry, there will be trouble somewhere in the world." Satan laughed, knowing trouble had already begun in the world, his world.

"After all, I am the Prince of the Power of the Air, the Master of Evil in the entire Universe." He drew within a hair's breadth from the guard. "I made that one up myself! Now will you let me in?"

Thunder boomed, along with a blinding flash of lightning directly over Lucifer, to remind him he stood on holy ground. Satan hissed but understood this and bowed, not in respect, but with the hatred he held in his heart for all things holy.

"May I now enter?"

The guards uncrossed their spears and allowed Lucifer to pass through the gate alone. Once Satan had passed, the gatekeepers stood firm with their spears crossed. The band of demons would not be allowed to enter. When they realized this, they fluttered off as they muttered under their breath.

As Lucifer approached the building, another large and powerful angel confronts him. Satan recognized him as one of his former colleagues.

"Oh, now what?" Sighing, he threw his arms out and stomped around muttering and mumbling under his breath. He spun around and through gritted teeth said, "I'm growing weary of all the delays."

The angel stood in his way, remaining silent until the rant is over.

"Will you please let me see your Master? I have other things to do today."

Michael, the archangel, replied, "We will enter together, Lucifer. You will give reverence to the Most Holy God or you will be removed from his presence. Do you understand?" The archangel's voice growled in all seriousness. "Heed the words my Lord has instructed me to tell you, Lucifer."

"Yes, I understand," Lucifer answered hastily. "Now let's go please. I've been detained outside long enough." He gestured with a wave of his hand as turned toward the door. They entered the building side by side and made their way down a corridor, where they approached two large doors.

When Satan entered, he sensed the power in the great hall. Although he sneered as he entered, he could feel the awesome glory and majesty throughout the throne room. A host of angels, elders, and people from all walks of life worshiped and praised their Lord with songs and shouts of praise. Satan stopped himself as he almost joined in the praise.

Large beasts each with six wings shouted, "Holy, holy, holy Lord God Almighty, which was, and is, and is to come." They flew around the great room giving God glory, honor, and praise. As they shouted, elders in white robes fell down before the throne, and worshiped him who lives forever and ever, casting their crowns before the throne saying, "You are worthy, O Lord, to receive glory and honor and power: for you have created all things, and for your pleasure they are created."

The praise and worship swelled with power forcing Satan to his knees. Michael, already kneeling before the throne, gave praise to his Lord and Master. Eventually a silence fell over the room.

Choral voices continued to sing praises to God accompanied by an orchestra somewhere in the kingdom. A roll of thunder rhythmically made its way through the room.

"The Master has stated that..."

"I know what he said," chided Satan. "Need I remind you I once ruled over you? Now, I wish to speak directly to the Master if I may."

"You will wait here." Michael turned from Lucifer to face the pure, white throne. He spoke with great reverence to the Almighty God. "My Lord, Lucifer has come before your throne requesting to have an audience with you. He states his business as urgent. What is your desire, my Lord?"

Thunder rumbled as the Almighty spoke to Michael.

"Yes, my Lord." The archangel turned toward Satan. "The Lord has granted you permission for this audience. You may speak, but bear in mind you will give him reverence or be removed. Do you understand?"

"Oh, thank you so very much." The reply dripped with sarcasm. "As if I don't know the rules around here!"

Lucifer turned to the throne. "How can you do such a thing as keep me from a soul? Do I not rule the air in which this mortal being exists? Why have you done this to me? Am I not the Prince of the Power of the Air? How am I to face my minions if I cannot show them I have the authority to rule over them? I do believe you have given me the authority to allow my army of demons to do as they please on the earth as long as I do not try to possess one of your precious saints." Lucifer made air quotes as he said precious.

He continued as he paced before the throne with wild gestures. "And yet, am I limited to now being selective in my choices since you will not allow me to gain acceptance of one measly man? I must protest this most disgusting command you have given to me. It is an outrage to say the least. I must ask you to give me the opportunity to fight for his soul. Just as you do not want any of those precious souls to perish and burn forever with me, I wish to take as many humans to my eternal destiny as I can.

He stopped pacing as he stared toward the throne. "Why do you stop me from this particular mortal? Are you afraid he will not turn from his ways and give his soul to you? Or is he one of the protected who will be allowed to preach during the great time of trouble? Do you just desire to keep him for another purpose? I wish to know why I am not allowed to tempt this mortal into cursing your name. But, then again, he already has, hasn't he?"

Silence fell over the room as Satan ceased his argument, rather pleased with himself with the way he presented his case. He paced back and forth across the floor, made of the purest marble while he awaited an answer from the throne.

Once again thunder sounded with a soft, melodious rhythm, and quickly built to a roaring crescendo. The elders maintained their posture of bowing down, their crowns still before the throne. The choir and orchestra continued to fill the air with praise. The beasts flew around the great room shouting their proclamation. Not even the irreverent spirit of Satan can diminish the love and praise toward the Almighty God. Through all of Lucifer's rants and raves, the love of God shines brighter and greater.

God summoned another angel to the front of the throne. He bent down to one knee, his head bowed, and waited for his instructions. The angel was large and muscular, with dark eyes, and cheekbones looking chiseled from stone. He was a warrior in the army of God who has been involved in many battles throughout his existence.

"Where have I seen this picture before?" Satan over-dramatized his words with grandiose gestures. "I suppose you're going to remind me of Job, aren't you? Would it be too much to ask for you to skip over that dreadful story? I do not need to be reminded again of how you were right about him. So please, spare me the agony of having to hear it again. I don't know how many times I've heard it, but I do believe I have the story down rather well, and I would rather spend the time . . ."

A single bolt of lightning flashed over the head of Lucifer, driving him to his knees in fear and reverence. "You are the Lord of all, and I thank-you for the opportunity to come before your throne." The confession came out weak, especially from one who, moments ago, felt so mighty. Satan cowered in the middle of the throne room changing his sarcastic attitude to one of humility, if only for a second.

The other angel remained kneeling in silence. He wouldn't raise his head even as Satan continued being so irreverent to the Lord, although his anger did burn within him. Gentle thunder rolled toward him. He stood and raised his head toward the Most High God. He was filled with honor at the request to come before the Almighty as he listens to the instructions from God in a voice only he could understand.

"Yes, my Lord, I understand the urgency of the mission. I will do my utmost to succeed. My Lord, if I may ask, how I am to complete such a task without failure? This serpent next to me is cunning and powerful and vile. He is able to inflict much damage on the man you request me to speak with. You know I will do whatever you ask of me without question. It is just that I am used to fighting, not talking and, well, my Lord, I do not know quite what to do."

God, once again, spoke directly to his trusted warrior.

"Thank you, my Lord. I will do my best not to fail you." He pounded his fist on his chest, "For the glory of the Most High God."

As he turned to leave, he stopped and looks back. "And yes, my Lord, I do recall Moses saying this same thing to you." He bowed his head slightly as he walked out of the throne room.

The moment he left the throne room of the Almighty God, another angel was summoned. This angel, although not large, had a spirit of meekness and servitude. He knelt directly in front of the throne and waited for his instructions. He was given a similar mission and was to collaborate with the warrior. The angel stood, bowed to his Lord, and left.

Off to the side, Satan impatiently tapped his foot. He sighed loudly several times trying to garner attention, then snapped, "Can we get on with MY business, now?"

———•———

Just outside of the building, the two angels met.

"Jareb, my friend." The large warrior grasped the smaller angel by the shoulders.

"It is good to see you too, Pithel (pronounced Py'-thul)."

"We have been given quite the mission."

"It always amazes me what the Lord will do for one soul."

"I agree."

"There is urgency for the souls of these men," Jareb added.

"So, we are to work together?"

"Yes. Our missions, although different, have many similarities."

———•———

Satan stormed out of the throne room, brushing past the two angels, as he mumbled, "I must have this soul in my possession to save face. I have lost way too many battles over the centuries. It is time for me to have a victory."

The devil began to devise his plan as he headed toward the guarded gate. An evil smile curled his lips as a plan formed in his mind. "Yes, but of course, it is almost too simple."

CHAPTER 1

"Maybe this isn't the best time to bring this up," Jack McDougal said, playfully.

"What are you talking about?" asked Judy, Jack's girlfriend of the past two years.

"You just seem to be distracted about something and I really need to have your undivided attention."

"Distracted? You think I'm distracted? I'm the farthest thing from distracted. I'm paying close attention to every word you've said to me," Judy said, returning the banter. "The question I have for you, Jack, is when are you going to say something worth listening to?"

"Now that's low." Jack gripped his heart. "Maybe I'll just keep my news to myself."

"Again, what are you talking about?"

Jack played coy, ignoring her question.

"Oh come on! Really? You're going to ignore me now?"

After he crossed his arms and turned away, Jack quickly spun back around and proclaimed, "I got promoted today. You are looking at Detective Jack McDougal of the Michigan State Police."

"Seriously?"

"Absolutely. Captain Bainer called me into his office just this morning and told me the good news."

"That's wonderful, Jack!" Judy threw her arms around his neck and congratulated him with a kiss.

"So now that I've been promoted I thought…" He let his words hang in the air.

"You thought what?" Judy interrupted.

"Well I thought it would be a good time to ask you again."

"Ask me what?" she asked.

"You know, about going to church with me."

"What?" Judy pushed him away and threw her arms up in the air. "Church? I thought you were about to take our relationship to another level."

"Can't we do both? I recall, you promised to go to church with me after I got my promotion and before one of us died."

"Well, the last time I checked I still had a pulse so there's still time," Judy teased. "And I think I said I can't go anywhere until my career settles down into something more permanent."

She crossed her arms in an unconscious defensive posture as she leaned against the door frame of her home. "And, yes, I did promise I'd go with you someday and I always keep my promises. So back off will you?"

They both laughed, Judy the sarcastic laugh, and Jack a defeated laugh. After a few moments Judy snapped her fingers and exclaimed, "Here's an idea: how about I just have the hearse swing by the church on the way to my final resting place?" She looked as if she were trying to win an award with her acting and carrying on.

Jack stepped back and as if looking into a camera stated, "And the award for best performance in a rejecting role goes to Judy Metcalf!" She gave him a gentle punch in the arm. "I still don't understand what your career and church have to do with each other." Jack took Judy into his arms and gave her their familiar good night kiss. "Don't be surprised if I ask you again before Sunday." His voice held both rejection and determination.

"I look forward to giving you the same answer again."

"Hey, persistency pays off doesn't it? And, if I might pat myself on the back, I am persistent with you."

As Jack left Judy's apartment, she followed him out. "I suppose I should congratulate you one more time on getting promoted, *Detective* Jack McDougal. It does have a nice ring to it."

CHAPTER 2

The morning meeting, at WGRT, started out like the circus had come to town and the animals were hungry. "This is out of control." Jim Delmark gestured toward his computer monitor and phone. "I haven't been able to get my first cup of coffee yet."

The old cliché of organized chaos had always been the way the staff described their duties. Today, however, began to look like a day when nothing would be going as planned. The tension started to thicken with the feeling of something about to explode at any moment.

Amid the brewing storm from the call-in desk, a sense of calm prevailed as if in the eye of a hurricane. The journalists and anchors sat around the oblong conference table and focused on their tasks given to them from Allen Stevenson, the assignment manager. They were all excellent multi-taskers at listening to Allen, checking their tablets and smartphones, writing teases, drinking coffee, and adding input to anyone who might or might not have asked for it.

"Here's another call!" Jim interrupted from his desk behind the table. "Some woman is trying to jump off a bridge downtown," he exclaimed, his deep voice resonating throughout the room. His future looked bright for doing voiceovers for whoever hired him after he completed his internship in six months.

"How many calls is that so far today?" asked Sarah Downing, on loan from the sales team. Jim answered with a shrug of his shoulders as he took another call.

He put his hand over the receiver as he said, "I know I'm only an intern here, but this seems strange. Do you guys keep records of the amount of stories covered in one day? I'll bet we've had fifteen calls just since seven o'clock this morning." No one paid any attention as some scurried off from the conference table to work on their assignments.

Jim had been right about this being an exceptionally busy day. A usual day would have close to seventy possible stories to cover with twelve coming in by phone for WGRT. Fifteen calls with all being possible major breaking news in less than two hours seemed incredible, even by the standards of the seasoned veterans working there.

"I've never seen this place so busy in all my years. This is just crazy," mocked a well-known and well-dressed anchor. "Why, we have enough material to fill the evening news for, for, for an entire show." Several people chuckled. Some shook their heads.

"Okay people, let's try to focus on today's assignments," Allen stated as he brought the meeting back to order.

"Seriously, though, there does appear to be a large number of issues breaking today," John Robertson stated as he pointed and winked at the intern, letting him know he was joking.

John was the evening anchor for station WGRT in Grand Rapids, Michigan and he liked to tell everyone so. He got up and left the meeting as he entered the news director's office. "I'm beginning to think we don't have enough people to cover everything going on today. These are some pretty big stories coming in, each being number one for the broadcast. How will we ever choose which ones will make it to air?"

"That's what I get paid the big bucks for, John," Al Tuinstra, the station manager, stated.

Back at the conference table in the newsroom Mark Salinger shouted, "Anyone care to bet it's a full moon tonight?" Mark had been around for over twenty years and had always been a skeptic. A growing number of employees at the television station believed full moons made things go haywire every month. Although they had no werewolf sightings, crime tended to go up, especially domestic violence.

Nurses in neo-natal departments of hospitals set the calendar by the cycle of the moon. They believed more babies were delivered then than any other time during the month. Police reported domestic violence rose during full moons. Psychiatric wards filled up fast when the moon shone at its brightest.

Mark's question, though, did get a laugh from the laid back group. The saying in the office was "if you could make this group laugh, then you should go professional."

Most of the people at WGRT took their jobs seriously, which meant they could be diagnosed as borderline workaholics, giving up life and limb to get a story straight before it went on the air. This strong work ethic, however, came at a price, with high burn out rates, and more than a few marriages ending, due to their work habits.

Mr. Tuinstra tried to get them to relax, by giving days off to allow for quality family and personal time, often only to see the person walk through the doors to finish a story started the day before. Somehow they always managed to stay the entire day. It was a difficult task to keep them away from the job for more than a day.

No one took the full moon bet.

After the meeting ended every photag, or photo journalist, left to cover the breaking stories. The station employed ten reporters, eight of which were on while two took time off. Everyone would be on call for any major news breaking stories. Al had already paged the other two reporters.

"Anything else, John?" Al asked as he rose from behind his desk and grabbed his sport coat.

"I have no further questions, your honor."

Mr. Tuinstra hurried out of the office as he gently nudged John out. "Be back later."

Being the star anchor of the channel 7 news team, John's ego told him that he was the real reason people tuned in to watch the WGRT news. He came from Santa Fe, New Mexico, after spending five years doing what he called "paying his dues as reporter, weekend anchor, and all around gopher boy." He considered it to be an invaluable experience he could not have gained elsewhere.

John had rugged good looks, a strong chin, and steel blue eyes, which caught the attention of the viewers. The eyes seemed hypnotic as people watched the news. John had taken full advantage of his looks throughout his career. The television stations he had worked for, whether in college as an intern, or afterward as a professional journalist, had hired him, not only for his talent, but for those piercing eyes.

He had won, what he considered the most prestigious award, the best-looking man on local television award, given by a ragtag magazine, who enlisted a group of viewers to watch television each day. Most of the female viewers agreed with their findings, and at one time or another, had stated they would die to have the opportunity to meet John Robertson. Of course, all of the women at the station said they would do anything to get him to leave them alone for one minute.

Aside from the arrogance, he did have the talent for the job. His ability to take an ordinary story and make it extraordinary was unrivaled. He had the uncanny knack to take a bad situation and make it tolerable.

During a live newscast a couple years back, a disgruntled employee from a nearby factory broke into the studio, after a particular piece was featured. The undercover story about drinking on the job during breaks had caused this man to lose his job. He stormed into the studio brandishing a pistol, which he pointed directly at John. Some quick thinking by the producer sent the newscast into a commercial break. The cameras, however, kept filming.

John sat behind the desk shocked to see the gun being waved in his face. The rest of the crew ran out of the studio seeking safety elsewhere in the building.

"You got me fired." The man paced back and forth, the gun trained in John's face. "I've worked there for fifteen years. I have a family to take care of and a mortgage to pay. What am I supposed to do?"

"Were you really drinking on the job?" John's voice was soft, but calm.

"What? What did you just ask me?"

"Did you drink on your breaks?"

The man paused in front of John, his head shaking from side to side. After what seemed to be an eternity, the man's shoulders slumped and the gun fell to his side. "Yeah, I did."

John's voice grew a little stronger. "Then first of all, I'm sorry you got fired. It's an awful feeling to have. Second, tell the truth about it. Own up to your mistake. That's what it was you know, just a mistake. Third, and I don't know if this is necessary, consider getting into some kind of rehab program to help you with the problem."

"I suppose you're right."

"Of course I am," John gave the man his award-winning smile and a wink. "I know of some good counselors you can talk to about this."

"Thanks. And I'm sorry I barged in here." The man set the gun down on the news desk. "It's not loaded."

"I appreciate both the apology and the fact that the gun isn't loaded. Just so you know, the police will have to take you into custody."

"Yeah, I know." At that moment, a police officer came into the room, handcuffed the man and led him out of the studio. John went right back to reading the news from the teleprompter as if nothing had happened.

Lunch, if anyone ever got to take a break, at WGRT started around 11:30. Some took an hour, some less. Most took none at all, depending on the news of the day. Today, with the late breaking stories it would be lunch on the go.

John grabbed his sport coat and walked toward the receptionist. "I'll be back shortly."

"You're leaving? Now?" asked the stunned and stunning, Stacey Reynolds, the newly hired receptionist.

"Yup, you need me to pick anything up for you?"

"I'm good, thanks," she replied, rolling her eyes and shaking her head in disgust. She had been in John's crosshairs the moment she'd been hired two weeks ago. Young and beautiful with deep green eyes and long dark hair, she had a smile that lit up the room. She also happened to be athletically fit, which John couldn't ignore. Several times she hinted bluntly, to John, "I'm not interested." John, not one to take "no", took it as a sign of possibilities.

Some of the women at the station warned her to beware of the prowling anchor. They promised to watch her back. Stacey had actually been dating the sports anchor, Bret Stewart, which is how she got the job. They decided to keep their romance a secret for a while not wanting to upset the delicate balance of the work place.

Nothing deterred John from flirting, however, and today was no exception.

"I have to keep trying, you know," John said, flashing his award-winning smile.

"You really don't."

"Someday you'll give in."

"Sorry, but it's just not going to happen." She didn't bother to look up as John leaned over her desk.

After all of the women who wanted the opportunity to go out with John Robertson, here was Stacey always turning him down. "Alright, then, I gave it my best shot. I'll be back shortly." He lightly slapped the top of Stacey's desk as he turned toward the door.

"Here we go again," Jim yelled from across the newsroom, his voice strained from all the calls coming in. His posture showed he was exhausted. All of his co-workers had to constantly remind themselves that, although he was striving to become a professional journalist, he was still a youth, green and tender.

CHAPTER 3

"Surprise, surprise, surprise. This one sounds like the prize winner." Jim said.

"Do you even know who you're imitating?" asked Mark.

"Of course I do. It's Gomer Pyle. My grandpa told me he used to watch that show with you." Mark ignored the "age" crack.

John stopped at the door to hear what story could possibly top the woman about to jump off a bridge.

"What's the scoop, Jim? We got a traffic jam on the freeway again? Another shooting on the Westside? What's so important about this one?"

"I'm not totally sure. It's just this gut feeling from the preliminary indications I'm picking up from the scanner." He kept his head down as he scribbled notes.

Everyone continued working even as they listened for the new breaking story.

"It's something about a hostage situation downtown somewhere. Here we go." He turned the volume up for the office to listen in.

The voice on the police scanner gave details about a situation at the bus station.

"Gunmen at Central Station bus terminal, unknown how many, three possibly four. Hostage situation, how many not known, initial reports indicate between ten and twenty. All units respond code 3 with local police, sheriff's department and state police."

Everyone at the television station froze, stunned by the news.

"Did she say Central Station?" asked Sheila Jorges, from a few pods away.

"I'm sure that's what she said," Jim replied.

"That's where Al just went to pick up his daughter." The office fell silent, concerned about this new incident.

Earlier, Al Tuinstra had announced his daughter, Amy, would arrive home from college today. His eyes beamed with pride, as he said, "I'll be leaving soon to pick her up at the bus station."

Amy, currently in her third year at the University of Minnesota, would always take the bus home from school. "I just feel more relaxed and can enjoy the scenery." She had also told her dad, "It's not *that* long and it saves you money." Al loved that about his daughter.

He had already left to pick her up. The entire staff feared she could be one of the hostages. Sheila grabbed her cell phone, scrolled to Al's name, and hit send, but got nothing. "Why am I not getting any cell reception?" she asked still looking at her brand new smart phone. "This is odd." She kept trying, adding her landline in trying to reach him. No answer.

Whatever the situation at the bus station might be, it had just become personal to WGRT. Everyone involved with packaging the story or putting it all together for the broadcast, would make sure it got covered properly, respectfully, and safely. No one wanted to put Amy, or any of the other hostages, in any further danger than they may currently be in.

Many couldn't move past the shock. Some sat crying together. Others became angry, asking why anyone would do such a terrible thing. Still others wanted to go to the bus station to rescue Amy.

Every time the scanner began to squawk, the room went silent.

"Guns have been sighted. Reports of doors being barricaded. No shots fired. Police and deputies have the area secured." A slight pause before hearing, *"All units approach with extreme caution. Suspects are considered to be armed and dangerous."*

Although in shock from the news, the staff still tried to cover their day's assignments. This, however, wasn't just another situation. This story had become personal.

"Um, Rich," Jim asked, from behind his computer monitor, "who do we have left to cover the story?"

Richard Stevenson rubbed his temples with his thumbs, painfully aware of the situation. "We don't have anyone near the Central Station Bus Terminal," Rich shouted in frustration. Every reporter of WGRT had been scattered throughout the region to cover the day's news. No one was in the metro area, other than those covering the woman on the bridge, which they couldn't leave.

Rich ran his hand through his thinning hair as the stories kept coming like waves crashing on the beach. This day was far from normal. "Okay, call Rex and tell him to begin wrapping up at the bridge and to be ready to move to the bus station as soon as they are cleared from the scene." The police had informed all the news crews to remain on scene in order to not spook the woman into jumping before the negotiator could try to talk her off the edge.

John's shoulders slumped and his chin fell to his chest. Slowly, he made his way back to his desk. Lunch no longer had the same appeal it did a minute ago. He rested his nose on the end of his fingers as he pursed his lips contemplating why the world seemed to be falling apart today. With a deep sigh, John called out, "Hey Rich, you need some help?"

"What do you think?" Rich kept his head down looking for ways to get a crew to the bus station. "Everyone's overbooked as it is, and completely out of the area. By then it could be over and we'll be left with no story. We got any volunteers to go out there and get a great story?"

No replies.

"Oh, come on people. There has to be someone who's tired of sitting around and waiting for the right opportunity to come along. Remember, this is for Al and Amy. Now how about a volunteer? How about you, John? You just asked who we had to cover the story. Well now's your chance to step up."

John heard the plea from Rich. He also thought back to his days as a beat reporter paying his dues, pounding the pavement. He had been a good reporter. In fact, as he would tell anyone who might ask, he was very good. He was always the egotist.

The stories he had covered before landing the anchor position ranged from the heart-warming human interest stories to large fires that had destroyed million dollar buildings to mass murders. The worst story he had ever reported on also happened to be the most gruesome, as well. A disgruntled employee had gone into work with an automatic rifle and just started shooting. Fifteen people died in that tragic crime, including the shooter, who shot himself after police arrived. The scene was horrible. Dead bodies lay everywhere, blood flowed and pooled while some blood splattered on the walls. Windows had been shot out and bullet holes could be seen on every wall inside Johnston Printing Company.

Still, heroes had emerged from the tragic event. One man had died while covering up another man, using his own body as a shield. Another man threw a woman down and landed on top of her just before the man turned and sprayed bullets near them, which saved them both as they pretended to be dead. The senseless loss of life from that day remained firmly etched in John's mind. The hostage situation brought back all those memories as he sat at his desk with his head buried in his hands.

He looked over to Rich. "Yeah, okay I'll go. Just give me a couple of minutes to prepare."

A few of the women nearby gasped as their jaws dropped. Then they applauded him for his efforts.

Peter Stallings, a former journalist, had been moved into a position of fact checker for WGRT. Without him first making sure everything was above board, nothing got on the news broadcasts. Peter had been moved into this position after he reported a story with misleading data. After it had aired, the station was sued, which cost several million dollars.

He stared at the computer screen thinking about Amy, whom he had known since she was born. He couldn't fathom what she must be going through being held hostage in the bus terminal. He prayed silently for God to protect her and get all the hostages out safely.

When Peter heard John volunteer to cover the story, he raised his hand and said, "I want to go too." He got out of his chair and walked over to Rich's desk.

"You sure about this, Peter?" Rich asked.

"I'm positive," he said. He lowered his voice as he leaned over the desk. "I need to prove that I can cover stories again. Plus, with two of us we can get more information."

"I'll buy that." Rich looked over at John. "You okay with him going?"

"Absolutely."

Peter grabbed paper and pen, his laptop computer and his smartphone, which he kept charged at his desk.

Over the years, Peter had been given the official title Director of Information, more affectionately known as the Guru of Information. To most, however, he was simply Mr. Info Man. Originally, he had not been fond of the position.

When he first came to WGRT, it had been his desire to be on the streets doing news stories and changing lives. One costly error had banished him from journalism. Peter didn't complain, however, because he needed the job and he discovered he actually enjoyed getting the facts right for the news. Plus, the work he had given him some very good contacts with other agencies in the community, especially with the police in the various precincts throughout the Grand Rapids metro area.

The police always held the stance of every case being under investigation and, therefore, 'no comment' would be the standard answer given to all questions. If any information was aired, it could be detrimental to the entire case, making the police reluctant to give anything to reporters. After months of working with Jillian Morgan, the spokesperson at police headquarters,

Peter proved over and over that he held to the standards set forth by the police. He had, therefore, established an excellent rapport with her and her with him. They had shared a common bond, having both graduated from the same high school, just several years apart.

Rich nodded to Peter, "Okay, get moving, but be careful out there."

Judy Metcalf had been stuck in the office as she recovered from an injury she sustained playing in a charity softball game. She claimed she had been given a clean bill of health, "but the doctor won't write me a note yet." She was fiery, young, and had a talent as a photo journalist for capturing amazing video.

Every day she would complain about not being assigned to go back out into the field. Every day Al told her to bring in the doctor's note. And every day she would humph off to do some menial desk work.

Even with her winning several awards for her work, she still remained inside the station waiting for her ankle to heal. "Hey, Rich aren't they going to need someone to run a camera?"

"Probably," Rich replied. "What are you trying to say?"

"Oh nothing, but I doubt very seriously either of them has ever held a camera, let alone actually worked one."

"Okay, I can see where you're going with this."

"I would love to go with them for the express purpose of shooting footage for this story," Judy said, as if she were back in grade school.

"So you're saying you're ready to go back out there running a camera?"

"Yes." she exclaimed, pointing at Rich. "You, sir, are a mind reader."

"Okay, you go too. All we got left is video only. Get your gear checked out from the equipment room and meet them by the back door in ten minutes. Let John and Peter know we'll have the live truck there as soon as we can. In the meantime, be careful and stay safe."

"Will do, Rich! And thanks."

No one else offered to go as they continued working on other responsibilities. Someone had to stay back and run the station.

Peter and Judy had been waiting for an opportunity to prove to their co-workers they had the skills to do field work. John, on the other hand, just wanted to prove to himself he still had the skills to report. Their emotions swirled, from excitement to fear, to anxiety and doubt. They had no idea what might happen at the bus station once they arrived on the scene.

CHAPTER 4

Law enforcement vehicles from the Grand Rapids Police Department, Kent County Sheriff's Department, and Michigan State Police, surrounded the Central Station bus terminal, all with lights flashing, the cruisers pointed nose to nose.

The sight caused the hostages inside to start to panic. They huddled together in a corner, holding hands in fear while at the same time trying to be brave. None of the passengers recognized the three men with the guns.

After the initial assault by the hostage takers, who screamed and flashed their guns at the fifteen passengers, the gunmen had not spoken. Occasionally they would glare and wave a gun, at the frightened passengers, but they hardly paid them any attention.

There were no demands. They made no attempts to harm any of the hostages. Still, the sight of a gun pointed in their direction stressed everyone in the bus terminal.

As more and more police surrounded the building, the gunmen stood behind a large support pillar and began to argue with each other in hushed tones.

"Now what do we do?"

"I don't know. We were supposed to get in and get out and that's all."

"Well, we're way past that now."

"Okay, you watch the hostages. You watch the outside for the police."

"What are you going to do?"

"Me? I'm gonna call the boss and find out what he wants us to do."

They hadn't planned this assault beyond the initial attack. Their arguing added to the hostages' confusion. A few of the passengers whispered among themselves as they tried to come up with a plan of escape. They had no weapons, but plenty of help waited just outside the building.

The gunman assigned to watch them overheard the whispers. "Hey, shut up!" He stomped over to the group and flashed his automatic assault rifle.

"You guys move over there." He pointed to another corner. "The rest of you stay put, and be quiet."

He walked back over to the man with the phone. "I say we just leave now. Nobody got hurt and no harm was done."

Their buddy, who acted as the lookout, chimed in, "I agree. I say we leave right now before this gets worse." He waved his gun at the windows and at the hostages as he made his point.

"We can't leave and you both know it." The man held his cell phone plastered to his ear. "We have to finish the mission or we fail." He was the largest of the three. He wore green army pants and jacket. His bulk had established him as the leader. "If we fail our part, then everything else will be a bust. I'm not getting the wrath of the boss on my back. No, we have to stay and stick to the mission."

Since this wasn't a democracy, the big man's orders stood. There would be no vote. But that didn't mean the trio could not argue or fight it out.

The man who watched the police outside said, "I don't want to face the boss either, but staying here is going to get us killed. Either way we're dead men." His greasy hair and scraggly beard dripped with sweat from the tension. "We gotta bail sooner or later. I'm seeing more and more police out there."

"What about you?" The big guy looked at the timid man who stood guard over the hostages.

He took off his beat-up Chicago Cubs baseball cap and scratched his head. "I agree about finishing the job here. I also think we have to get out of here before this gets any worse. All we were told to do was to take hostages here at the bus station so that Anti-Pro could get some publicity." He pointed with his finger to the hostages. "We did what we were asked to do. With the police showing up, I'm betting the news people aren't too far behind. I say we hold up a little while longer, you know, until we see the cameras and the reporters then we bolt."

"Now that sounds like a plan," stated the greasy haired man.

"I can agree with that too," said the big man.

"Just in case, though, I suggest we take one of them with us."

"Okay," the two agreed.

"Go ahead and choose," the big man said.

He studied each of the hostages. "I choose her." He pointed his gun at a young woman. "She looks like a very good prospect to me, if you know what I mean." He walked over to her as he waved his gun at the others and grabbed her by the arm. The woman didn't fight, didn't panic, and didn't cry. She just got up and walked with him.

"What's your name, honey?" he asked.

"Amy. Amy Tuinstra."

"Well, Amy Tuinstra, it looks like it's your unlucky day." The trio of gunmen laughed. Some of the hostages cried. Amy just stood quietly.

She finally turned to the man who firmly held her arm and stated, "Look, I'll be your hostage if you promise to let these people go."

"What did you say?" asked the big man, slowly walking over to her.

"I'm protected by God. I'll be okay with anything you try to throw at me. So, go ahead, take me, but let them go."

The man who held her arm put his gun to her head and spoke softly, "We'll talk about letting the others go, later. But how can your God be with you if you're with us? What if your God fails you?"

Amy did the unexpected. She began to pray, "Lord, I know you hear me right now. We are in need of your help. I know you will be with me and will protect me with your love and power. I pray you will protect us all from these men who wish to harm us. . ."

"Shut up." The big man raised the butt of his gun to hit her before she could finish. "No more praying."

"I've already prayed," Amy said quietly. "And I know my prayer will be answered."

CHAPTER 5

Judy had worked a camera before her injury, which seemed to be a lifetime ago, but had really only been three months. She felt confident in her ability to handle this today without any problems. "It's just like riding a bike," she told Jack several weeks ago, when asked about her desire to get back in the field.

The equipment room sat near the back of the station, close to the back door for easy access to those needing to get equipment fast. The overzealous equipment manager, Arnold Milton yelled, "If you're not going to fill out the requisition form, then you're going to be responsible for any damages on any of the equipment you bring back. I don't care if it's the smallest scratch."

"I'll be sure to tell Richard you said that. I'll also be sure to tell Mr. Tuinstra when I see him at the bus station."

"You do that. And be sure to let them know those orders came from me."

"Just give me the camera and battery packs, Arnold. The guys are already waiting for me outside."

"I told you I need you to fill out the request form first," he shot back.

Judy wasn't in the mood to be harassed nor did she want to be stuck jawing with Arnold. "Look, if you want trouble, then call up Rich and ask him, but I'm taking the equipment whether you like it or not. Do you understand?"

And with that she picked up a camera and two battery packs, making sure each had full charges. She started lugging the equipment, heading for the door, when Arnold yelled from behind her, "Hey Judy."

"No time to chit chat Arnold."

"You're gonna need these." She turned back just as Arnold tossed two blank tapes. She caught one, dropped the other.

"Thanks, Arn. I'll be sure to be to take care of everything."

"You do that, Judy. And take care of yourself too." Deep down, Arnold was just an old softie.

———— •◄► ————

Peter stashed his notebook, two pens, and mini-tape recorder into his laptop bag. He walked over to Jim who continued to monitor the police scanners as well as the situation at the bus station.

"Anything new?" he asked.

"This story just keeps getting bigger and bigger with every passing second." He paused to take a sip of his now lukewarm coffee. "The entire area's been cordoned off. No one's allowed near the site. The perimeter is over a block away."

Peter grabbed Jim's notes and quickly made a copy of them. "Keep us updated. I'll have the radio on at all times."

<hr>

John, ever the professional, took a detour to the men's room to comb his hair. "If I'm going to be in the eye of the public, then I'm going to have to look good."

Everyone in the office rolled their eyes, some even let out a chuckle, while one unnamed, brave soul sighed, "What an egomaniac."

Although true, John's large ego could take over his thoughts, he did play the part of being an excellent anchor. The staff always put up with his strange idiosyncrasies. Now they would get to see if he was as good a reporter as he always said he was.

Alone, inside the men's room, John stared into the mirror. "I hope I'm able to this." He felt apprehensive about going out into the field again. Inside the station, he carried an air of confidence. Inside the men's room, however, he wasn't so sure of himself. Still he wouldn't let his co-workers down nor would he let on to his fear about going into a hostage situation. So he covered up his feelings by primping. He did have to keep his reputation intact.

CHAPTER 6

John met Judy as they headed to the parking lot. She slung the heavy camera with the two battery packs over her shoulder. Behind her she dragged cables and bags of miscellaneous equipment. She hinted rather bluntly to John, "I sure wish we had a cart for all this *heavy* equipment. My *back* is *killing* me from all of this *heavy* stuff."

She might as well have been talking to the clouds. John completely ignored her call for help. He walked absorbed in thought as he mapped out the best way to cover the situation. Judy groaned and grunted as she waddled like a penguin.

They headed to the garage where Peter had checked out a van to transport the three self-made reporters to the scene. Company policy stated, "If you cover a story for WGRT, you must use a company vehicle. No exceptions, ever." The only vehicle left was the oldest van in the fleet. The old white van had many dents and dings on it, but still carried the letters WGRT shown in big block letters on all four sides.

"That's the most important part of the van," Al always stated, usually followed by a moment of laughter.

Judy, huddled in the back with her equipment, said, "This van is really embarrassing." Peter pulled the van out of the parking lot and headed downtown to the Central Station bus terminal.

On the way, John suggested assignments to the newly formed team. "If you two are feeling like I am, then you're nervous and a bit scared about what we're walking into." John hoped Peter and Judy would understand how he felt.

"I'll be honest," Judy said. "I'm a bit on the rusty side with all this equipment. I've only been sitting at that lousy desk for a few months. You'd think this would be a piece of cake." She fumbled sliding the tape into the camera.

"All I've done for such a long time is information gathering," Peter said, his eyes glued to the road. "I've always wanted to get back out and try my hand at doing some kind of field work, but of all days and of all the stories. . ."

"It does make things a bit more complicated knowing Al's daughter could be one of the hostages. Either of you ever met Amy?"

"I've known her since she was a little girl," Peter said. "Now she's all grown up."

"How about you Judy, you ever met Amy?"

"I have never had the pleasure, just seen her picture in Al's office."

"Well, I'm sure you'll like her when you finally do meet her," John said. "So, Judy, when we get to the Central Station, why don't you try to get as many angles of the building as you can. Peter and I will work together to gather as much information as we can."

"That sounds like a plan to me," Judy said.

"We don't have enough radios to be able to keep in contact. If you need to get in touch, just text. Go as quickly as you can and we'll meet back at the van." Judy and Peter both agreed with the plan.

Peter recalled a story. "The last story I covered was something about a dog stuck in a drain pipe just outside of an abortion clinic. I always thought it was so ironic. The entire community came to the aid of this little dog, which was commendable. But right behind them, little unborn babies were being killed without a second thought. I think that's what put me in the office on such a permanent basis. They had way too many calls from angry pro-choice viewers." Peter gave a nervous smile as John and Judy each just rolled their eyes.

"I thought it was some kind of lawsuit that stuck you in the office," Judy said.

"Now that was uncalled for." Peter wagged his finger but with a warm smile.

They each put on their professional faces and worked to hide their fear. The radio crackled to life. Jim's voice filled the van. "The S.W.A.T. team's on the way. They're going to surround the bus station. You might want to hurry and get there before they do."

"Thanks, Jim. Unit 13 clear," Peter stated. A new wave of fear washed over the trio as they realized this was not a hoax or prank, but the real thing. "We're getting close." The air in the van heated up even as the air conditioner pumped out a cool breeze.

Judy thought about where she might position herself to get the best angles to shoot footage. She looked around at the buildings surrounding the area, now cordoned off by the police. All the buildings blocked her view instead of helped her. She looked for open windows and doors of neighboring businesses. She wanted to be able to focus her camera lens on a spot inside the bus terminal to look for movement. She hoped to catch a shot of the gunmen and the hostages inside. Secretly, she hoped to get some footage of Jack with his new promotion to detective.

John, in a sarcastic voice, offered her tips to help her get the best shots at the scene. "Make sure you have plenty of power in those battery packs," he said as he turned in his seat.

"Yeah and make sure you focus the lens before you start shooting," Peter added.

"Hey, I said I was rusty, not brain-dead. I remember how to do this job." Judy knew they had been joking, but she also wanted them to know she was in control. "But thanks for the tips. They just might come in handy if I forget to take the lens cap off of the camera."

"Oh, yeah, you should never do that," John quipped. All three laughed, easing the tension.

"You two just make sure to take the caps off the ink pens!" Judy went through her supply inventory while she attached the power cord to the camera, rechecked the VHS tape, and moved the camera around on her shoulder, getting used to the weight. As she finished, she gave a quick glance at the guys as she checked the lens cap. She felt ready to go the second they stopped the van.

"I have an idea," Peter said to John. "How about you work the law enforcement people and I'll check the crowd?"

"That's a good idea. We can cover more ground that way."

"I'll see if I can get in touch with Jillian Morgan, my contact with the police. Although I'd bet she's pretty tight-lipped right about now."

"Thanks, Peter, that'd be great," John said.

Peter turned his thoughts to his assignment. Mr. Info Man shouldn't have any trouble getting something, he thought. He knew the secret to success in this business would be to get details no one else could get. He practiced his questions in his head. "Got any names for me?" "Do you know if any shots have been fired?" "Has anyone been injured?" "Do you know if any of the hostages have been able to escape from the bus station?" "Have the gunmen made any demands yet?"

He recalled his first day in Journalism 101. Find the right person to talk to is the key to getting the right answers. Don't forget the five Ws; who, what, when, where, why, plus how.

As they neared the scene, Peter radioed Jim back at the station for any last minute details.

"Hang on, and I'll get right back to you."

Peter felt his heart beat harder as they neared crunch time and the risk factor increased at the unknown of the scene loomed over the three. He struggled to put his fear aside as he knew they had to get the jump on the other networks.

John prepared himself to be the face of WGRT once again in front of the camera. He wanted to have a decent story to present to the viewers, who would tune in later to the news. He would need to gather as much detail as he could get. Later he and Peter would sift through everything to make the story compelling and human. Outwardly, he felt confident of his skills and wouldn't be afraid to share this with Judy and Peter. Inside, however, his nerves were shot from the stress and pressure of reporting.

John babbled on to Peter and Judy about some sort of technique he'd learned while in New Mexico. Neither of them listened to him. They were too consumed with their own tasks.

CHAPTER 7

Law enforcement vehicles sped past as they neared the bus station. Fire trucks and ambulances lined up on every street ready to jump into action. Officers put the yellow "DO NOT CROSS POLICE LINE" tape around the perimeter and used barricades to keep the growing crowd at a safe distance.

Peter slowed the van just beyond the barricade as he scanned the area for a place to park the large vehicle. A rival station had parked their van right up against the barricade, the live tower protruded from the top. "It figures they're already here," Peter said.

The air inside the WGRT van grew thick with anxiety as they each began to realize the dangerous situation they were about to step into.

With the van stopped, Peter closed his eyes and prayed silently, *O Lord, I pray that you keep us safe today as well as those inside the bus terminal. Be especially close to Amy Tuinstra. I pray this in Jesus' name. Amen.* As he opened his eyes he felt peace flood through his soul which gave him the sense everything would work out today.

"Hey, say a prayer for me too, buddy. Don't go hogging all the holy stuff." John laughed trying to lighten up the tense mood in the van. It didn't work. Instead, his joke made the air thicker, seemingly choking all three of them. "Come on, I was only kidding. You can hog the prayers if you want to." He felt he only dug the hole deeper. He finally did the only smart thing...he shut up.

"If ever there was a time for a prayer, I think it would be now." Judy was shocked as she heard herself say that.

———— • ————

As peaceful as Peter felt by his prayer, he also sensed a powerful, evil sensation in the air.

Unseen by the three, the demons of hell tried to intercept Peter's prayer from reaching its destination. The devils knew it was impossible to keep the prayer from getting to heaven's throne, but to keep Peter from praying again was possible.

Their plan was to keep Peter away from John and Judy so he wouldn't talk about his faith.

"Keep them apart for as long as possible." The orders were barked from a very large, shadowy creature that stood on the hood of the van with the rest of the hoard perched on the roof. "Remember we are not allowed to kill them nor can we take possession of their souls today. We are only to influence them to follow our master's bidding. We must not fail. We must fight to the finish with those angelic warriors who most certainly will be appearing here today, especially after hearing the prayer of this saint. Why did he come with them? Who failed in keeping him off of this story?"

The demons snarled at each other. Fingers pointed in all directions. No one confessed.

"They must not win. Do you understand?"

The band nodded their heads in agreement as they began to howl like a pack of hungry wolves. Their captain commanded them to stand by. As the howling turned into laughter, a terrible stench filled the air. A thick, greenish smoke accompanied the acrid smell, signaled the time of their mission was at hand. They skittered away from the WGRT van to their assigned positions around the bus station.

———◆———

"Pull over here, Peter." Judy pointed to one open parking space near the barricaded street. Peter eased the WGRT van into the parking spot. All three sat still as he shut the engine off. Something kept them from getting out. None of the three could tell if their fear of what could happen kept them sitting still.

Judy's emotions rose to the surface and a single tear rolled down her cheek. John noticed and said, "We're going to be okay today."

"I know," Judy said. "I'm just a bit nervous that's all."

"Me too," John said.

"Don't think I'm full of confidence," Peter stated. "My nerves are shot."

"Okay, let's just get what we need to get and meet back here in an hour," John said. "If we need to do more after that, we'll make a plan then. Agreed?"

"Agreed," both Peter and Judy said together.

———◆———

Just outside, three demons, left to guard the van, leaned with their backs against the doors so the journalists couldn't get out. A laugh rose in the air as they worked through their prank while the reporters finished up their last minute preparations.

Peter opened his door with ease as Pithel and Jareb, the angels assigned to this mission, broke through the barrier of the demons.

"Leave or be banished," Pithel said. "It doesn't matter to me what you choose."

"You'll pay for this." The demons decided to live to fight another day and flew away.

CHAPTER 8

John and Judy followed Peter as he stepped out of the van. Judy adjusted the camera on her shoulder and made sure the cables had been secured on her belt. John and Peter looked around for people they might be able to get information from.

John spotted an officer giving out orders. "I'll start with him and then go down the block." John pointed down the street heading towards the bus station.

Peter nodded. "I'll start with her." He pointed at one of the bus drivers.

"Good choice." John said. He reminded Peter and Judy to meet back at the van in one hour. They synchronized their watches.

Judy shot a test shot to focus the lens and to try some maneuvering making sure she remembered how to handle the camera. "I took the lens cap off, if anyone cares to know that." John and Peter both smiled. John patted her on the shoulder as if to say "good job." They were ready to tackle the story of her life.

———◆———

Peter walked over to the bus driver, who stood next to a barricade. He introduced himself to the woman. "Hello, I'm Peter Stallings with WGRT news. Can you tell me what's happening inside the bus station right now? I know there's a hostage situation, but do you have any inside details or information you might be able to share?"

The woman, with the name Angie on her name tag, looked at Peter with a blank expression, but gave no answer.

"I know this is a troubling time," Peter said in a softer tone. "I just want to tell people what is going on here."

Realizing the reporter wasn't going to leave, she started to answer the question. "Well, the last I heard there are three men inside the station armed with automatic weapons."

"Any word on what they want?"

"No, they're just in there with hostages. It's really strange if you think about it."

"How so?" asked Peter.

"This isn't the hub of the city that it once was. A few years ago, this old bus station would have a bus pulling in and out every minute it seemed. Now, with all the planes and cars, bus travel just isn't what it used to be. That's why this is so strange to me. If you want to get attention go to the airport or the train station, but you don't go to the bus station. It just doesn't have the glamour it once had." Angie appeared tired to Peter.

"How long have you been driving buses, Angie?"

"Close to thirty years," she answered with pride.

"Do you still think bus transportation is useful?"

"Absolutely. It isn't the fastest trip in the world, but it's cheaper." Angie looked over at Peter and said, "Let me tell you about driving a bus." She talked but Peter wasn't interested at this moment. He still had questions to ask about the current situation.

He endured Angie's stories about how great the country appeared from the driver's seat of a bus. She spoke of the panoramic views of mountains, valleys and grand rivers and all the charming little cities and great people she had met over the years. She talked about what felt like to drive into a sunrise and later that day drive into the same sun as it set. Peter pretended to listen waited for a break to ask his next question. He checked his watch. Thirty minutes until he had to be back to the van.

He interrupted Angie's story to ask, "Have you heard if there is any plan to get the hostages out?"

"Nope, I haven't heard anything about no rescue attempt. My guess is they'll try to wait them out, could take hours, even days. You know how the police operate sometimes. Makes you wonder if we really are safe out here. We certainly aren't safe today, are we?"

With that Peter thanked Angie for her time and for answering his questions. He began looked around for another potential source of information.

John Robertson didn't get anywhere with the police officer. Every question asked had been answered with the statement, "I cannot divulge any information at this time." John quit asking questions and just stood around listening, hoping to catch a tidbit here and there. Other officers came and went giving information and getting new instructions from the officer.

Most of the details coming in were old news to John, but he stood by waiting to hear something useful. The most important piece of information he had garnered had been that no dialogue between the gunmen and the police had taken place. It seemed odd to everyone present. "Why would they not make some kind of demand?" John overheard one officer ask.

"Good question," John said out loud. The officer, who asked the question, turned and looked at him. It was a moment of eye contact John had been waiting for. The officer didn't come over and talk with John, but a connection had been made.

Any reports of movement by the gunmen inside of the bus station came to this officer, Captain George Bainer from the Michigan State Police. There just weren't any good, juicy, fresh pieces of information coming in. Time is the key factor in this story, John thought. He knew they needed to have time to prepare and package the story before the evening news. If they stayed out here too long, they wouldn't get back in time. He looked down at his watch. Twenty minutes left.

The gunmen, huddled away from the hostages, began to work on a plan of how to get out of the bus station. They kept Amy close by as they talked about making a run for their van parked out back.

Amy sat quiet, looking over at her fellow hostages. Some cried while others sat defiantly, ready to pounce if the occasion happened to arise.

The small, wiry man who suggested she be their hostage grabbed Amy and pulled her down the corridor. The other two men walked backwards with their guns trained on the hostages as they headed toward the back door.

Amy didn't try to resist, feeling it would only get her hurt. She calmly went along with the man toward the back exit. The other two caught up, looking over their shoulders to make sure they hadn't been followed. As they walked up, the grimy man tried to hit Amy with the butt of his gun, but the big man pushed the gun causing him to miss. "Why do you want to do that? She's being cooperative."

"She is now, but what if she stops?"

"We don't want to leave a trail of blood for anyone to follow." The big man shook his head as they moved toward the back of the building.

The other hostages stayed in place as instructed. "You make a move and we'll shoot you all."

CHAPTER 9

Judy shot video footage all around Central Station. She dodged police officers, who she knew would tell her to get back behind the barricades. They would say, "You're putting the hostages in danger if they see you pointing that camera at them."

"I've heard it all before," she thought. Being a professional, Judy felt she had to get this footage for the public to see. She handled the camera as if she had never stopped doing the job, getting the best shots using small movements. She got everything she could from the front of the building.

The equipment grew heavy as she lugged it around to the back where the buses sat parked. As she filmed two empty buses she realized the hostages inside the station should be boarding them.

She moved with purpose behind the station and found a great angle to shoot. The perfect place was next to a stinky dumpster. It offered her protection while being in direct line with the back doors. From her vantage point she could see policemen positioned around the building as well as see inside the terminal.

As soon as the lens focused she saw people moving toward the back of the station. She immediately recognized who she was looking at. One man carried a gun while holding a woman. Two other men brandishing guns ran up next to the man and woman. She zoomed in on the rear doors of the building.

The closer they got to the back door, the harder Judy focused. She pointed the lens directly on the face of the woman. "That's Amy." She took a deep breath to help her regain her composure in order to continue doing her job.

She thought about leaving her camera perched on the edge of the dumpster so she could rescue Amy. Judy wanted to help, but didn't want to cause Amy to be harmed, or killed, over something foolish she might do.

Instead, she did the only thing she could remember to do, something she had learned from another photojournalist. "Keep shooting until the story ends."

Reluctantly, she stayed put and kept the camera focused on the three men. The longer she stood there recording video, the more determined she was to get great shots of the three men. She also remembered what Jack had told her of using everything about a person to identify them, things such as; tattoos, piercings, scars, hair, teeth, height and weight, and clothing. Judy zoomed the camera in tight on each of the men's faces. She checked her watch, knowing time had become her enemy. "One minute longer. That'll give me five to get back to the van."

The back door of the bus station inched open. As the first of the three men stepped out, Judy whispered, "This shot's for you, Amy."

———————

Heavy perspiration dripped from the officers as the predicted extreme heat hit in early June. The sun bore down relentless with tenacity as the officers stood ready behind the bus station in their dark uniforms waiting for something, anything to happen. Average temperatures should have been in the upper 70's for this time of year. The thermometer, from the bank sign across the street from the bus terminal, read 85. Everyone felt miserable because, not only did the temperature soar, but the humidity accompanied it.

Judy panned the camera through the parking lot and the parallel street trying to see where the gunmen might go. Several vehicles sat parked nearby, one of which, she thought, might be used as the getaway vehicle.

She glanced at her watch and saw her time had expired. She pulled out her cell phone to get a message to John and Peter. Before she got the opportunity to type anything, the gunmen headed directly toward her. She set the phone down and kept filming.

Over her shoulder she knew one of the vehicles had to be the gunmen's. She made her way from the dumpster to get by a beat up white van. "This is not smart. This is not smart." She moved in stealth mode, not wanting to alert the gunmen or the police officers of her presence.

———————

In the front of the building, next to a GRPD utility truck, Peter and John compared notes.

"We don't have anything new here, Peter." John sighed feeling the weight of failure.

"I know. We could've gotten this from the radio."

"What do you think about what one officer said of this possibly being terrorist related?"

"It would need to be verified by some reliable sources before I would air that on the news tonight."

"I agree. Come on, let's keep digging."

"Thankfully, nobody's been shot."

"It is odd, though, that no demands seem to have been made. It's like this just turned out to be a robbery gone awry and now the gunmen have no way out."

"That might make this situation more dangerous, with the odds of someone getting hurt increased."

"Desperate men do desperate things," John overheard one officer say.

Peter checked his watch. "We gotta get back to the van, John."

"I know." John sighed again as he began to walk. "There's no point staying here anyway. We're not getting any information from these guys."

As they headed toward the WGRT van, John stopped and rubbed his chin. "Okay, when we get back to the van, let's see how Judy did. If she didn't fare any better, then we come back here and press harder."

"I agree." Peter took out his handkerchief and wiped his forehead. "This heat is a killer."

"You're not kidding there. I can't wait to get back into the van with the a/c kicked up."

"On the positive side, we managed to walk all the way down the block as far away from the van as we could possibly get." Neither could muster the strength to laugh.

They walked with their heads hung low, in exhaustion, from the heat, and because they felt they had failed to cover the story properly.

"I don't know if we've got enough to fill up a two minute spot let alone to be able to take the lead story tonight," Peter said, as they slowly made their way back.

"It's been rough going. Talk about trial by fire. I didn't think I was that rusty until I got out here. I think I'll stick to reporting the news someone else finds. It's a whole lot easier."

Peter chuckled and agreed working behind the scenes inside the television studio was much easier.

CHAPTER 10

Pithel and Jareb walked unseen next to John and Peter accompanied by two other warrior angels, Josiah and Mikael. Moments before, Pithel spoke, "Our mission is from the Almighty. We must not have any interference. Is that clear?"

"Yes," both Josiah and Mikael said together.

"We must allow events to take place. You are to only assist in keeping those fallen angels at bay."

"We will not fail, Pithel," Josiah stated, with Mikael agreeing.

"For the Almighty," Pithel exclaimed.

"For the Almighty," Josiah, Mikael and Jareb said in unison.

"Then here is our mission from our Lord. He wishes this reporter come to know him as his Lord and Savior. He has asked me to convince him of our Lord's existence which at this time this mortal doubts. Josiah, as the guardian who has watched over him, you know he does not believe in our Lord."

Pithel reached out a powerful hand and placed it gently on Josiah's shoulder, "How difficult a task you have had, my brother, in trying to keep him from dying before he accepts Jesus into his heart. You truly are an exceptional warrior."

Josiah only nodded his head in gratitude.

Pithel turned his attention back to the mission. Jareb stood by his side, his focus on a window from the building next door. The building, an old warehouse, abandoned by its owners many years ago, had rotted floors, broken windows, several patches of missing brick, and a lack of business. The five story building had deteriorated like the rest of the neighborhood.

———◆———

On the third floor, a lone figure stood just out of sight, watching the crisis next door. He held a fully loaded automatic rifle in his trembling hands.

Sweat poured from every pore in his body, soaking his shirt, dripping into his eyes, and rolling off his chin. He stood breathing heavily, arguing with his conscience about his orders.

"If I fail, my boss will kill me. But if I go through with it, then I'll get shot by the police."

He had joined a group, formed to protest the capture of a man known to most of the country as David Hartley, which was not his real name. His birth certificate read Joseph Hart. The group turned violent, after David had been taken into custody, just over three weeks earlier.

The group, called Anti-Pro, vowed to do anything and everything to get their leader freed from federal custody. Never mind the alleged crime, from eight months earlier, of killing a woman who refused to join him in his newly formed ministry. The group had declared war on Grand Rapids, the city where David had originally formed his group.

The man, in the building next door to the bus station, had been ordered to kill fifteen people for the release of their leader. This had been part of the vow; fifteen people killed for every week David Hartley remained in custody. This would be the first test of the group's fortitude. They felt the government would release their leader because otherwise innocent people would die. The government, however, stood its ground in dealing with threats, domestic or abroad, and would not bow to terrorist groups.

This man, chosen to take the first shot in their new war, had never been a violent man. He had been taunted into doing this deed by the other men, who were too cowardly to do the job themselves.

He shook his head and blew air out of his lungs, to clear the thoughts disturbing him. Slowly, he brought the rifle to his shoulder and took aim into the crowd. His shaking hands made the task of keeping the gun steady difficult.

His orders had been clear. "Make this a random shooting." The hostage situation next door didn't matter to him. For him, it was an added bonus to make his job easier to complete.

"I'll show those three idiots who the coward is. Next time they'll think twice before telling me what I will and won't do. I do what I say I'll do."

Five police cars blocked the road where John and Peter found themselves stopped. Behind them, a huge gathering of people pressed up against the barricade and squad cars to get a better view.

"Getting through this crowd is impossible," Peter said. "We'll never make it back to the van on time."

Without a second thought, John stepped in front of the first squad car as Peter followed. They held their press credentials high. "We're only going around the car and right back behind the barricade." The officer standing by waved them onward.

The moment they stepped in front of the police car, gunshots rang out. It sounded like the start of the Revolutionary War and the famous "shot heard 'round the world."

For hours nothing happened around the scene. In one second shots erupted followed closely by complete and utter chaos. Shots rained down on the crowd from seemingly every direction.

John and Peter found themselves in the proverbial no man's land. They sprinted to find safety behind the cars. Pithel and Jareb each guided a bullet to hit John and Peter in the exact same spot, right above their right ears and more to the back of the head. They both fell to the ground instantly.

Shots continued from all directions, with everyone shooting at everything. The scene was surreal. The police took aim at the bus station, believing the three gunmen inside decided to make a break and run for it. Shattered glass sprayed everywhere. Bullet holes filled the walls.

CHAPTER 11

As the hostage takers neared the back doors, they slid to a stop, crashing into each other.

"Is that gunfire?"

"What's going on?" screamed the small man. He tightened his grip on Amy's arm.

"I don't know," shouted the big man. "They just started shooting at us. Get moving." They pressed on to the back of the building, ready to make their escape.

Next door in the warehouse, the man continued firing away. No one realized it was him doing all the shooting. He sprayed bullets high and low, back and forth, into the crowd.

Pandemonium reigned as bullets flew and ricocheted off the pavement. People stampeded in all directions as they trampled over each other to seek shelter. No one noticed the two fallen reporters in the street. Pools of blood encircled each of their heads.

Judy, shooting footage by the van, heard the gunfire from the front of the building. As she looked through the camera lens into the bus station, she could see the gunmen look out the door, confused and but not shooting. A puzzled look washed over her face, as she scampered to get her gear, and go where the action took place. "I wonder who they're shooting at. The bad guys are back here." She adjusted one of the cables on her belt, which had tangled around her feet.

All of the police officers who had stood guard behind the bus station immediately took off running. Judy could hear the frantic voice on their radios. "SHOTS FIRED. SHOTS FIRED."

She ducked her head, before peering around the side of the van, to be sure the coast was clear, getting ready to make the dash to the front of the bus station. One step out from behind the van, she saw the gunmen crashing through the doors, with Amy as their hostage. Judy threw herself back behind her hiding place, turned the camera toward the fleeing gunmen. They headed right at her.

She looked over her shoulder and realized the van she'd been hiding next to was their getaway vehicle. It was an old white Chevy cargo van, full of rust, no hub caps, and no windows sitting less than a hundred yards from the back door of the station.

"I was right. This is their van!" She turned the camera toward the white van, to get the shot of a lifetime, and to "impress everyone back at WGRT." She also wanted to gain the respect of her peers.

Before she could get the camera pointed and focused, a bone-chilling crunch came down across the back of her head. She fell sprawled on the ground into a state of unconsciousness. The camera went flying underneath a car parked nearby. The record button remained in the 'on' position, continuing to shoot pictures of whatever crossed the path of the lens.

One of the three gunmen tried to grab the camera, but the sound of footsteps changed his mind. Instead, he raced to catch up with the other two with Amy and now Judy in tow. Amy knew the deputies would see the camera, eventually. She only hoped the woman now crumpled next to her had been able to get pictures of them along with the van.

The door of the white van slammed shut and the driver pulled away, squealing the tires as he left the area.

"Are you trying to get us caught?" asked the big man. He biffed the back of the driver's head with an open hand.

"What're you talking about?" He rubbed his head.

"You just squealed the tires. Why not just get out and yell *here we are* to the police?"

"Oh, yeah, I didn't think about that. Sorry."

One of the deputies, who began to run towards the sound of the gunfire, heard the squeal of tires. His initial thought was of someone trying to get out of harm's way. He turned to see the vehicle but saw nothing. "I'll check it out when the area is more secure," he thought as he headed to the front of the bus station.

———————————•———————————

Within five minutes of returning to the back of the bus station, Deputy Jake Daniels, who had always been ribbed about his name, hovered near the camera he'd found under the car. He was careful to not touch it in case there were fingerprints. He radioed the commanding officer, who continued trying to sort out where the original shots had come from only moments earlier, and told him about the camera.

"Secure the area, Deputy Daniels. I'll send a detective and the forensics team your way."

"Yes sir." With the area secure, Jake turned his attention to the rest of the area. He came to the conclusion the gunmen had fled to a vehicle somewhere near the dumpster. Though he was not an expert, he surmised this from the angle and the trajectory of the camera, the operator had been within fifteen feet from where he now stood.

He also noted the tire marks, left by a vehicle, just a few feet farther from the dumpster. Jake couldn't come up with any more information before the forensics team arrived. He pointed at the camera wedged under a car. He also showed the tire marks as he explained his theory to anyone who might be listening.

Derrin Andrews, a technician on the forensics team, reached under the vehicle and grabbed the camera with a gloved hand.

"It's still recording." He hit the 'off' button.

"Get the video to the truck ASAP," commanded Beverly York, team leader. "And see what was filmed before it ended up under this car."

Derrin hurried back to the truck. The rest of the team continued to scour the area for clues, including tire marks.

CHAPTER 12

Only after the bullets stopped bouncing off the steamy, hot pavement did the eerie silence give way to the brave souls who came to the aid of the wounded. Everything stopped as quickly, and as suddenly, as it had begun. It was like a fast moving thunderstorm hitting without warning, with wind, rain, and hail, which ends moments after it begins, going from total turmoil to perfect peace.

Law enforcement officers converged into the open with caution. With guns drawn, they began to secure the area, being hyper vigilant with every move. The officers scoured the area for the shooter or shooters. They also cleared the way for EMT personnel to move in to tend to the wounded.

Everything moved in slow motion. The relentless heat on the pavement gave the sense of the horrific scene being merely a mirage. Bodies on the streets assured the rescue personnel of the reality before them.

The EMTs, paramedics, fire fighters, and other first responders had been told to stay in the safe areas with their heads down. This included Bill Jones and Katlynn DePores, from the Grand Rapids Fire Department. They were eager to get to the wounded.

Bill always followed procedures by the book, took the order to stay down seriously. Katlynn also tried to be cautious, but always stood willing to take more chances. As opposite as they were in regards to safety, when it came to the wounded people, they were a great team.

Katlynn had her gear in hand and wanted to get moving. Bill reminded her of what their training instructor had told them, "Safety must always be on the top of your list. It's the first rule of any rescue operation. This includes your safety. You're no good to anyone needing medical attention if, because you rushed into a situation, and you end up on the ground next to them."

"Come on, Bill, whoever did the shooting is long gone by now. We gotta get out there and start helping people."

"I know you're right, but I don't want to get shot because we ran into something that isn't over yet. I got a wife and kids to think about."

"You can sit here if you want to, but I'm going. I really could use your help."

Reluctantly, Bill began to inch forward next to Katlynn. "Let's at least move slow and keep our heads down," he sighed.

"Deal."

Soon, officers deemed the area to be safe enough to allow the paramedics to come out and help the wounded. With the 'all clear' signal given, fifty paramedics, firemen, and other police officers approached those injured. Bill and Katlynn ran to the two men just in front of a police car that had been riddled with bullet holes.

"Gunshot wound to the head," Katlynn said to Bill.

"Same here. You getting any pulse?"

"Yes, but weak. Lost a lot of blood already."

"This one too. We better get them moved fast if they have any chance at all of surviving."

"I agree." Katlynn reached for her radio and called for two ambulances. She gave a brief description of the injuries each man had. "Ambulances will be here in less than a minute."

Both continued working on the men, covering the wounds to staunch the bleeding, get other vital signs, and stabilize the patients for transport. They were limited as to what could be done while the two men lay in the street.

———◆———

Two ambulances arrived at the same time as other medical personnel jumped in to help get the victims ready for transport. The man who assisted Katlynn pointed out, "That's John Robertson of WGRT news."

"What?" The announcement threw off Katlynn's attention as she did a double-take, shocked she didn't recognize her favorite news anchor.

"This is Peter Stallings from WGRT." The medical technician helping Bill held up the name badge.

"Quit gawking and get them loaded right now," Bill yelled. It snapped everyone back into focus. The EMTs responded by getting back to work. "Every second counts right now." They had the victims loaded and gone within a minute of Bill's reprimand.

As soon as the ambulance pulled away, Bill and Katlynn looked around for other wounded. All they saw were blood stains spotting the streets as the wail of the last sirens faded away.

As Bill and Katlynn made their way back to the medical equipped fire truck, they learned five people had already died. Three others had very serious wounds, which included the two they had assisted. Most of the EMTs felt sure there would be more dead before the end of the night. Many others had minor injuries, all expected to make full recoveries. Those pronounced dead at the scene by the county coroner had been respectfully loaded into waiting ambulances and transported to the morgue for identification by the next of kin.

Bill sat on the curb next to the van, exhausted. Katlynn grabbed two bottles of water, handed him one as she sat next to him.

"Tough day."

Bill grunted in acknowledgement.

They both just sat quiet, calming down from the adrenaline rush of the bullets and the victims. It felt longer than the three hours they had been at the bus station.

"Why aren't they dead?" Bill recalled his days of service in Iraq. Today's massacre had brought back memories of his days serving as a medic in the war. He continued to get treatment for PTSD.

"Those two men aren't going to die. They're going to live long and normal lives." Katlynn had always been a firm believer in the power of positive thinking. It's something her father taught her when she was a little girl, "If you want something bad enough, all you have to do is think positive thoughts and it will be sure to happen."

"I hope you're right, Kat. I hope you're right."

CHAPTER 13

In the warehouse next to the bus station, the lone figure sat quietly, waiting for the police to clear out before making his exit. His hands shook uncontrollably as he relived what he had just completed.

He took the rifle apart and put it inside the large duffle bag he carried his weapon in. Zipping the bag shut, he laughed to himself as he mumbled, "Boy, oh boy, Jimmy, you sure did it now. That was good. They dropped like flies out there. And those cops, those cops shot at anything that moved in the bus station. They never realized that it was me, Jimmy Morten, doing all the shooting from here. I'm going to get away scot free and those three boneheads next door are going to take the heat. They don't even have a clue."

He shook his head as he lifted the bag onto his shoulder and started to leave. He knew those who had made fun of him before sure wouldn't be laughing when he got back and told them about what he had done. Jimmy headed for the staircase, small dust trails kicking behind him.

———— ◆ ————

In the shadows, on the far side of the warehouse, a large beastly creature glowered. Its eyes grew narrow and intense like an old alley cat perched and ready to jump on the prey. Saliva dripped down from fangs protruding from its elongated lips forming a sinister grin. "That could not have gone any better. My master will be pleased."

———— ◆ ————

"Jimmy has left the building." The door latched behind him as he rushed through the parking lot. With a heightened sense of paranoia, he peered over his shoulders trying to appear relaxed. He slowed to a casual walk as he neared his pickup truck. When he looked up, his heart skipped a beat as he met the eyes of a weathered middle-aged man standing between him and his truck. Jimmy hoped to get by without talking.

"You got any change, Mister?" Jimmy's head dropped at the sound of the voice. He noted the tremor in the extended hand. "I sure could use some change so I can eat today."

Jimmy's eyes met the old man's. They were gentle and kind, putting Jimmy at ease for the moment.

"What? Oh yeah, change. Here's a couple of bucks. Now beat it."

"God bless you, sir."

"Glad I could help. Now really, I have to get out of here right now." Jimmy stepped around the man as threw his duffle bag into the bed of the truck. Sweat poured off his head from his chin, into his eyes, and one drip off of his nose. He climbed into the red Ford F-150 pickup truck, took a deep breath, started the engine, and quickly left the area.

———◆———

The shadowy figure, still on the third floor, watched as Jimmy took off. He let out a gut-wrenching laugh as he gloated in this victory for his master.

"That was rather enjoyable." The beast spoke into the empty warehouse, "Humans are such easy prey these days." He then disappeared to report to his master of his successful mission. He knew he would be rewarded handsomely for not only a completed mission but success.

The rest of this most important battle now belonged to his comrades who waited nearby for this part of the mission to be completed. The beast reappeared momentarily, to give instructions to the anxious and unruly hoard.

"Your task is to make sure those two reporters don't survive. You are also to see that those angelic warriors would stay away."

———◆———

In the middle of the nearly empty street, four large angels stood shoulder to shoulder, unseen by humans. "We have achieved a victory on this battlefield today," Pithel stated. "This is the plan our Lord has laid out for us." Thunder rolled to his ears. He excused himself and separated himself from Jareb, Mikael, and Josiah. A band of other angels lined the perimeter ready to fight, certain to come under attack by the blood-thirsty devils in the vicinity.

"It always feels strange," Mikael said, "how when something evil is in the air, it spreads over many people at one time. It causes grief to everyone in the area."

"But on the other hand," Josiah interjected, "it's just as amazing when a good deed can produce other good deeds. Look at the way they helped each other here."

"Humans can be easily swayed," Jareb lamented. "Whether they give in to the evil or hold on to that which is good, is up to them to decide." He turned to look toward Pithel. "I have seen many evil men turn to good and good men turn to evil deeds. That is why we must continue to be vigilant in our mission."

Both Josiah and Mikael agreed.

As Pithel stood alone, he listened to his Master.

"Yes, my Lord. The first portion of the mission is complete as you have commanded. The demons, however, are doing all they can to thwart the victory. In spite of their interference, we have prevailed." Pithel never hid his disdain toward the forces of darkness.

"I await further orders from your throne to complete this mission. I, and my fellow warriors, will do our utmost to give you all of the glory, my Lord." Pithel knelt down on one knee as he spoke reverently before the Almighty God. From where they stood, Jareb, Josiah, and Mikael also knelt.

Another rumble of thunder pierced Pithel's ears.

"Yes, my Lord, I will wait for the reporter, John Robertson, outside of your kingdom's walls. I will also be aware of the evil one."

He walked back to his friends. "I will see you soon Jareb. Josiah and Mikael, I thank you, and the legion of angels you have brought with you, for your assistance today." With that he left to his next destination.

Back at the WGRT van, the demons felt the weight of their lost victory. They argued over who should be blamed for this blunder, pointing fingers at each other.

"What did you do, Albus?" Their captain stood large and brooding as he yelled into the face of his much smaller subordinate.

"Me? I followed your orders, sir. That's what I did." He cowered after saying that, expecting to be pummeled.

"Maybe this is what our master's plan is," interrupted another devil squatting on top of the van.

"To lose a battle to them?" The captain snarled as he pointed toward the army of angels in the street. Moments later the arguing turned into shouts. Fights broke out throughout their ranks which caused further dissension.

The fight stemmed from the incident of the two reporters being shot but not dying.

"They should both be dead. Not dying, but dead." The captain pushed his way into the middle of the fighting demons. "Who was assigned to see to it that their injuries were fatal?" He looked around for the guilty party. None of the defiant demons stepped forward.

Albus, always the mischievous one, spoke up, "Look, it doesn't matter what happened here today. Yes, our master will be upset. But remember, the battle has only begun. There are more of us than them." He jerked his head toward the angels. "We just have to get to the reporters first." Laughter filled the air as the pack of demons stopped their fighting and patted each other on the backs.

Their leader gave instructions of next part of their mission. "Be ready to move to these fallen reporters immediately. We must work harder to secure the victory. There will be no breaks until further notice."

The devils grumbled at the order. The fighting started back up. They scattered as Pithel flew through the middle of them as he left the region.

"Come back here and fight us, you coward." Albus shouted, after he thought Pithel had vanished. "I didn't think he would be brave enough to fight me. Why I'd beat him from one side of the universe to the other without even working up a sweat." He began to wrestle himself as if fighting the angelic warrior, not realizing Pithel had come back and stood behind him with his arms folded across his massive chest.

The rest of the demons backed away slack jawed at the appearance of the mighty warrior.

"Psst, Albus, look behind you," pointed one of the demons in the pack.

"What?" responded the self-wrestling demon. "Do you think I'm gonna fall for that?"

"But he truly is behind you."

Slowly Albus turned and faced the massive Pithel. He cowered to the ground with no place to hide.

"You wish to fight with me, little creature?" Pithel's voice boomed.

"No, not really. I was only joking around. Don't you angels have a sense of humor?"

"We will meet up at a later time, creature." Pithel vanished from view.

All the demons laughed, jeered, and mocked Albus. It brought out the most hideous and evil side of him. He proceeded to wreak havoc on a little dog walking by at the wrong time. The demon entered the body of the dog and sent it into the street in front of a speeding car, instantly killing the dog. Albus was shaken from the blow of the car, but soon got up and left the area.

"Well, at least it wasn't pigs," one of the demons said.

CHAPTER 14

Law enforcement officers assisted the hostages in leaving the bus terminal and getting to a place of safety. Each person needed to be debriefed. Counselors were also on hand.

"We need to know everything you were able to see and hear during the situation," Officer Ken O'Conner of the GRPD stated in a matter-of-fact fashion. "Things such as what the men were wearing, scars, tattoos, even color of eyes and hair will all assist us in being able to capture these criminals and prosecute them. It will put an end to what you have had to endure here today."

The officers moved cautiously around the group of former hostages, giving them time to unwind and collect their thoughts. They wanted the people to realize the police were on their side. Refreshments had been brought in with assistance from the local Red Cross.

The police felt it was important to show they cared especially with some recent bad press the departments received. It was after a riot broke out over a court ruling that an officer had shot and killed a young boy who had allegedly pulled a gun on him. The evidence showed the boy had only pulled a piece of fruit from his pocket.

At the trial the jury acquitted the officer stating, "He had acted in proper manner due to the area of the city being known for drugs and gang activity." The residents of the neighborhood took to the streets, turned over and burned several cars, looted every business within a five block radius, and injured countless people. The protest lasted two days.

The former hostages, who sat inside a local high school cafeteria, started getting restless.

"When can we go home?"

"I have to get to my children."

"Why are we being held here?"

As the people peppered the questions towards the police officers standing guard at the doors, in walked newly promoted detective Jack McDougal from the Michigan State Police. He stopped, just inside the cafeteria doors, where he abruptly turned towards a group of officers who were talking softly.

"According to reports, three employees of WGRT were involved today."

"Yeah, I heard John Robertson was shot along with Peter Stallings."

"I also heard a woman named Judy Metcalf was taken hostage."

"Excuse me, Roger?" Jack interrupted. "Who did you say was taken hostage?"

"What's that sir?" responded Roger Owens.

"Did I hear you say the name Judy Metcalf?"

"Yes sir, Judy Metcalf," Officer Owens stated.

"From WGRT?"

"Yes, from WGRT. We found her camera behind the bus station still shooting footage for the news."

"Thanks, Roger. I need a minute before I talk to the people here." Jack sat in shocked silence as he absorbed the terrible news.

"Detective McDougal, is everything all right?"

"Oh, yes, yes everything is fine. Were there any other hostages?"

"Yes. According to everyone here, a young college girl has also been taken hostage. We have been informed her name is Amy Tuinstra." Silence hung in the air as the tension seemed to intensify. "Sir, are you sure you're all right?"

"Yes, I'm fine. I'm just thinking about the next few steps. Tell the crime unit to hold onto the film from the camera for me."

"Yes sir," Bill replied.

———◆———

Jack left the high school to look at the video from Judy's camera. On his way out, he gave instructions to get the information they needed and to get the people out of there as quick as they could. "They've been through a lot today. No need to make them go through any more." As he got into his car, he thought about how inexperienced he felt at not having many opportunities in hostage situations in his five years with the Michigan State Police.

Now, on his first case as not only a detective, but lead detective, he had to investigate a crime involving someone he loved. He prayed as he started up the car that God would protect Judy and Amy and to give him the strength and wisdom to find them. He put the car in gear and drove back to the Central Station.

Jake, the deputy who discovered the camera, pointed Jack to the forensics truck.

"Thank you, Deputy Daniels," Detective McDougal stated. "I need you to stand by while I look at the tape. I might have some questions for you. Also find out if anyone on the forensics team saw the tape yet."

"Yes, sir." Jake walked towards some of the forensics team.

———•———

The video from the camera started with basic shots of the bus station from various angles. Jack sat alone in the truck working the fast forward button. The camera zoomed in to get a tight shot of one of the gunmen.

"Good job, Judy." Jack gave a small fist pump. She was able to get very good facial features of the man pulling Amy Tuinstra along. The other two gunmen ran up behind them. Judy zoomed in on their faces as well. "Wow, Judy, you've done some amazing work here."

Finally, the camera picked up voices growing louder, as the picture began to shake violently and crash to the ground. The lens caught a momentary glimpse of Judy unconscious and then dragged away. Jack's anger boiled over seeing the woman he loved harmed and then taken hostage.

Jack stepped out of the truck and asked, "Deputy Daniels, has anyone seen this video?"

"No, sir. They waited to allow you to see it first."

"Good. And thank you. Now can you please ask the team to join me in the van?"

"Right away sir."

———•———

"Thank you for letting me see the tape first," Jack said to the assembled team of forensic specialists. "Now I want you to see it to get your impressions of what you see taking place." He had learned the first impressions are to be considered some of the most important work a detective has to work with.

He had picked up that tactic from the veteran detective who trained him, his father, also Jack McDougal. Jack was not Jack Jr. because his father did not want him to be called Jr., so he named his son with his father's first name,

Albert, while his own middle name was Allan. The other officers, however, still called him Jr. He didn't mind since his father had been a great detective. In fact, he considered it an honor to be referred to by his father's name.

Detective Jack Albert McDougal left the crime scene and went back to the makeshift shelter to check on the debriefing of anyone left at the school. He wanted to make sure the officers didn't pressure these innocent people. Jack did have a compassionate side, especially for the victims.

He would be tough, however, when he had to be. When a crime had been committed, Jack worked tirelessly to make sure the person who did it was caught and brought to justice. His father had given him those pearly of wisdoms just before he died of cancer less than one month ago.

A special crime unit from the Michigan State Police entered the Central Station after Jack gave the okay. They were to search for more evidence in the area where the hostages had been held.

CHAPTER 15

The two ambulances drove away, sirens blared and lights flashed, en route to St. John's Hospital. A team of doctors and nurses stood ready to accept the first two gunshot victims being brought in. Each ambulance driver responded with the accelerator pressed to the floor while they dodged heavy downtown traffic.

In the first ambulance, George Meyers radioed, "Victim male, 35 years old, heart beat erratic but holding, breathing is weak controlled by respirator. Skin color is pale, cold and clammy. Victim appears to be in shock."

The voice on the other end of the radio, Dr. David Howard, ordered, "Keep the pulse as steady as possible. Continue checking all other vitals. Get him here ASAP."

"Roger that. ETA less than 2 minutes. Unit 47 out."

The second ambulance carried Peter Stalling. His condition mirrored that of John Robertson's. The EMT, Jeff Mallory, riding in the ambulance numbered unit 15, knew the answer would be the same as he listened to Dr. Howard respond to unit 47.

Both ambulances sped up.

"This is really bizarre," stated Dr. Howard to his colleagues, "two gunshot victims and both shot in the head in what appears to be the exact same spot. I think we have something very freaky going on today. I chose the wrong day to take an extra shift, didn't I?"

Most of the gunshot victims the doctor had dealt with over his career had never ended well. To him, gunshot wounds equaled death. His concerns swirled around whether either man could be saved or if their efforts would be a foregone conclusion. No matter, he and his team would do their utmost to save the patients, regardless of the injuries.

"This will take precise directions and an enormous amount of team work," he said, rallying the assembled teams. "That includes all the doctors, if we are to have any chance of success today." Dr. Howard divided the staff into two teams.

"We'll be working in rooms five and six. Keep the curtains open enough for us to be able to go back and forth as necessary. Kelly, call up to the OR and have them on stand-by. Everyone else, get in place and let's rock and roll." He walked with the orderlies to the doors as they waited for the ambulances. On the way, he turned to two nurses and ordered, "Have syringes ready to get blood immediately. I also want STAT labs done." The nurses nodded and hurried off.

As the rest of the teams waited near the doors of the ER, sirens could be heard getting louder. "We're going to be making some very fast and difficult decisions, so be ready for anything." He paused and then looked at each member of the teams, "It's up to us whether these men will live or die today. Let's pray we help them to live."

———◆———

Pithel waited near the entrance of St. John's Hospital next to the staff. The sirens shut off as the ambulances turned into the loading area. The angel stood alert as his mission continued. Jareb joined him, along with four other warriors, who had come along with him.

"They have such archaic modes of transportation," Pithel spoke under his breath. "My brothers, the battle continues here. We must not and we will not fail." Jareb and the four angelic warriors each put a hand out, like a basketball team in a huddle. Pithel joined the circle and placed his massive hand on top.

"We are prepared for the fight, Pithel."

Pithel posted each warrior in strategic places. "Mikael and Gideon stand guard in room five. Josiah and Oramni, you will guard room six. When they move, you move with them. You are to never leave their side. Be vigilant for the devils. They will try to gain access to these souls. We are strong, but so is the enemy. The Almighty God has given us enough power to overcome."

The warriors moved into position, swords drawn as they stood alert and ready to do battle. Jareb spoke to Pithel relating what he overheard Dr. Howard say about the survival of the two men.

"That doctor said it was up to them, the doctors, whether these men live or not."

51

Pithel shook his head and asked, "Does he not know that only our God can give or take life, not a human?" He sighed. "Still, I understand the doctor's intent."

———•———

Unit 47 pulled in first. The team of doctors, nurses and orderlies met them at the door. The head nurse, Angie Tyler, gave the orders, "Room five." They pushed the gurney to the room. Only the machines hooked up to John Robertson kept him alive for the time being. The moment the gurney rolled into the room everyone moved in constant motion.

Orders came in rapid fire succession.

"Get him on the monitor stat."

"Call the trauma team," Dr. Howard barked at the nurse he pointed toward. She ran out to make the call. Dr. Howard went on with the orders without missing a beat.

"Run Lactated Ringers wide open and start two units of O-negative blood."

The room looked like complete chaos with no organization whatsoever. Everyone in the emergency room, however, knew their job without question. They worked together as a team to save the life of the victim. They had been informed of who the victim was before his arrival. They had elated thoughts initially of being able to meet a celebrity. Those thoughts quickly faded as they remembered their motto of: "Any patient is a patient, no matter their lot in life." This team would be counted on to save John Robertson's life.

More orders came from Dr. Howard, "Hyperventilate him to keep the brain swelling down and start Mannitol." A nurse carried out the task to perfection without any mishaps.

"Get him intubated on a #7 ET tube. Then bag him and get him to CAT scan."

Within thirty minutes from the time John Robertson arrived, orderlies wheeled him to the CAT scan room where the monitors showed minimal amounts of blood in the ventricles of the brain.

"Get him to the third floor right away." The trauma team stood by prepared to receive the patient.

———•———

Peter Stallings in Unit 15 had arrived in the ER less than two minutes after John Robertson. His team of doctors and nurses worked on him in room six. The orders from Dr. Jalinski, sounded very similar to those given in room five. They prepared him for surgery after his CAT scan.

———————•———————

After Peter had been wheeled to the third floor for surgery, the doctors in the emergency rooms talked about the chances of survival for each man.

"If I were a betting man I wouldn't give either one a very good chance of survival. Those were some pretty nasty gunshot wounds," Dr. Jalinski stated. The staff all agreed the odds had been stacked against the two victims.

Dr. Howard added, "Even if they survive the surgery, returning to a normal life is even slimmer odds." He sighed heavily as he continued, "They will probably be 'vegetables' on feeding tubes soaking the insurance companies for all their worth."

The doctors had become cynical and hard-hearted from all the patients that had come through the emergency room throughout the years. Many patients had survived their ordeals to go on to live normal lives. Others, however, either died from their injuries or illnesses or ended up unable to function 'normally' after they came to St. John's.

The doctors and nurses learned to safeguard their emotions as to not get emotionally attached to any of their patients in case they did not make it. It's the way they dealt with some very traumatic incidences.

"I apologize for that last comment," Dr. Howard said. "You all performed great in there. Good work everyone." He turned to go to his desk to begin typing his orders into the computer.

CHAPTER 16

After three hours of grueling surgeries each, both John and Peter had, for the moment, survived. The doctors, with hopeful optimism, constantly examined the men. All of the staff worked in silence, going about their jobs with skilled precision.

In the recovery rooms, nurses kept watchful eyes on the monitors, tubes, and machines, hooked up to the men. The doctors feared the men could go into cardiac arrest, not uncommon for a traumatic event like this. They also monitored for brain swelling to either continue or begin to relieve slightly. The doctors gave the standard answer of "Too early to tell."

As time crept by slowly, it became apparent neither man would regain consciousness any time soon. Several doctors came in to assist with the assessments. Each agreed being in comas was the best course of treatment for now. After further consultation, none of the doctors could determine if the comas had been a result of the surgery or of the wounds themselves. It had been known to happen as a result of traumatic events.

"How long do you think this might last?" Dr. Jalinski asked Dr. Howard.

"I have no idea. But it may not be a bad thing right now. Having both men in comas will give their brains the opportunity to reduce the swelling as they rest." Comas had been known to last minutes, weeks, or, in some rare cases, years.

"Let's get them transferred to the ICU." Dr. Howard suggested. The nurses and orderlies began making the arrangements.

———◆———

Pithel knew why they were in a coma. It was part of his mission from Almighty God.

CHAPTER 17

On a deserted two lane highway in the middle of nowhere, the white van sped out of the city. Night had fallen and the only light came from the beams of the headlights hitting the pavement twenty feet in front of them.

Perched on the top of the van, with dark, leathery skin and glowing yellow eyes sat the demon assigned to monitor those inside. He was to make sure the van reached its destination which had been predetermined by his commander. As of this moment the van remained on course to a house far from anywhere.

Inside, the men rode in silence, exhausted from the long, trying day. In the back of the van, the limp body of Judy Metcalf lay crumpled on two tires and a toolbox, moving only with the bumps of the road and with the breathing of her body. Dried blood matted her hair where she had been hit.

She remained unconscious from the blow to her head. She never got the opportunity to see the video footage. She never knew if she had gotten the license plate number of the van. She never knew she had been hit in the head.

Amy Tuinstra sat on an empty milk crate behind the driver. Her hands and feet had been tied together. She sat calm as she prayed for protection and for a way of escape. She knew she didn't possess the power to overcome the men by herself, especially being tied up.

Next to her, but unseen, sat a large angel with a bright white robe and a razor sharp sword, drawn and ready for action. No harm would come to Amy for now. Her prayer had been answered.

Although the highway had been deserted for miles, it was just a matter of time before another vehicle approached.

"We're gonna have to get off the road soon," the big man said. "By now they've got to be setting up road blocks."

"Not to mention any possible patrol cars," the greasy driver said.

"Keep an eye out for a place to turn off. We'll start going on the side roads." Being night, they struggled to see any roads, until after they had already passed them. They didn't dare risk hitting their brakes, which would light up the road behind them, in order to turn around.

The demon on the top of the van had his razor-sharp talons through the roof and onto the steering wheel, guiding the vehicle wherever he wanted it to go without the driver knowing anything about it.

"What a rush. Woo. Who's the coward now? Come on, tell me. You guys didn't think I had the guts to pull it off did you. Well, I showed you." Jimmy rehearsed the way he would tell the rest of the group he had gotten involved with, known as Anti-Pro.

He drove his pickup truck down the highway, waved his arms, pounded on the steering wheel, and yelled out the window. The rush hour traffic barely moved. He turned the radio on as he hoped to hear about the shooting. He felt sure his friends in Anti-Pro would be ecstatic about what he did. The one most proud would be William Bennett, the current leader of the group.

"I can't believe I actually pulled that thing off. And I really can't believe I'm going to get away with this clean scot free. Nobody, and I mean nobody, saw me shooting those people. It was like shooting fish in a barrel."

In the back of the pickup truck a devil rode with fiery darts tossed deep into the heart and mind of Jimmy Morten. A thick gob of drool dripped from its tongue, as a smile bent the corners of its misshapen mouth. "I control you now, Jimmy."

In the wake of Jimmy's pickup, evil drifted over to other vehicles. A Chevy cargo van swerved into the path of a small car both caromed into the center barrier with major damage to both vehicles and to everyone inside.

Other bizarre events, such as flat tires, radiators overheating, fender-benders, and road rage, affected people and their vehicles as Jimmy drove past. Few were left untouched as one incident led to another in a chain reaction. The large demon in the back of the truck laughed at all the destruction and carnage on the highway. Jimmy drove on, oblivious to everything behind him.

CHAPTER 18

Before they left the recovery room on the surgical floor, another team of doctors examined John. Each agreed his condition had stabilized, but they remained cautious to upgrade his condition from critical until the effectiveness of the surgery became known. He would remain in the Intensive Care Unit under constant surveillance.

After the exam an orderly wheeled him from the recovery room up to the ICU. As the elevator doors opened, a nurse directed him to room #2. A team of nurses walked beside the gurney to monitor the life support machines and making sure nothing became detached during the transport from one floor to the other.

Word of the famous anchor's arrival to the floor spread like a virus. Unlike the recovery room, the buzz of voices grew as the gurney rolled down the hall, the face of the celebrity bandaged and unrecognizable. The nurses quickly put aside their star-filled eyes and got back to their patients.

Still, they found it difficult not to talk about the reasons they watched the WGRT news, while they checked his status. They couldn't agree on what drew them to him.

"It's his hypnotic eyes. They just pull me in and I can't look away. I just love that about him," exclaimed the lead nurse, Deb Nolanski, who along with nurses Julie Schmidt and Andrea Mills, made the room ready for the his arrival.

"I like his deep voice and that smile," fawned Julie.

"Come on, girls," Andrea interjected, "You know it's his rugged good looks." They all giggled like schoolgirls.

"I just wish we didn't have to meet him like this," Deb sighed as she turned back to the seriousness of the situation.

"We need to do whatever we can for him," Andrea said. She readied the blood pressure cuff and heart monitor finger clamp. "I mean, we do the best we can with everyone in the ICU. For some reason I can't explain, I just feel the need to try harder with Mr. Robertson."

"I feel the same way, Amy." Julie nodded and shook her head. "That also includes the other reporter coming here, Peter Stallings."

The nurses who stood in the halls, made a path as they stared in disbelief as the gurney was wheeled into room #2. They peered into the room mouths agape at the unrecognizable figure that lay in the bed.

Seated at a circular desk, immediately outside the room, a nurse continuously scrutinized computer and video monitors from all the machines attached to John. Any change, no matter how minor, would send teams rushing into the room to check on their patient. All in all, the Intensive Care Unit had eight identical rooms. Each had the same monitors, both in the room as well as at the main desk. All the rooms had windows which allowed the staff to keep a constant visual on their patients, but no sunshine would ever be allowed to enter through the glass.

The three nurses in the room, along with the orderly, secured the brakes on the bed, before John was transferred from one bed to the other. Once this task had been accomplished, the team worked diligently to change over the equipment of the temporary machines from the ER and surgical unit to the permanent equipment in the ICU. The changeover took less than thirty seconds, as the nurses worked in tandem, which included detaching and reattaching the monitors and life support machines as well as moving IV bags from one pole to another.

"Check his vitals," Deb ordered, back to all business.

With only a slight nod of her head, Julie methodically worked through the check list; heart monitor beeped steady, tanks released oxygen regularly through the tube affixed under his nose, temperature remained constant. "All vitals are normal," Julie reported.

"Andrea, check his IV and make sure the medication is set at the prescribed dosage."

Andrea did as requested. "Everything is working properly with the medication administered as prescribed."

Deb inspected the tubes attached to his arms, chest and head as part of the cross-checking as a precautionary measure. She also looked at the machines monitoring various activities, such as brain waves and heart rate and blood oxygen levels. She examined the medication pathways to be sure they consistently dripped properly into his body via the IV line attached to his arm.

All the beeping, buzzing, and dripping kept a constant rhythm going which, under other circumstances, might have been very musical; instead the noise meant John Robertson remained alive by life support machines.

"Good work, everyone," Deb stated to the nurses and orderly. "Let's get ready for Peter Stallings." One nurse remained at the nurses' station to monitor all the machines in room #2.

Although there are male nurses at St. John's, none had been on duty when the celebrity patient had come into their care. It would be safe to say none of the female nurses would allow any of the male nurses near John Robertson without getting first opportunity to treat him. All of the nurses, however, were aware of the seriousness of the injuries and the state the man was in right then.

"I just can't believe that's the same man I watch the news for," Jerri Koslinski said.

"I know, poor man," Anne Delman added. "It doesn't even look like him."

They made their way toward the next room, where they would be assisting the lead nurse when Peter Stallings arrived momentarily.

All the tubes, machines, and bandages wrapped around his head made John look more like a monster rather than a celebrity. Dr. Howard, still considered the lead doctor after being the first to take the call from the paramedics, came into the ICU to bring the staff up to speed the patient's progress.

"As you can all know from the seriousness of the injury sustained from the gunshot to the head, the chances of survival, let alone recovery, is very low. There's been significant swelling in the brain along with hemorrhaging. We are hopeful the surgery stabilized these issues. We won't know the results until the swelling is reduced and he comes out of the coma."

Almost as an afterthought, he added, "One more point, we believe the coma wasn't a result of the surgery nor was it induced by the doctors. As far as we can tell this is from the natural cause from the trauma. I'm sure you're all aware this is the body's way of trying to heal itself by shutting down."

Some of the nurses, after they heard the prognosis, hung their heads to say prayers, while others wept quietly. Many thought about other patients who had passed through the unit with similar if not worse injuries, and those patients had survived. The team of doctors, nurses, and other staff members knew if this man was to have the best chance to live, then everyone would have to do their job and to it with a great amount of efficiency.

Before Dr. Howard had left the ICU, the staff went back to doing their jobs, although they had never actually stopped. They made sure every patient, not just the new celebrity patient, had the correct dosage of the prescribed medications administered. They made sure all the vitals were normal and the machines continued to work properly. They also made sure each patient was as comfortable as they could be, all things considered.

Still, everyone on the unit took a special interest in John Robertson. It couldn't be helped. Perhaps having a local celebrity got them feeling star struck. Or maybe another presence was at work in the intensive care unit this day.

Pithel asked Josiah to stand guard over John Robertson in the event of unwelcome visitors entering the room. "I want no interference from the forces of evil. You have been given great power from the Almighty to withstand any attack they most certainly will try against my ward. Josiah, my friend, we must prevail." Pithel, used strong gestures as his fist pounded into his palm. He also pointed his finger into the air as he gave instructions to Josiah. After the room was secure, he looked into the eyes of the angel, "Do you understand the importance of this mission, my friend?"

With a nod of his head, Josiah said, "Yes, Pithel. I am ready to fight against any of the fallen angels who dare enter this room."

"Thank you, Josiah. I know I can trust you and your judgment as you are a most loyal warrior to the Almighty God."

Josiah turned his attention to his task without another word being spoken. His hand rested on the hilt of his sword as his eyes continuously swept the area. He was also charged to keep the hospital staff focused on John Robertson's room.

Pithel had requested and been granted the assistance of other angels to stand guard in the rooms of the other patients on the unit. He placed them in each of the other six rooms of the ICU.

"It is not my intention to put any other human's life in harm's way while the battle for John Robertson and Peter Stallings ensues."

Josiah wanted to give the staff the feeling of John Robertson being a very special patient. He worked to instill that this case needed more than their expert medical abilities, but also their true, genuine concern and care. He wanted the nurses to come into the room continuously, which would help keep the demons from being able to launch their attacks.

So far his mission had been successful as the nurses kept a steady stream in and out of the room. Some of the nurses even had business in the room, such as checking John's bandages or the continual monitors of the machines and IV bags. Josiah also knew some of the nurses prayed for the healing of the man. "Those prayers are very powerful indeed," he thought, pleased with the results so far. He gave thanks and praise to the Almighty for this blessing.

CHAPTER 19

Peter Stallings unexpectedly opened his eyes. Confused, he furrowed his brow, when he didn't recognize or understand where he found himself. Looking around, he saw he was sitting outside on a well-manicured lawn in a very peaceful place. Wherever he was, he felt warm and safe.

As he looked up at the bright sky he didn't feel the need to shade his eyes. The temperature of the place felt perfect. Oddly, he felt no pain but knew he had been injured.

Over his shoulder he glanced at an enormous wall that went on forever. Not only could he not see either end, he couldn't see the top. He reached back to place his hand on the wall. It felt very smooth as he touched it with no signs of any erosion or breaches. Peter leaned forward as far as he could, where he saw a large gate which he thought could hold his whole house and then some.

"Wow." He leaned back against the wall, still confused as to where he had ended up. "Maybe I'm dead," he said.

He looked out from the wall to the terrain around him. Gently rolling hills with the greenest grass he had ever seen met his eye. "Now that would beat Sam Jorgeson's yard any day of the week." The soft, green grass had been manicured to a perfect length.

"It smells like someone must have mowed just this morning. I'm sure glad I don't have that job." Peter relaxed with his hands clamped behind his head.

There wasn't a single cloud in the bright, blue sky. He was a little perplexed when he couldn't see the sun, but let the thought pass. Peter took in a deep breath of air so clean it almost hurt his lungs. As he continued to assess his situation he also remembered where he had lived for most of his life.

"There's no smog, no loud stereos, and no sounds of violence. No sirens and no one ordering me around. It's just peace and quiet. Maybe I really have died and gone to heaven."

He discovered he could not stand up or move around. He could move his arms and legs just not from this spot. As he contemplated where he might be and how he got there, soft music drifted into his ears from the other side of the wall. The music sounded joyous, like a celebration might be taking place. "Maybe a concert's started," he thought. He couldn't make out the words, but the music was definitely joyful.

As he sat, questions popped into his head. *"Where am I?" "Have I been kidnapped or something?" "Who would do such a thing to me?" "And why would they bring me here?"*

"Peter."

Fear replaced his feelings of peace. Peter thought of the worst case scenario. "My kidnappers have come back for me."

"Peter." The voice sounded again. "Do not be afraid. No harm will come to you."

"W-w-who's t-t-there? W-w-what do you w-w-want with m-m-me?"

"I have been sent from the Lord to strengthen your walk of faith with Him."

"I-I-I d-d-don't understand," Peter stammered.

"You will view the world in which you live, being allowed to see those things which are invisible to human eyes, but seen through spiritual eyes. You will see the world this way, so you may know the Lord is in control and know he has a task for you. I will stay by you to help you see this through as well as to give you instructions from the Lord, as he has asked me to do."

Peter pressed himself against the wall unable to speak as he trembled.

The voice continued. "You will see things in the present as they happen at that moment. This will not be future events nor will it be the past. Only the present will be seen by you."

"This is some sort of drug-induced nightmare," Peter thought. "Either that or I've seen Scrooge one too many times."

"I assure what you are experiencing is real. I have been sent by the Almighty God to help you, to guide you, and to instruct you, so that you might be stronger in your walk with him."

The voice stopped. Peter, still confused and frightened, scratched his head as he tried to make sense of what might be going on. "Okay," Peter said, "if you're real, then what's my son doing right now?"

Silence after Peter's request lasted less than a millisecond. "Behold."

Instantly, Peter found himself in the food court at the mall. The place was packed with teenagers. Loud music played through overhead speakers.

Girls talked about the boys, giggling and pointing all around the large area. Many of the teens sat with their ear buds listening to their own music while testing on their phones. The whole scene looked unruly, yet most of the kids were well behaved.

Peter moved through the crowd easily enough, seeming to go right through groups that stood around drinking sodas and eating junk food. In the middle of the food court, Peter found a kid playing a game on his cell phone. The boy, dressed in ripped blue jeans, a Detroit Lions t-shirt, and matching ball cap, was surrounded by some bigger boys looking over his shoulder.

Upon closer inspection, Peter realized he was looking at his son, Paul. The bigger boys around him did not appear to be the kind of boys Peter approved of his son hanging out with. These boys wore their hats sideways, sagging pants, and what Peter knew from the news to be the apparel of gang members in the area.

Peter also saw two monstrous creatures with long, sharp teeth and skin so dark and thick it looked like leather jackets, walking up behind his son. As they drew close, they transformed into two young girls, both very attractive with bubbly personalities and big smiles. They moved through the boys to stand on either side of Paul, along with several unseen creatures, as he continued to play his game. One of the creatures stuck a talon into the game. Paul got angry at not achieving the high score he hoped to get. He pounded the tabletop.

"What's going on?" Peter asked, not sure he wanted to know the answer.

When the voice did not reply, Peter yelled, "Where are you?"

Still no answer came from the voice. Peter instinctively began to pray for his son to be protected from the demons, and not allow them to influence him, as they now tried to do. As he stood by his son, two very large angels with swords drawn appeared. They moved the demons, putting themselves between them and Paul. The fiery swords showed the demons they had come prepared to fight. The demons thought twice about their attack against the angels as the warriors guarded the boy playing the game. The two girls quickly vacated the area leaving Paul alone.

Reluctantly, the demons snarled, hissed and howled as they backed away in retreat. Fights, between other teens, broke out all over the food court, as the devils moved toward the exit.

Paul kept playing the game. He barely noticed anything had happened around him, including the attractive girls who had stood next to him moments ago. He just kept his attention focused on his phone, allowing it to control his mind. The gang of boys around him became more involved in the game by giving Paul encouragement as they appeared to enjoy watching Paul play.

Still Paul just played the game without attention to those around him. He made it look like he was alone, even though he had several boys around him. Peter felt his son's pain of loneliness. He bowed his head and prayed for his son's welfare. He also gave a prayer of thanks for his safety.

Peter opened his eyes back up and found himself back against the wall. He thought about the entire situation and came to the realization his prayer had worked immediately. He prayed for Paul's protection and angels appeared even as he prayed.

"That's amazing. I never imagined prayer worked that fast." He paused for a moment still reflecting on what he had witnessed and learned.

"Hello?" he yelled into the air. "I believe you are who you say you are. Will you please talk to me now?" He knew his voice had been heard and it would only be a matter of time before the voice of the unseen person spoke to him again.

CHAPTER 20

At the Eastside Baptist Church, reporter Harry Nickols, a rival from the television station WOZD, waited patiently for Pastor Joseph Thompson.

"Do you know when Reverend Thompson will be back?" Harry paced in the tiny office. "I'm on kind of a tight deadline here."

"The pastor is out on a visit and should be back directly." The church secretary sat behind her desk, eyes glued to the computer monitor, never glanced up as she continued to type.

Harry came to the church to do a story about the reporters shot the day before. He knew Peter Stallings attended Eastside Baptist Church. The story would be in the human interest category with the angle of showing that journalists are regular people who often find themselves in dangerous situations. He'd waited close to an hour and was quickly running out of what little patience he had.

Harry liked to appear old-school with the look of a stereotypical reporter. He wore a brimmed hat, tweed suit coat with matching tie. He had a slight build complete with wire-rim glasses thin mustache and nasal tones when he spoke.

"Ma'am, do you know if the reverend will be much longer?" he asked again.

The secretary never took her eyes off the monitor.

"I don't mean to be impatient, but I have to get this story to my editor soon." Inside, Harry seethed with anger at the obvious stonewalling going on. He didn't like being inside churches, no matter what day it might be.

"I don't keep the pastor's schedule," she replied in a dry tone.

"I understand that. Is there a way to possibly call him?"

"He told me he would be gone for about two hours and it's getting pretty close to that now. I'm sure he'll be along any minute. But if you prefer, you can make another appointment. I know Pastor Thompson would be glad to speak with you."

Mary Williams had been the church secretary for the past two decades. Grey hair had long ago overtaken her black hair, but her skills continued to be sharp. She also had made herself the unofficial guardian of Pastor Thompson's schedule. Her fingers were a blur on the keyboard. She made very few errors, although she told folks, "I don't make mistakes; the computer just can't keep up with me." Mary also had great multitasking skills as she continued to type, answer the phone, and assist Harry Nickols, who continued to stand in front of her desk.

"I think I'll give him ten more minutes and then I'd better be going."

"Suit yourself," Mary replied.

Harry sat down in the small waiting area, twirling his hat on between his hands. He glanced at the literature spread out on the coffee table, which also had a bouquet of dusty, artificial flowers. He briefly thumbed through a magazine called Christianity Today but was not interested in anything it had to offer. There was a short stack of the current Our Daily Bread books on the table.

***

Harry let out a sigh just as his ten minutes ran out. As he stood to leave, Pastor Joseph Thompson crashed through the door like a running back hitting the line of scrimmage.

"Sorry I'm late, Mary, but Mrs. Stallings really needed to pray." As he spoke he turned to see Harry in the waiting area.

"Pastor, this is Harry Nickols from WOZD-TV. He's been waiting for quite a long time for you. He would like to have a few minutes of your time." Mary pointed a boney finger toward Harry. He walked toward the Pastor with his hat in his left hand and his right extended to shake the hand of the Pastor.

"Harry Nickols? Yes, I've heard of you. Didn't you do that story on churches being cheaters of the government because they don't have to pay taxes?" One thing about Pastor Thompson was his bluntness. He didn't believe in beating around the bush.

"Well," Harry replied uncomfortably, "yes, I am." He sighed before he added, "But that was a long time ago, when I first started reporting. Since then I have retracted that report with another story showing the constitutionality of churches being exempt from taxes." He fished hard for the right thing to say to the large Pastor Thompson.

"What can I do for you, Mr. Nickols?"

"You can call me Harry. I'm covering the shooting from the Central Station bus terminal. I would like to talk to you about Peter Stallings as I understand he's a member of your congregation. I would like to do a story about the yesterday's tragedy, as kind of a follow-up."

"As a follow up to what, Mr. Nickols?"

"I only want to show the human side of the story. I want to let people know about the victims involved."

"It's against my better judgment," Pastor Thompson said. "But come on into my office."

Harry followed the pastor through an old wooden door, into an office furnished with a large oak desk, piled high with books, mostly Bible commentaries, as well as an open Bible in the middle. "What would you like to know about Peter?"

"Well, what kind of things did he do around the church? Was he an active member? Did he live the life of a Christian every day or was he one of those hypocrites that comes on Sunday and that is all?"

"A couple of things before I answer your questions, Mr. Nickols."

"Sure."

"First, you talk about Peter in the past tense. He isn't dead. Second, sounds like you're rather bitter toward God yourself, Harry. Are you sure you're doing this for Peter, or are you doing this for you?"

Pastor Thompson's gaze locked onto Harry's eyes as he looked into his soul. Pastor Thompson was a giant of a man who, before he became a pastor, played football for a Division I university as an offensive lineman. He chose the ministry over playing professionally. Yet in spite of his tremendous size, he had a gentle and meek spirit. He always had the knack to know what people thought as they spoke to him about spiritual things. This included Harry Nickols.

Harry felt nervous across from Pastor Thompson as he squirmed in his chair. "Well, I'm doing this for Peter. You are right, though; I am upset with God."

"Tell me about it."

"He took my parents from me, when I was only ten years old, in a car wreck. I've never forgiven God for doing that to me." Harry could barely control his anger as he spat out the words.

Pastor Thompson replied, "Maybe we should talk about you instead of Peter. Would you mind doing that Harry?" Pastor Thompson's voice softened a bit toward Harry.

"Maybe we can. But first I have to finish this story." Harry felt desperate to change the subject.

"I have an idea, Mr. Nickols. The best way for you to understand Peter Stallings is to attend one of our weekly services. You see, Peter's been a great member of this congregation for many years and is very well respected. Our next service is tomorrow night and I think the best way for you to cover this story is to see just what makes him tick. After you attend the service, I will be glad to answer any other questions you might have about Mr. Stallings." Pastor Thompson looked Harry Nickols square in the eyes as he asked him one final question, "Will I see you tomorrow night, Harry?"

"Um, well I, uh…" Harry struggled to find an excuse, but came up empty. As his shoulders drooped he said, "Yes, I guess you'll see me here Pastor Thompson." He surprised himself with that.

They spent a few more minutes going over times and some of the other little details that would not interfere with the service in any way.

CHAPTER 21

John remained in a coma aided by the life support machines. An IV bag delivered medications as a breathing tube gave him oxygen. Bandages covered his head as if he had been mummified.

In an instant, his eyes snapped open. What he saw around him didn't make any sense. He closed his eyes and opened them again. No change. Everything looked crystal clear.

"This is some medication they have me on." He knew he had been injured at the bus station. He figured he had been brought to a hospital. He also thought he may have had surgery.

Although everything looked clear, he was confused about the 'how.' "I don't understand how clear my thoughts are. I know everything that happened to me."

He began to look at his surroundings. There were no machines, tubes, or bandages attached to his body. "Exactly where am I? I have to be having some sort of reaction to the meds." He recalled a story he'd reported on about strange reactions people have during and right after major and traumatic surgeries. "How is it I can remember that particular story?"

Lying on his back he saw a cloudless, blue sky. The sunshine was a perfect 80 degrees with a slight breeze and no humidity. He sucked in air so pure he almost gagged, not sure his smog-infested lungs could handle it.

"I'm definitely not in Grand Rapids, Toto." He then noticed where he sat, which was in deep, plush, green grass.

He rubbed his eyes. "This is some kind of hallucination. Where in the world am I?" He shut and opened his eyes trying to get back to reality. "I was sure I was in a hospital? This must be some new-fangled treatment: healing, nature's way to a faster recovery or something. I'll have to make a note to do a story about this place after I get out of here. And I better make sure my insurance covers this kind of treatment."

He closed his eyes again as tight as he could, and then, after a few seconds, opened them as he continued to test his perception of reality against what he suspected to be a delusion.

"Nothing changed. This can't be possible." He looked at his arms and noticed he had the ability to move them. His legs moved without pain, but he couldn't stand up. He found he could get to a seated position.

Once sitting upright he looked around and whistled in amazement. "This is the most beautiful place I have ever seen in my life. I only wish I knew where this place is." He ran his hands through the plush green grass. "It looks and feels like shag carpet, only it's organic. And the air is so pure. I definitely don't think I'm in Kansas anymore."

Looking farther out, he can see a wall, which by comparison, made the Great Wall of China look small. The enormity is breathtaking even from so far away, which he estimates to be twenty miles. "I can't see either end. It just seems to go on forever."

From this distance, he could clearly identify three large gates. They appeared to be closed. Studying the gates he noted they had the look of pearl. "That just can't be right. There are no pearls that big." As he sat and stared at the wall and especially at the pearl-looking gates, he thought, "Maybe if I could get a closer look at the gate I might be able feel like I have a little bit of reality left in my head."

He tried to lift himself, but his legs wouldn't work. He sighed, "It could be worse."

CHAPTER 22

Al Tuinstra used his cell phone to call the television station in the waiting area outside of the ICU. It had become second nature for him to stay in touch about various events and breaking news stories. Today, however, everything was personal.

He spoke with his assistant, Jamie Maris. "Have Susan Reed and Bill Meyer ready to take the evening news broadcast onto the air."

"Yes sir," Jamie replied as she typed the e-mail.

"Also let everyone know the evening broadcast will go on as scheduled. Like the saying goes, 'the show must go on.'"

Al waited while Jamie passed the messages around to the staff.

"Everyone is getting ready as we speak, Mr. Tuinstra."

"Thanks Jamie," he said quietly and close to tears. "I'm sure everyone knows about John and Peter. I don't have any more information to pass along other than they both went through surgery and are currently in the ICU. Let people know to pray for them."

The shock and strain had taken its toll as his emotions spilled over. "And if you would be so kind to let everyone know Amy and Judy have been taken hostage. No one knows where they are..." Emotions overtook him after saying his daughter's name. He took the phone away from his head as he choked down his tears. "I'm sorry about that, Jamie."

"We all know this is a difficult day, Mr. Tuinstra. You just take care of yourself, and we'll take care of the station here. You're all in our thoughts and prayers."

"Thanks, Jamie. I'll keep you posted if there are any changes here. Let me know if the police call with any news."

"Yes, sir."

"I trust everyone can handle the evening news without me tonight?"

"Everything will be just fine."

"I'll check back with you later." He shut his cell phone and turned back to face the family of Peter Stallings. John Robertson didn't have any family in the area. They had been called by the police, however.

———◆———

Everyone at WGRT, working or not, had heard about John and Peter. They also knew Judy and Amy had been taken hostage. Words like *disbelief* and *disturbed* were used to describe their feelings.

No one spoke. No one worked. How could they? Three of their co-workers had been injured or taken, while their boss had his daughter taken. Like a ship adrift at sea, the staff sat quietly not knowing what to do.

Al Tuinstra's call helped get them back to reality. Slowly, life came back into the station as people tossed information back and forth, sharing what they knew. The tip line rang steady, mostly from well-wishers. No new information came in.

All the social media outlets the station employed brought in the real tips, although none verified as of yet. Facebook brought in pictures, Twitter accounts gave captions of what took place, and e-mails poured in one after the other.

Journalists on other assignments returned from their stories. They felt they had somehow failed in not covering the Central Station story. Others gave words of comfort reminding them it was an exceptionally busy day. There could have been no possible way to know what might happen next. Still, they took little comfort knowing when one hurt all hurt. That came in part from the family atmosphere Al Tuinstra had tried to exhibit at the station.

Marianne Johnson, one of the secretaries, had her home burned to the ground several years ago. Everybody pitched in to help her and her family get back to normal by donating money, food, and clothing. Others even helped rebuild the house. They all felt a sense of accomplishment at the end of the project. Marianne's family threw a huge party to thank all of her fellow-employees. That was the family attitude of WGRT. And this tragic event would not go on unmarked by the family.

CHAPTER 23

Inside John's hospital room, monitors went crazy as the nurses ran around trying to figure out what had happened.

"I don't understand," Andrea said. "He isn't moving around and everything checks out normal. So why are the monitors going off?"

Deb called the doctor. "We have a really bizarre incident taking place here. The monitors are signaling the patient is having some sort of attack, but he's perfectly still and all vitals are normal."

"I'll be right there," stated Dr. Leonard Mockman.

Fifteen minutes later, Dr. Mockman told the nurses, "There's nothing to be alarmed about." He looked at the monitors, checked the chart, and had examined John. "Apparently, our patient cried wolf. Keep monitoring him and let me know if there are any more changes. As of right now, he's perfectly fine. Well, for his condition anyway."

Dr. Mockman left the room to continue his rounds. The nurses went to the monitoring station baffled at what took place.

Josiah could only chuckle quietly. He had seen Pithel set off the alarms to throw the demons lurking nearby a little curve. He gave Pithel a look of accomplishment. Pithel waved back to Josiah as they continued their missions.

The demons stood nearby. They had been there since John Robertson had arrived, ordered to stay near him at all times. "And don't let him out of your sights for any reason. Is that clear?" barked the captain. Ten of the devils crowded into the ICU. Their master did not want this mortal to have the opportunity to hear about Christ without having an equal chance to keep him.

"As long as he remains unconscious, we have nothing to worry about," he said.

"Just be sure he doesn't wake up...ever."

They knew a human had to accept Jesus before death. So far they kept their eyes on him, at least physically. These demons were hard pressed to sit still for very long. They felt the need to cause trouble while stuck in the ICU.

They spilled an entire tray of blood being rushed to the lab for testing. Another little demon distracted a nurse passing medications so the pills got mixed up. Before the nurse passed them, another demon tripped her spilling all the pills. The nurse started over again and every patient received the right medications.

———— •◆• ————

"This is a very strange night," said Barbara, a fifteen year veteran nurse.

"It all started when our two celebrities came on the floor," Charlotte replied. She always seemed to be working. "I don't know why it is, but there's an evil feeling here tonight."

"I felt that, too," Joan said as she walked up to the desk. "There's definitely something wrong here tonight."

All the other nurses gathered at the nurse's station agreed something weird was going on, but no one was quick to say it might be some sort kind of evil power.

"Well, whatever's going on here, make sure you do the right things," Deb ordered. "Double check everything, medications, name tags, doctor's orders, and then recheck. Don't let something go wrong because something frightened us into doing it."

CHAPTER 24

"I don't feel any pain," John said reaching to feel the back of his head. There was neither a bump nor a bandage. He took in a big breath of the clean, fresh air enjoying every moment of it. "I just can't get over this. I'm amazed at the progress of modern medicine. I don't think I ever want to get better if this is what life is like in the hospital."

As he continued to look around, he felt a wind blow by him. It blew his hair back but not enough to break his concentration from the beautiful sights. "I have never had such a peaceful and quiet place to relax before..." He yawned and started to fall asleep.

"Why are you here, John Robertson?" The voice boomed through the air causing John to cover his ears and shake in fear. He had no idea what to do say or do. He tried to hide by covering his head with his arms.

The voice thundered again, "I ask you, John Robertson, why are you here? Answer."

John tried to regain his professional composure as the anchor for WGRT. "I'm not sure..." he cleared his throat and tried again. "I'm not sure why I'm here. I don't even know where here is."

When no response came, John begged, "Please, don't hurt me. I'm hurt already and I don't think that I could take any more pain right now."

The voice rang out with an uproarious laugh. "I am not going to hurt you, John Robertson. I am here to comfort you. Do you feel the pain of your human body? No. As for where you are, you are at the threshold of heaven."

John went from fear to confusion. "I must be having a reaction or to the medication and I'm having a bad dream."

"You are not dreaming, nor are the drugs having this kind of effect on you, John Robertson. What you see and feel is real. It is not part of your imagination, as you would wish to believe. As I stated earlier, you are at the threshold of heaven. You are actually looking at the walls of heaven with the gates of pearl from a hill a little more than twenty miles from those gates.

But the sad part is this may be as close as you ever get to enter those gates. That is truly a shame."

"How do you know my name? And who are you? Where are you for that matter?" John looked around, trying to find the source of the voice. "Please don't play games with me right now. I'm confused already and I can't take anymore. I'm tired and I'm hurting from the surgery." John continued to question reality. He wanted to see the person behind the voice.

"Yes, John Robertson, I will show myself to you. And I will reveal to you the purpose of the mission my Master has given to me concerning you. But first I must..." The voice stopped abruptly.

———•———

John screamed out as sharp pain shot through his head. It was unlike any pain he had ever felt before, including the gunshot. He grabbed at his head as he rolled back and forth on the plush grass.

———•———

In the ICU, his body lurched upward with involuntary convulsions. The monitors went wild inside the room and at the nurses' station. The warning signals showed the tubes connected to his body had become unattached. A very erratic heartbeat registered on the electrocardiogram monitor, while the oxygen tube had been ripped from his mouth.

Doctors and nurses raced into the room. They worked feverishly to reattach the tubes and wires. Within seconds, everything went back to normal. John's body relaxed. The machines resumed their normal rhythmic tones.

"What's going on in here?" Deb Nolanski sighed, "This sort of thing just doesn't happen. It's like some sort of horror movie taking place in here."

———•———

She wasn't too far off with that statement. Only the horror part would not take place inside the room, not with Josiah on guard duty.

The large angel had a small battle with the band of demons who felt they could take on one warrior of the heavenly host. They soon realized the power of even one angel, given the power of the Almighty, is able to conquer anything the evil one can throw at him. Josiah quickly repelled the unclean spirits from the room of John Robertson and brought order back to the Intensive Care Unit.

———— • ————

Back at the threshold of heaven a confrontation took place that John could only hear. The familiar voice rang out, "You will leave him be while he remains in my presence or you will face the wrath of the Almighty God. Now be gone from this place immediately." The voice sounded like it came from a large being.

A moment of eerie silence followed until a voice pierced the silence in a tone that made the hair stand up on the back of John's neck. The voice sounded snake-like hissing, with every word. "We have just as much right to him as you do, warrior. He has already chosen. You cannot take him now. We choose to stay here to make sure you do not interfere with our master's plan for this man."

"You may stay if you desire. To do so, however, you will have to fight me. This day the battle belongs to the Lord God."

John could only scrunch into a ball, still holding his head in pain, as he listened to the stand-off.

"Need I remind you, the saints pray for this soul even as we speak? That, demon, gives us power you can only dream about."

"Demon? Did you say demon?" John's question was ignored.

"Do you wish to test my power, warrior angel?" The voice seemed to be coming from the top of John's head.

"I will try your power? Before I do, know this. My Master has given His power to me. Now do you wish to test the power of your ultimate creator? If not, may I suggest you take your band of evil packrats and leave this place immediately before I give you a firsthand look at this power? Now be gone with you." The angelic warrior had started to get a little perturbed at this confrontation. He stood ready to fight.

The silence seemed to go on for eternity as John waited to hear an answer. Finally, this hissing demon snarled. Other strange hissing and guttural noises could be heard as the leader spoke, "This day may belong to you, Warrior, but the soul of this mortal man you guard belongs to us. We will have him."

With that, the demon released its grip on the skull of John Robertson, retracted its talons and flew back to the place it had come from along with his hoard.

One of them flew close enough to Pithel to be struck. Pithel sent the slimy creature miles ahead of the others. Its scream was loud enough for the entire kingdom to hear.

As the demons fled from region, John asked, "What's going on with me? Please tell me. Oh God, please take this pain away from me."

One of the demons knew what that meant. He flew at lightning speed to get away. "I'm not getting destroyed," he yelled as he disappeared.

The intense pain subsided immediately. John lay back and rested comfortably once again.

———•+•———

The monitors began their rhythmic sounds with the beeps and buzzes and drips, all normal readings. The room, filled with the medical team, collectively scratched their heads as they stood in wonder about what just happened. John's vital signs went back to normal and it appeared as if no crisis had ever started.

———•+•———

Josiah stood firm by the side of the human he had protected since birth. He would need to be even more vigilant as the next few days would be very troublesome for John Robertson. He joined his thoughts with Pithel's as the battle for the soul of this man went forward. He prayed Pithel would have the wisdom and strength to work with John.

Josiah knew his assignment would be difficult. Many times the guardian angel thought John would die from the things he'd done. He drew the memory from John's mind of how the man had abused his girlfriend as they dated, both verbally and physically. She only wanted to help John with his career.

Carrie Williams had been a wonderful woman with a strong Christian background. She and John met during their freshman year of college in an economics class. John had those eyes and Carrie fell for him right away. They dated for a couple of months, usually on the week nights since both worked on the weekends. They both studied journalism and both worked at the college's television station on the weekends doing whatever was needed at the station. Carrie always encouraged John during those times, always being supportive.

John, however, wasn't always there for Carrie. When her father died during their junior year, John didn't speak to her. He didn't try to comfort or support her. For a time he wouldn't even look at her. John's attitude changed toward Carrie as she talked about the hope and peace she had about seeing her dad again in heaven.

While Carrie left to attend her father's funeral, John began drinking. He claimed he couldn't handle the pressure of having her gone for so long. In all actuality, however, he had given up on life. The bottle gave him peace and comfort.

When she returned he would yell at her for the simple things, like forgetting to call when she said she would or not telling him that she had gone out with her girlfriends without first checking with him. A little time passed and he seemed to settle down. One night, however, after a heavy round of drinking, Carrie came by to see how he was doing.

Josiah recalled John saying, "Get out of here and don't ever come back." He then literally threw her out of his room. John never saw Carrie again. She transferred to another school and went on to have a great career in Pittsburgh, PA.

Josiah shook his head as he thought about those days. He rejoiced the day John gave up drinking a few years later. He worked up the courage to call Carrie several years after both had graduated. He apologized for what he had done to her. She actually forgave him and they established a friendship once again.

Through the years Carrie prayed for John to find God's will for his life. John told her he would one day listen to her, usually laughing it off. Carrie continued to pray for John which was the reason he was still alive.

"Our prayers are worth so much to God," Josiah thought.

CHAPTER 25

"The pain you felt, John Robertson, came from a demon trying to take over your body as you lay in the hospital bed." Pithel had not yet revealed himself. John still cowered. "They wish to cloud your mind and destroy your soul so they can manifest themselves in you forever. For now, however, they are not allowed to take your soul. They must wait until we finish our business. The choice will then be up to you. For only you can decide what your future will be."

"Business? What are you talking about? I'm not here on business. I'm here to recover. In case you haven't realized this, I was just shot in the head. Business will have to wait until. . ."

In mid-sentence, a huge figure materialized before him, blocking the light. John cowered as he shook in fear. He covered his head to shield himself from the being. "W-w-what are you?"

"Do not fear, John Robertson, the Almighty God has sent me to you. I am not come to harm you, but to minister and to comfort you. We are to have a very serious talk. You see, I am to be interviewed by you, John Robertson."

"Interviewed? By me? Are you insane? I'm in no shape to interview you. I don't know anything about you. I'm totally unprepared for this." John rambled on and on.

The large angel let loose with a laugh from the belly.

"What are you laughing at? This isn't funny," John protested. "Now who are you and what do you want with me?"

"Yes, I suppose introductions would be appropriate. I am Pithel, warrior in the heavenly host of the Almighty God." He grabbed John's hand, nearly crushing every bone in his massive grip. "I have been assigned to meet here with you to be interviewed. This opportunity is very rare, so I suggest you accept it. There have been very few times throughout history that an angel has been interviewed. Sure, we have been seen on earth by humans and even conversed with them. To sit down and have them ask us any questions, however, is really a rarity."

"Look, I have absolutely no clue what you're talking about. Quite honestly, you're really getting on my nerves." John tried not to show his fear. "How am I supposed to interview you? I don't even know you, let alone anything about you. Just what is a warrior in the heavenly host?"

"That's a very good first question. You'd better have your pen and paper ready. Once I start talking, I have a difficult time stopping." The angel let out with another belly laugh. "Oh, John Robertson, this may prove to be a better mission than I first thought. I must admit that I do like this, conversing here with you."

After he settled down next to John, he began to answer the question. "Now about your question, 'what is a warrior in the heavenly host?' Well, the first thing we do is to give praise to the Almighty God, our Lord and Master. Then we fight for the saints as we are commanded. We fight against the forces of evil as you have witnessed a few moments ago.

"We also minister to the saints, comforting them in times of distress, carrying out tasks to help them through difficult times, and healing them when they are sick. There are times, however, when we get to carry them home. That is a most joyous occasion for us, as you can probably imagine."

John shook his head, not being able to comprehend how death could be such a happy event.

"Then there are times when we must fight for the souls of people in order to keep that evil serpent, Lucifer, from taking control of them. We do all we can to protect them, but humans can still choose for themselves whether or not to accept the Lord."

He paused for a moment as he looked at John, "That is why I am here, John Robertson, to protect you from the evil forces desiring to feast on your soul. You are being given the opportunity to learn about the love of Jesus. Your friend, Carrie, who you remembered moments ago, is still praying for you as we speak. Her prayers, along with others, are the main reason you still live today. She remains fervent in her prayers for you. Carrie is a wonderful woman whom the Lord has used mightily for His work."

John gave Pithel a puzzled look. "How do you know about Carrie? What's going on here?"

"I've already told you."

"Do you honestly expect me to believe you're some kind of angel I'm supposed to interview? This is crazy," John said throwing his arms out.

"Okay, where are the cameras? This is some kind of sick joke being played on me isn't it?"

He cupped his hands and yelled, "Come on out, you guys, I'm on to you." No answer came, only the breeze flowing by. He turned to Pithel, "I'm in the psych ward aren't I?"

"Whether you believe me or not, I suppose, does not matter at this moment." Pithel threw his hands in the air at not being able to convey the message of truth. "I am who I say I am, an angel of the heavenly host. My mission from the Almighty God is to be interviewed by you."

He locked eyes with John. "How am I to complete my mission if I cannot get you to believe even the simplest of things, let alone the deeper meaning of your soul? Perhaps the wicked one is right about you. Maybe you are too far gone. If so, then not only am I a failure, but you will be given up for eternity."

His massive hands clamped onto John's shoulders. "Oh, John Robertson, you must believe that what I tell you is the truth. I am here only to help you for the sake of the Lord. He desires to have you for His work, but you must be willing to accept Him as your Savior. Now, please tell me what I must do to prove to you that I am an angel."

"I just don't understand why I've been chosen for this interview," contested John. "There must be another reporter out there who has a much better work ethic than me. I mean, I work for a small market television station with no attachments to the major networks. You know, no ties with the big boys. Besides, most of the time I'm a pretty good guy with no major hang-ups to contend with. Okay, once in a while I get a big ego. But so what, everybody in this field has ego problems here and there. I'm no different than they are. So why me? Why did I get chosen for this thing? Couldn't you find anybody else?"

Pithel interrupted John. "Please stop with the excuses. You sound like Moses at the burning bush. Just tell me what I can do to prove I am an angel from the Almighty God. That is a simple request, don't you think? Come on, let me tell you something or show you something that nobody knows about. I'll amaze you."

Pithel's taunting got to John as he pondered what he could ask this 'angel.'

"I'll tell you what, if you can tell me some secret I have that nobody could possibly know then maybe I'll believe you're an angel. And I'll believe I am to interview you. Do we have a deal?" John felt certain this creature, man, being, or whoever he was could not possibly know anything about him. Not enough to convince him that all of these shenanigans could be nothing more than a fraud. "What do you say to the deal...um...Pither is it?"

"That's Pithel. I accept your proposal. As for your question to why you have been chosen, I do not fully know the answer yet."

"I knew it," John said, pointing his finger at Pithel. "You're a fraud."

"May I continue?"

"Of course," John said, crossing his arms letting a smug look of satisfaction cross his face.

"You are a difficult one to deal with," Pithel stated. "I assure you, you have been chosen by the Lord God Almighty Himself. He does have a purpose for you. He has given you many opportunities and, perhaps, one last chance to accept Him as Lord and Savior. My Master is very gracious to you mortals, even after the way he was treated while living there.

"He has been watching you for quite some time now and knows you have become very skeptical in your beliefs even he exists. I do not understand how you cannot believe in my Master's existence. I am sorry not only for the grief it brings my Lord, but for the pain it may end up causing you in the very near future. That is very difficult for me to understand. Gratefully, I have the task of helping you to believe in the Lord."

The large angel stopped talking and drew in a deep breath. "As for your request to share a secret about your life nobody else knows about. . ."

"This should be good," John stated, still feeling confident of this being a ruse.

"How's this?" Pithel asked. He paused for dramatic effect. "When you were fourteen, you were going to use the telephone in the kitchen to call up one of your friends. You picked up the receiver and overhead your father talking to a woman. Something about meeting her later and that she should not call the house anymore. You did not tell your mother because you knew it would break her heart to hear her husband was cheating on her. And from that day until now you have never told another living soul. And because of this, you have harbored some very bitter feelings toward your father. Does this satisfy you to believe I am what I say I am? Or is there something more you need to help you believe?"

CHAPTER 26

John sat still, totally stunned as he heard the story. "That was more accurate than even I remember." It had taken place so long ago, to hear this being given so much detail, cut deep into his soul.

The thousand yard stare came over John as he thought back to his childhood and that awful day. His father never came home unless he wanted something from his mother. She worked so hard to keep the family together. She was a beautiful woman, he thought. She had long dark hair and strikingly bright blue eyes. It seemed she just could never keep her husband home long enough to please him.

Then one day while his mother went out shopping for the groceries, John intercepted a call for his father. A woman's voice he didn't recognize asked for Bill, his father. When his father answered, John heard him tell her she shouldn't have called the house, but that he was glad she did. They talked for as John listened in on the extension. Pain shot through his heart as he realized his father was cheating on his mother.

Pain turned to anger and anger to resentment towards his father. They had not spoken since then. His mother also carried the pain deep in her heart. It finally ate away at her until she became ill, eventually passing away from a broken heart. The death of his mother and the pain his father had brought on him had caused John to become hard hearted toward people who treated other people in a harsh manner. It dawned on him at that moment. I did the same thing to Carrie. He had not spoken to his father in over ten years, including at the funeral for his mother. His father tried to make amends, but John would have no part of it. He claimed, "It's too late for apologies, Dad."

Over the years, John tried to cover up his pain by working hard on his career, followed closely by drowning it with alcohol. The memory still haunted him each and every day.

As Pithel told the secret to John, it came to him so clearly as if it had happened at this exact moment. To John it was horrifying to relive that awful scene again. "John Robertson, are you convinced yet? Answer please."

John shook his head to clearing away the memory, "What was that? Oh, um, yeah, I think that will suffice. How did you know about that?"

Pithel laughed again, "Oh, John Robertson, you are the skeptic, aren't you? As I have said, I am an angelic warrior in the army of the heavenly host. I have been sent here by the Lord God Almighty to allow you to…"

"Yeah, yeah, yeah, I get to interview you. I get it."

"It is his desire to have you here through the means of your gunshot wound to the head, which you have now. He has allowed me to know everything about you in order to complete my mission. As I sit here with you, however, I still feel you do not believe me. Not to worry, though, by the time we are finished you will believe that I and my Master are not only real, but we both care about you."

CHAPTER 27

At St. John's Hospital, Dr. David Howard explained to Al Tuinstra about the seriousness of the injuries John and Peter had sustained. Al, still in shock over Amy's abduction, struggled to focus on the conversation.

The doctor had been amazed at the similarity of the men's wounds. "They are so close in the proximity," Dr. Howard said. "The chances of survival, let alone recovery, are very slim. If they do survive the initial trauma, the odds of either living a normal life again are very minute. I only mention it to let you know you might need to begin looking for a new anchor. I'm sorry to say this so bluntly, but since this is business, you should know what they are up against."

The two men shook hands. Doctor Howard left to complete his rounds. Al returned to the waiting area.

Al Tuinstra, a thin man with a receding, gray hairline, wept quietly as he processed the information just given to him. Only a few hours before, he'd learned the hostage taken by the gunmen was Amy, his beautiful daughter. One of the worst phone calls he ever had to make took place as he drove to the hospital, when he called his wife, Beth, to tell her. He also included the news about Judy being taken as well. The reaction from Beth was worse than he'd expected. The phone dropped and he could hear her crying.

"Beth? Beth." he yelled. It took her a few minutes but she had been able to compose herself long enough to hear what had happened.

"The police assure me they are doing everything they can right now," Al said. "Right now I'm at the hospital checking on John and Peter."

"When are you coming home?"

"As soon as I finish up at the hospital." They said their good-byes and told each other to pray.

Amy being taken, the phone call to Beth, and John and Peter being in the ICU, both on life support, had already worn him down. He didn't think he would be able to stand anything more.

His thoughts returned to his only child as he sat in the waiting area of the ICU. Amy, now a senior in college, had just turned twenty-two years old. He still considered her to be his little girl. As tears streamed down his cheeks, he prayed.

"Lord, keep Amy in your protective care. And give Beth and myself strength, along with my staff at WGRT." Words weren't able to express how he truly felt, but he knew his prayer had been heard by the Lord.

As he finished praying, he stood to stretch his legs. He thought about the relationship he had developed with his newscasters, especially Peter Stallings. Peter came to WGRT eight years ago when Al had just started running the operations at the station. The transition had been a difficult time for both men as they had each moved to the area without fully understanding what they had gotten themselves into.

The station had lost its contract with one of the major networks. The entire staff had been replaced with inexperienced people in the broadcasting field. That's when Al met Peter. They shared ideas about how to run WGRT in order to get the higher ratings the new owner sought. Even though they didn't see eye to eye on every issue, they maintained a relationship that reached beyond the television station.

Al attributed it to the faith Peter had introduced him to in the second year of their working together. He remembered Peter saying, "If you want to be the best you can possibly be, then you must have a relationship with Jesus Christ." The way Peter explained it not only sounded simple but not pushed on Al. A few days later, Al recalled, he received Christ as his Savior.

From then until now they'd had a fellowship past work and even beyond friendship. It included God and their entire families. As Al thought about that, a peace washed over him that gave him assurance of everything turning out all right. "The Spirit of God can do wonders for the soul, especially in difficult times like these," he thought.

Al turned to go to the elevator when he saw June Stallings, Peter's wife, still in the waiting room, still praying. He'd talked with her before Dr. Howard came to the unit.

"She's a very strong woman," he thought. He pressed the 'down' button and headed to the cafeteria to get two cups of coffee.

Tears rolled down June's face as she waited by herself in the family area of the ICU. She prayed constantly for him to be brought back to full health. She couldn't think of losing Peter like this.

CHAPTER 28

On the mark of six o'clock, the WGRT evening news theme music began to play, followed immediately by a screen that read Breaking News behind the two anchors. Susan Reed looked into camera 1 and began.

"Good evening, I'm Susan Reed filling in for John Robertson." As she looked into the camera, she controlled the teleprompter with her right foot just below the desk. "We begin with late breaking news. It's a story hitting very close to home for us at WGRT. Earlier today, three gunmen took over the Central Bus Station, holding twenty people hostage, in a three hour stand-off with police.

"As police worked to negotiate the release of the hostages, gunfire erupted killing three people, injuring seventeen people, eight of which remain in critical condition. Two of those critically wounded are WGRT anchor, John Robertson and our information technician and field correspondent, Peter Stallings. It has been confirmed that two hostages have been abducted from the scene, one of those being Judy Metcalf, WGRT employee. Jeffery Samuel is standing by, live at the Central Bus Station, to give us an update. Jeffrey."

"Susan, I'm standing just a few feet away from where, earlier today, gunmen opened fire on police, and the gathered crowd of onlookers, while they worked to rescue the hostages being held inside the bus station." Jeffery Samuel stood off to the side of the live truck as he broadcast his report.

"According to witnesses, the shooting began without warning or provocation from the police. As the bullets flew, our teams of reporters, covering the late breaking story, apparently were caught in the middle of the crossfire. It has also been confirmed by police that Judy Metcalf, a photo journalist for WGRT, has been taken hostage by the fleeing gunmen. Jeffrey Samuel reporting. Back to you, Susan."

"Jeffrey, what, if anything, are the police saying about the three men?"

"The police have informed me that the gunmen remain at -large and are considered to be armed and extremely dangerous. They have very little information to pass along about the men, only that there were three and all wore old, dirty clothing. It isn't clear if anyone got a good look at the suspects as they fled due to the shooting. It is believed, however, the camera belonging to WGRT has been recovered behind the building where Ms. Metcalf had been shooting footage for the story. Officials hope the camera might have captured video footage of the men in order to identify and catch them. No information about the video has been released as of this time. When more information is available, we will pass that along to you and our viewers."

"Thanks, Jeffrey. Both Peter Stallings and John Robertson are listed in very critical condition at a local hospital. No other details are available at this time. We do ask that you keep them in your thoughts and prayers."

Bill Meyer, looked into camera 2 and continued, "As we report the tragic news from the shooting and hostage crisis at the bus station, there is more to the story. WGRT has learned that, not only have the gunmen abducted Judy Metcalf, they have also taken another hostage, Amy Tuinstra. This is another blow to the WGRT family, as Amy is the daughter of station manager, Al Tuinstra. At this time, no one is certain of the well-being of the two women. Police have given the description of the vehicle as a white panel van, perhaps heading south out of the city of Grand Rapids. If you see this van, you are asked to call police immediately. Susan."

The exchange went perfectly as Susan spoke to the camera, "When we return, we will continue coverage of this tragedy, along with the other news of the day."

"We're clear," said the voice from the control room. Commercials filled the screen; the cast caught their breath, as the director readied everyone for the next segment.

Al Tuinstra watched the news from the waiting room as he sipped his coffee. It felt strange to watch the news outside of the studio. Through all the concerns for John and Peter, Judy and Amy, he had been pleased with the news broadcast and the way the crew pulled it all together.

The commercials ended, and Susan Reed began the segment of the newscast, "From St. John's Hospital, we have this report from Lori Orenthal."

"Doctors at St. John's have been busy all day long, not only with the shooting victims from the bus station, but also from many other crimes and accidents occurring throughout the day. After speaking with hospital director, Alex Morestin, I've been told this has been the busiest day in fifty years. It's something the hospital hopes doesn't happen for at least another fifty years. I've also been informed that due to the large number of people needing medical attention, blood supplies of all types are critically low. Anyone wishing to donate blood should contact the American Red Cross as soon as possible. As to the condition of John Robertson and Peter Stallings, they are listed in very critical condition with both in the Intensive Care Unit. Doctors cannot say what the chances of their survival or recovery are at this time. We are waiting and hoping for the best. Susan."

"Thank you, Lori. Once again, we'll keep you informed of any further developments that occur before the late edition of the news tonight."

Bill Meyer and Susan Reed continued with all the other news stories from the day. All seemed to have very little impact in comparison to the lead story. Of all the stories covered, only fifteen had been broadcast with two dozen newsworthy items never getting air time. It didn't matter tonight. This night, the news was about John, Peter, Judy, and Amy.

As the news ended, Bill Meyer stated, "I've always wanted to be the anchor, but not like this. I sure didn't think getting through my first opportunity would be this difficult." The entire station sat quiet, emotionally drained.

Usually as the credits ran, staff would bolt for the parking lot in between newscasts. Tonight, however, most everyone stayed. Some of the non-essential people quietly slipped out to be with their families. When the broadcast ended, only a few eyes remained dry. They felt sure many viewers cried during the news as they heard about their friends and family, victims of this senseless crime, not to mention the others injured and those killed at the scene.

"Why did this happen?" Bill shouted, unable to contain his emotions. "What's the meaning of something as terrible as this? Just who are these people anyway? Don't they care what they do to the lives of their victims and the lives of everyone around them? I can't deal with this anymore."

Betty Smith, from accounting, the wife of a minister, tried to explain, "Sometimes God allows people to go through very difficult and often tragic events in order to show us that not only is he real, but he cares for us so very much."

"You call this caring for us?" Bill asked. He threw his arms out in frustration.

Betty continued, "I remember when my family went through a tough time. My sister had leukemia and her health began to fail very rapidly. The doctors told us she didn't have much longer to live, less than six weeks, he said. As you can imagine, we were devastated by this news. Soon, however, we realized her time with us, although short, she was on borrowed time. God was still in control. Within the six weeks she passed away. You probably wonder how this could ever turn out as a joyful event, don't you?"

Bill, confused, only nodded.

She continued. Her voice still had a slight accent from Kentucky even after living in Michigan for over twenty years. "Well, I'll tell you how. My father and my brother had never been very close since my brother dodged the draft by moving to Canada. When the war ended he came back home, but my father never truly accepted him back because of what he'd done. When my sister died, Rick, that's my brother, began to cry uncontrollably so much so that my father held him in an embrace. I'll remember that sight forever.

"Since then my father and brother have been the best of friends. You see, Bill, sometimes it takes tragic events to get us in touch with the important things of our lives. I don't claim to know what's going on with John and Peter, or with Amy and Judy, but I do know that God will work it for the good."

Betty turned back to her desk as she began to pray again. Bill tried to take in all she'd said. No one else joined the conversation. No one argued about Betty's religious views or tried to outdo what she presented. They just sat shocked and confused, hugged, held hands, and cried. Some prayed, others thought about their colleagues. They also knew there was another newscast to get through tonight.

CHAPTER 29

Angelic warriors, who stood guard at WGRT listened as Betty Smith shared her words of encouragement. The demons inside the studio had been completely overpowered by the prayers of the saints this night, not only from those at the television station, but from all the viewers praying as well.

"The power of prayer is a mighty tool when used properly," one of the warriors, Jariel, stated as his sword arced through the air, causing a devil to flee. "We have had a victory today," he said. "Be diligent, for it is only the beginning."

A few stubborn demons, however, did not leave until they had stirred up more trouble. As the saints continued to pray, the angels gained strength. The brightness of the Lord began to shine through the room, which began to drive away the evil presence.

Jariel, with his sword drawn, stood among those demons, foolish enough to remain, and proclaimed, "This night belongs to the Lord and to the saints. You are to leave this place immediately or face the wrath of the Almighty God."

"You underestimate our power, warrior," exclaimed one brave demon. "We, as well as you, have strength given to us by our master."

"You are no match for the power of the Almighty God, especially when the saints pray."

Arguments and small skirmishes broke out between the two spiritual factions. As the angelic warrior's power increased by the prayers and from the throne of God, the demons began to cower and take flight. Others defiantly clenched their fists and raised their voices in anger as they pointed fingers at each the angel's faces.

The anger spilled over to the staff of WGRT as arguments started over things like who would have to clean up the room tonight or who didn't make the next pot of coffee. Emotional outbursts took over the room for a short time.

The demons could have left, should have left. Jariel had warned them fairly. "The prayers still being offered to God are giving us even more power."

The demons, however, decided to hold their ground. "This is our territory as much as it is yours. And we have every right to defend it."

The angels received approval to remove the demons from the building. They were outnumbered two to one, but had been given the power of ten angels. In terms the demons could understand, Jariel said, "We have been given strength from the Almighty God. You must leave now."

Demons flew all over the room, just not of their own freewill. One brave devil, charged at a warrior, talons out, ready to plunge them into the angel's skull. Instead, as he made his approach, the angel turned, grabbed him by the feet, and spun him around several times before letting him go sending him back to the pits of hell.

Jariel swung his sword at any demon who dared approach. He'd cut the talons off of one demon, sent another off to cower in a corner, where another angel finished him off. One demon had his wings sheared off, rendering him helpless and useless. As he lay in agony, another angel came by and mercifully ended his stay with a powerful swing of his sword.

The air reeked with the foul stench of dying evil spirits. As soon as the battle ended, however, the room cleared and the air went back to normal. The staff also began to come back to their senses. Jariel stood by, sword still drawn and grateful for the victory gave praise to God.

Thunder rang out over the city that rattled windows and set off car alarms. Some looked up for thunder clouds; others looked for a low flying jet. Still others went on about their business not paying any attention. High atop a tall building, Pithel looked toward heaven, his head bowed as the Almighty God spoke to him.

He listened intently to every word spoken to him. "Yes, my Lord, I will carry out my mission for your glory."

The thunder crashed again as Pithel stood up, ready to leave.

"You are incapable of doing anything right." Satan stood millimeters from the face of his subordinate. "How could you allow one angel to keep you away from that human? Did I not equip you with enough power to not only overthrow one angel, but the entire army of angels all by yourself?" Satan paced back and forth. "I cannot stand this type of failure from someone who is supposed to be one of my top leaders. I find myself questioning whether I can trust you for any task or not."

"Please, master, give me another chance," begged the failed captain. "I promise I will not fail you again. That angel had just received more power from the praying saints. That is why I could not get to the reporter. I tried to get to him . . ."

"Stop giving me excuses. I want results." Satan shot back, loud enough to be heard all across Hell. Some demons listening nearby snickered while Satan disciplined their comrade.

Satan pointed his finger in the face of his leader and said, "I want victory. I will not tolerate anything less. Is that clear?"

He tapped his other finger on his chin as he paced back and forth. "You want to try again? All right, I'll give you one more chance. But if you fail me again I will personally cast you into the pit for an entire millennium. Your new task will be to stop the saints from praying. Is that simple enough for you or would you rather I send you to a daycare?" Satan asked sarcastically.

"I will do my best, master." He vanished before Satan started yelling again.

"Do not fail me." Satan shouted to the empty space.

CHAPTER 30

From the back of the white van, Judy moaned quietly as she regained consciousness. Her head lopped back and forth with the movements of the van. Her eyes opened in slits only for a moment before closing again. Minutes later she was able to open her eyes fully.

Her head throbbed to the point she thought her head would explode from the pressure. She had little range of motion as she realized her wrists and ankles had been tied together. She had just enough slack to feel the top of her head, where an egg-sized lump had formed just behind her left ear.

Her vision, still blurry, forced her to squint in order to see anything. She turned her head with a slow and quiet motion to not arouse suspicion. Judy understood she was in the back of a van but didn't remember how she got here. The knot on her head had not registered to put that together with being tied up inside the van.

When she looked around, she saw a young woman seated behind the driver, tied up as well. Judy noted a vacant look on the girl's face, but she appeared to be looking in the direction of the three men. It was bizarre from Judy's point of view.

As her head cleared more, Judy tried to free her hands, but the pain intensified to the point she has to remain still. "Make no mistake about it, Judy Metcalf will not only get through this nightmare, but I will get even with them."

Judy has always been a fighter. If not for the cords, she would take on the whole bunch. She continued working on the knots with small, limited movements in case anyone in the front of the van looked back.

The woman up front hadn't realized Judy had come to, which is how Judy wanted it. If she had been seen moving around, it might cause the men to panic and do something to make things worse. Judy watched closely, but the woman did not move a muscle. "Come on, Metcalf, think. Find a way out of this. Stay alert." In her head she screamed to keep from losing consciousness, "Find a way to beat these sorry specimens for humans."

———•———

"Play it again," Jack ordered. "Slow it down and try to get tighter on the license plate."

"Sorry, Jack. It's just not a clear view."

Jack had lost track of the time as he watched the video over and over. Frustration set in as he tried to find something, anything, to lead him to the gunmen. So far, there was nothing new.

As he watched it again, he thought of Judy, which fueled his intensity to solve this case.

He opened his cell phone and called the crime lab, hoping Bill Owens might still there. "Come on, Bill, pick up the phone."

As he started to take the phone away from his ear, Bill finally answered, "Yeah?"

"Anything new?"

"Not yet," Bill replied. "We're still working on compiling everything. There just aren't that many clues to work with yet."

"Okay, Bill. Tell the guys I appreciate the work they're doing on this. Keep me posted if anything turns up."

"Sure thing, Jack." The phone went dead.

Jack turned back to the video player, "Okay, Don, play it again. There's something we're missing."

Nothing more could be done except to wait for another clue to pop up. APB's had been put out to all law enforcement agencies across Michigan and surrounding states, with a description of the white van and the three men with two hostages. "Don't worry, Judy. I'll get you back safely. You too, Amy. That's a promise." Jack wanted this to be true.

CHAPTER 31

Peter sat against the wall as he thought of Paul seated at the mall. He didn't think the answer to his prayer was so unusual, but how fast the prayer had been answered. "I am just amazed by the immediate response I got from God himself."

Music played again on the other side of the wall. The music didn't play all the time, but it played often. When it did play, it was obviously joyful music like a celebration.

Peter turned his head to the left and screamed as he found himself face to face with a stranger. The voice, however, sounded familiar. "Welcome, Peter."

"H-h-hi." After a moment of staring into the face of the angel, he asked with mild trepidation, "Who are you and where am I?"

"I have been sent from Almighty God to help you strengthen your faith. My name is Jareb of the heavenly host."

"Wait a minute. Are you telling me you're an angel?"

"Yes, Peter. You are seated against the wall of heaven. You are not inside the gates yet, since you are still alive on earth. I assure you the Lord has a place prepared for you when the time comes for you to enter his kingdom."

Peter stared in disbelief, at the meek, gentle face that glowed with the glory of God. Peter felt calm as his anxiety disappeared and peace overtook him. "So why am I here?"

"To see your present life through spiritual eyes. You will see events taking place in the physical world you would not normally be able to see, such as what you witnessed with your son. I am to help you to understand that you don't wrestle with flesh and blood, but against principalities, against powers, against the rulers of the darkness of this world, against spiritual wickedness in high places."

"But I already know that."

"In the physical world, people fight against themselves in order to feel better about themselves. In the spiritual world, there is a battle raging for the souls of men and women that, if it could be seen, would scare human beings to death. You, my friend, have the rare opportunity to see that world."

"Are you being honest with me? Are you really an angel? And is this really Heaven?" He patted the wall behind his head.

"Yes, Peter, I am being honest with you."

Peter scratched his head as he scanned the scene before him. He decided that until he could prove this wasn't an angel or heaven, then he would believe what Jareb told him.

"Come, we must go." Jareb stood.

Instantly, Peter realized he could move, stood and followed the angel.

"Where are we going?"

"Follow me, and I will show you what you are to see."

CHAPTER 32

Jimmy Morten pulled his pickup truck off the main road onto a two-track dirt road. Thick trees lined the road, formed a dark canopy overhead. He drove two miles, before he reached his turn off, which looked like it led to nowhere.

The trees grew dense, the driveway narrowed to the point he thought me might lose his side mirrors. He turned his headlights on bright because nothing, not even sunlight, could penetrate the jungle-like foliage. His truck hit ruts and holes that bounced him up and down in the cab. "When are they ever gonna fix this dadgum driveway?" Jimmy asked through gritted teeth, as he rubbed his head after hitting the roof.

He slowed down for some larger holes not wanting to risk a broken axle. After another three hundred yards of slow going, the narrow driveway opened up. "I can't believe anyone could live out here, but the proof is right in front of me."

A two-story, red brick house jutted toward the sky in the middle of the clearing. The severely peaked roof had old green shingles, some missing, some loose. The dark brick structure had four windows on each side, all shuttered. One shutter hung precariously on one hinge.

"This looks like the Addams Family Mansion." Jimmy joked to himself. He pulled the truck around to the back door and parked in the circular drive. He grabbed his bag from the bed and walked in through the screen door, which slammed shut behind him from the strong spring.

Jimmy ambled through the kitchen into the living room. There a man and a woman turned to look at him, but never spoke. The room had been furnished with over extravagance. Two crystal chandeliers, too large for the room, hung from the cathedral ceiling, lit the handmade Persian rug made specifically for this room. Leather furniture had been placed in groupings to allow for maximum eye contact. Antique tables, sitting between the sofa and two recliners, were filled with folders and note pads. Everything had been placed in a certain order with meticulous scrutiny. The room had recently been sterilized and cleansed from all impurities. It had the smell of disinfectant but a musty odor lingered.

And yet, with all of the beauty of the room, the two sat huddled around a 10" black and white television. They turned back and continued watching the news.

The moment the news ended, Jimmy spoke excitedly, "Did you see the story? Did you see it?"

"Which story do you mean?" asked Elaine, rising from off the sofa. She had long dark hair covering her entire back that flowed gracefully as she walked towards Jimmy. Her kept dark eyes fixed Jimmy's face.

"Oh, quit playing around. You know what I mean. The shooting at the Central Bus Station? Where the people got shot and killed? Didn't you see the story?" He stood still as he looked back and forth between the two of them.

"Yes, Jimmy, we saw it," replied Bob from a recliner, directly in front of the tiny television. He never looked at Jimmy as he spoke. "You did do what you were ordered to do. For that I must commend you. On the other hand, you may have started what could very well be our downfall. Are you prepared to live with that, Jimmy?"

Bob finally stood up. He had a portly physique, along with a small strip of hair around his bald head. His eye brows had been shaped to make a 'V' in the middle of his forehead. He walked over to Elaine and played with her hair. Jimmy thought about what he'd been told.

"Look, Jimmy, it's not that we don't appreciate what you did." This voice caught Jimmy by surprise, as it came from behind him. He spun around to see William Benning, the leader of Anti-Pro. "It's just that we're concerned for the safety of Mr. Hartley. We don't want anything to jeopardize his well-being. Do you understand what I'm saying?"

Jimmy couldn't speak but did manage to nod his head. It felt like he had been slapped in the face as reality set in.

"Bob and Elaine, would you please check on our other projects while I talk with Jimmy in private?" They left the room no questions asked. Jimmy started getting nervous sensing trouble might be on the way for him.

He spoke hastily, "Mr. Benning, I wasn't trying to make trouble. Honest. I only want to help our cause. You said if Mr. Hartley was not released on time then people would have to die. I believed you and I did what you ordered me to do."

"Jimmy, relax, you're not being punished. You did good. You helped send a message that will not to be taken lightly. I wanted to talk to you alone because I have another special assignment for you. It will include killing just one more person. Would you do that for me? For Anti-Pro?" William Benning's tone became be very hypnotic.

Jimmy fought to stay in his right mind, but heard himself answering, "Yes, Mr. Benning, I'll do whatever you need to further our cause. Who do you want me to kill?"

"Come with me and I'll show you."

They walked through a room, set up as a shrine, and into an office. Above the door the title "High Priest of the god, Re" had been engraved on a stone mantel.

Re was the Egyptian sun god. It was said he rescued his people from certain destruction. According to followers, victory was certain if all commands of Re were followed.

As they entered the office, William shut the door. He turned to the picture of Re and placed his hands together and bowed slightly to his god. Jimmy walked past without doing anything.

CHAPTER 33

Jareb brought Peter to a familiar place, Eastside Baptist Church.

"This is my church," Peter exclaimed. He saw his pastor and his boss together. Jareb spoke, "Listen."

———◆———

"Why does God allow us to go through such deep dark valleys like this, Pastor Thompson?" Al Tuinstra struggled to understand everything that had happened to him, his family, and his staff. His job dealt with reporting things like this to other people. Now those same events had hit way too close to home.

"You know, Al, people have asked that question for centuries and never really been satisfied with the answer," the pastor began. "God Himself does not tempt us, but he allows Satan the opportunity to bring certain circumstances into our lives to see if we'll be faithful to God or whether we'll give in or give up. I know you remember the story of Job."

Al nodded.

Pastor Thompson continued, "He was faithful to God, but Satan thought he could break him. God allowed Satan to take Job's every possession in this world. And, according to the scripture, Job was a very wealthy man. All of his livestock, all his barns, and all ten of his children were taken from him destroyed or killed in less than a day. But he remained faithful.

"God then allowed Satan to take Job's health but not his life. He had painful boils from head to toe to the point his face was unrecognizable by his friends. Job's own wife said, 'curse God and die.' But Job remained faithful. And if that wasn't enough, Job's friends came along and accused him of sinning and hiding things from God and not confessing his wrongdoing.

"You see, Al, we sometimes have to go through hardships in order to gain the rewards of the life that is to come. When all was said and done, Job received double everything that had been taken away from him. God won't let you down. Stay faithful."

"Sounds easy when you say it like that, but what about real life?" asked Al as he shrugged his shoulders and threw his hands out.

"You must pray. Ask the Lord to give you strength and wisdom to overcome this terrible trial that's come to your family."

Pastor Thompson paused a moment. "Rest assured, Al, you're not alone in this. Our entire congregation is praying around the clock for Amy and your staff. We've also called other churches and they, too, are praying. The power is there. We just have to wait for God to answer it. And, believe me, God will answer these prayers."

"I appreciate your wisdom, pastor." He left the pastor's office and slowly walked out of the church. He needed to head back to the hospital and also call the station. He had to admit he felt better after he talked with his pastor. Yet, as a father, he still felt the pain of his daughter missing, but the helplessness that he could not do anything about it.

Tears ran down his cheeks as he thought of the wonderful memories he, Beth and Amy had shared. He also realized the many times he had not been there for his family. He allowed work to come first in his life, not his family. He had worked at being a better father over the past few years. He knew he had a long way to go before he felt he'd become a good father.

"By the way, Al," Pastor Thompson shouted from the steps of the church, "a Harry Nickols has been snooping around trying to get some information about Peter. He's supposed to be at the service tonight hoping to get a firsthand look at what Peter does outside of the news. Do you have any advice I can give this Mr. Nickols? I don't want him disturbing you or June."

"Old Harry, huh?" Al said while he walked towards the pastor. "That's interesting, Pastor. Let me think. No, there shouldn't be any trouble with Harry. If he bothers you just let me know. I'll call the station manager at WOZD-TV. We go back a ways."

Al grabbed hold of the pastor's hand and shook it, "Thanks, Pastor Thompson, for everything."

———•———

Peter turned to Jareb and asked, "Is Harry Nickols going to hurt my family?" He felt he had to know his family would be safe from any more problems while he stayed in the hospital. "I know there are other important things, but I have to know about Harry. Please tell me, Jareb."

"I have been assured that your family will not be harmed by Harry Nickols. There may be other, greater dangers for your family that might have greater consequences to you and your loved ones as Satan is allowed to infiltrate their lives. You must pray passionately, Peter. You must pray with perseverance for their protection."

Jareb allowed that to sink in before he spoke again. "Come, we have much to see." They walked through the walls of the church building. Peter didn't flinch, but just walked on through.

CHAPTER 34

In the front of the darkened van, the three gunmen-turned-abductors discussed their plans. "Look, we're all tired. Find us some place to stop for a quick breather," the big man said. It sounded more like an order than a request. "There's not a lot out here, so we shouldn't be noticed. We need to stretch for a little while."

No one argued about being exhausted. The van stunk from the three men, who hadn't showered in a while, now coupled with the two women, and the Michigan heat beating down on them. The humidity, mixed with the hot air, blew inside the windows. Although difficult, they had all become accustomed to the stench.

The men yawned constantly as the day's events caught up with them. The radio played country music. Once in a while a news bulletin would break in to inform the listeners to be on the lookout for a white van with three men and possibly two women. The listeners were told to call police if the van had been spotted.

Just as another report started, the driver turned the radio off. "I'm tired of hearing about it," he sighed. "I just want to know who did the shooting. It wasn't us, was it?"

From behind him he heard, "Yeah, how is it we were in the back of the bus station and the shooting starts in the front? Are they crazy or something? Someone could have gotten hurt." He took off his glasses and cleaned them with the bottom of his dirty white T-shirt, which only smeared the lenses, making them nearly impossible to see through. He put them back on as he continued his thought, "You know, we pushed him pretty hard, calling him chicken and coward and all. I wonder if he had anything to do with this."

"You mean Jimmy? No way," the driver said. "He's too much of a wimp to do anything like that. And if he did, he put the whole plan in jeopardy."

The big man riding shotgun analyzed what was being said, as he scratched his head through an old greasy hat. "It doesn't matter what happened," he said, "or who did it. The police are after us now because we have something they want. We got us some hostages." He let out a sinister laugh. The talking stopped for a while.

Several signs passed by with city names. Billboards advertising "roach motels" and "greasy spoons" lined the miles in-between. No one spoke again inside the dark van.

Amy was the only one alert. She tried to look out the windows to see where they were headed, while at the same time she kept an eye on the men. All her thoughts circled back to their plan and how this might affect her and the woman behind her. She prayed silently for God to keep them safe.

Her mind raced through memories of her life, moments spent with family members hugging her after she scored the game-winning run to win the state championship in softball. Memories of being comforted after her best friend had been killed in a car crash. Amy thought on anything she could to find some peace.

She then thought back to her days spent in church. She thought about how her parents had always force her to go to the services and to learn about God and to memorize the scriptures. Now, as she sat on a milk crate, she thanked God for her parents, because it helped her through this nightmare. She had no idea what might happen next, so she prayed and planned.

The driver spoke, breaking the silence. "Do we have any clue where we're supposed to be going? We've been driving for hours and we haven't gotten anywhere. And I'm really tired of driving. I sure could use a little relief if you know what I mean."

"Look, I told you to find a place to stop," said the big man. "Our orders were to get to someplace safe before the police catch us. There'll be time to rest later when things blow over. Try to contain yourself and keep driving. I'll tell you when to turn off of the highway."

The driver let out a sigh but did as he was told. He kept his eyes open for a convenience store somewhere along the highway.

Highway hypnosis took over as he drove. The thumping of the tires, the rhythmic hum of the engine, and the constant stare at the white lines on the highway all contributed to him going into a trance. The highway didn't end and didn't offer any places to stop.

———•———

Behind the passenger's seat, the third man fell asleep hunched over on an old paint can. He was the youngest and the least willing to be involved. A bump in the road jarred his head up and slammed it back down on the can. He rubbed the side of his face. "What're we going to do?"

The question was sincere and showed the fear he harbored over the deed they had done. He knew society doesn't look kindly to men who took hostages and shot people. He went on a rant, "We just can't run for the rest of our lives. They'll find us and then we're going to spend the rest of our lives in prison. And for what? To help someone we've never met before? He's never helped us any. This is crazy. I told you guys I didn't want to do this. But you both said nothing would happen. We would just go in, wait for the phone call and then get out of there with no problems. Well, I think we missed the call and now we've got some major problems. Wouldn't you agree?" His rambling struck a nerve.

"Shut up," the big man yelled. "We haven't been caught yet. We can't panic like a bunch of scared turkeys before Thanksgiving Day. We've gotta stay calm and lay low until they get tired of searching for us. Then we leave either the state or the country. I'm not quite sure which just yet. Now I don't want to hear any more talk of how stupid this was. Do you understand?"

The man seated behind him gave a quick nod of his head, but didn't say anything. He could hear the instability in the voice of the so-called self-proclaimed leader in front of him when he tried to make a plan without thinking it through.

Of course, being the biggest of the three apparently did have its advantages. The big man stood six feet, two inches and weighed close to two hundred-fifty pounds. He had a big head with a thick unshaved beard with cold dark eyes and a mustache hanging over his lip. His greasy, black hair fell to the middle of his back. It must have been days since it was last washed. His willingness to always let it be known he was the man in charge might be something that could come back and bite him later, if and when they got caught.

———•———

In the back of the van, Judy tried to hear what the men said. She wanted their names and any detail she might be able to glean. The talk had stopped after the big man yelled. She also tried to see their faces, but without any light in the van, it was useless. While she lay on the floor of the van, her head propped up on a few dirty, greasy rags, she let her mind wander off to her youth. She thought about her childhood as she grew up in a small town in Missouri. Her parents were so deeply in love it was impossible to see a tragedy soon entering their lives.

Her dad had been out of work but had found a job with a construction company building a highway just a few miles away from their home. He'd been working on a bridge over a small creek, smoothing out wet concrete when a co-worker approached driving a steamroller used to press the asphalt. She had been told her dad looked up at the heavy machine and saw the driver grab his chest. He was having a heart attack. The driver slumped over and the steamroller to veered directly toward her dad.

Before he could react he was pinned to the side of the fortified bridge. That day changed the lives of Judy and her mother forever. The tears never stopped flowing after that horrible day. Neither had ever fully recovered from the incident. They only learned to live with the pain.

Judy came back to reality as she felt tears roll down her cheeks, only now the tragedy would be her own death by the hands of three dirty men. The thought of being killed strengthened her resolve to somehow get out of this situation. She became more determined to hear names, plans, anything she could take with her in order to get these men convicted.

CHAPTER 35

At St. John's Hospital, Detective Jack McDougal continued his investigation. At the moment he sat next to Peter Stallings' wife.

"Any news on how he's doing, Mrs. Stallings?" The question was sincere. He hated to see anyone suffer, not only the victims but also their families and friends as well.

She shook her head and in a weak voice said, "The doctor told me the chances of Peter recovering are very slim. They don't give either of them much hope." She broke down in tears as she had so often since the shooting.

Jack put a hand on her shoulder and held out a box of tissue, trying to comfort her. He had become acquainted Peter and his family over the past few years. Peter had been to several press conferences with Jack, as he gathered facts for news broadcasts. Their respect for each other stemmed from their ability to trust each with information that needed to stay confidential until the crime had been solved or the news leaked to another source. Jack found by sharing some facts each had gathered they were able to solve some important cases.

Soon the business relationship turned into a friendship. They knew to be careful to not compromise any cases by giving out too much sensitive information that might damage an investigation. Nor did they wish to endanger themselves or others by either hiding information or reporting it too early. Peter had gotten into some hot water with his boss for doing business like this but had built a respect with Jack McDougal.

Jack spoke to Mrs. Stallings, "You know I'll do whatever I can to bring whoever did this to justice. I promise you they will go away for a long time."

"Oh, Jack, this is such a shock," she said biting through her tears. "We never imagined in our wildest dreams something like this would happen to Peter. How could someone shoot him and John like that? Did they provoke anyone? I tell you, Jack, if it weren't for the prayers of the church right now, I honestly think I'd have a nervous breakdown."

Jack didn't have an answer. He sat quietly and let her talk. He knew her devotion as a good, godly woman was well known throughout her community. She knew the scriptures and how to use them in appropriate ways, which meant she never beat God into people but allowed God to work through her to those she talked with.

Her faith helped her through many difficult times before. It gave her peace few around her understood, but everyone wanted. She could usually handle the toughest situations by holding on to her faith.

Several years ago her sister Emily's house burned to the ground taking the lives of her two small children. The entire family of three brothers and two other sisters felt sorrow but didn't know what to do to help. June took control, kept the family from falling apart, and gave everyone tasks to help Emily.

Three months before the fire, her sister's husband had run off and left her alone with her two daughters. Then the fire had brought down the rest of her world. Emily felt alone in this world. If it hadn't been for June she would have killed herself. She couldn't take care of her basic needs, like eating, sleeping, and keeping herself clean. She would just lie on the sofa at June's, feeling the weight of all her losses. June finally told her to stop feeling sorry for herself and get on with life. It wasn't something June wanted to say. She knew how much Emily hurt. What June said, she said in love.

This tragedy, however, didn't just hit too close to home. It actually hit home. This time it was Peter, the man who had swept her off of her feet in college, the man who helped to raise their two boys, and the man she loved with all of her heart. This was Peter, the man who seemed to be invincible, the man who could fix anything, and the man who loved her with all of his heart. It tore her up inside in spite of her faith in God.

"I'll check back later to see how Peter's doing and you, too. You know, you could go home and rest. You'll need your strength over the next few days." He knew she would be polite but tell him 'no.' Still, he asked, "Can I give you a ride home, June?"

"Thank you Jack, but you know I can't leave without knowing how Peter's doing," she stated as she gained the strength to continue. "That's my man in that room and I will not leave until I know he's going to be all right. But I appreciate your kind offer, Jack. I just might take you up on that later. But for now I can't leave."

Jack nodded understanding and stood up to leave.

"You could do one thing for me, Jack."

"Whatever you need, Mrs. Stallings."

"I would really appreciate it if you or another officer could check up on Paul, our youngest son. He's been getting into some kind of trouble lately and we're not sure what it is. I think it's gang related. Could you do that for Peter and me, Jack?"

"I'd be happy to do that. I'll have the local guys send an officer over there as soon as I get back to the station. I'll be sure the officer is discreet so he doesn't scare Paul," Jack stated as he wrote down the request. "Take care," he said as he turned towards the elevator.

June Stallings began to weep before Jack could get the elevator doors shut; his eyes welled up with tears of his own. He wasn't afraid to let his emotions show, especially when it came to crying and when it came to his friends.

While the elevator descended, he thought about his next move. It had only been a few hours since the shooting, but he felt the trail had gotten cold already. He hoped and prayed something would pop up to help. He knew something had to be on the video tape from Judy's camera. After numerous viewings of the video and a break, he went back to see it again.

"Oh, God," he prayed, "I need your help on this one." He lifted his eyes toward the ceiling of the elevator. "Help me to find the people who took Judy and Amy and shot Peter and John. Those are my friends in the ICU. And, well, you know how I feel about Judy. I have to do all I can to find them but I can't do it alone. I ask you to guide me and lead me to them. Show me where to begin. And, Lord, place your healing hand on the life of Peter Stallings and John Robertson. Give comfort to their families and friends. Give me strength to complete this task. Amen."

The elevator door opened on the first floor. As he stepped off of the elevator, he ran into Pastor Joseph Thompson. Jack filled him in on June Stallings in the waiting room. They also talked a little about the investigation.

As they shook hands, Pastor Thompson told Jack he and his entire congregation would pray for Jack to have wisdom and guidance as he tracks down the men who did this. The pastor stepped into the elevator and pressed the button for the third floor. As the doors shut, Pastor Thompson said, "You'll get 'em, Jack."

Both felt peace knowing they helped each other. Jack investigated and Pastor Thompson prayed.

CHAPTER 36

Judy had just closed her eyes when the van suddenly turned off the main road. She crinkled her eyebrows together as she heard them say something about this road not being on the map. Amy sat still on the milk crate and stared out the window. The men went quiet as they traveled unknown territory.

The narrow dirt road lined by trees and deep ruts might only be used by farmers. The road did not get much use. The van jumped up and down between the grooves that jostled everyone inside.

The driver finally yelled, "Look, store or no store, I have to stop and I have to stop now. I've had to go to the bathroom since the bus station. I can't wait another minute."

"You're driving the van. Stop suffering," the big man said. "In fact, stop right here if that's all you have to do."

The van eased to a stop in the middle of the road. The driver slammed it into park and bolted out the door. He barely made it to a tree not more than two feet off the road. The other two laughed at their buddy making such a scene. Moments later, they stood right next to him doing the same thing. They didn't laugh anymore.

As soon as they left the van, Amy turned to Judy and whispered, "Hey, hey, wake up."

No response came.

She tried again, "Wake up. Hurry." She kicked a small plastic container towards Judy trying to wake her up. It hit her shoulder and jarred her awake.

"Why'd you do that?"

"Shhhhh." Amy hissed. "They're outside for a minute."

"What are they doing?" Judy asked, not sure what was happening. She shook the cobwebs from her head.

"They're by the trees, just a few feet away," Amy whispered. "Are you okay?"

"I'm a little banged up, but yeah, I'm all right."

"So what should we do now?"

"Right now, we shouldn't do anything but stay alive. We're going to get out of this. As long as they keep busy they won't be thinking about us too much."

Judy tried to sit up a little so see out the window, but the cords restrained her from even the simplest of movements. "For now, try to get their names and any plans they might talk about. Oh, and memorize what they look like, facial features, scars, tattoos, anything that will help identify them later."

"I've already studied their faces, but I haven't heard their names yet. I don't want them thinking I am doing anything that might make them angry."

"That's good. Just try to stay calm."

"Here they come," whispered Amy franticly.

Judy put her head back down to look like she was asleep. Amy stared out the window. The van door opened.

"Hey Tom, what about these two?" asked the young guy pointing to the back. "What if they have to go too? Do we let them go or do they suffer?"

Amy and Judy both heard the name Tom. They had to contain their emotions when they heard the name after just talking about it. In their hearts they celebrated as they seared the name in their minds.

"Let 'em suffer for a while longer," Tom said.

"Whatever."

As they drove on, the road twisted and turned underneath the summer foliage, hiding the van from everyone looking for them. The two in the front seats grew weary as the weight of what they had done had turned them into fugitives. Behind them, the young one fell asleep again, this time leaning against the side of the van. Although they tried to keep the macho persona intact, they were running scared.

It might have been the heat, it might have been their clothing, or perhaps it might be they hadn't bathed for days that caused the odor inside the van to become almost unbearable. The wind blew their long, greasy, unkempt hair around also blew the stink around.

When they spoke they used rough, vile language. Thankfully, they grew too tired to speak.

Judy's pain had done her more good than she realized. Her body needed rest in order to heal as much as possible without proper medical attention her head needed. The pain kept her from doing something that might make the men upset.

Judy had never been known for being soft-spoken. She would speak her mind when the need called for it. Some called her mean-spirited; others called her passionate; still others said it must be her Irish heritage. If asked about these characteristics, Judy would reply "yes" to all three being true. Tied up in the back of the van, her head throbbing, sleep was a good thing.

CHAPTER 37

As the mid-week service began, people made their way to their seats. It seemed most had a favorite place they had picked out for themselves ever since the building was built. The Johnsons sat behind the organ next to the window. Mrs. Hattie Mae Wilson always sat on the fifth pew next to Alicia Jones. Both had been widowed for many years and had become very close friends.

Near the back of the church, a thin man sat, looking out of place, after having been welcomed by several people. Harry Nickols came to the service at the Eastside Baptist Church as he'd promised he would do. Pastor Thompson didn't believe he would show up. Mary Williams, the church secretary, sat across the aisle from Harry and gave a friendly smile, Harry returned the same. He had come to the service as agreed, but he continued to be angry at God.

Pastor Thompson spoke after the singing finished. "As you all know, and are praying for, Peter Stallings and his family are going through a very difficult time right now. Peter and his co-worker, John Robertson, were both shot this week down at Central Station. Another co-worker, Judy Metcalf, and Amy Tuinstra, daughter of Al and Angie Tuinstra, have been taken hostage." Harry noticed the Tuinstras sat to his left a few rows ahead of him.

Pastor Thompson continued, "My brothers and sisters, when one of our family hurts, we all hurt. Tonight, we all hurt, along with the Stallings and Tuinstras. We must pray for them, not just tonight while we are assembled together. We must pray until they are restored back to health and with us here once again among their family. Tonight, we must pray and pray hard. We as a body of believers must unite our hearts in prayer and overwhelm the throne of the Almighty God together, tonight."

The gathered folks gave their approval in a variety of ways.

"Brothers and sisters, Brother Stallings and Brother Tuinstra and their families have been faithful members of our congregation for many years.

They've labored together with us in the good times and the bad times. It is our turn to lift them up in prayer and ask the Lord to perform a miracle in their lives tonight."

———◆———

In the back of the room, Harry squirmed. He sat lost in memories from another time. He remembered sitting in a room filled with people as a small boy in northern Michigan. People cried as he sat in the hospital waiting room. Harry didn't understand what had happened at the time. He then remembered his father came to find him. The words remained fresh in his mind, "Harry, God has taken Mommy away from us." The words sounded angry and bitter.

Since then Harry had been bitter and angry with God for taking his mother when he was so young. Deep in his heart, however, he knew there had to be more to the story than *"God just took her away."* There had to be an explanation, Harry just never tried to find it out.

It wasn't long after his mother died that his father couldn't handle life anymore. Harry remembered coming home from school and being met by his grandmother, who told him his father had died too. This only added to Harry's confusion about why God did this to him. He vowed right then and there to never step foot inside a church again. He also vowed to do all he could to get even with God for taking away his parents.

Through his reporting, Harry got, what he called "even with God." He covered stories of crimes committed in churches. He would go after any clergy for any small offense with the ferocity and tenacity of a grizzly bear. Ministry after ministry was ruined with deep satisfaction. Until this moment, while he listened to Pastor Thompson talk, he had acted to ease his pain by destroying God. In his heart, however, he felt emptiness, a sense of shame instead of vengeful pleasure. He didn't understand what was happening to him.

When the service ended Harry went up to Pastor Thompson.

———◆———

"Well, Harry Nickols, I'm really surprised you came to the service tonight. I thought you'd try to find some other angle on Peter and skip church altogether. It's good to see that you are a man of your word."

"Thanks, Pastor. Believe it or not, I really enjoyed the service tonight. I got a feeling for what Peter's life is about. I still want an opportunity to talk with you about him and other things as well. Would that be all right with you?" Harry's tone sounded different as he spoke with the pastor.

"Sure, Harry. I promised that if you came to the service I would talk with you if you still wanted to do so. And, as you are, so am I a man of my word. Name the time and I'll make room for you in my schedule. By the way this is Al Tuinstra, Peter's boss at WGRT. You may wish to talk with him as well."

Harry shook hands with Al as he said, "That'd be great, if it's all right with you, Mr. Tuinstra. I'd like to call you perhaps tomorrow and set up an appointment with you."

"Call my secretary and she will set up a time for you," Al said. He gave Harry a business card.

"Thank you, sir. I have to get another story completed before my deadline. Thanks again, Pastor Thompson. I'm sorry to hear about your daughter, Mr. Tuinstra. I hope she gets back safely."

"Thanks, Harry. I appreciate that."

They all shook hands once again and Harry left the church. The Tuinstras walked close behind him. Pastor Thompson prayed silently for Harry. He turned the lights off in the main auditorium, locked the doors and headed home. "It was a good service, Lord, a very good service indeed." He whistled a favorite hymn as he drove down the road.

CHAPTER 38

Pithel and Jareb sat a good distance from John and Peter. Pithel said, "All is going according to the precise plan of the Almighty God. As of now, John and Peter remain in the hospital comas. Their co-worker, Judy, along with Amy, are being held hostage in the back of a van."

Jareb stated, "Satan has started his attacks on all those directly and indirectly involved. His followers fight against the heavenly warriors for the rights to one soul."

Jareb shook his head as he thought about that. "One soul. It is hard to imagine that one soul is worth all this effort. I know the Almighty said he is not willing that any should perish, but that all should come to repentance."

"He meant every word of that," Pithel chimed in.

"That is the precise reason he allowed his son to die," Jareb said to complete the thought.

"Well, from here the mission only gets tougher," Pithel said. "Satan will complicate things as he tries to win a victory for the soul of these humans. Our part of the plan is beginning to unfold as we speak with the reporters."

The angels turned their attention back to the mission.

———◆———

"We must win at any cost. Do you understand?" Satan gave his best motivational talk to his gathered army. They stood before him but didn't pay attention; instead they played and fought. After a few moments, Satan had had enough, "*Silence*. I want it completely quiet or I shall take my wrath out upon you."

"For wanting silence, he sure is yelling pretty loud," one foolish devil chimed. That comment did not set well with his master. Satan cast the poor soul to the lowest part of hell.

"Does anyone else wish to challenge me?" None dared to move or even breathe until their master calmed down.

"Good, then shall we continue? We simply cannot fail. We must prevail against the other side. Distract this reporter. Do not allow him to hear the gospel. When that angel, Pithel, begins to talk about God's love, we must attack. Never allow him to hear about Jesus." Satan let out a deep sigh, "Now go and bring me the soul of this reporter."

The legion of demons howled and screamed as they fled from the presence of Satan. Flames leaped into the air from the nostrils of the more talented, as they made their way to the place where Pithel and John Robertson talked.

CHAPTER 39

Rebecca, a young nurse, finished her exam of Peter and found everything normal. She left the room to type her information into the computer. Across the hall, in a small meeting room, Dr. Peterson sat with Peter's wife.

"Mrs. Stallings, I wish I could tell you something to lift your hopes, but I'm afraid I can't. As of now the prognosis remains unchanged. I must tell you that the odds of your husband coming out of the coma, let alone returning to a normal life, are extremely slim. The bullet lodged itself in the right frontal lobe of his brain after entering just behind his ear. He has major swelling in his brain. We can't tell what the extent of the damage is due to the swelling. Until then we'll keep him sedated and under a very close watch to prevent any further damage as the best we can." Dr. Peterson stood after he gave the dire news.

"I'm truly sorry for what you are going through, Mrs. Stallings. I hope you know we'll do everything in our power to help your husband."

Dr. James Peterson, regarded by many as the doctor with the best bedside manner, found it difficult to speak with Mrs. Stallings. He did his best to give the highest amount of hope, but knew in his heart it was just a matter of time before her husband would be dead. He knew his words didn't bring her comfort. He really spoke them to soothe his own conscience for not being able to do any more for her husband.

His words, however, fell on deaf ears as June concentrated on her husband. She wanted so desperately to see him, to touch him, to hold him again. Pastor Joseph Thompson sat beside her as the doctor gave the news, which didn't leave much hope. He put his soft, strong hand on her shoulder as tears continued to flow. The pastor didn't have any words to give her comfort. He could only pray the Holy Spirit would comfort her and give her peace.

Dr. Peterson broke the silence. "You can go in now, Mrs. Stallings." Before he finished the sentence, June had already made for the door to her husband's room. A team of nurses turned into John Robertson's room as she passed by. The pastor and doctor watched her enter the room. Neither man spoke.

Pastor Thompson sat back down and prayed. He hoped this wouldn't be the last time she would see her husband alive. He prayed for strength for her and the family. He finished his prayer and looked toward Peter's room. He bit his bottom lip as his emotions finally got the best of him.

As June entered the room, the sounds of machines rhythmically beeping, buzzing, ringing, and dripping hit her ears. Tubes in his mouth, wires attached to his head, chest and arms, and bandages made it impossible to tell if this could truly be her husband. With all the equipment, she thought Peter no longer looked human, but like some futuristic machine constructed by doctors. June's resolve allowed her to look past it all and see Peter. This was still the man she fell in love with. This was her husband of twenty-five years.

In fact, if asked, she would say she was even more in love now than the day they got married. She reached out to touch his face, scratchy to her fingers as she gently ran her finger across his cheek to his ear, the only part of his face uncovered. Tears ran down her face falling onto Peter's bandages as she looked over her husband.

She remembered the day Peter proposed. They walked hand in hand along a stretch of beach near the Lake Michigan shoreline looking into each other's eyes. They talked about their future. She could still hear Peter say, "I want to make enough money so we can retire early enough to enjoy the golden years of our lives."

"What's my man going to do for me today?" she recalled asking. The sun had almost set as they strolled along the sandy beach. The lake's waves were gentle on this very beautiful night. As the sun, a huge red ball, slowly disappeared over the horizon, long shadows of Peter and June fell behind them. Peter looked nervous as they stood and watched the final rays of the sun.

"Look, June, I want to give you the best life I can. I'm just afraid my best won't be enough," Peter said almost in tears.

"Peter Stallings, what on earth are you talking about? I've never asked you for anything like that. In fact, I have no clue what you're talking about."

"Oh June, you are so beautiful. I'm the luckiest man on earth to be with you." He fidgeted while trying to get his words out. "I guess what I'm trying to say is. . . is. . ." Suddenly he fell to his knees, giving June quite a start.

"Peter, are you all right? What's the matter with you?"

"June, will you marry me?"

The look of confusion on the face of June Johnson quickly turned into a face of joy. "What did you say?" Her voice sounded soft and full of love.

"Will you marry me, June Johnson? Please say that you will. I don't think I could go through this agony of proposing again."

"Oh, Peter. Yes, yes, I will marry you." She threw her arms around his neck and hugged and kissed him.

"If I'd have known you'd react like this I'd have asked you sooner," Peter chided his now bride-to-be. She gently slapped his arm before kissing him again. Six months later they stood in the front of the church, exchanging their vows in a beautiful traditional wedding. That was twenty-five years ago.

June stared into the face of Peter as all of those memories of the golden years turned to anger. "How could I ever enjoy those years without you, Peter?" she whispered into his ear. "We've done everything together. When our friends' marriages fell apart, we stood strong and firm vowing not to end up like that because of our love for each other."

She wiped a tear away with the tissue she carried as she continued, "We dedicated our home to the Lord the very day we got married. And through the good times and the bad times, we stood on our faith in Jesus. And each and every time he brought us through, those struggles making us stronger than before. But now I don't know what to do."

Other thoughts raced through her head that clouded her mind and brought doubt with confusion. This was not something she had been accustomed to having invade her soul. Then again it wasn't everyday she faced the possibility of losing her husband.

Fear of the unknown, the shock of seeing her husband in pain, did not begin to describe her feelings. She felt weak and alone as she thought about the possibility of losing her man. Even earlier in the waiting area when Jack McDougal talked with her, she had still been in good spirits. Now, as she looked into Peter's bandaged face, his wounds brought her to the brink of falling over the edge. She did the only thing she could think to do.

"Oh, Lord, I know you are in control. And I know you have a plan that I don't understand. Please, God, don't take Peter from me now. I know it's selfish of me to ask this, but I'm so scared to lose him. All those times I thought I was strong, I wasn't. I am only strong because of Peter and because of you. I have no strength right now and I don't know why this is happening. Give me the strength to get through this and through all I don't understand. I pray this in the powerful name of Jesus. Amen." She shed more tears.

CHAPTER 40

In the hospital bed Peter convulsed violently. Alarms rang out from the monitors and machines sending a message of major problems. Nurses and doctors ran into the room immediately checking Peter, trying to find out what might be causing the convulsions.

A nurse escorted Mrs. Stallings out of the room to give the medical team the space needed to do their jobs. More machines rolled into the room to be used to restart Peter's heart if necessary. An injection was given to him to stop the seizure. Each nurse had a look of worry on their faces, fearing this might be the end of Peter Stallings' life.

Next to the machines, and just above the head of Peter, a battle raged. A little demon had unexpectedly entered the room and managed to pinch off a tube from one of the machines used to keep Peter alive. Two others demons stood guard to keep Aremus from getting too close.

The two guards were way out of their league in facing Aremus. He once took on fifty of the strongest demons hell could ever hope to throw into a battle. He came out of the fight unscarred and with the hides of fifty demons. Three would be no contest.

Aremus sounded his warning, "You are not welcome here. He is protected by the Almighty God as a saint. You will leave immediately or I will force you to leave. Choose now, demons."

"We'll stay and finish our mission and you will not touch us. Now, back off angel or face the wrath of our master." hissed the demon, dripping saliva as he inched his way toward Aremus. "We will be victorious in this battle."

"You speak with confidence. Yet you talk as one who underestimates the power of the Almighty God. If you do not leave now, I will throw you out of the room by the power which you underestimate, the power of the Almighty God."

None of the demons moved. One, however, moved his eyes to see over the head of Peter where a fourth demon pulled on the tubes and wires.

"We will not leave," snarled the leader of the small band.

"Very well, have it your way." Aremus drew his sword, raised it above his head and with one swing, sent the leader back to hell. The other two charged at him simultaneously. With one more swing, Aremus sent them both back to hell to face their master.

"This is too easy. Next time, at least make it worth my while." He turned to face the fourth demon who hovered over Peter's bed. "You may leave of your own freewill or I can dispatch you back to the pit along with your friends."

"I'm going, I'm going."

"Wise choice," Aremus stated with his sword pointed at the demon's throat.

Before they could put the needle back in Peter's arm, the convulsions stopped. All of the monitors and machines went back to normal readings. Peter rested peacefully, as if nothing had happened. The nurse with the syringe was ordered to hold off on the injection.

The entire medical staff stood astonished and perplexed. One nurse could be overheard saying, "This is a miracle. I thought he was dead for sure this time."

The nurse, who had escorted June out of the room, went over to explain what had happened, although she couldn't explain how the seizure had stopped.

Peter relaxed against the wall after the ordeal in the hospital room, and thought about what Jareb told him moments before ago. It may have been a dream. It definitely wasn't reality. "I know he told me this is the wall of heaven. And he did show me what Paul has been going through. How can this be real, though? Maybe if I shut my eyes really tight, I'll be back in the hospital bed. Then again, why would I want to be there?"

He shut and opened his eyes anyway. After a few tries, he began to believe it could be real. It seemed the more he shut his eyes and opened them, the more vivid the colors became around him. The sky became bluer and the grass greener. Flowers in the fields shone in bright and vivid reds, yellows, oranges, and violets as the fragrance of them wafted to his nostrils.

"I've never smelled anything like this." He shut his eyes one last time thinking the place would disappear and he'd be back in the hospital bed.

As he clenched them tight, he prayed a simple prayer, "Lord, I have no idea what's happening right now. I feel so weak, so helpless, so totally out of control. You promised you would be with me always and would guide my footsteps. I just want to understand and believe all this. I also pray you would give strength and comfort to June and Paul. Protect them with your loving power."

He opened his eyes as a strange sensation overcame him. Peter continued to pray. "For some reason, I feel you are very near, like you're right next to me in a very real, physical sense. Show me what you want me to do. Thank-you for sending Jareb to talk to me. In Jesus' name. Amen." Peter looked to his right and found Jareb seated next to him.

"Jareb." Peter shouted, shocked to see the angel next to him so suddenly. "You have to stop popping in like that or I might end up with a heart attack to go along with the bullet wound." Peter placed his hands on his heart, feigning like Fred Sanford as he quoted, "It's the big one, Elizabeth."

"I am truly sorry, my friend," replied Jareb, chuckling as he watched Peter waving his arms. He grew more serious as he stated, "You will be safe as well as your family."

"How can you be so sure?"

"There is no need for you to fear, Peter, for the Lord has chosen you to be used of Him."

Peter doubted reality again with whomever it was seated next to him. For all he knew, this could be all part of some weird dream caused by the drugs the doctors had prescribed for him. "If this is a joke, it isn't funny."

"Peter, be of good cheer and comfort. I come to you with a message from the Most High God." The angel sat calm as his eyes penetrated deep into Peter's soul. "I am here to help you."

Peter went from almost believing back to unbelief. "Okay, guys. This isn't funny anymore. Come on in and talk to me." Peter sounded annoyed. "I really don't feel like playing games right now."

Jareb spoke again, "The pain you are suffering from now will not end your life. Nor will it cause you any permanent damage. You will recover fully. Through your pain and suffering, however, there will be many who will turn to Christ. The Lord himself has spoken this to you, through me, as I am his messenger. He has brought you here, amid these trying circumstances to instruct you as to what his will is for you. You will also be strengthened through your struggle while you remain here.

"In a short while I will return. I will be here to minister to you throughout your time here in the heavenly realms. You and I will walk through phases of your life as they take place at this present time. You have already experienced a portion of this with your son, Paul. You will be encouraged to pray and to serve the Almighty God on a higher spiritual level. For now, Peter, you must rest. We will begin our journey together shortly." Jareb finished speaking and vanished.

"Wait a minute," Peter yelled. He received no response. In the background, celebration music continued to play. As he listened to the music, it sounded like two choirs, one constantly and the other periodically. He thought they both sounded joyful, so glorious in their songs. Peter thought it must be some sort of party. "That can't be for me," he thought. He didn't understand why joyful music played in the hospital anyway.

He began to relax again as he settled into the calmness all around him. No telephones rang telling him another killing in the city needed to be investigated. No one asked him to get the latest stats on how much violent crime had risen in the past ten years. He actually felt at peace.

Peter thought he would enjoy it for at least a moment. His mind went back to his prayer from a short while ago, when he prayed for guidance, comfort, and understanding. He realized he had received guidance and comfort by way of the angel, but the understanding had not come to him yet. "Wow," he thought, "prayer really does work." With that said, he fell asleep and rested.

CHAPTER 41

Jack McDougal came back into the room as June prayed. The medical team continued to check on Peter regularly. There had been no seizures. Jack had been gone less than two hours, but he felt burdened to be with June and what she went through.

"Has there been any change?"

"Jack? What are you doing back here? I thought you're supposed to be out looking for the men who did this." Although happy to see a friendly face, she felt confused about this particular visitor not out doing his job.

"I have law enforcement from all over the entire state searching. They'll call me the second they hear anything. I wanted to see how you're holding up."

"Thanks, Jack. I'm doing all right, really. I just don't understand why this happened to Peter. He was only doing his job, not hurting anyone. Why? Why did this happen?"

Jack understood the frustration as he said, "It's pretty common to feel the way you do. You can analyze everything and not be able to see the reasons for something like this. But for now, there isn't anything to see. So far, we have no reason for the shooting."

Jack, sincere in his quest to make the burden as light as possible for June, said, "I sent an officer to see Paul. He hasn't gotten back yet, but I think he'll be able to get through to your son. He's one our best officers and counselors on the force." His words fell short as Mrs. Stallings seemed to be elsewhere with her thoughts.

"They told me he may not live another day, Jack. They told me that, even if he does live, he won't be the same. How do they know what God can do? How can they know that my God will not answer my prayers and the prayers of his people praying as we speak right now? Tell me Jack, what makes them think they can tell me God will not perform a miracle in Peter Stallings, and even in the life of John Robertson. He can do it, you know, for all things are possible with God. Do you believe he can do miracles, Jack?"

Jack allowed a small smile to creep across his lips as he spoke, "Now this is the June Stallings I know." Her faith could move mountains and give hope to all those around her. This was the June Stallings Jack is familiar with being around. Only this June Stallings had sorrow, hurt, and anger. Jack didn't have to answer her questions she reeled off. He knew them to be rhetorical.

He remembered a story that seemed appropriate right now. "June, about two years ago I worked on a case similar to this one, people being shot and abducted. I remember a woman who reminds me of you, in that she had faith in Christ, too. She prayed for a miracle for her son. He'd been shot in the stomach and had internal bleeding. She, like you, had been told her son would not survive the gunshot wound.

"She prayed and she prayed. When everyone else had given up hope, she still prayed. Her church, and even her pastor, stopped praying, but not her. She prayed around the clock non-stop, for her son to be healed. A couple of days later, the doctors, who had said her son wasn't going to survive, said he was only alive now due to being on the life-support system. They said they he wouldn't survive without it. She continued to pray even as she gave them permission to pull the plug.

"They removed the life-support system and after a couple of days, her son still lived. In fact, he began to improve. When her church heard he had improved, they started praying again. Her son improved even more and faster than the doctors could understand. She just kept on praying.

"Within two weeks after the doctors had said that her son wouldn't survive, he walked out of the hospital on his own two feet, not feeling any effects of the bullet that had gone into his stomach. It was truly a miracle."

Jack put a hand on June's shoulder as he continued, "I told you that to tell you this; You have the faith get you through this. You have to keep praying without stopping, even when those around you quit. You, however, have one advantage the other lady didn't have."

"What would that be?" June asked curiously.

"You have me on your side. And I won't quit praying either. Together we will get through this thing, no matter what the outcome might be. We both know God has a purpose for this happening."

June sat by the side of Peter's bed and looked at her husband, placed a hand on his cheek. "I haven't stopped praying, Jack. I would love to have your company in praying for my husband. I know my Lord will see me and Peter through this. We'll be stronger in our faith. Even more importantly, through this someone may come to know the Lord as their personal Savior.

What more can we ask for? The Lord did give me this man for such a long time and here I am trying to be so selfish with him. Shame on me."

"I don't think you're being selfish at all. And there is no reason to shame yourself." Jack stated firmly. "I think you're doing some heavy duty fighting for your husband. And I believe the Lord will answer your prayers very, very soon. You just wait and see."

CHAPTER 42

In the middle of the woods, sunlight faded and bounced off a picture window on the old house that cast deep shadows into the trees. The hair on the nocturnal animals stood on end as they hissed, howled, and barked while they passed by the house.

Inside the house, Jimmy sweated as he sat on the sofa. He shivered while he stared into the fire. He ran a fever and felt his shirt had soaked completely through. "I don't get how I'm sweating when I feel so cold. I feel like my blood has quit moving through my veins." His skin was a shade of blue.

"Oh, Jimmy," William Benning spoke softly as a log in the fireplace cracked. "I'm sorry you're feeling this way. There's nothing more we can do for you right now. You need to understand, what you did yesterday was very harmful to our cause. You may have begun the downward spiral for Anti-Pro. In order for us to protect ourselves, we must not allow you to go on."

"Well, I can just stay here for a while." Jimmy realized as he spoke what William Benning meant by him not being allowed to go on.

"No, I'm afraid that's not a possibility at this time. There is only one solution, Jimmy, and that is for you to stop existing." William Benning's tone was ice cold. He stated this like it is the most normal thing in the world. He didn't blink as he looked in Jimmy's eyes. His entire visage became a sinister stare.

Jimmy visibly shook as he stood up from the sofa and stumbled toward the door. He muttered incoherent things like "I gotta go now," and "My boss is expecting me." The spring on the door creaked as Jimmy pushed it open. It then slammed shut as Jimmy ran to his truck. No one inside the house followed.

"There's nowhere for him to go. He'll be dead before the sun sets, which is just moments from now." The three people in the house watched Jimmy make a desperate attempt to flee from what they knew to be his impending death.

"Did you see his face when I told him it was better that he was dead? That was classic." William Benning proclaimed.

———•———

Jimmy turned the ignition key only to have the engine not turn over. "Come on," he urged the engine on. He tried again, this time with his foot through the accelerator. The engine roared to life. He slammed the gear into reverse and quickly turned around. He put the transmission into drive and the truck lurched forward. Jimmy didn't slow down for the potholes he had been so careful to dodge when he entered the driveway.

Constantly looking over his shoulder, and in the rearview mirror, he expected to see William, Elaine, and Bob coming after him with knives over their heads, ready to kill him. No one appeared to follow him. He felt a moment of relief, but not enough to slow him down from leaving the creepy place. It helped him to breathe.

Desperation washed over Jimmy as he drove down the long, narrow driveway. He felt, more than saw that he wasn't alone inside the truck. His eyes were wide with fear as despair overwhelmed his mind. The hair on the back of his neck stood on end. He couldn't see the demon of death next to him in the cab. Through all the holes in the driveway, the truck bounced up and down, barely missing trees. Jimmy's head slammed into the roof over and over again. The demon sat motionless and waited for the final command from his master.

"What have I done?" Jimmy yelled, as he neared the two-track road that lead to the main highway and to the city.

The windows steamed up inside the truck. He rolled down the window to get some fresh air. The cool wind woke him up.

"Oh, God, I've really messed up this time," he spoke softly.

The devil sat next to him and cringed as Jimmy mentioned the name of God. Jimmy continued, "I don't know if I can live with myself after what I've done to those people at the bus station. But I don't know how to make it right."

The demon of death sensed Jimmy might be trying to repent for his evil doings. This must be the moment to strike.

"If I wait any longer Jimmy here might actually get to the forgiveness part and send the heavenly warriors in to rescue him from my grip."

The demon reached over and grabbed Jimmy's hands. Jimmy cranked the steering wheel sharply to the right as he cried out in pain. The tires hit loose gravel and the pickup truck fishtailed. Jimmy over corrected the skid and the truck veered into the thick grove of trees. The truck smashed head-on into a large oak tree. Jimmy's head impacted with the windshield since he hadn't take the time to fasten his seat belt. His head snapped back into the headrest and then dropped forward, unconscious from the blow. His chest hit the steering wheel so hard he had several broken ribs and shattered the steering wheel. The horn sounded momentarily from the impact until he slumped over in the seat.

The demon of death felt he had dealt the necessary blow, dripped saliva on Jimmy's head to leave his mark on the body. He howled with pleasure over Jimmy's body before he flew off for his next mission.

The road Jimmy made his escape on rarely had vehicles on it. He or his truck would not be found until William, Elaine, or Bob decided to leave the house to get supplies. They had stocked up only days before Jimmy showed up with his news. Weeks might pass before they would need more supplies.

CHAPTER 43

Peter thought about June and his family and the worry they must feel about him. Jareb told him his family would have peace, comfort, and safety while he recovered. "He sounded so believable with his smooth, reassuring words. It must be true." When he realized his family would be taken care of, he felt he could actually rest.

He scanned the rolling hills once again, this time with a fresh perspective. Mile upon mile of meadows filled with bright and colorful flowers. Not a cloud in the sky and the perfect temperature in the air. "Richard Edmore and the WGRT weather team would be out of a job here," he chuckled.

Trees looked taller and fuller with the foliage symmetric. Fresh air and a gentle breeze, coupled with the warmth, made for a beautiful day. As he took it all in, a tinge of guilt swept through his thoughts. "How can I enjoy being here, in this beautiful place, while my family suffers, wondering if I'll live another day? It just feels wrong to be feeling happy and free right now." He sighed as his shoulders to droop. "I hope Jareb comes back soon. I could use some answers to these questions."

Wondering how to contact Jareb, he resorted to the old tried and true way; he cupped his hands around his mouth and yelled, "Hello? Jareb, can you hear me? Hello. I have some questions for you. Can you come back and talk with me?"

There was no response; only a breeze blew through his hair. Subconsciously, he bowed his head to pray.

The soft voice of Jareb broke the silence, "Peter, I have returned to begin our journey. Are you ready?"

Peter sat speechless from his prayer being answered so fast again. "Before we go, Jareb, how can I know my family is being comforted? And how can they know I'm going to be all right?"

"Another angel from the heavenly host has been sent to your family, Peter. I know this angel delivers good news better than any other angel in the kingdom."

"How can you know that?"

"Because my friend once showed himself to a group of shepherds and told them of the birth of Jesus. That is how I know."

Peter pondered that thought for a moment. "I guess that would qualify as knowing."

"This angel, along with others from the Almighty God, have been commissioned to give them peace and comfort as well. Would you care to see for yourself?"

"That would be nice, yes," Peter said solemnly.

"Observe what the Lord allows you to see."

Peter could not have blinked fast enough as he found himself next to June by his hospital bed. He did a double-take as he saw himself hooked up to all the life support machines. "That's me," he exclaimed. "It's kind of freaky."

June prayed as she gently held his hand. A large angel prayed next to her while he guarded her from the enemy. Peace filled the room, and Peter knew June would be just fine.

"Your wife does not understand the battle taking place here. Yet she is one of the strongest saints living, one the Lord has looked upon with great joy."

Peter stood next to his wife while Jareb spoke. "At the same time, her faith is being tested to make her stronger, just as your own faith being tested. She, along with your son, believes you will completely recover, although those around her are skeptical."

"Thank you for allowing me to see June, Jareb. This is a great comfort to me." Peter paused and turned to look Jareb in the eyes as he asked, "Are you sure this isn't some weird scientific experiment?"

Jareb, not known for laughing, smiled as he replied, "I assure you what you are experiencing is very real. This is not a dream. This is not from any drugs. You, Peter, are at the very threshold of heaven. You have not entered at this time since you are still living, although you are already part of the kingdom. You are in a place of comfort. You are also being given the opportunity to understand the power of the Almighty God."

"But why me?"

"This is so you might strengthen your walk with your Savior, Jesus Christ. As we walk together you will see your life from a heavenly point of view. Through this experience, it is the prayer of Jesus that you will become a strong warrior for Him."

"Me? A warrior?" Peter sat confused by what Jareb had just told him. Another question came to mind, "But how will the Lord use me?"

"That is something I cannot tell you. It is something you need to find for yourself as the Lord guides and directs you. I assure you once again, Peter, you have been brought here to be strengthened and encouraged by the events that will come to pass shortly. For now, Peter, you must continue to rest. You will need your strength for the journey that follows. The next few days will prove to be a time of urgency and importance to you and the lives of your friends, as you will see. They are now on their own separate journeys filled with dangers which may help them to, perhaps, choose their own final destiny."

"What destiny would that be? Please tell me so that I might know."

Jareb did not answer the question. Instead, he said, "I am sorry, Peter, but my Master calls for me. I will return soon to continue the journey. Until then rest, and be of good courage."

He stopped, just as he began to vanish, and said, "I am to tell you this, Peter, you must pray. Pray with all power and without stopping. This is most urgent." Jareb vanished once again.

Peter, seated back against the wall, started to pray immediately.

CHAPTER 44

"Look, John Robertson, I really am an angel. Did I not just prove this to you by telling you your hidden secret?"

John nodded his head, shocked and amazed, in acknowledgement of his secret being revealed. "But how can I know for sure you're telling me the truth? I just don't understand how you can sit there and tell me you're an angel without me thinking that you're some sort of a lunatic. Think of it from my point of view: I'm a reporter who deals with a lot of 'psycho' people throughout the day, some who are just trying to get on the six o'clock news, claiming to be some sort of hero; others say they're the 'savior of the world' when really they're just crackpots out on the streets. Now you're here telling me you're an angel. How can I know you're not just another crazy person trying to get on the news? Tell me that."

"My, you really have become cynical, haven't you, John Robertson? What more can I do to prove myself to you, if you already have it in your mind that I am just another, as you put it, 'crazy person'? There are some things you must take on faith."

"What do you mean?"

"Jesus illustrated what I mean so wonderfully. Do you believe there is wind, John Robertson? Of course you do. If you did not then you would be the crazy one. Have you ever seen the wind? No, you have not. And yet it is obvious it exists."

"Okay, where are you going with this?"

"When you sit down in a chair, do you test it to make sure it will support you before sitting? Of course not. You sit down trusting the chair will hold you. It is simple faith. And as of right now, John Robertson, you have no faith."

Pithel pointed his finger at John. "You used to have faith. Remember when you went to Sunday School? When you were eight years old, you attended Mrs. Wilson's class, in the basement of the First United Methodist

Church. You sat in the front row very willing to learn. Do you remember that, John Robertson?"

John sat dumbfounded as he found himself back in the classroom.

Pithel continued, "One Sunday, when Mrs. Wilson taught a lesson on how Jesus died on the cross, you listened very closely. You wanted to ask your teacher a question, but your mother needed to hurry home before dinner burned. Do you remember that day, John Robertson?"

"Yes, I remember. Mrs. Wilson said Jesus didn't just die for the whole world, but that he died specifically for me," John spoke as he saw the memory clear as day. "I liked her a lot. She was always so nice and happy. How did you know about that day?"

"As I have been trying to tell you, John Robertson, I have been sent to you from the Almighty God to talk with you. You refuse to believe. Must I tell you more before you accept me for who I am?"

"All right, all right I believe. I believe."

Pithel laughed with great joy with such intensity it shook the very knoll they sat on. "Oh John Robertson, you do make me laugh." He held his sides from the deep laugh. "I see you believe in your mind, but I know that in your heart you still have doubt. Perhaps, as we spend our time together, your doubt will be put to rest."

Pithel's stopped laughing and turned serious. "Let me once again explain to you what is happening here, which is the purpose of our meeting. You have been brought here to this place to be given the opportunity to interview me, an angel of the heavenly host. It is an opportunity not many humans are given, so, once again, I strongly encourage you accept it. This is to give you one more chance, maybe your last chance, to believe in the Lord Jesus Christ."

"My last chance?"

"He has taken notice of you, John Robertson, and he has a special task for you. But he can only use you if you accept him as your Savior. You see, God is mighty and great and not willing that any would perish, but that all would come to repentance." He stopped long enough for that to sink into John's head.

"Now, John Robertson, you may begin the interview. Any questions you might have I will answer to the best of my ability."

John sat without a word. He couldn't think of a single question even though hundreds ran through his mind all at once.

"Oh, John Robertson, can you not think of a single question for me?" The roar of laughter filled the air once more.

After a few minutes to organize his thoughts, John decided he would start with a general question to help him get his thought process flowing.

"All right, Pistol, tell me about some of your adventures. Tell me your greatest adventure."

The angel laughed again. "Oh John Robertson, I am enjoying myself. First of all my name is pronounced Pithel, not Pistol. As for your question, I have been involved in many adventures. I remember a time, roughly 6,000 years ago or so, take a couple of hundred years either way," he chuckled. "I accompanied my Lord to the wicked city of Sodom."

John found himself next to the angel in the center of the city, which bustled with all sorts of activities. Markets stood opened. Children ran through the street playing games. Cheerful music sounded from several different venues.

"For an ancient city, this is quite the happening place," John said as he admired the layout of the city.

"Yes, it is. Anyway, we went to warn this man, named Lot, of the impending destruction of the city because of their horrible wickedness." They stood and watched the man with the downcast look on his face. "Lot had been the man of God in the city until he gave up trying. My Lord had been very patient with this wicked people, but they refused to turn from their ways. After a while, my Lord must deal with sin." The large angel clenched and raised his massive fist into the air.

They continued their walk until they reached Lot's home. Many men stood outside the house yelling, making threats toward Lot.

"My Lord and I found Lot at home. We forewarned him of the coming destruction. As we spoke to him, the men of the city yelled louder, begging Lot to turn us over to them. Lot stepped outside to try and reason with the men."

"I will not give them to you. Don't you know these are men of God?"

"If you will not give them to us, then we will come and take them."

"They pressed in harder to the door, shouted louder to have us be given to them."

"I will not give them to you. I will give you my two daughters if you will leave these men alone."

"No, send out the men to us!"

"The crowd became violent. My Lord and I pulled Lot into his home and shut the door behind him while we stood outside with the wicked men of the city."

John cringed as the men pushed at the door, threw stones, and shook their fists in the air.

"We then smote the men with blindness. Look at them, John Robertson."

John witnessed the men as they tripped over themselves, crawled on their hands and knees, ran into houses, trees and rocks, unable to find Lot's house.

"That was truly a tragic situation to be part of, I must admit."

John anticipated the rest of the story with eagerness. Pithel did not disappoint. They found themselves next to Lot, his wife and two daughters as they were forcefully pulled out of the city.

"God would not allow the city to be destroyed until Lot and his family were safely outside the city and into the mountains. They had strict instructions to not look back for any reason."

John watched as Lot's wife turned back to catch one last glimpse of Sodom. She immediately turned into a pillar of salt. He also saw the fire pour out of heaven like water over a waterfall. He shielded his eyes at the intense brightness and heat.

When he looked again, the entire city of Sodom, along with city next to it, Gomorrah, was completely gone. The entire region sat empty on blackened earth.

Pithel peered over at John, who stood with his mouth agape at the scene before him. "Do not look so distraught, John Robertson. The people of these cities had been given plenty of opportunities to turn from their wicked ways, but they refused. They became so involved in their evil ways nothing could turn their hearts back to God. The Almighty God will only tolerate so much wickedness before carrying out that which he does not want to do."

Pithel looked John in the eyes as he continued. "Let it be known, John Robertson, it truly grieved his heart to have had to destroy Sodom and Gomorrah. But also know this; the Lord will get the victory in all that he does. He will receive the glory due unto his holy name."

CHAPTER 45

As he looked John in the eyes, Pithel asked the next question, "Would you like to hear more of my adventures, or do you now have another question you would like to pursue?" Pithel sat silently and waited for a reply.

John pondered about what his first real question might be. He found himself intrigued, however, by the story Pithel had just told him and decided to hear more of his adventures. "I think, before I ask a question, I would like to hear more of your adventures. I remember Mrs. Wilson telling us about Daniel and the lion's den. Were you a part of that story?"

"As a matter of fact, I was there. I must be quick to point out, though; I was not the one who shut the lion's mouths. Oltheus, my good friend, did that work."

Moments later they stood inside a palace.

"Where are we?"

"We are in Babylon. This is the palace of King Darius, who you see sitting on his throne."

"This place is amazing." John gazed in awe at the splendor of the ornate craftsmanship of the walls, ceiling, and floor. "But why did you bring me here?"

"This, John Robertson, is to show you that I am an angel of God. It is also to allow you to be a part of the story."

"Okay, I guess. You aren't going to throw me into the lion's den, are you?"

Pithel laughed heartily as he patted John on the back. "You will be safe."

They watched several of the leaders as they conjured a plan to destroy Daniel. John found himself able to understand their language. "How is it I can understand what they say?"

"I have given you the ability to know the language of the Chaldeans."

"Oh."

"*King Darius, live forever. We wish to honor you by passing a decree for the kingdom to only come to you with their petitions. Only you, King Darius, will be able to grant their wants and needs. No one will be allowed to call upon their God, but to pray only to you my king."*

"I will grant this." King Darius had a pleased look on his face as he signed the petition into law and sealed it with his ring.

Pithel pointed at Daniel, who, off to the side, witnessed this law being passed. The assembled leaders bowing as they left the throne room.

John and Pithel now stood in the room of Daniel as he knelt next to his open window praying to God. "He knew about this horrible law and yet he's doing this?" John spread both hands toward Daniel as he prayed.

"Yes, he knew about the law. After all, he is the third highest leader in all of Babylon."

"Then why is he praying with the window open?"

"Daniel decided to remain faithful to his God rather than to obey the law of the king."

Shortly after he completed his prayers, a band of soldiers sent by those envious leaders brought Daniel to stand before King Darius.

"King Darius," spoke one of the leaders. *"Did you not pass a decree stating we may only ask you for our petitions to be granted?"*

"Yes, that is true."

"Then why is it that Daniel has disobeyed this command?"

Pithel pointed at King Darius and said, "He just realized he has been deceived by evil men."

"Daniel is this true?" asked the king.

"Yes, King Darius. I pray only to the living God of Israel."

"King Darius," interrupted the leader, *"there is but one decree for such a crime as this. Daniel is to be cast into the den of lions."*

"Leave me," King Darius yelled in anger.

"But, my King…" The king waved a hand to cut off any further words.

"Guards, remove everyone from my throne room." The soldiers marched in formation, spears pointed towards the leaders. One of the guards placed Daniel in a room away from the mob of leaders.

"This is where the king tries to find a way to get Daniel out of this punishment, but fails to find a way out." He summons the guard to bring Daniel before his throne.

"Daniel, my friend, I have been deceived by wicked men. I cannot go back on the law."

"I understand, King Darius." Daniel remained steady and calm.

"I know your God, to whom you pray, will save you from the mouths of the lions."

The king had the other men brought back into his throne room. He acknowledged the law he passed and then informed his guard to carry out the sentence.

John and Pithel stood near the mouth of the den as the guards approached, followed by the king and the leaders. One of the guards rolled back the stone to the den as the other guards shoved Daniel inside.

"Set the stone back in front of the mouth and seal it with my ring," commanded King Darius.

John witnessed the king pacing throughout the night. "This palace is usually filled with celebrating each night," Pithel explained. "Tonight, however, there is no music, no food, nor any guests."

Pithel brought John back to the den early the next morning. He saw King Darius run to the lion's den and commanded the stone be removed. He yelled, *"Daniel, are you there? Did your God deliver you from the mouths of the lions?"* His voice shook from fear and sorrow as he waited to hear anything.

"King Darius, live forever. My God sent his angel to shut the mouths of the lions. They have not hurt me at all."

John stood with his hand over his mouth in amazement. "I know this story from the Bible, but to see it really happen…Wow." Tears ran down John's cheeks as he watched Daniel walk out of the den as he patted one of the huge lions on the head.

"Hold on, John, there's a bit more you need to see."

"Guard, bring me those men responsible for this decree. Bring their families as well."

After they arrived, King Darius told them, *"You have brought shame on me and this kingdom. I hereby command, by royal decree, that you and your wives and children be cast into the same den of lions."*

John watched as the guards once again carried out their orders. The roar of the lions caused John to step behind Pithel. The lions tore those evil men to pieces when they hit the floor.

Pithel brought John back to the knoll outside of the City of God.

"Wait a minute. Where do you fit into this story, Pithel? Didn't I ask for you to tell me one of *your* adventures? I didn't see you anywhere near Daniel or the lion's den?"

"It is true that I was not directly involved. I was there, though. I, just like you, witnessed the entire miraculous event. I did get to play a small role. When the guards threw those responsible into the den, I was allowed to give the lions a little extra push in, shall I say, their appetite." His belly shook as he laughed loud enough to be heard throughout the kingdom.

"I am sorry, John Robertson, if you feel as though I tricked you about this particular story. I do not blame you if you are upset about this. There is something you should know about Daniel. As he prayed in front of his window, Satan tried to tell him to give up and give in to the king's commandment. As you witnessed, he endured to the end and was rewarded by king Darius as well as the Lord God. So I say to you, John Robertson, endure the pain and the persecution that have come your way in order to fulfill the mission of God."

Pithel finished the story along with the lesson it had brought. He then listened to another voice from somewhere. John couldn't hear anything. The expression on Pithel's face made it very clear that someone spoke to him.

"I must leave you for a short while. I have been instructed to have you rest for a time while I must attend to some other issues elsewhere. I will be able to explain to you later what has happened and what is going on at this very moment. Rest, John Robertson, rest well."

Pithel left as his final words hung in the air. Wind from his rapid departure caused John's hair to poof back. John sat back against the hillside and fell asleep.

CHAPTER 46

Winding around a blind curve on the narrow, dirt road, the van kept up its speed. Without any warning, the driver slammed on the brakes and the van ground to a halt. Dirt and loose gravel sent a plume of dust high into the air as well as inside that choked the passengers. Aside from the coughed -up dust, two of the three abductors found themselves pressed flat-faced against the windshield. The driver laughed hysterically at his friends as they peeled themselves back from the glass.

Doors flew open, followed by slams hard enough to shake the van. The men decided this would be the time and place to hash out their differences. None of them knew what they were about to argue about, but that wouldn't stop them from getting involved.

Amy had somehow stopped just short of her face being planted into the back of the driver's seat. She wasn't sure, but it felt like a strong arm pulled her back at the last possible second. She regained her balance and sat back on the crate.

Judy slid all the way to the front of the van, along with all the trash, a toolbox, and anything else not properly secured. She ended up between one of the men and Amy. Her head hit the crate while her feet kicked the young man. Thankfully, he was too busy peeling himself off the back of the seat to notice.

After they angrily left the van, Judy tried to roll close enough to hear what men said just outside. Every move added another abrasion to her bruised and battered body which included a new contusion on her head. The pain felt sharp, but she refused to allow it to keep her from working on a plan of escape.

The new bump on her head began to throb. "Well, at least the pain lets me know I'm not dead," she thought. She made eye contact with Amy, as their abductors stood off to the side of the van. Amy had a peaceful expression on her face, which Judy could not understand. *"How can she sit there and look so calm?"*

Judy whispered, "Where are they now?"

"Just outside," Amy whispered back.

"Can you hear what they're saying?"

"No, but I'm trying." Amy strained her neck forward to hear the conversation. She leaned down toward Judy and whispered, "They're about two feet away from the front. It sounds like they're arguing, but I can't understand them."

Judy nodded. "Okay, just keep listening for names and places."

Amy asked, "Did you hear the name Tom a while back?"

"Yes, one down, two to go."

"I'll keep listening," Amy said. She prayed silently as she turned back toward the open window.

The three men stood in front of the headlights as they ranted and raved. The driver stomped around and flailed his arms about, frustrated by what the big man had just said. Amy could see each man stood away from the others, shaking their heads. Coupled with the tone of their voices, it was evident each of them had a different plan. The volume in their voices rose and Amy could finally understand what they said.

"This whole thing is so messed up."

"It's beyond Murphy's Law."

"What?"

"You know, anything that can go wrong will go wrong?"

"Shut up with that kind of talk."

"Get back to the issue," ordered the big man as the other two bickered.

"I just don't think it's right to keep them if we don't need them." The young man pleaded his case to his partners.

"We need them for insurance."

"I agree. We don't know what we might run in to."

Judy tried to raise her head up, but the ropes intensified the pain that forced her to back down with a thud. Amy reached back but couldn't get to her. The raised voices of their arguing drowned out the noise.

"Look, Billy, we have to complete this thing. Do you want Benning on our backs? I don't." The big man let his emotions and fear take over as he yelled at the other two.

Amy looked at Judy and held up two fingers as she said, "I just heard the name Billy. He's the driver."

"Great job." Judy said through gritted teeth.

The men kept up the argument, which by now continued to get louder and more intense.

"It's not that I'm against what we did. It's what we're doing now that concerns me. When we agreed to do this job, we were told no one would get hurt. As far as I know, there are at least three people dead and a whole slew of people in critical condition who might die. And here we have with us the woman reporter who may or may not have gotten our pictures. We also have the girl we took for insurance. I'm telling you, this has bad written all over it. We're being used as bait for some other purpose. I don't know what's really going on, but we're in way over our heads."

"I agree with you," said the only man still unidentified. "But my question is what're we going to do? We can't run forever."

None of the men had an answer or a plan yet. The argument stopped momentarily as each thought about the next move to make.

Tom, the big man, said, "All right, so we already have at least three people dead, maybe more by now, what's one or two more?"

The other two men's jaws dropped.

"What are you suggesting, Tom?"

"Do I really need to spell it out for you?"

"You can't be serious. There may be people dead back at the bus station, but we weren't the ones who did the shooting."

"Look, I'm not saying kill them right now. I'm saying it needs to be considered. That's all."

Judy and Amy clearly heard this part of the conversation. Fear took over their emotions. Judy's mind raced to form an action plan. She worked harder to free her hands from the cord. She glanced up at Amy, who had closed her eyes and looked to be praying.

CHAPTER 47

Jack McDougal returned to the bus station as the first rays of the sun lit the sky. He combed the area for any anything his investigative team might have missed. He felt both hopeless and helpless, in his search for clues. Time was not an ally.

After he circled the building, he returned to the on-sight command post. His team had all arrived to continue the hunt. As he entered the post, everyone sat or stood quietly.

"Talk to everyone; employees, drivers, passengers, people in the neighborhood. Ask them again what they saw and heard." He ran a hand through his crew cut hair, frustrated about not being able to find any other leads. "We need something, anything that might help us, and we need it right now. Do you understand?"

"Yes, sir."

"All right, then get to it. Oh, and a couple of you talk with the hostages again. Maybe they remember something else after having more time to think about it."

———————◆———————

Plain clothes officers and uniformed officers alike scoured the neighborhood. They spoke with businesspeople and residents of the area, asking them what they saw. No one had any new information to offer.

The officers started with a two block radius from Central Station. They had less than four hours to find a lead. Although rushed, the investigators remained thorough in their investigation.

Officers Larry Buitman and Sarah Pulker walked back from the northwest area, near the outer perimeter from the scene. They walked with slumped shoulders and heads down. The thought of failure overtook them by not finding a single lead. As they returned, the officers continued to scan the streets. They walked past an alley, one block from the bus station.

"Hey." A man's voice called out.

"Where'd that come from?"

"Somewhere in the alley."

Not being able to see anyone, they instinctively placed a hand on their weapons. After the shooting and no one apprehended, no chances would be taken.

"I'm over here...in the doorway." The male voice came out weak, shaky, and weathered.

Larry pointed to the small, arched door as the officers moved cautiously in that direction.

"Sir, have you been drinking?"

"Not today."

"Hands where we can see them," Larry stated with his hand still poised on the handle of his gun. Sarah stood to the left of her partner, ready to pull her revolver if necessary.

"Yes, sir." The old man raised his hands.

"Do you have any weapons on you, sir?" Larry asked.

"No, sir."

"Why'd you call us over here?" Larry continued taking the lead.

"Aren't you the police?"

"I'm sure you can see by our uniforms we are the police," Larry quipped as he realized the man would be no threat.

Sarah interjected, "Yes, sir, we are police officers."

"Well, I have some news for you." The man stated and thrust his finger into the air.

"News about what?" Sarah had taken over when the man seemed to connect with her.

"It's about that shooting yesterday. Are you interested?" The man's eyes grew big like he had a big secret he wasn't supposed to tell.

"Of course we're interested," Sarah said. "Do you know something that might help us find out who did this?"

"Yes. Yes I do."

"Would you be so kind as to tell us what it is?" Larry asked sarcastically.

"Larry, be nice," Sarah scolded.

"Thanks, ma'am." He continued to look at Sarah. "Well here's what I know. Yesterday I wasn't feeling too good. I lay down to take a little nap behind that old warehouse; you know, the one next to the bus station."

"Yeah, I know where you're talking about," Sarah said.

"I'm not sure, but I think I had the flu or something."

Larry rolled his eyes. The smell of alcohol said it wasn't the flu. "Sir, have you been drinking today?" Larry asked.

"No, sir, I already told you, not today."

Sarah said, "I'm sorry to rush you, but we need to report back. You said you have information about the men who did the shooting yesterday."

"Men?" asked the man with a quizzical look on his weathered face. "There was only one man."

"What are you saying?" Larry asked, intrigued by this tidbit of information. "Are you saying there was somebody else involved?" Initially, he thought the old man might be just trying to get another drink. He changed his mind as soon as he heard what the man said.

"Well, I don't know if I can say somebody else was involved. All I know is that I saw one person. He came right out the back door carrying a gun case. He put it into the back of a red pickup truck."

"Did you get a good look at him?" Sarah asked.

"I got more than that," he said proudly. "I got a five spot out of him." The old man took out a five dollar bill and showed it to the officers as he continued. "He was pretty nice to me. I think I scared him though."

"Sir, we need you to come with us to the command post and talk to the detective in charge." Sarah spoke carefully to not scare him off. "Would you be willing to do that for us?"

"Sure," he said. "Say you wouldn't happen to have some extra change you could spare, would you?"

"You really panhandling an officer?" Larry asked.

"No harm in asking, is there?"

"I'll see what I can do," Sarah said. "After you talk to the detective."

"Well, what're we standing here for? Let's get moving."

Officers Buitman and Pulker picked up their pace, the old man in tow, as they made their way back to the command post. They both smiled over the lead they just discovered.

CHAPTER 48

"Go check on him," yelled William Benning. "Make sure he's dead. Do you understand?" He barked the orders to Bob and Elaine, who seemed hurt to have to do such a ghastly deed. Both stood in front of William Benning's desk with their arms folded as they pouted.

"Why do we have to go?" Elaine whined. "Can't you find someone else to do it? I mean, really. After all the things Bob and I do for you around here, to have you ask us to go look for a dead body is absurd."

"I agree with Elaine," Bob said. "We've worked very hard to get where we are in Anti-Pro. I think we're above having to do such menial and disgusting tasks like that."

"Are you two finished whining yet?" William's agitation had reached its peak. Elaine looked down at the rug. Bob stood by quietly fiddled with the back of the sofa and acted as if he wasn't interested in the conversation.

William sighed as he said, "I need you to go because no one else knows what's happened. We don't need anyone here messing things up more than they already are. Now, please, will you go look for Jimmy Morten's body? It shouldn't be too far from here, probably just off the dirt road near the end of the driveway. I'm not asking you to touch him or anything. Just make sure he's dead. It's that simple."

Reluctantly, they agreed to go. As Elaine opened the screen door, she shouted, "I refuse to touch it for any reason. You got that?" The door slammed shut behind her.

William Benning shook his head with a smirk. If Bob and Elaine had seen it shivers would have gone up their spines.

<hr>

The argument continued outside the van. "What do we do about those two?" asked the young man whose name Judy and Amy had not heard.

"I say we kill 'em right here and right now," the cold-blooded remark came from Tom. "That way we're through with them and we can get on with our mission, which now is to stay alive."

"Don't you think that killing them will end up making things worse for us?" asked Billy. "I say we tie them to a tree somewhere and let them try to survive out here on their own. That way it technically won't be our fault if they happen to die. We weren't there, so we couldn't have killed them."

"I guess we're at a standstill. Allen, what do you think?"

Inside the van, Judy's and Amy's ears perked up as they heard the third name. Billy, Tom, and Allen, three names they would never forget. Amy smiled at Judy with three fingers. Judy smiled back and blew out a puff of air in relief.

Back outside, Allen gave his point of view. "Well, I'm just not too sure yet. I see the points both of you are trying to make. On one hand, killing them now could make our escape less of a burden, as we would be rid of them. On the other hand, it's kind of harsh to kill the two women who are here against their will. It's not like they've been any trouble."

He scratched his head and pushed his glasses back up after they had slid down his nose. "Still, on the other hand, tying them up out and leaving them to fend for themselves would be a way for us to say we didn't kill them. I say, we take a little more time to think about it and try to come up with something we can all agree on"

"Okay, I'll go along with that for now," Tom said.

Billy then said, "Let's find a place to stop. I'm way too tired to keep going tonight."

Amy and Judy hurried to get back into their previous positions before the men got back into the van.

As the men climbed back inside, they didn't pay any attention to the women. They plopped back in the same positions as Billy put the van back in gear. Dust kicked up high into the air as they sped farther down the road. The high beams only shone twenty feet and made Billy's reaction time to curves tricky because of how tired he was. "How come you two don't drive?"

Allen responded. "I lost my license last year. Remember when I got stopped for drinking on my birthday? In fact, they hauled you in with me because you had an open container inside a moving vehicle."

"Yeah, but under the current circumstances, driving without a license should be the least of your worries. If they catch us, you're going to fry with me, you know. What about you, Tom, how come you aren't offering to drive any?"

"I'm too tired to drive." He offered no other explanation.

"I still think one of you should take over for a little while. I need to get some rest. By the way, we're running low on gas. We'll need to stop anyway within the next few miles."

"Where we going to stop?" Tom asked. "There's nothing out here." He pointed his finger at Billy and said, "Why didn't you say something earlier? If we run out of gas in the middle of nowhere you'll be joining the ladies back here."

Billy squirmed behind the wheel as he glanced at the gas gauge. "I think we'll be alright," he said.

———◆———

Judy, scrunched near the feet of Allen, studied his features. She noted he had a small face with a long nose which didn't seem to fit. On his head, he wore an old dirty baseball cap with the Detroit Tigers baseball logo on it. Once in a while he would take it off to show an almost bald head. His voice had a high, squeaky pitch. Judy memorized his every feature, something she learned from Jack. She thought about how Jack had taught her to do surveillance work.

"When you're tailing someone, the most important thing is to not let them know it. You want to stay back a few car lengths, changing it up every once in a while. Try not to look at them, but act like you're trying to find an address or a landmark of some kind. That way they might think you're just lost. If you're following them on foot, stop and look into store windows trying to make them think you're shopping. And if you're sitting across from them, use your peripheral vision so they don't catch you staring at them."

"Jack is so good at his job," Judy thought. "I wish he were here right now."

CHAPTER 49

Officers Larry Buitman and Sarah Pulker introduced their man to Jack.

"It's very nice to meet you, sir. The officers say you have information about what happened yesterday. Can you tell me what you told them?"

"Well, as I told these officers, I saw a man getting into a pickup truck and driving off right after the shooting. I'd been behind the old abandoned warehouse, you know, taking a little nap, when he came out of the building. It was strange, though, because I could hear him whistling and talking to himself about how brave he'd been. I didn't understand any of that."

"Go on." Jack listened intently.

"Anyway, I asked him if he could spare a little cash. I was running a little short and getting pretty hungry. I think I startled him. He turned around real fast, expecting to see someone else is what it looked like. When he saw no one with me, he took out a five dollar bill and gave it to me."

"Anything else you can remember?" Jack asked.

"He was carrying a shotgun bag which he threw in the back of his red pickup truck. He told me not to tell anyone that I'd seen him."

"Officer Pulker said you might be able to identify him. Is this true?" Jack felt some relief at finally getting a break. It wasn't what he expected to hear, however.

"Sure, I could. But it didn't look like he had done anything like that before, the way he was carrying on and all. I would bet he'd never committed a crime before in his life, except for a traffic ticket or something. It would probably be better if I described him to you. Maybe one of those guys who draws the pictures could help me."

"Sure thing," Jack said. "Sarah, call down to headquarters and get Ben Smith to come down here with his sketch pad."

"Yes, sir," Officer Pulker responded.

"Thanks, Sarah." Turning back to the gentlemen, he asked, "You hungry?"

"Well, I haven't eaten yet today," he said.

"I'll take that as a yes. Officer Buitman will take you to that diner over there after we finish our conversation." He turned to Officer Buitman. "I'll call you when Benny gets here."

Larry nodded in agreement.

Jack turned back to the man. "How is it you know he had a shotgun? And how do you figure he'd never committed a crime before?"

"Well, sir, I didn't always live like this. In fact, I served as a major in the first Gulf War. When I returned home, I found out my family had been killed in a fire, all of them. I had nothing left and nowhere to turn. After a while, I just gave up and turned to the bottle. Now, I can't get away from it. But it's all right; I still know who I am."

"Well, sir, may I ask what your name is?"

"My name is Jones. Robert Jones."

CHAPTER 50

"I'll be nervous if we still have the women with us when the sun comes up. I say we do whatever we're going to do pretty quick." Billy stared as he talked.

"So what's the verdict? Kill them or tie them up?" Tom asked.

From behind them, Allen exclaimed, "I've been thinking about that. I say we tie them up. I really don't think we want to kill anyone. We have other things going on that are far more important than killing women." Allen looked at Amy and continued, "Besides, I promised her I wouldn't hurt her and I have to keep my word."

"All right then, it's settled," Tom said. "Find a spot for us to get rid of them."

"Why not right here? It's about as far in the middle of nowhere as we can get," said Billy.

They all agreed and Billy eased the van to a stop in the middle of the narrow, gravel road.

"Allen, get your girlfriend," Tom teased. "I'll get the one back there. Billy, find some more cords. Oh, and bring a couple of those rags so we can blindfold them."

They all hurried to do their assigned tasks. Neither Judy nor Amy resisted. They found it difficult to walk, however, after being in the same position for such a long time. It didn't matter to the men. They practically dragged them over to a clump of trees.

"That looks like a good spot." Tom pointed to a clump of trees a few yards off the road. "Bring her over here, Allen."

Moments later, Amy and Judy were tied to separate trees and blindfolded. The knots in the cords fell at a place where neither could easily reach it. "Keep a little slack in the knot so they can eventually get free," Allen said. "At least it gives them a chance to escape."

"Yeah, let's leave a little slack," Billy teased Allen. "I think Allen here likes that one." He and Tom laughed, while Allen stormed back to the van.

Billy became serious again and pulled out the pistol tucked in the waistband of his pants. He struck Judy on the back of the head again and knocked her unconscious.

Allen, who stood by the van, yelled at Billy, "Why'd you do that for? She wasn't doing anything. Just don't do that to her." He pointed at Amy.

"What if I do? You gonna to stop me?" Billy taunted Allen as he walked toward Amy.

"Yeah, I'll stop you," Allen said as he ran towards Billy. "You're not going to hurt her, Billy."

Billy raised the pistol to strike Amy. "What're you going to do? Aren't you going to try and stop me, Allen?"

Allen moved to get between Amy and Billy. "Look, Billy, I said don't hurt her and I meant it."

Billy bared his teeth and laughed as he swung the butt of the pistol towards Amy's head.

From just behind him, an unseen arm reached out and guided the pistol into the tree. Billy crumpled to the ground in pain and yelled, "My hand's broken."

Allen turned to Amy and whispered in her ear, "I'm sorry I chose you. I don't know why, but I felt drawn to you somehow. I can't explain it. Anyway, I'm sorry about this, and I hope you get away." He turned and walked toward the van as Tom helped Billy get to his feet.

"Okay, we're done here. Let's go," Tom yelled. "Allen, you're driving. I don't think Billy can manage it." As he climbed in and yelled, "We'll see you two pretty ladies later."

CHAPTER 51

"Okay, Pithel, why don't you tell me one more of your stories. I think I'm almost ready to ask some real questions."

"I would be glad to tell you another adventure, John Robertson." He thought back through time. "I have a great story to share with you. Come with me."

They stood outside a little mud brick building that sat between some hills. The air was hot, the ground barren and scorched.

"The king of Syria wanted to get rid of a prophet named Elisha. He was one of God's faithful servants."

John's eyes lit up. "I remember that story, too."

"Yes, I can see that. Let's hear what the king is saying." They stood in a palace in Syria.

"Who is the traitor among you, telling of my plans?" The king stood, furious at the leaders of his army who had not been able to destroy the army of Israel.

"Your majesty, it is not us, nor any of your loyal subjects. It is that prophet Elisha who warns the army of Israel to move before we can get to them."

"Then bring him to me!"

John and Pithel moved back to the little house.

"Look at the size of that army." John looked astonished at the thousands of soldiers. "This is all for one man?"

"Yes. The king is very angry for not being able to defeat Israel."

"This just doesn't seem right."

"It turns out all right." Pithel pointed at a man who had just walked outside the house. "That is Elisha's servant, who walks with him everywhere the prophet goes." They watch as the servant stretched before he washed his face. When he looked up, John saw the color drain from the man's face. The entire Syrian army filled the hillside next to the small dwelling, ready for the command to attack.

"That's the same army we just saw."

"It is quite an impressive sight, seeing such a vast army like that."

The shocked servant ran back inside, shouting, *"Elisha the Syrian army stands outside."* Elisha just shrugged it off, confusing the servant. *"Did you not hear me? The entire Syrian army is just waiting for us to step out so they can kill us."*

"There are more with us than with them." His servant gave him a look that said he had gone completely mad.

Elisha prayed. *"Lord, open up the eyes of my faithful servant that he may see."* The man became even more confused. Elisha turned to his servant and said, *"Go look outside!"*

John and Pithel walked with the reluctant servant. "Now that's not something you see every day." John had put his hand up to shield his eyes from the bright sunshine in order to see the other army. Behind the Syrian army, the entire mountain was filled with horses and chariots of fire.

"Are you in that army?" John asked as he stared at the impressive sight.

"Yes, John Robertson. I am driving one of the chariots. We struck the soldiers with blindness, and Elisha took the entire army captive. You see, the Lord will get the victory in ways that would seem impossible for men."

"You were really there? It must have been awesome to be with all the warriors and chariots of fire. And how did that servant go out and see nothing but the enemy ready to attack but looks again only to see the army of angels behind them?"

"It was another amazing victory for the Almighty God. He works in ways we don't understand, but he does have a purpose. I am to help you with find the purpose he has for you."

CHAPTER 52

Judy's head lopped back and forth as she regained consciousness. A strand of drool fell from her lip as she slurred, "I'm really getting tired of being hit in the head." She wanted to rub the sore spot. She heard Amy groan as she worked on the cords.

"What happened?" Judy kept her voice low in case the three men still lurked about. A chill went through her as she realized she could not see. "Are we still alive?"

"Yes, and they're gone," Amy said, "They tied us up and knocked you out. Are you all right?"

"Other than another knot on my head, I think I am. Boy, does my head hurt." Judy sucked up the pain to work on her escape. "How 'bout you, are you okay? And are you having any luck getting free?"

"I'm not hurt. Billy tried to hit me but somehow missed. I've worked a little slack in the cords but still can't get loose."

"Do you have any idea where are?"

"I tried watching, but no, I have no clue where we're at. All I know is that we're somewhere southeast of the city. I don't know which way they went after they left us here. But I'll tell you one thing."

"What's that?" Judy asked.

"I'm glad they left."

"Me too," Judy agreed. "I would much rather be tied to a tree in the middle of nowhere than be anywhere near those clowns again."

"I was getting scared when they talked about killing us."

"Well, try not to think about that. Let's work on getting free from the trees. Then we'll figure out where to go from here." Judy tried to sound courageous. "I think with just a little work I can get out of this knot. My boyfriend taught me how to get out of things like this."

"He taught you how to get out of being tied up to a tree?"

"I'll admit it wasn't the best first date. I honestly thought we would never stay together. And now look, here we are in the middle of who knows where, and I'm using what he taught me. What a guy."

"Is he a cop or something?" Talking helped keep their mind off their current situation.

"As a matter of fact, he is a cop. He's actually a detective, and I know he's looking for us right now. By the way, my name's Judy Metcalf. What's yours?"

"Amy Tuinstra. It's nice to meet you even though we haven't really met yet." Amy gave a little chuckle to Judy who chuckled back at her.

"You wouldn't happen to be the daughter of Al Tuinstra would you?"

"Yes, I am. Do you know my dad?"

"This is too incredible to even begin to believe. Your father's my boss. I work at WGRT. Your dad told us you were coming home today. We heard about the hostage situation just after he left to come get you. We all hoped your bus hadn't arrived yet."

"My bus actually got in early," Amy said.

"How's that for rotten luck." Judy told Amy about the exceptionally hectic day and how she had come to be at the bus station. "All the other reporters were covering other stories happening at the exact same time. That's when I, along with John and Peter, rushed to the bus station. That reminds me; I wonder if John and Peter are okay?"

"When the shooting started, they'd already brought me to the back door, waiting for the right moment to make the run for the van. So you're a photo journalist at WGRT?"

"That's my job," Judy stated in a weary voice.

"Well, it's nice to know someone who works for my dad. Is he a good boss?" She continued to loosen the knot.

"He's really great, except he wouldn't let me get back to my job since I hurt my knee playing in a charity softball game." She mocked, "Get a doctor's note."

"That sounds like my dad."

"He doesn't think I can hold up under the pressure of lugging a heavy camera everywhere with all the bending, standing, and turning all the time. I'm kind of hoping this story will be the break I need to show him I'm more than ready to go back out."

"Are you good at what you do? I'm not implying anything, just asking," Amy said sounding like she might be offering an apology.

"I'm pretty good at shooting footage. I've won a few awards over the years. I'd pat myself on the back if I could undo this knot." They both laughed as they relaxed, even in their predicament.

After a few minutes of silence, Judy said, "I'm just about loose. Just a couple more. . ." She grunted as she strained to free herself. The force of the knot breaking free sent her falling forward, landing face first on the ground. "Ouch." She ripped the blindfold from her eyes as she spit dirt from her mouth. "I'm free. Hang on and I'll untie you."

Judy stood up on weak, wobbly legs as she worked on maintain her balance. She made her way over to Amy and removed her blindfold before she untied the knot. Amy fell forward into Judy, who caught her. They embraced each other like long lost sisters.

"Come on. I don't want to be out here if they decide to come back."

"Which way should we go?" Amy asked as they made their way to the gravel road.

"I don't really know."

In the road, Amy said, "We need to go this way." She pointed down the road. "I remember we came from that direction. There's nothing between the main road and here. But I'm sure there's a town not too far from here. There has to be. Nobody would build a road that leads to nowhere, would they?"

"I don't know about that," Judy replied with skepticism at Amy's reasoning. "If you're sure that's the way to go, then I'll go with your instincts. Just make sure that you're sure. Okay?"

"All right, I will. Maybe we should pray a minute. That always helps me." Amy prayed in her heart for God to give her and Judy guidance as they began this long, hard journey together. When she finished, she opened her eyes and the direction was very clear to her now. "Yes, this is the way to go. Come on."

CHAPTER 53

The women headed down the road, hoping to find a town or a farm. They walked close to the edge, ready to dive in the bushes if they needed to. Amy continued to pray for safety. Judy kept a vigilant eye as her head swiveled in all directions. She expected to see the headlights of the van right behind them.

Their journey seemed to take forever but in reality had only been close to two hours. They stopped for another rest when it dawned on them that they hadn't eaten since the ordeal began. Now their energy level started to wane. Judy looked at Amy, who sat calmly.

"How come you look like you're at peace?" Judy asked. "I mean, throughout this whole ordeal, you haven't once seemed to be afraid. It's like you have this, this, I don't know, this look that says you don't have to worry about anything. It's like you know everything's going to be all right. I just don't know what it is about you." She threw her arms out in frustration at not being able to find the words she wanted to say.

Amy began to laugh, "I know what you're trying to say, Judy. What you see in me really is peace. I am afraid, but in my heart I have peace because I know God will keep me safe. I don't know why we're here, and I honestly wish we weren't, but I know we're not alone. God's with us." She smiled at Judy with genuine tranquility that literally emanated from her soul.

Judy scrunched up her forehead as she pondered that. She didn't have anything to say. Instead, she felt now was the time to figure out how to stay safe. She knew the men would be back for them. They needed to be able to survive out here.

As they started to walk again, Amy thought back on her short life. She'd lived in Grand Rapids her entire life. She only knew of country life from she and her family went to visit her grandparents in Nebraska. They would visit every other year or so as she grew up. Those trips ended almost ten years ago when her grandparents had died within two years of each other.

She recalled some fond memories at their little farm house. The place would be crammed full of every relative in the family when they heard that Al and his family had come home to visit. Even now Amy could taste the fried chicken, corn bread, and fresh vegetables along with some kind of cobbler. It seemed that fifteen ladies all jumped into the kitchen where they would camp out cooking all day long. They would tell stories, share news with each other, and would have a great time doing it. Amy never thought of cooking as fun until being in that kitchen.

All the cousins she liked always showed up to the farm. They would play games, hiding in the cornfields, exploring the old barn for treasures, running around on the three hundred acre farm. They would somehow manage to find ways to get into trouble, like forgetting to shut a gate, letting the cows get out of the pasture, or rolling the tractor into the little pond. "Those were some great times," Amy thought.

———————

Judy's life had been very different from Amy's. She moved to Grand Rapids after she graduated from the University of Texas. Before she left for college she lived with her mother in St. Louis, Missouri for twelve years.

Memories from her childhood were often difficult and painful. She couldn't dwell on them long because of the hurt they brought. Judy's parents divorced when she was only eight years old and from there her young life spiraled downward. After her dad left, she thought her life lacked meaning. Her mother tried very hard to stay out of poverty, but somehow the more she worked the deeper in debt they went.

The only good memory she had was of her grandmother. Grandmama Williams was the sweetest little lady in the entire world. Judy considered her the poster of what grandmothers should be like, the perfect stereotype. From her gray hair always pulled back into a bun to the flowered apron that went from her chest to her knees to her little round glasses that always found their way to the middle of her nose. Judy considered her grandmotherly plump, to which Grandmama Williams said while she laughed and hugged her, "It's so I can give you more love." Judy loved the times she had been allowed to stay over at Grandmama Williams' home. Of all the people Judy admired most in this world, Grandmama Williams topped the list.

"We have to find a phone," Judy stated back in the present. "Those guys grabbed me so fast I couldn't get to my bag, which had my cell phone in it."

"They took all of our phones at the bus terminal."

"I need to call Jack to let him know we're safe. And we need him to come and get us."

"I think we need to find something to eat too," Amy exclaimed, "I'm feeling really weak. I haven't eaten since before I got on the bus for home."

"Okay. Try not to think about food right now. We'll find something soon, a town, a house, somewhere."

They traveled on down the road. The wind picked up and chilled the women. They shivered and huddled together as the strove forward. The wind blew harder and made them colder. Amy prayed for warmth and a place of safety. Judy scouted the area.

CHAPTER 54

Bob and Elaine reached the pickup truck and circled around it from a distance.

"Where is he?" Elaine asked as she timidly looked through the truck's window.

"Shouldn't he be in the front seat?"

"It's going to be dark soon, and I don't want to be out here looking for some dead body."

"Knowing Benning, he's gonna want all the gory details about what Jimmy looked like when we found him."

They each took a side of the truck and searched for Jimmy's body.

"He's gone," Bob said.

"Do you think someone else already got to him?" Elaine asked frantically.

"I don't see how that's possible. No one's been here except us."

"Then where is he? Do you think that he's not dead?"

"It's the only thing that makes sense. But if that's the case then he couldn't have gotten very far."

"Why do you say that?"

"I'm sure he's hurt pretty bad, judging from what his truck looks like. It's amazing he could even survive this."

The truck sat mangled, wrapped around a huge oak tree. Glass from the shattered windshield had been scattered everywhere. The hood of the truck had become embedded twenty feet up into the tree. All four tires had been blown out from the rocks and broken tree branches.

"Somehow Jimmy survived this," Bob said.

"He won't be happy." Elaine looked at the house as she started walked away from the truck.

CHAPTER 55

Since his fall, entrance into heaven had never been an easy task for the once highly exalted Lucifer. He stood face to face with the same guards, impatient as always. "I want another audience with the Lord God Almighty."

The guards stood firm as they detained him and awaited authorization.

"Oh, please hurry up, will you?" Satan groaned and tapped his foot. "Must you always keep me from seeing your Lord? You know he has never turned me away before and he most certainly will not turn me away this time. Now be good angels and let me pass before I get angry and turn my evil unholy angels on you."

After what seemed like eons, the guards uncrossed their spears to allow only Satan to enter. A sentry of heaven's guards escorts him to the throne room. Satan shook his head in disbelief. "Does your Master not trust me?" He took his time and smirked the whole time at the angelic guards surrounded him.

As he entered the throne room, he curled his lips and snarled at the continual praise. The presence of God drove him to his knees. A crystal clear river flowed through the room which began at the throne. It watered the trees of life planted on both banks.

One of the angelic guards gave direction, "You may speak."

"Thank you so much," came the snide reply. He waved the warrior off and turned his attention to the throne. "What kind of game are you playing with me? You know you have given me power over the earth, and yet you keep me from being allowed to use that power."

Silence filled the throne room as the Lord spoke. No thunder rang, no lightning flashed, the voice spoke clearly. Everyone heard the words spoken to Satan.

"Yes, I have given you the power of the earth, but right now you are not on the earth. You are in the Heavenly Kingdom. Therefore, you have no power here. Do you understand?"

The question did not need an answer, Satan knew.

Satan half ignored the question, "You have deliberately kept me from taking the soul of this reporter by tricking me into thinking he would die. Instead, you take him away and hide him from me. Am I to stand by silently, while he is being converted by one of your saints without even so much as any effort? I think not."

He paused as he expected to hear rebuke from the Lord. "My Lord, I must insist that I be given the opportunity to persuade him to come to me. Are you not sure he will convert to you even if I am allowed to work on his soul?" Satan's eyes narrowed as he spoke as he knew he was close to crossing the line. "And then there are those others with him. There is the saint, already in your possession, who you have been instructing to strengthen his faith. And let's not forget the women involved in this fiasco. One is your saint, the other is still mine."

He turned and pointed his finger, toward the throne. "Do not think I do not know what you are up to. I know you have put them together so your saint can witness to the other. Rest assured, I will not give up so easily. I will fight for their souls."

Satan ceased from his rant. "Not bad," he thought. He paced the marble floor as he continually peered at the throne. Soon an angel went to Satan to deliver a message.

"The Lord has instructed me to inform you of the following: You have owned this man throughout his entire life without so much as lifting a finger to keep his soul. The moment my Master moves to gain his soul is when you begin to fight. You may own his soul right now, but the battle now belongs to the Lord. It is a power you cannot overcome. Only the man can choose to follow you through his own free will. The attempt to gain his soul will be made without any further interference."

Satan shook with anger when he received this news. He stomped as a child would have a tantrum, and shook his fists. "I do not believe this. This is absolutely wrong. I insist I be allowed access to his soul." His words went unheeded as the Lord had already spoken.

"You are free to leave now," the angel stated. The guards who escorted him into the throne room stood by, ready to escort him back out.

"I will not stop my attacks. I will have his soul. Do you understand? Do you hear me?" The doors closed as the guards led him out.

CHAPTER 56

Inside Peter Stallings' hospital room, the continuous sound of the machines kept a rhythm that was both melodic. The sound lulled June into a much needed sleep. Until now, every time she would doze off, a staff person would make enough noise to wake her back up. She smiled and nodded to each person as they would check the monitors, IV's, and all the wires attached to Peter. They would change the bandages occasionally, as well as restock the cabinets and empty the trash cans.

June remained by his side for all but eight hours in the last two days. She would go home only to change clothes and freshen up before she returned. She was determined to stay here until he was out of danger. "After all," she told the nurses, "he's only in a deep sleep. He'll be back, you just wait and see."

In truth, Peter lay in very critical condition. Amazingly, he began to stabilize in the last few hours with the aid of the life support systems. The doctors continued to believe there wasn't much hope, but they kept this to themselves. "No need to give her a false hope," Dr. Peterson stated out of range for June to hear. While huddled around the monitoring station he said to the nurses. "The next forty-eight hours will be the most critical. Everything depends on the swelling."

In their hearts, the entire staff hoped for Peter and John to survive. But the nurses knew the chances of survival were so slim that some of the personnel had started to fill out the paperwork for a person who dies while in the hospital.

June had never been satisfied with the answers given from the staff and wasn't shy about telling them. She stayed right next to Peter's side in a flower-patterned dress and sat on the padded wooden chair as she prayed.

She refused to believe she would be going on through life without Peter. In her heart she knew there must be a deeper meaning to all this. But, she thought, as always when caught in the middle of life, the meaning gets buried somewhere, even lost. Nevertheless, she prayed believing God would hear and answer her prayer. She believed in being passionate about prayer.

———◆———

Peter's body remained still with the exception of his chest and stomach, which all worked on the life support machines. Somewhere else, however, his eyes remained open. He contemplated what to do next with his back against the wall. Jareb had told him to pray. He did pray, for a few minutes anyway.

"I just don't understand what's happening. I know I said I believe Jareb is an angel, but, come on, this has to be some kind of a dream. It has to be the drugs the doctors gave to me so I can rest. But this seems so very real."

The voice of Jareb called out. "Peter." It echoed against the wall with great resonance. "I have come to you to give you more instruction from the Lord."

"Jareb, where are you?" Peter looked around for the angel. "Show yourself."

Jareb materialized next to Peter as he looked the other way.

"Ah, Jareb. You almost gave me a heart attack." Peter grabbed at his chest as he gasped for a breath.

Jareb began, "When I left you a short time ago, you had been given instruction to pray. Yet you have not done so in the way the Lord desires. This is one of the reasons he has sent me to you. I am to instruct you in the proper way to pray."

"I don't understand. Isn't prayer supposed to be what I feel?"

"You must give your whole heart, not just your mind, to prayer, Peter. Earlier, when you prayed, you spoke the words you thought God wanted to hear. Your heart, however, did not agree with your words. Even still, with just your mind and words involved, you saw the effects of that prayer, didn't you? God answered you, but not to the fullest extent he would like to answer."

Peter sat reflecting on what he knew to be true. "You're right, Jareb. I didn't put my whole heart into it. In fact, I don't think I put any heart into my prayer."

"The Lord desires you to know your prayers make a difference in your life and of those around you. The lives of John Robertson, Judy Melcalf, Amy Tuinstra, and your family can be affected by your prayers, Peter. If you do not pray with your whole heart, however, it may be an effort the devil can easily overcome."

"I thought I knew how to pray. I've been doing it for years. I admit there've been times when praying didn't mean all that much to me. Other times, though, my heart has been heavy and it feels like I'm praying to the walls with my words going no higher than the ceiling."

Turning back towards Jareb he asked, "So you're supposed to show me how to pray properly? How about answering one of those prayers?" Peter turned to anger at being accused of not knowing how to pray.

Jareb asked, "Did you pray for comfort earlier, which was given to you? Did you pray for your family to be comforted, which was also given to them? You still do not believe in the power of prayer. Soon, Peter, you will know the mighty power you hold when you use it to pray as God instructs you. I am to allow you to see what it is you pray for. Behold. . ."

Peter saw two beings in the distance. As he focused on them, he recognized one of them.

"Hey, that's John." He also saw another angel, much larger than Jareb. They sat on a hillside. The angel's hearty laugh seemed to put John at ease as they spoke together.

Moments later as Peter watched them talk, a band of demons circled around the two. They darted towards John, picked at his soul, while they tried to avoid the sword of the angel.

"John, look out." Peter was too far away to be heard. A razor-sharp talon sunk into the skull of John. Peter hear the scream. The other demons kept the angelic warrior distracted while their comrade worked to complete its mission.

Jareb compelled Peter, "Peter, it is you who can defend your friend."

"How can I do that from here?"

"Pray, Peter, pray now. Pray with all your heart."

Peter found himself back against the wall where he panicked, unable to find the right words to pray. He could still see the horror in the distance. "God, protect John from those attacking demons. Remove them from where he is."

As he prayed, the huge angel sent a demon through the air. It passed within inches of Peter's head and smashed into the wall. Peter felt the wind and smelled the foul stench that followed. The demon looked Peter in the eye with an evil look that seemed to say "It's your fault that he did this to me."

"That's incredible," Peter exclaimed. "Not only did my prayer get heard, but I saw it being answered." He realized this had been part of Jareb's instructions and began to pray more. He didn't stop as he had been prone to do, but stayed focused and didn't daydream. He watched as all the demons departed in defeat. John rested comfortably.

CHAPTER 57

Jimmy moaned as consciousness returned. He toiled to focus on where he was, only to remember that he had driven away from...his mind became clear as the name of William Benning crossed his memory. It all flooded back to him: the shootings, driving to the farmhouse, and William Benning's threat to kill him.

He looked back to see the destroyed pickup truck wrapped around the tree. "How did I get here?" Intense pain shot through him as he tried to move his arms and legs. As much as they hurt, nothing felt broken, until he took a deep breath. "I must've some broken ribs." Slowly and carefully, he lifted his head enough to notice blood seeping through his pant legs.

He laid his head back down, exhausted from the effort it took just to lift it a couple of inches. "I have to get out of here before Benning comes looking for me." He began to crawl away from the wreckage. Every inch was difficult because it felt like an elephant stood on top of him.

He had no idea how far he had gone when he heard the voices of Bob and Elaine. He froze for a second before he made his way under some thick foliage. He knew what they would do if they found him, so he hoped he could stay hidden.

After they left, he worked himself out from under the thick underbrush. "I don't know how they missed me." He'd only gone a few feet before the pain of his bruised and battered body put him back into unconsciousness. A short time later he came back around and continued his arduous journey through the woods. New scratches from sharp tree branches and thorn bushes cut into him as he moved along the ground.

Blood began to drip from a new cut above his right eye after a branch seemed to jump out and poke him. The pain in his chest increased as he thought he may have cracked or broken another rib. His arms were heavy as he pulled his body along the rough terrain.

"I have to make it." He willed himself to move towards the road. "I have to tell someone what's going on here."

To occupy his mind, he thought of people who had been positive influences in his life. His mom and dad had always taught him to do what was right, even if it hurt. He remembered his eighth grade English teacher, Mrs. Tipper, who said, "You can choose to do good or you can choose to do bad. No one chooses for you." He felt like he'd let them all down as he lay flat on his belly in the middle of nowhere.

Every few feet he had to stop and rest. Sweat poured down his face and stung his eyes as it mixed with the blood. He looked and listened for Bob, Elaine, or William, but so far there were no signs of them. He knew they would be come back.

In front of him he saw nothing but trees. Behind him he created a very well-marked path. For some strange reason, as he took a break with his face in a pile of dirt, he began to pray. He couldn't remember ever being taught how to pray, but tried anyway. "Dear God, I need help. I've done some bad things that I need to make right. I know what I did was wrong. Please forgive me. Don't let William Benning find me. If he does then no one will ever know the truth about what's happening. Please God, help me." He lapsed back into unconsciousness for the third time.

A short while later, Jimmy's eyes opened with his face down in the dirt. He had a renewed strength and determination from somewhere deep within his soul. He began to move forward again.

A large hill up ahead with a huge rocks sticking out of it separated him from the main highway. "If I can reach the highway. . ." he blacked out again from the pain.

As expected, William Benning chewed Bob and Elaine out when they returned before they found Jimmy's dead body. His face turned red, and his jowls shook in anger, "You get back out there and find that body. And this time if you fail me, I will have your heads in glass jars. Do you understand?"

They ran from the room and shut the door behind them. "That man is insane," Elaine snapped at Bob. "I can't believe he's losing it over somebody like Jimmy Morten."

"Well, I can sort of understand why he's upset. He's going to have to answer to somebody higher up. If we don't find Jimmy, not only will he be in trouble by his superiors, but I think the trickledown effect reaches us."

They huffed back down the two-track road to where the truck crashed into the tree. Bob circled around the truck and saw the path Jimmy had made.

"Well, look at this." He pointed in the direction where the green plants were flattened. "I believe we've found the way our dead man crawled." He headed down the path. Elaine reluctantly followed him. She complained every step of the way.

"This is ridiculous." She didn't see the branch snap back at her after Bob let it go. "Ouch, what'd you do that for?"

"Sorry. I wasn't paying attention." He grinned but didn't look back. He knew a welt formed across Elaine's face. "Try to keep up with me, will you?"

———◆———

Jimmy winced and wheezed as he scrabbled at the dirt, He had finally reached the peak of the hill where he hoped his expedition would end. As he raised his head to look over the crest, his shoulders slumped, "This is going to be impossible."

The downside of the hill had more rocks, fallen trees, and seemingly no way down. He collapsed as exhaustion and pain overtook his adrenalin-depleted body. Every breath became more erratic and difficult. Blood continued to seep through the scratches and cuts.

Now he fought to keep consciousness. He knew if he closed them he might never wake up again. The fear of William Benning and his goons in the woods weighed heavily on his mind. "I don't want to be around when they show back up to finish me off. They already know I'm a dead man. I'm just not dead yet."

Jimmy rolled over on his back, which made it easier to breathe, and looked up toward heaven. He confessed, "I really messed up this time. I know I don't deserve to ask you for help, but I don't where else to go. When I was a kid, I only went to Sunday School a couple of times. Lying here, I can hear the teacher still talking about how Jesus died on a cross for us. Somehow I can still hear her saying that we could go to Heaven too by asking Jesus to come into our hearts. I remember I wanted to do that, but my dad was in a hurry to leave. I hope it isn't too late for me to do that because right now, I want to do just that."

He coughed up some blood. Sharp pain pierced his ribs. He closed his eyes and slept. For the first time in his life he felt at peace.

CHAPTER 58

Jack asked Robert Jones one final question. "Do you remember anything about the pickup truck? The color, make and model?"

"I know for sure it was red," he said with certainty. "I'm not as sure, but I think it was a Chevy."

Jack stuck his hand out and grabbed Robert Jones' hand. "Thank you for your help today."

"Glad to be of service." As the man walked away with Officer Buitman, he shouted back, "There's one more thing."

"What's that?"

"I got the license plate number," he smiled, many of his teeth missing. "Would that help you at all?"

"You'll never know just how much that will help," Jack smiled, amazed at the lead this man gave them.

"Uh oh," the old man sighed as his shoulders slumped. "I forgot the last number. Is that bad?"

"I think we can manage." Jack wrote the numbers down and handed them to an officer. "Get the name of the owner ASAP and get it out over the wire."

The officer nodded and hurried off. Jack turned back to the old man, "You know there may be a reward for this."

Officer Buitman led the man out of the command center and headed to a nearby diner for the promised meal.

The lead brought new life to the entire investigation team. Everyone felt the energy change as it went from doom-and-gloom to a glimmer of hope. The pessimists still doubted they would find the two women unharmed or even alive. The optimists found their silver lining.

No one could tell who the most excited person in the command post was. He sat alone in a corner with his head bowed and thanked God for the new amazing lead.

As he finished, Jack had to wipe away tears from his cheeks as he thought of what Judy and Amy might be going through. Although he had faith they would be found alive and well, he had to work in the world of reality, which told him they might be found dead. So many years of law enforcement with so many crimes ending up as losses for the victims and their families had made him skeptical about their safe return.

He caught his breath and stood up. "All right everyone, listen up. It's not time to celebrate yet. There's a lot of work to do. We still have two ladies to find and killers and kidnappers to catch."

The smiles in the room remained in place as the officers slowly returned to their work. "We're just excited to finally catch a break, Detective McDougal," Officer Walter Moore said.

"Believe me, I want to celebrate, too. I just can't do that until we solve this case. We need a successful investigation where the women return safe and the bad guys get caught. Is that too much to ask?"

Jack's motivational speech hit the hearts of the team assembled to solve the crime. Everyone went back to their tasks, some to the phones, others out to the scene, still others to the place where the pickup truck had last been seen.

Jack left the command center to go back to his office. His thoughts returned to Judy's camera and the video she had shot. "There has to be something I missed." An idea came to him like the proverbial light bulb going off. He radioed ahead as he sped back to the office.

CHAPTER 59

The light, refreshing rain turned into a heavy downpour. The women were drenched as they scrambled to find shelter. Now they were chilled to the bone from the wet clothing. The hot sun, currently behind dark thunderclouds, created sweltering humidity. They sat huddled close to each other for warmth. They sank down in a grove of trees for a safe haven to wait out the storm.

As soon as the heaviest of the rain stopped, they ventured back to the road. A steep hill rose before them. "This is draining me, and I didn't have any energy to begin with," Amy said. They leaned on each other as they pulled and encouraged one another to keep going.

Judy dropped down on her stomach. "Go on ahead, Amy. I just need a little breather."

"I'll go scout it out and come right back." Amy sloughed up the hill. On the way she prayed they would find help soon.

Judy climbed up behind her. "I hate to admit it, but I'm getting too old to keep up with you."

A few steps from the top, Amy turned back to Judy. "Come on, you can make it. We're just about there." She finished the climb and waited as Judy huffed and puffed to join her.

Judy remained on the ground, breathing heavily as Amy stood over her. She rolled onto her back, looked up, and saw Amy in tears. "What's wrong?"

"It's the most beautiful sight I've ever seen." She reached down to help her friend up. Judy leaned on Amy, and turned to see a tall, white steeple of a little country church greeting them.

"I could swear I saw this exact same church on a postcard somewhere," Judy stated. "Let's get down there."

The hill they just climbed seemed to be just as steep going down, but the renewed energy of finding a place of safety made the way much easier. The rain turned the gravel road to mud. The women ended up sliding down the hill on their backs.

"Just like a roller coaster." Amy yelled. At the bottom, they hugged and laughed at the sight of themselves, soaked from the downpour, and now covered in mud. Still, they felt safe. They ran over to the little white church, unaware of the day or of the hour. There were no cars in the parking lot.

Judy walked up to the doors as she asked, "Do you think they have to lock their doors out here?" She half grinned as she turned the knob and the door opened. "I feel like Goldilocks going into the three bears' house."

Amy stayed outside a few moments longer as she looked around the grounds and the building. "What a beautiful place this is. Thank you, Lord, for bringing us here."

She strolled out by the road to read the name on the sign, Zion's Hill Baptist Church. The schedule of the services along with the name of the pastor, Rev. Jim Troutman, had been written underneath. "I hope we get to meet some of the people who attend here." She traced the letters of the church name.

Having found a refuge from their danger put the women at ease, if only for a moment. The possibility of the men coming back loomed large. Judy stuck her head out and called to Amy, "We should stay out of sight, just in case." Amy nodded and walked toward the building.

Judy stood in the back of the little sanctuary. She sighed in relief for the first time since this ordeal began. The pain in the back of her head, however, felt like a bass drum that reminded her the nightmare wasn't over.

Judy started to search the small building to find a phone and food. Instead, she found a drop cloth near some buckets of paint. She laid it out on the back pew to keep her muddy clothes off the cloth. She tucked two hymnals under her head for a pillow. The moment she put her head down she fell into a deep sleep.

Amy walked in the small sanctuary with a smile. She found a folding chair covered in paint, which she gathered was used as a ladder. She brought it to the front of the sanctuary and sat to pray. "Thank you, God, for bringing us here. It's warm and peaceful." She felt an urgency to pray, but exhaustion took over and her chin fell to her chest in sleep.

CHAPTER 60

Peter could still see John Robertson in deep conversation with the angel. They both gestured from time to time as they pointed and waved in all directions. Peter noted the distance from where he sat and where John was. "I wonder why John is so far away from the wall?"

As he pondered this, he realized the battle was for John's soul. "That's why the demons are hovering over him. They're trying to take his soul away from him. No wonder Jareb told me to pray."

Music from the choir rang out again. He thought they were singing praises to God. Everything he had ever been taught about prayer now became more than just lessons. "I'm supposed to pray, so I better get started."

He cleared his head of distractions that raced through his head in order to concentrate. He started to pray for John Robertson, for both his safety and his soul. He then prayed for Judy Metcalf not knowing what had happened to her at the bus station. His prayer also included comfort and peace for his wife June. He prayed for Paul to make the right choices for his life. This time he didn't stop to look around or to think of other things. He found himself focusing on praying diligently.

The voice of Jareb spoke to him, "Peter, your prayer, along with those of other saints, has reached the ears of the Almighty. Be of good cheer, the Lord will have a great victory this day. The battle belongs to him."

"Jareb, where are you? Come and sit with me again. Please, I want to thank you for what you've taught me."

Jareb replied, unseen, "I am unable to come to you right now. I can, however, give you more instruction. Peter Stallings give reverence to God. Continue to pray for those around you. The Lord will do mighty things through you if you remain faithful to him and do what he bids you to do."

The angel's voice faded as Peter sat alone. There choir sounded again with jubilant celebration. "I would love to be a part of that choir."

As Peter contemplated prayer again, a Bible verse popped into his mind, "For we wrestle not with flesh and blood. . ." He realized he was part of that fight. This wasn't some test; this was the real deal. He discovered the battle included his soul, to keep him from being faithful to God. He sensed the necessity to pray, but this time he wouldn't stop.

"Not only must I pray for those around me, but I must also pray for God to guide my every step and thought. Now I can see what I've been doing." He sat and thought about his past. "For so many years I just played church. I never committed myself to do the work of God. I thought that showing up, saying a few simple prayers, and giving a few dollars would be enough. How wrong I was."

CHAPTER 61

The white van parked behind a broken down barn that allowed the men to get some rest without fear of being seen. Billy changed places with Allen to get back behind the wheel. Tom had not moved. They slept in the seats. Allen took advantage of the space and stretched out on the floor. He used the spare tire for a pillow.

They slept for two solid hours when the first rays of the sun hit the windshield. The bright light caused Billy to stir. He grimaced in pain. He tapped Tom on the shoulder, "Yo, Tom." He was careful not to startle the big man and risk a punch. "Tom, wake up. It's time to go."

Tom snorted, not able to focus yet. He rubbed his eyes with the back of his hands as his head cleared, "What's the matter?"

"I've been thinking."

"That's not good."

Billy ignored the comment. "We shouldn't have let the women go. I don't know what we were thinking when we thought the chances of letting them fend for themselves would be a good idea. We need to go back and either get them or finish them off. They know too much about us."

"Why are you so worried? Even if they do talk to the police, we'll be long gone before then."

Allen stirred from the back, "What're you guys talking about?"

"The women," Tom shot back. "You think we should go back and get them? Or do you think we should keep moving before we get caught?" Tom peered over at Billy, who squirmed behind the wheel as he held his swollen hand. "Ol' Billy here thinks they're not only gonna be okay, he thinks they'll turn us in to the police. I think he's still too angry about his hand being broken to think straight."

Allen sat up, stretched his arms high over his head as he gulped in air. Lines had formed on his face from the tire that read 'GOO.' With a stern look on his face he asked, "Why would we want to go back into more danger? If we made a mistake by letting them go, it's a bigger mistake to go back. But

I'm willing to risk it if you guys are." Allen yawned and scratched his head. "Yeah, I think Billy's right. We have to go back and get them, but we won't kill them." He put his head back down on the tire and dozed back off to sleep.

"All right then, let's go back. Do you remember where we left them?"

"No, but I would guess they'd head to that little village we passed." Billy started the van, turned around in the field behind the old barn, and headed back to the village.

———◆———

Pastor Joseph Thompson strode up to the pulpit. "As you all know, Peter Stallings, one of our long time members, was shot while at the bus station this past week. He, and his co-worker, John Robertson, also shot, remain in critical condition at St. John's Hospital. They, along with their families, are in much need of our prayers." He paused as the message reached the ears of the congregation.

"Also involved in this terrible crime is Amy Tuinstra, the daughter of our brother, Al Tuinstra. She just got back into town when the whole thing started. She, along with Judy Metcalf, also of WGRT, has been taken hostage. As a body of believers, we need to bind our hearts together and lift our voices to God to heal and protect."

The ladies started saying, "That's right."

The men began chimed in, "Preach on, pastor."

"These people are depending on us to pray for them while they are incapacitated."

"Keep going, preacher."

"The Lord will honor the prayers of his faithful children. When we call on his name, he will deliver those of his children from the torments that they are in."

"That's right."

"I say unto you, pray. Pray without ceasing."

"Come on."

"Preach, pastor."

"Do not stop until we know that God has not only heard our prayers, but he has answered them."

The choir broke into a prayerful song while the pastor paused to collect his thoughts. When the choir finished he continued, "Let us now take some time to uplift these people and their families in prayer." The entire congregation prayed for healing and protection for Peter, John, Judy, and Amy as well as their families.

CHAPTER 62

In the throne room of heaven, the Lord heard the prayers offered up by saints. The winged beasts flew around as they shouted their praises to God. The white-robed elders fell on their knees and praised the Almighty God. "He is worthy of honor and glory and praise."

Thunder and lightning shot out from the throne as God accepted the praise while Pithel was summoned to come before him. Only Pithel understood the call, as the instructions from his Lord and Master were for him alone.

<hr>

Pithel told John, "I must go before the Almighty God as he has requested my presence. I will not be gone long."

"Can I go with you, Pithel?"

"I am sorry, John Robertson. You are not allowed to enter into his kingdom at this time. That is not my decision. It is one you must make when you return to your physical body. I must go at once." Pithel vanished as fast as a snap of the fingers.

<hr>

Before the throne, Pithel bowed with his face to the floor in reverence. As the praise continued, God spoke to Pithel. The angel raised his head and looked toward the throne. "Yes, my Lord, I continue to speak with him."

"Does he question why he is where he is?"

"Yes, my Lord, I feel he is very close to understanding the purpose of being here. He has asked about my battles and other stories of history, which I have been happy to tell him of those great victories given to you. I feel he will soon ask about Jesus and what he did. I am fully prepared to tell him about that dark day and also about the grand and glorious day that followed." Pithel waved his arms around in a grand motion as he spoke about the Son of God.

"Then proceed. Be mindful of his time being short."

"Yes, my Lord, I will continue to do your bidding. For your glory, I will do my utmost to not fail."

Pithel stood and left the room to return to his mission.

———◆———

Pithel reappeared next to John Robertson. John immediately asked, "What did he want? Are you in trouble?" As John Robertson rattled off the questions, Pithel began to laugh.

"You have been a reporter for how many years and you only wish to know if I am in trouble with my Master? Oh, John Robertson, you do refresh my spirit. No, I am not in trouble. But you may be if you do not get on with this interview. Our time grows short."

Pithel's voice became serious as he spoke about who was in trouble. "My Lord will not keep you in your present state much longer. You must be returned to your physical body soon. I would like to suggest you begin asking me some more serious questions."

John sat, stunned at the tone of voice Pithel used. "Well, I, uh," he stammered. "Then tell me why am I here. Is that serious enough?" John tried to lighten the mood but the question came out too serious.

"Yes, John Robertson, it is time you know why you are here." Pithel took a breath. "The Lord has great plans for your life. He can only allow those plans to be used if you give yourself fully to him. He desires to have you in his service to further his kingdom. He cannot do this if you refuse him, which is your choice."

Pithel's gaze bore deeply into John's eyes and into his soul, "You see, for a long time he has desired to have you in his care. My Lord never pushes anyone into making a decision they do not wish to make. Why anyone would not want to accept the love of Jesus is beyond me. He is a great and loving God and very patient. But his patience can only go so long before Satan is allowed to take over the battle for the souls of men."

"Am I in that battle right now?"

"Yes. The battle for your soul is being fought as we speak. Those sharp pains you felt earlier were devils from hell fighting for your soul. They are being held at bay while you are here. After you return to your physical body, however, they will be allowed to fight once again for your soul. The choice will then be up to you. Although my Master does not desire you to perish, he will allow it, if that is your desire. John Robertson, I do hope you realize what you are facing if you do not wish to accept my Lord."

"Does hell really exist, Pithel?" John asked.

"Yes, it does. It is more horrible than you could ever imagine. It is not only the fire that torments you, but also all the evil deeds you have done while on the earth. Any afflictions, pain, or suffering you may have will stay with you forever. Hell is very real."

Pithel bored into John's soul with his eyes. "I suggest you consider your decision carefully. You must understand my Lord loves you and every person that has ever lived or will ever live. He has set forth his plan which cannot be changed or altered. If someone does not follow his rules they will pay the penalty. There is another way though, and it is the only other way. That is through the blood of Jesus."

John interrupted with his hand raised in a halting motion. "Wait a minute, please. I'm writing down what you just told me. That's some pretty heavy stuff. I think it will be great in the story."

"You do not have to write this down, John Robertson. It has already been written for you. Have you never read the words my Lord has given to you? It is the information you need to understand what I have told you. Please know these are not my words but the words of the Lord God Almighty. I am only his messenger. I am very grateful for the opportunity to speak to you on my Lord's behalf."

CHAPTER 63

"Ernie, play it again. I'll tell you where to stop." Officers who had worked the case had gotten more video footage from several surrounding buildings and other news organizations. It had been two days since the shooting and abduction. Jack McDougal had found a new enthusiasm after the lead had come in from the man in the alley. "Not only do we have to I.D. these guys, but I think we have to determine where the bullets came from."

So far no one had been able to identify the three guys from the bus station. It sounded like they had never done any crime before and then vanished before anyone could get a good look at them. Jack thought back on the first few hours after the crime had been committed.

"You mean to tell me you couldn't find one fingerprint anywhere inside the bus station?" Jack fumed at his forensics team upon hearing this bit of news. "Then you need to get back there and try again." The team leader nodded quietly and headed back to the scene.

All the hostages had been interviewed, some of them several times. None of them heard anything considered to be a valid lead. "They never said anything around us about their plans," Lindsay Miller told police. "It's like they didn't have a plan to begin with."

"If they said their names, then I just didn't hear it," Murray Sizemore stated. "They kept things pretty close to the vest, other than yelling at us and then taking that young woman as a hostage."

Their clothes and facial features had been identified, but those could be seen from the videotape. It did serve as a way to see if the hostages had remembered the incident clearly. "By now they surely would have changed their appearance," Jack said as he stared at the monitor.

"Stop it right there," Jack shouted to Ernie Caldwell, borrowed from the IT department. He had transferred the video to a digital format that made viewing easier. "Back it up a few frames. Slow."

Ernie hit tapped the left button on the mouse to slow the picture down to go frame by frame until Jack saw what he needed to see. "Right about here," Ernie said as Jack looked over his shoulder.

"Just a bit more, Ernie. Come on, be there." Jack focused intensely as he stared at the monitor. "Stop right there." Jack pointed at the monitor. "See that? Can you clean up this picture some more, Ern?"

Ernie typed some commands on the keyboard to the computer. Within seconds the picture had become much clearer. "How's that, Jack?"

"Not bad, but it still needs to get a little clearer. I need to see the top right corner." As Jack ran his fingers through his hair, Ernie worked to make the picture clearer. The IT tech tapped the enter button, and the image became crystal clear. Jack whistled and patted Ernie on the back as he stared at the picture. "Look what we have here, Ernie."

Ernie saw it clear as day. "It looks like we have ourselves a second shooter."

"Or a lone gunman."

From how the gunshots hit the targets, it was obvious they came from a high angle. On the third floor of the building, next to the bus station, the figure of a man could be seen pointing and firing a gun into the crowd. Fire could be seen coming out of the barrel of the gun.

"Can you get a still picture of this?" Jack sighed with relief at having another piece of the puzzle solved.

"No problem. When would you like it?" Ernie asked.

"As soon as possible, please."

"Here you go." Ernie handed Jack the photo.

"Ernie, you're the man." Jack said as he reached out and shook his hand. "I think we have a big break on our hands, and I don't want to sit on it."

Jack went over to his desk to check for any messages that may have come in and to grab a quick cup of coffee. The captain walked into his office unexpectedly.

"Look, Jack, we've got everyone out looking for the women and those creeps. Go home and get some sleep," said Commander Bill Jamison, who had been on the force for thirty years. He started as a street cop who had patrolled, handed out traffic violations, and settled domestic disputes. He worked his way up through the ranks all the way to the top. Even after several years of not being on the streets, Bill still had the compassion for those serving on every level. "By the way, Jack, that's an order."

Jack admired his boss. It helped that he had worked with his father.

CHAPTER 64

Judy slept on the back pew of the little church almost to the point of being unconscious, which might not be a stretch when she considered all the hits she had taken. It had been so long since she had had any amount of quality sleep. She dreamed of being lost on a road where she wandered endlessly without ever finding help.

Even further into the dream, she had to run from people who chased her. It felt like she knew someone followed her, but she never saw anyone whenever she turned around. She heard herself say while in the dream, "I'm just being paranoid." Yet the shadows that haunted her seemed real. She kept running as she searched for something, or someone to help her find peace and safety.

On the pew, she thrashed, wriggled, and turned. In her mind, she grew very uncomfortable. Every so often, she would swing at the shadows that chased her.

Throughout the entire dream, the shadows seemed to be the most real. She could feel them, waiting for her to take one wrong step, as they reached for her soul. She kept running on and on, unable to stop and rest. Her breathing became heavy and sweat soaked her shirt. The shadows kept coming, drawing closer and closer.

"Jack," she yelled out still asleep. "Jack, please, I need you. Help me, Jack." Her tossing and turning increased as she still swung at the shadows. "God, please send Jack to help me." After a few moments she fell back into a deep sleep again.

A hand slowly reached down and nudged Judy on the shoulder. No response. The hand reached out again; this time it lightly poked Judy's shoulder.

"Miss, it's time for the evening service," a voice called out quietly. The hand gently shook her shoulder while the voice grew stronger and a little louder, "Excuse me, miss, it's time for our evening service to begin. Wake up." Judy moaned and snorted as she began to arouse from her deep sleep.

Up front in the small sanctuary, an elderly man woke Amy up. Her eyes opened into small slits as the man spoke softly, "Miss, we're about to start the evening service. Please wake up."

With a long stretch of her arms that forced the man to step back, Amy opened her eyes. She yawned as if she tried to swallow all the air in the room. She had blurry vision as she rubbed the sleep out of her eyes. She found herself face to face with a man who looked down at her. "Where am I?"

"Good evening," the man said with a warm smile. "You're in the sanctuary of the Zion's Hill Baptist Church." He scratched his head as he asked, "How long have you and your friend been here?"

"I'm sorry for breaking in to your church, sir, but we were kidnapped," Amy said as her head cleared. "They turned us loose somewhere around here. Judy and I walked for what seemed like forever before we found this beautiful building."

Amy rambled as she spoke with the man with the kind face. "I hope we aren't doing anything to upset you. That wasn't our intention. Would it be possible to use a telephone maybe after the service tonight? We would like to call our families and tell them we're okay."

"That would be fine, dear," the man said. "In fact, you should probably call before the service begins. What did you say your name was?"

"My name is Amy. Amy Tuinstra. And my friend's name is Judy Metcalf. We're from Grand Rapids, where we were taken hostage in that bus station takeover. Did you hear about that in the news?"

The man's mouth fell open as he asked, "That's you?" The elderly man turned and yelled, "Martha, would you please bring this young lady to the office and let her use my phone?" He handed Martha his cell phone. The woman, presumably his wife, made her way to where Amy sat, and carefully lifted her by the hand.

"Come with me, dear, I'll show you to the office."

Amy nodded. "It's been so awful the last couple of days. We've been tied up in the back of a van for I don't know how long, without food or water or knowing where we were. We thought sure they were going to kill us. They finally tied us to a tree and let us go. We got free and walked until we found, well, you. You don't happen to have any food here, do you?"

"I'll see if I can find something for you to eat, dearie."

CHAPTER 65

Judy sat up in the back pew and listened to Amy tell the story of their abduction from the bus station, the van ride, and being left tied to trees. She wiped the sleep from her eyes as she yawned and stretched her aching muscles.

The elderly man made his way to the pulpit while a woman sat down at an old upright piano. She started to play familiar hymns as people filed into the building.

Fifty people inside the little building made it look full. As they began singing, Amy ambled back to sit by Judy. Amy sang along when she knew the song. Judy sat still and just listened. Both felt a peace come over them as they realized they might just be safe now.

After a couple more songs, the people sat down. The man on the stage reached over to a chair and grabbed hold of his Bible. He apparently doubled as the music man and the pastor.

"That has to be Pastor Troutman," Amy whispered to Judy. "I read his name on the sign out front."

He looked to be near seventy years old with only a few strands of gray hair left. His stature appeared frail, like the smallest breeze would carry him off through the trees. He began to speak and it became obvious the frailty didn't match his heart. He spoke with confidence, but also with compassion commonly referring to the people as God's sheep in his pasture.

Judy listened as much as her attention span would allow. After being hit on the head three times, tied to a tree, and everything else she had been through, she was completely exhausted.

Her mind drifted in and out of semi-consciousness, filled with all kinds of thoughts. From working the camera outside of the bus station, to thoughts about cooking, to childhood memories, that all ran together as she tried hard to listen to the pastor speak.

She heard some things the pastor said such as, "God works in our lives through adversity." She also heard him say, "He will not give you more than you can bear." The pastor then said, "Give him your heart and he will save you."

A confused look came over Judy's face as she thought about that statement. Soon, however, she nodded off into another deep sleep, unable to stay awake any longer.

The white van sped through the dirt as fast as Billy dared to go. "Come on, Billy. We have to find them before they talk to the cops," Tom yelled directly into Billy's ear less than a yard away. "How far do you think they could've gotten since last night?"

"Well, if they weren't able to get a ride then they wouldn't get too far. I'd guess they could've made it around ten miles at the most." Billy put up his fingers as he said, "They were hurt, cold, and hungry, but then again, I've seen stranger things happen than two women traveling a long way in a short amount of time. If they got any adrenalin flowing, they could possibly make to that little town we went through last night."

"Well, I hope they make it and that they're safe," Allen shouted from the back of the van. "I promised that girl she wouldn't be hurt if she cooperated with us. She did everything we asked her to do without so much as raising her voice. I hope they make it."

Tom and Billy shook their heads as they chuckled from the front seats.

"And then we can go directly to jail without passing go, right?" Tom retorted. "That's just like you to go soft on us, Allen. Just so you know you're in this thing all the way with us. So don't even think about trying to double-cross us. We won't hesitate to kill you." Tom turned his head and gave Allen an evil glare to show he meant every word of his threat. Allen sat quiet in the rear of the van as it continued down the road.

CHAPTER 66

"Peter." The smooth voice of Jareb called. Peter sat deep in thought against the wall that separated him from being inside heaven itself. "Peter," Jareb said again. "I have been observing you as you pray. I have come to show you how your prayers are being answered by the Most High. He wants you to realize his great and awesome power. See what he is doing."

As Jareb spoke, Peter immediately stood outside a church located in the country. A service was in progress. People sang and praised God with their voices. Peter heard a sudden hush from the other side of the wall, as all of heaven stopped to listen. The heavenly choir joined with the small congregation.

The small gathering sang "How Great Thou Art" with such a sweet sound that God added the sound of thunder that rolled through the portals of heaven right to the little church. Angels filled the sanctuary to unite with the people as they praised God. Peter sat speechless as he listened to the inspiring sound.

Peter pointed at the two women who sat in the back row. "Hey, I know those two. Those are my friends, Judy and Amy. But wait a minute, what are they doing there? Shouldn't they be home or at their own church?" Peter's brow crinkled as he looked at the scene. "Is this real?"

"Peter, you must watch as your friends are about to face another test of their faith. Amy is protected from Satan. Your friend Judy, however, is not. She is currently feeling the power of the Holy Spirit as the minister speaks to the congregation."

"She does look like she is in deep thought about something."

"They are about to encounter another terrible event in their lives. It is important you pray as they go through the next part of their trial. You must pray with constant passion as the Holy Scripture states."

As Peter continued to watch the service, a white van pulled into the parking lot with its lights turned off. The tires crunched the gravel as it rolled to a stop. Three men, dirty and mean looking, got out of the vehicle and made their way to the building. The back doors of the church crashed open into the door stops.

———◆———

Through her peripheral vision, Judy saw just as the men jerked the door open. She pushed Amy down under the pew when she realized their worst nightmare had just come true.

"They're back," she whispered as she ducked her head down as well. They sat trapped in the back row. The small church building offered no other escape routes, no rooms leading out of the auditorium, not even an open window to crawl out of. They stayed low and hoped the men wouldn't see them.

The men wielded their guns and swung them back and forth as they looked through the small congregation.

"Gentlemen, may I help you?" Pastor Troutman asked in the middle of his sermon.

The men ignored him as they continued to search for the women.

"Gentlemen, please. This is a house of worship. We're in the middle of our evening service. Now if you wish to join us, you may take a seat; otherwise I must insist you leave."

That seemed to strike a nerve. Tom looked up at the pastor and took aim at his head. He would have pulled the trigger but a strong force took hold of the gun. The barrel slowly turned toward the floor.

"Look, we got no beef with you," Tom said with a crooked smile. "We're just looking for our friends. We think they're here with you. Now, if you'd be so kind as to show us where they are, we'll be happy to leave. But we're not leaving until we have them with us."

As he spoke, Billy looked down at the pew he stood next to. "Well, look what we have here." He said as he reached down and pulled Judy up by her arm. "Jackpot." Amy stood up next to Judy.

"We did some thinking after we drove away," Tom said. "Letting you two go wasn't one of our brightest moments. So we thought we'd swing back by, pick you up, and take you along with us the rest of the way." Tom waved the gun around and gestured toward the back door. "I hope for your sakes you haven't told anyone about us yet. That would have been a very bad mistake. 'Cause if you told anyone about us, then we would have no use for either one of you. We'd have to get rid of you. So the million dollar question is: did you talk to anyone?"

Both Judy and Amy stood unmoved. Judy spoke for the first time since being taken by them, "We got here just before the service started. We didn't have time to talk to anyone and we won't talk to anyone." She knew that last part never worked, but she felt she had to try. "You just go on your way and leave us here. We won't talk to anyone."

Billy and Tom laughed. "Oh, we believe you," Billy said.

Allen jumped in the middle of Billy and Tom and said, "Look, guys, we don't need both of them. Let's just take her." He pointed his dirty finger at Judy and then moved toward Amy. "I gave my word to her, remember? And I keep my word."

"But, Allen, if we leave one of them, she'll call the police on us."

"Well, then take someone else in her place."

"And who do you suggest we take? The organ player?" Tom chided. Billy laughed at the joke.

"Take him." Allen pointed at the pastor, who stood still behind the pulpit in bewilderment.

"Allen. I think you're on to something there." Tom said. "I think we can do that. We take the old man and the redhead. We leave the other one here so Allen can keep his word." Tom and Billy laughed. "If we hear or see any cops we kill them both without so much as blinking an eye. I like it. What do you say, Billy?"

"Sounds good to me, but we have to get going. I'm not comfortable being here," Billy said. "I feel like I'm being watched."

Tom went over to Billy and whispered something in his ear. Billy laughed as Tom stepped back from his ear. They gave each other a high five as Tom barked out orders to tie up everyone in the church while he took Judy and the pastor to the van.

Billy and Allen found some rope used to tie off the little balcony when it wasn't needed. They started to tie up the people. Ten minutes later the entire congregation sat back to back all bound together.

As they stood and admired their work, Billy walked up behind Allen and knocked him out with the butt of his gun. Allen crumpled to the floor with a loud thump. Billy took a piece of the rope and tied it around Allen's wrists before he regained consciousness. After Allen was secure, he darted out the back door to join Tom, who had taken Judy and the pastor out to the van.

Everyone in the church sat as quiet as the proverbial mouse. No one dared to make a sound until they were sure the men had really left. They heard an engine rev as gravel flew which told them what they needed to hear. They felt relieved for themselves, but were beyond disturbed since they had taken their pastor.

The silence was broken when someone in the congregation started to sing. Amy recognized the song and joined in for a moment. Soon, however, she prayed for Judy and Pastor Troutman and the peril they now faced. Allen stirred, his head lopped back and forth while he groaned in pain. His eyes opened, glazed over with dilated pupils, while his face showed no signs of recognition of what had happened. He dropped his head, back into nothingness.

"Where do we go from here, Tom?" Billy asked when he felt they had finally gotten to the end of their crime spree.

"I think it's time we go see William Benning," Tom replied. "I'm very sure he's getting anxious to see us over at Anti-Pro headquarters."

CHAPTER 67

"I can't believe what I just saw," Peter exclaimed. He pressed his hand to his forehead, shocked as he turned to Jareb. "What just happened? You have to do something." Peter didn't know how to react when he saw Judy and the pastor being taken from the church.

"You must understand that the ways of man are not the ways of God. You must know why he has called you here to learn about your walk with him."

"You're saying this is part of his 'mysterious ways?'" Peter asked. "And what do you mean, 'my walk with Him'? I'm doing just fine with my walk."

Peter's anger spewed out like hot lava from a volcano. "I go to church every Sunday. I tithe every Sunday. I do extra things around the church. I pray, although I don't pray as well as I should as you've so clearly pointed out. I do whatever I can to help other people. So just what do you mean by what you said about my walk?" He turned away to where he saw the other angel with John. "Is John over there getting the same talk as I am?"

"What happens with John is for him. You are here to focus on the things you need to work on, which is your walk with God."

It frustrated Peter as Jareb kept his voice so calm and steady. He turned his head away from the angel.

"It is true you have been faithful walking with the Lord. You, however, are not complete in your walk with the Lord. You must learn to serve him with your whole heart, soul, mind, and strength before you can understand what he has in store for you."

Jareb placed a hand on Peter's shoulder. "Do not misunderstand, Peter. You are walking with the Lord. I have been sent to tell you to strive to walk closer to him than you have ever walked before."

Jareb vanished once again and left Peter alone. Initially, he continued to fume from how the angel talked to him. The longer he thought about it the more he felt everything said had all been true. "I thought I couldn't do any better, but now I know I have to be stronger." He closed his eyes. "God, forgive me of my pride. I know I can do more for you and with a better heart."

CHAPTER 68

At the Eastside Baptist Church, Pastor Joseph Thompson strode up behind the old wooden pulpit. The choir ended by singing a hymn about prayer. The congregation was moved to do just that. Pastor Thompson felt the Holy Spirit move in the room, so he began his sermon with his head bowed.

"Our Great Lord, Father God, we humble ourselves before your throne knowing we alone are not worthy to kneel before such a great and loving God, but through the blood of your Son, Jesus Christ. We ask tonight, here at Eastside Baptist Church, that you would send the angels of heaven to protect us from the wiles of the devil and allow the Holy Spirit to move freely among us and give us the power from on High. We ask tonight for continued healing for Peter Stallings and John Robertson as they remain in critical condition. And place your protective hand on Amy Tuinstra and Judy Metcalf as they have been taken by evil men. We know, Father, through all this your will must be done. Thank you for being so great and so mighty and for giving us your only begotten Son, Jesus. It is in Jesus' name we pray. Amen."

In the back of the auditorium, Harry Nickols sat for the second time in a week. He took more notes for his story on Peter Stallings, while at the same time he listened to what the pastor said.

Pastor Thompson was in rare form tonight. His sermons had always been good food for the soul. This night the soul was being fed T-bone steak not chopped beef. He let the power of God speak through him with Harry Nickols being the one to benefit most from the message.

Harry didn't realize his pen had stopped as he gave his attention to the pastor. He could only sit and listen. For the first time in his life he heard how Jesus loved him. He took it personally. "Jesus loves me," he thought, "but how is that possible?" The sermon lasted less than twenty minutes, but Harry thought it had been much longer. It wasn't boring or difficult to listen to: on the contrary, the message moved him in such a way that time seemed to stop in the room.

———•———

"We have a problem." William Benning's voice cracked as he spoke to his unnamed superior. "We cannot seem to locate Jimmy Morten's body. He seems to have survived his accident."

A muffled voice on the other end of the phone questioned Benning. "Have you sent any of your people out to locate his body?"

"Yes. I sent Elaine and Bob through the entire woods, but to no avail."

"Then I suggest you go out and search again. Everything we do from this point forward depends on you tying up the loose ends out there." The voice grew tense through gritted teeth. He went silent to give emphasis to his last words. "And get rid of those two incompetents you hired to do your work. If you fail, Benning, you will end up just like those two. Do I make myself clear?"

Benning's face turned ashen as sweat poured off his forehead. He struggled to find his breath. "Yes, sir. I won't fail in what you have asked of me."

CHAPTER 69

Jareb met with Pithel away from the two reporters. Jareb spoke, "Things are moving along as planned. Peter continues to learn his life is not meant to be lived only with outward actions. He is learning how his whole heart must be given completely to the Almighty God."

"That is good progress," Pithel stated. "Has he seen how his actions affect those around him?"

"Yes. He has been able to see the pain and suffering of his family as well as Amy and Judy. This has been effective in showing him he must be stronger in his faith."

"Yes, I can see how that would be helpful for him to see," Pithel said. "John Robertson has been more difficult to this point. He only asks about what I have done for God. He does not seem too concerned about his own soul yet. He has been able to relive some of his childhood memories, which included him seeing a friend from when he was a youth. I pray this will be something that will turn him toward God."

"I will continue urging Peter to pray for John," Jareb said. He then reported, "Amy's faith is strong thus far. She is learning the way of following Christ is not easy, a point she already knew, but had never had tested this strongly."

"I agree with your assessment. Do you think she will be able to survive this ordeal?"

"I do believe she is strong enough, yes."

Pithel then added, "Judy is beginning to learn that the love of God reaches far deeper than she ever thought possible. It is hoped the pastor now traveling with her will be able to speak to her about God's love as he works on her heart along with us. Harry Nickols has been able see the Lord God is a God of love, not hate."

"For the most part, the demons have been kept away from Peter and John," Jareb stated.

"Yes they have, except for a few small skirmishes. We must remain vigilant knowing they will not give up without their battle. I must go and continue my interview with John Robertson. Our fellow warriors are to remain standing guard while the battle is being waged. We must be victorious for the Almighty God. May God be praised."

———————◆———————

A speechless and angry Satan paced back and forth as his demons told him of the happenings at the Zion's Hill Baptist Church and with Judy Metcalf. "Master, she is being influenced by those Holy Words."

"I can see that. What are you doing about it?"

"We are providing distractions by bringing back memories which have haunted her for years. We have entered her nightmares as well. Then we brought back the abductors who have taken her again. We feel this should keep her in your fold. She cannot hold out much longer before she comes to join us here forever."

"Why do I put up with such incompetence from you bumbling idiots?" Satan hissed, not impressed with the report. "Why did you bring back the abductors? They will most certainly have to take that saint girl. Now I suggest you get back to her and do not let her out of your sights for even one moment. You will not lose this woman. Do you understand?" Satan's words grew louder and more intense with each syllable he spoke to his cowering demons.

As he finished, one of the demons spoke, "Master."

"What?"

"The men did not take the protected woman."

"Now that is finally some good news."

"In her place they took the pastor." The demon quickly vanished before Satan exploded.

CHAPTER 70

Memory after memory swirled through John's head, especially those from his childhood. "Things seemed so simple back then." He relived the memory of playing with his friend, TJ. They grew up as neighbors. Only a few homes separated their homes in the small housing development.

They played for hours, everything from army men to dodge ball to teasing the two girls who lived across the street. John smiled as he remembered how the girls always seemed to be nice enough to never move when they threw water balloons at them. They thoroughly loved hearing the girls scream after getting doused by water. Of course, later they would tell their parents, which started the phones ringing at the boy's homes. "We were such naughty boys," he chuckled.

John also recalled the girls, Amanda and Jennifer, continually asked them to go to church with them. TJ and John would always say "no way" not so much because it was church, but because, well, they were girls. "We're not going anywhere with you." They would chase them away and start playing again.

One week, during the summer, TJ's family went on vacation, which left John to fend for himself. The girls, like clockwork, asked him about going to church. As if it had happened just yesterday, John heard himself saying, "Okay, I'll go with you. But you have to promise to never, ever tell TJ." The girls agreed. The next Sunday John went to church with them.

John leaned back into the hill with a smile on his face, almost laughed, as he thought about that Sunday. Seeing Amanda and Jennifer in his memory, he realized they were the cutest girls on the block, and there he was, right between them. He didn't remember much about the lesson taught that Sunday, something about forgiveness.

"Do you wonder where Amanda and Jennifer might be today, John Robertson?" Pithel interrupted the memory.

John sat up, startled at the sudden appearance by the angel. "Yes, I do actually. And how did you know I'm thinking about Amanda and Jennifer?"

"Who do you think caused you to remember this particular memory, John Robertson?" Pithel laughed as he gave John an all knowing look.

"Very clever, Pithel."

"About those two girls, Amanda is a wife and a mother of two beautiful children, a boy and a girl. They live in Tulsa, Oklahoma, where her husband is an engineer. They are very happy." Pithel reveled about the happiness Amanda had found. "She and her husband are faithful members of their church and have been saints for a very long time. Do you know Amanda still prays for you, John Robertson?"

"I'm very sure she does," John replied sarcastically. "What about Jennifer? Where and what is she doing?"

"Jennifer's life, I am afraid, has taken a different path. After she graduated high school, she went to a college in Kalamazoo, Michigan far from her home. There she met a man who only wanted to use her. She became pregnant by that man. The stress of having a baby while in school was too much for her to handle and, very sadly, she aborted her baby." As Pithel spoke about the incident, a tear ran down his chiseled cheek.

"The man never spoke to Jennifer again and never claimed any responsibility for his actions. Rest assured, John Robertson, he will be held accountable for those actions. Jennifer dropped out of college. She could not face the torment of going back home, feeling she had disappointed her parents, although they love her as much as they ever have. She remains in Michigan."

John looked the angel straight in the eyes, eyes filled with compassion. "Pithel, what about abortion? I mean what happens to all those babies?"

Pithel looked into the distance at the kingdom walls, and tears welled up in his eyes, "Oh, John Robertson, my friend, that is a very good question, worthy of your profession as a journalist." Pithel turned to face John. "The Almighty despises that which happens to his children, the horrible murder that takes place in such despicable ways. Yet because of his great love and his gift of a free will, he allows this to take place. Those who partake will pay for their sins, John Robertson. But you must realize that even in such horrible circumstances, there can be great joy."

"Joy?" John snapped at the angel. "How can there be joy over abortion?"

Pithel laughed so loud it echoed off the walls.

"Is that funny to you?"

"No, that is not funny. There is joy because one of God's little precious lambs has come home. You see, John Robertson, when one little child is taken from the earth, the child immediately comes into the waiting arms of Jesus where they find comfort and joy for eternity. They never have to go through the hardships of life on earth, but only have to enter into the joy of the Lord forever. Do you know what all those little children are doing right now, John Robertson?"

John shook his head.

"They pray for their parents to find truth and peace. They pray to God for their mothers and fathers to find the love of Jesus. They pray their parents will find forgiveness for what they have done. There have been many times their parents have turned to the Lord for forgiveness and eternal life. All the children praise God for his tender mercy toward their family."

Pithel's eyes beamed with joy as he continued. "The reunions that take place when a mother or father comes to the Kingdom after turning to Jesus are absolutely incredible. They embrace and shed tears of joy as they are introduced to their parents for the first time." Pithel wiped a tear from his face with a forefinger. "I hope you will one day get to witness one of those reunions."

"Wow, that's really amazing. I know I'm changing the subject here, but do you know where Jennifer is now?"

"As I said, she still lives in Michigan, in Holland. She is working at a bank during the day and she has a cleaning job on the weekends. She just recently began to attend church again." Pithel raised a finger in the air. "That is a good start on her road to recovery. I believe she will be well if she stays on the right path."

"She lives in Holland?" John asked with surprised. "Will I be able to find her when I get back to my regular life? Would you help me? I think I would really like to find her and maybe help her out. I know it would be great to see her again."

"I will check with my Master about helping you find her," Pithel stated. "But first we must complete our interview. Now, what is your next question?"

"I know I've asked you about your adventures of Bible stories. And I know I've really been stalling. I'm honestly getting very close to having some questions formulated in my small, feeble brain. So, while I'm almost ready to ask you some questions that will be a tad more challenging, would you indulge me with one more story?"

Pithel sensed the request to be a sincere one. He also knew time would quickly become a factor. He put his finger on his chin as he thought for a moment. "I believe I have a story you will find most interesting. It concerns one of my Lord's great saints, George Evans."

John had a puzzled look as he said, "George Who?"

"George Evans. George was a great man of God while he walked this earth. He walked very close with God. They had great times of fellowship. This was not always the case with George. I remember a time when he had a serious problem with strong drink. His family had left him, and he had absolutely nothing in this world, no money, no job, and no friends. Nothing he did ever turned out right.

"Then one day George decided he could not take his life any longer and decided to end it. He lived in New York City right near the infamous Brooklyn Bridge. That is the place he chose to jump into the river below. The Lord sent me to George's side to fight for him at this low moment in his life. As I arrived at the bridge, the forces of evil had George on the edge and ready to give him one final push. I helped George fight through anguish, despair, alcoholism, loneliness, and many others tormenting him on that bridge. All in all, close to fifty demons had invaded the very soul of George.

"But there is nothing more powerful than the Word of God as his love takes over the life of a poor helpless soul. That night George fell off the Brooklyn Bridge. Instead of falling into the river below, he ended up falling backward into the street. His life was spared from death that night. Shortly after, another man of God driving over the bridge stopped to help George. The man helped George get into his car, where the man told him about the Love of God. George accepted Christ into his heart right there on the bridge. It was a most precious victory. Anytime a battle ends up with a soul coming to Christ, it is a wonderful victory."

John listened to Pithel tell this story so magnificently. He thought he could actually see George stepping off of the rail and get into the car of the unknown man of God.

"After George accepted Christ we sang praises for I don't know how long," Pithel said with a look of joy. John felt the love Pithel had for the Lord. He sensed nothing could ever come between them. Never once did he hear a complaint of he battles he had fought for his Master.

John knew his questions had been lame, especially for someone who was supposed to be a great reporter, at least in his own mind. He found it difficult to formulate a series of questions, especially when he doubted the authenticity of the person he talked to. "Is he really an angel? Am I truly at the threshold of heaven? Is this some cruel hoax being played on me?"

"I want to believe this is all real, that you're real. And I really want to believe God's love is real." He knew he needed to get serious with his questions. John turned to Pithel after a long silence and said, "You know I still have doubts about who you are and about God don't you."

"Yes, John Robertson, I do." The warrior nodded his head.

"I'm trying to believe. I want to believe. I still need more time. Could you give me some time to think about the questions I have for you?"

"If this is what you require to believe in God's love, then I will give you more time. You must know, John Robertson, I cannot give much more time. Soon you will be back in your physical body in the hospital. I urge you to be sincere about your questions. I will go now and attend to some business the Lord has asked me to look into. I can give you only one hour before I return. We must begin our discussion at that time. Choose your questions carefully. Your eternal existence will depend on them."

"Thank you, Pithel. I'll put careful thought into what I ask." A wind blew John's hair.

CHAPTER 71

Jimmy Morten rested under some thick brush just off the road. He had made it half way up the hill, but couldn't go on without rest. Pain shot through his body every inch of the way, but he felt determined to finish his task. He was glad he had not passed out again.

He tried to put things right as he made his way along the rough and rocky terrain that tore at his flesh. "I know I haven't done anything good in my life, especially lately. I hurt some people, even killed some people, for no reason whatsoever, except to make William Benning happy. Please, God, forgive me, if that's even possible. Help me to get away from here so I can try to fix this mess."

He found the strength to continue his journey as he reached the top of the hill. From this vantage point, he saw a road. Just a short way farther down was a gas station. At that moment, Jimmy felt as if God crawled right next to him to help him finish this journey. His hands and knees bled from the rocks, sticks, and thorns.

— • —

Bob, Elaine, and now William Benning searched the woods for Jimmy's dead body. They started by his pickup truck. From there they formed a line that fanned out ten to fifteen feet from each other, as they followed the path Jimmy had made.

"He must be hurt pretty bad," Bob said. He pointed to the blood along the trail.

"How could he get so far while losing this much blood?" Elaine asked. "There's no way he can survive out here half-dead."

"Will you two shut-up and keep looking?" William snarled. "It's bad enough you incompetents couldn't find him, and now you have to add your own thoughts to this mess. The next words I hear from either one of you had better be 'here he is.' Do you understand?"

The stress to find Jimmy's body weighed heavily on William. The people he answered to wanted immediate results. They didn't care how they got those results. The promise of him being punished if the body wasn't found began to take its toll. It only added to the pressure he had already felt since the shooting and the abduction. He continuously wiped sweat off his face with his now soaked handkerchief.

William was quickly losing control of his senses as the situation spiraled downward. As hard as he tried to cover his despair, Elaine and Bob both knew he was under the gun, both figuratively and literally.

They searched the woods for hours as they looked under brush, around rocks, even up in the trees, all to no avail. Nothing turned up. "Jimmy must still be alive," Bob stated. "I don't know how but he must have survived the crash."

William glared at Bob with a sinister sneer. His facial expression changed from that of a stressed out person to someone who had completely lost his mind. "I told you not to speak unless you found the body. Yet, you still speak." William's speech pattern came in harsh strong tones. "You will not speak to me again, ever." He wagged his finger in their faces as he spoke.

Bob and Elaine stood frozen in place, fearful of what William Benning might do. They slowly backed away to put as much distance between them and Benning.

"Where do you think you're going? Don't think you will be able to leave without my permission. Do you want to leave now?"

Bob hesitated but then nodded to say he wanted to leave right then.

"Then I give you my permission to go." As William Benning spoke, he pulled out his 9mm revolver and took aim at Bob. One shot rang out, and Bob fell to the ground lifeless.

Elaine screamed as she turned and ran through the woods in wild abandon.

"Where are you going, Elaine?" William mocked. "Come back, I won't harm you. It was Bob causing all the trouble, not you. I still need you to help me."

Elaine looked back over her shoulder as she ran through the woods. William started to follow her. He could just see the back of her head bob up and down. Her fear propelled her through the thick woods. William ran a few more yards, stopped, raised the gun and fired.

A moment later, Elaine fell to the ground, dead. William bent at the waist with his hands on his knees, the revolver still in his hand. He breathed very hard as the sweat dripped from his head. His teeth clenched tight, and his brow furrowed in evil anger as he yelled, "You may both leave."

Jimmy heard the two shots, which sounded like they had been fired right behind him. He felt sure they had been fired at him. He somehow knew the shots came from William Benning. He felt a surge of adrenaline course through his body as his desire to get to a phone increased while this nightmare closed around him.

For reasons he didn't understand, he thought about Superman and how he always got through tough situations. Jimmy tried to think like the man of steel as he worked harder to get to a phone before he was discovered by the Benning.

"I'm no man of steel." A realization he felt with each new cut in his flesh. The distraction allowed him to focus on his task as the pain ripped through his body with every inch of the way. He drifted in and out of consciousness as he drew closer to the gas station.

He closed his eyes and prayed again, which he found odd since he had not prayed this much in his entire life. He sensed that, each time he prayed, a strange, calming peace came over him. *God, please protect me from William Benning. Please don't let him find me. He'll kill me if he does. I just need to be able to call the police. I have to get to a telephone, I just have to. Hide me from him. Make me invisible to him long enough to make it to the gas station over there.*

He turned his body in the direction of the gas station. At least a quarter mile stood between him and his target. He crawled like a soldier in enemy territory, while he tried to not get caught. He continued to pray, confessing everything bad he had ever done in, what he described as "my whole miserable life." He realized this might be the only opportunity he would have to confess his sins before God. *God, I know I've done a whole lot of horrible things in my life.*

Besides those I've talked about before, I have cheated on tests, stolen from my parents and I've always been mean to Riley Malone, who lives down the street from me. My parents are so disappointed in me. They don't even want me to come home and see them. I really miss them. If you will help me get through this, I'll try to make things right not only for my life, but for theirs too. I need your help to do it because I can't do it on my own. All I ask is that you give me the opportunity to prove that I'm serious about this. I don't want to be a part of William Benning's group, Anti-Pro. They only want to hurt people and I don't want to hurt anyone anymore.

Jimmy stopped to rest as he labored to take a breath. Every muscle and bone hurt from the crash and his escape. He remained still and quiet as he closed his eyes for a moment. The gas station looked to be farther away than he thought, which brought doubts that he would actually be able to get there before he died.

"Maybe I won't make it after all." He blacked out again.

CHAPTER 72

Some of the congregation of Zion's Hill Baptist Church dared to look at Allen as he began to stir. A couple of the members were angry to see he had started to come to. They weren't shy in letting their thoughts be known.

Allen's head rolled back and forth as he didn't comprehend where he was. He thought Billy and Tom had put him in the back of the van. As his eyes adjusted to his surroundings, however, he knew this wasn't the case. "Where am I?" he asked.

"You're still in the church, young man." The woman's voice shook, not in fear but from age and with some anger. "You took quite a wallop on your noggin. Are you okay?"

"Yeah, I think so," Allen tried to reach up to feel the bump only to realize his hands had been tied to a chair. His head throbbed with each beat of his heart. "Did they leave me here with you?"

"Who do you mean?" This came from an elderly man seated next to the woman who had spoken earlier, presumably her husband.

"My so-called friends."

"I'm afraid so. They took that red-headed woman along with Pastor Troutman. They left you and her here with us." He used his head to point at Amy, who sat tied up across from the elderly man.

Allen craned his head up and saw Amy across the circle, tied to her chair. He called over to her, "Did they hurt you?"

"No."

"I'm sorry I got you into this mess."

Amy tried to show compassion towards her captor, but struggled with her emotions.

Allen continued. "I just felt like I was supposed to choose you. It felt really weird, strange. To be perfectly honest, I never even saw you until I grabbed you. I suppose it doesn't matter much to you, does it?"

Amy finally found her voice. "You know as hard as this is to say, I'm not angry with you. In fact, I'm glad you took me and not someone else from the bus station."

"Why would you say that?" Allen fiddled with his cords to free himself. The small congregation listened to the conversation as if it were a tennis match.

"I've been thinking about this since you threw me inside the van. I have Christ in my heart, and I know he's been protecting me from you and your friends. If you decided to kill me and he allowed it, then I'll be going to see him sooner than I thought I would. I'm not sure, but I think I'm here for some purpose, like I'm to complete a mission of my own."

Amy thought back to the Bible story of Shadrach, Meshach, and Abednego and the way they stood up to King Nebuchadnezzar. They pretty much said the same thing she had just told Allen. They said they wouldn't bow to the idol. They knew their God would rescue them. Even if he didn't save them, they still weren't going to bow down to his idol. It made her glad to know she was in good company with those three men.

"Right now I'm not completely sure what that mission might be, but I know I'll do my best." She had a heart of kindness towards the man who had put her through so much terror in the past forty-eight hours. "I think that I'm going to pray for you, Allen. I'm going to pray for you to know God's love toward you, no matter what you've done to me and these people."

Amy turned to the rest of the small congregation tied up with her and asked, "Will you pray for this man's soul right now? Pray for him to find Jesus tonight while he is here with us."

The people, although taken aback by the request, began to pray for Allen with their hands tied behind their backs. Some prayed quietly, others voiced their prayers verbally.

Allen didn't know what to do. Never in his life had he heard a request like Amy had just asked of the church people. He knew he wasn't in charge any more, if he ever had been. All he could do was to listen as these people prayed specifically for him.

CHAPTER 73

Against the wall, Peter thought about John Robertson, whom he could see in the distance. He had never gotten to know his co-worker all that well. Everyone thought of him as just another hotshot passing through town on the way to larger television markets.

He thought about the times he shook his head whenever he would see John flirting with another woman in the building. He remembered saying to Al, "No woman is safe in this building as long he's in it." Now as he looked at John, his heart filled with compassion and the realization John needed the love of God.

His thoughts then turned to his wife and son. He couldn't imagine living without either of them. June had been so faithful to him all these years, standing by him during some pretty rough times early on in their marriage. "She grows more beautiful every day." Paul, however, had been hanging out with some bad kids recently.

Peter could see his son's heart filled with compassion for those kids. One time a neighbor had called over to Peter and started with the line "I need to talk to you about your son." Peter thought when the neighbor had started the conversation with those words, that what followed wouldn't be good.

"Your son was so helpful yesterday when I dropped a bag of groceries on the sidewalk. Paul not only helped me pick everything up, but he offered to go back to the store for me to replace what had been broken." Peter recalled swelling up with pride for his son's actions. "You should be very proud of your son."

Peter had a difficult time speaking at that moment as his throat constricted from his emotions. Now was the time that Paul needed his father around. "Maybe he's hurting because of me getting shot."

At this particular time, Peter couldn't do anything physically to help any of his friends or family. The only thing he could do was what Jareb had suggested . . . pray continuously. He started to pray again.

A short while later, Jareb's voice interrupted him, "Peter, there is something you must see."

Jareb stood beside him with a look of urgency in his eyes. "Behold."

Peter's eyes opened to a scene of a white van on some back roads moving very fast. The van swerved at a high speed almost out of control. Peter could see inside of the van. There, he saw Judy and another man tied up in the back while one man drove and the other remained quiet.

Peter heard the older man speak quietly to Judy, "Young lady, what is your name?"

"Judy."

"Where are you from?"

"Grand Rapids."

"How did you manage to get here, so far away from the city?"

"I, and Amy, the girl who was with me in your church, were taken hostage from the bus station a couple of days ago."

"Can you tell me what happened?"

"They took people hostage inside the Central Station for some reason. There was a long stand-off with the police. Then gunshots were fired. The strange thing is that these guys didn't do any shooting."

"Then what happened?"

"They took Amy from inside and then they found me in the parking lot. They hit me on the head and that's all I remember until we got left out in the middle of nowhere." The pastor looked at her kindly while he listened to her story.

She continued "For some strange reason they stopped a few miles from where your church is located and tied us up to a tree and left us. Oh, and they hit me on the head again. When I came to, I got my hands free and then untied Amy. We started walking down the road until we came to your church, which by the way, you have the most beautiful steeple I have ever seen. I think Amy had prayed just before we went over the hill and saw the steeple. Talk about coincidences."

"Hey, shut-up back there." Tom yelled. He turned to Billy and asked, "When we going to be at Benning's place?"

Billy shrugged his shoulders. "I don't even know where we are."

From the back of the van, Tom heard, "We're just trying to stay calm by doing some small talk. We'll be quiet if it bothers you," Pastor Troutman politely said.

"It bothers me, okay? We have some thinking to do up here so just keep it quiet."

The pastor ignored Tom and looked into her face. "Judy, do you know Jesus?" The question was direct, without any hint of judgment.

The question caught Judy off guard. "Well, I know who he is, if that's what you're asking. I mean, I know what he claims to have done and everything. I'm not quite sure what you mean."

"Well, since we have nowhere else to go and we're all tied up, would you mind if I told you about Jesus and what he wants to do with you?"

"Do I really have a choice?" Her words sounded angrier than intended. She softened as she realized a part of her was interested. "You can tell me about him, but I can't make any promises what I'll think."

"Fair enough."

CHAPTER 74

William Benning crammed his belongings into two old beat up suitcases. Time had run out. He had to disappear immediately. Three boxes had already been filled with all the documents he knew could either get him arrested or be used to keep him from getting killed by his superiors.

Panic showed in his hands, which trembled as he tried to wipe sweat from his brow with the back of his hand. He couldn't think straight as he rushed to get everything. He had no rhyme or reason to how he packed, only the urgency to throw it all into the back of his Lincoln.

As he ran through all the rooms in the old house, William could feel he wasn't alone. Whispers filled the halls that called his name. Several times he whipped his head around, thinking someone had come up behind him only to find he was alone. His eyes filled with fear as he moved forward. His round face had turned an ashen white.

Suddenly, sounds of sinister laughter filled the room that mocked and taunted him. He couldn't see anyone in the empty room except for himself. As the laughing continued, he filled his arms with as much as he could carry and ran out the back door. The spring on the door squeaked its familiar noise as it slammed shut behind him. William Benning never heard it. Panic, fear, and the urge to hide took over his mind.

From a dark part of the house, devils laughed as William ran to his car. The scenes of him shooting Bob and then Elaine kept haunting him, torturing him, mocking him. He couldn't stop the shaking or the contorting and convulsing as he thought about what he had just done.

On his back, two demons dug their nails into William Benning's soul, causing him to react the way he did. Other demons simply waited around for their opportunity to control what this man did next.

———•◆•———

Peter smiled as he heard Pastor Troutman share Jesus with Judy. "Tell her, Pastor." He felt like he was right there with them in the back of the van. Pastor Troutman quietly yet directly told Judy about the love of Jesus. He listened as Pastor Troutman quoted Scriptures and gave illustrations to Judy. Judy seemed to be taking it all in.

Peter looked around the rusty old van. It was filled with odds and ends like an old tire, an alternator and a fan. He saw quite a few tools scattered around. Most looked like they had seen better days and had now been condemned to live out their remaining days inside of the old van. Then something else caught his eye. Seated directly behind the pastor a strange being watched the old pastor as he spoke.

The creature nodded and shook his head as he listened to the stories being told from the Bible. Peter thought the being must be an angel. He couldn't prove it. There weren't any wings on its back or a bright halo shining around its head. It was the sheer size of the huge, hulking creature. Peter then saw other angels who appeared as he looked at the creature. They created a wall between the men in the front of the van and the pastor and Judy. Each had their swords drawn, ready to protect any who dared interfere.

In the front seat, Peter saw the two men surrounded by hideous beasts. "Obviously demons," Peter thought. They whispered into the ears of Billy and Tom while they drove down the road. They tried to get them to stop the talking behind them.

"You see, Judy, Jesus isn't willing for anyone to die and go to hell, but wants everyone to know him as their personal savior and have eternal life. That's what he wants for you. He wants you to know you can be forgiven from all you've done. You can be healed from those deeps wounds you keep harbored down in your soul."

Those last words struck Judy straight in the heart. She knew she had some 'things' that, no matter how hard she tried, would never go away. She had never forgiven her parents for divorcing when she was so young. All this time she had built a wall of hatred between them and herself. She had tried to tear the wall down but never had the courage to do it. She had too much pride. But the words Pastor Troutman spoke gave her the hope she had been looking for.

In the front of the van, the demons got jumpy. They fought amongst themselves, which meant they needed to stop what was happening in the back of the van. The three very large angelic warriors stood between them, armed and ready to fight if they dared to move toward the back while the pastor spoke.

Still, the demons knew they had to do something. They had to stop the Holy Spirit from convicting Judy's heart or they would have to give their master news of another loss. They did not wish to face him again. Slowly, they inched toward the back as they climbed over the seats and stood directly in front of the warriors.

———◆———

Peter knew a fight was about to break out. He began to pray. "God, give strength to these you have sent to protect Judy and Pastor Troutman. Allow the pastor to continue telling Judy about your love."

———◆———

The demons, now moved closer to the angels, hoping to get by them without a fight. That wouldn't be an option. If they wanted to get to the pastor and Judy, they would have to go through the angels. They continued to press forward.

They edged their way toward the angels, who held them at bay. "Ten demons versus three angels hardly seems fair," said one of the pesky demons. The angels, however, had the power of the Almighty God on their side. They also had the advantage of having saints praying.

With one swing of a sword the battle began to rage. The demons flew, dove, and swung their swords, attacking the three guardian angels. The sound of metal on metal filled the back end of the white van. Dust, dirt, and debris filled the air.

The angels spoke to each other. "Enid, watch your flank. Bartok, two are overhead." It sounded like the dogfights of fighter pilots.

Demons were everywhere, mostly on the floor or sent back from where they came from. Enid fought fiercely as he warded off the attacks of four of the largest demons as they each surrounded him in a feeble attempt to throw off his guard.

Bartok saw the demons around Enid, and with one swing of his mighty sword, sent two of the creatures back to their master. They would face a much greater challenge going home with another loss. Bartok turned and took out one of the fiendish beings as he began to help his friend.

"Aeretus, take care of these devils while I help Enid." Bartok knew Aeretus could take care of himself. It angered the demons, who began to lose control and make mistakes, which led to their eventual demise.

"Yes, Bartok, with the power of the Almighty, I can dispatch these few fallen angels. I do believe, however, that Enid can take care of the matters in front of him as well as I can."

———————•◆•———————

Peter pressed his back into the side of the van as the battle ensued. He wondered how in the world Judy could concentrate on what Pastor Troutman said with the noise of the battle from inside the tiny compartment of the vehicle.

At that moment he realized she could focus because the battle wasn't happening in the world but in a spiritual dimension. He then noticed two other angels next to Judy and the pastor, keeping them from the distractions.

Aeretus took one massive swing and delivered the three demons back to their eternal death. He moved closer to Enid to help end this fight. Enid had just sent another pesky little demon into the night right out the top of the van with a piercing blow directly under his chin. Only two demons remained until Bartok took his sword and cut them deep enough to send them back to the abyss.

CHAPTER 75

The battle in the van ended, and as the air cleared from the stench of the dispatched demons, a stillness settled over all the occupants for the first time since the bus station. No demons were left to intrude as Pastor Troutman spoke to Judy.

Aeretus, Bartok, and Enid, listened as the pastor told Judy about the love of Jesus. They began to pray for the soul of Judy Metcalf. Peter sat in awe until he realized that he, too, should be praying.

He began to voice his prayer for Judy with all his heart. He prayed she would find salvation this day even while tied up in the back of that old rusty van. He didn't see when it happened, but he found himself with Enid standing over him. The angel had put his massive hand on Peter's shoulder. Aeretus, Bartok, and Enid joined him bound together as prayer warriors.

They considered Peter to be a warrior with them. As the humble Jareb sat on the one side, and Enid, the massive warrior on the other, with Aeretus and Bartok behind him, Peter felt honored but knew the battle was far from over. Much more prayer needed to be done. He also recognized all the glory going straight to the throne of God.

He now understood what Jareb had taught him. He realized there was more to being spiritual than just showing up and going through the motions. He recognized it wasn't merely words, but actions along with those words. "Faith without works is dead," the apostle James had said in his book.

Peter now understood that being a man of God and of faith wasn't a practice for life nor was it a way of life . . . it was life itself. It was giving God every part of one's heart and soul, body and spirit. It was putting himself in line with the Almighty God for the purpose of serving and praising him.

"Jareb, my friend, I believe I'm finally beginning to understand what my purpose is in life. It's to give praise to the One who gives me the words to speak, the breath to breathe, the Almighty God. After that, everything else will fall into place. I just have to be willing to sacrifice my all to his will."

"Very good, my brother. The Lord will use you mightily. You will be a greater warrior saint on the earth." Emotional tension filled the voice of Jareb as he spoke of his Master, the Almighty God. "Yes, you will be a great warrior saint."

He pointed to the pastor and Judy and said, "Listen."

———————•———————

Judy's voice sounded weak and shaky as she spoke, "Pastor Troutman, what do I need to do?"

"About what, dear?"

"How do I accept Jesus? I've never heard him explained to me the way you just did. Now it all makes sense to me."

"Just tell him you want him in your heart because you believe in him and need him."

———————•———————

"HALLELUJAH." Peter sounded like his team had just scored a touchdown in the Super Bowl. "That's awesome. Praise God."

"Yes, Peter, praise the Almighty God," Jareb spoke softly. Peter looked at Jareb, who had tears flowing down both cheeks as he watched this new birth. "This is truly a great day for Jehovah."

CHAPTER 76

"Expect to see an old sign post advertising 'Smith's Farm Fresh Eggs' on the left; just past that you will go right. When you get to the old broken silo, veer to the left. You'll have to watch for the Miller's white horse, he tends to wander out of his corral every now and again. The silo is painted a faded red and the property is surrounded by a white rail post fence." The woman's voice quivered as she gave the directions to the church. Yet, recalling the vivid details she had given, for Jack, was as clear.

"Right after the silo, there's a dirt road coming up over a hill and right into town. You'll know you're right when you see the steeple of the church at the top of that hill."

"Ma'am, you have been a tremendous help in calling me. I'm going to ask you to speak to one of my officers now. He'll ask you about details of what has happened to you. Before I let you go, however, I have just one more question; can you tell me about the woman they left with you at the church?"

"Why, yes. She's young, college age, I believe, with darker, blondish, brown hair. They took the other woman along with our pastor."

"Can you tell me the name of the woman there with you now?"

"Just a minute." She put the receiver against her chest and called out. Jack could hear her yell across the room, "What's your name, dear?"

Jack heard some muffled voices and the shuffling of chairs. "Here dear. It's a Detective McDougal." The woman handed the receiver over to someone else.

"Detective McDougal, this is Amy Tuinstra."

Jack's demeanor fell not hearing Judy's voice. He cleared his head with a shake. "Amy, it's good to hear you. Are you okay?"

"I'm fine, a few bumps and bruises, but nothing serious. They came back and took Judy and Pastor Troutman. One of the three men got left here after he tried to defend us."

"Did they hurt Judy or the pastor?"

"Judy's been hit on the head and knocked unconscious a few times. Other than that she's like me, with bumps and bruises. When we walked to the church, after getting free from being tied to the tree, we were tired and hungry, but we both moved okay."

"I'm glad you are doing all right, Amy," Jack said. "We're on our way to the church. I'll call your parents as soon as we hang up and let them know you've been found safe. Now, can you give me any details about the men? We know they're driving a white van and have headed south. We don't have any other leads to go on, though."

"Give me just a second to remember." She thought back on everything she had seen and heard while behind the driver. "Their names are Billy, Tom, and Allen. Allen is the one tied up here. I don't know their last names. Allen took me from the bus station. Then they found Judy in the parking lot. That's when Billy first hit her on the head with the butt of their gun, knocking her out. After they dragged us to their van, they drove off."

She looked up at an imaginary place on the ceiling as she recalled the next event. "Judy and I were tied up in the back of the van for the entire night. Judy came to after several hours and seemed to be good. She probably has a concussion from all the hits she took though. We seemed to drive forever before they stopped to rest."

When Amy paused to think about other details, Jack quickly asked a leading question. "Did they hurt you at all at any time?"

"It's weird, but they never put a hand on me except to help me. They hit Judy at least three times, the last time after she was tied to the tree. They argued again about killing us, but Allen told them he promised no one would hurt me, which they didn't do. Praise God that carried over to Judy as well," she added.

Amy went on with her account. "Something strange happened as they tied me to the tree. Billy, the one who hit Judy, raised his gun to knock me out. When he swung it at me and hit the tree, I'm pretty sure he broke his arm. I don't understand how he missed. I mean, he stood right next to me and had put the butt of the gun on my head to mark the spot. There's no way he should have missed."

"What happened next, Amy?"

"Well, they left us tied up in the middle of nowhere. After a short while, Judy managed to get loose and untied me. She told me you taught her how to get her hands free. We rested for a few minutes before we started walking. We had no idea which direction to go but knew there was nothing between us and the main highway. So we started walking in the direction the men had gone, hoping they wouldn't be just up ahead. I don't know how long it took, but we finally climbed a hill and saw the steeple of the church. And here we are." She gestured as she waved her arm around the room as if Jack stood right in front of her.

"What happened next, Amy?" Jack asked to help keep her focused.

"We fell asleep inside the little church. These nice people woke us up for the evening service. Then the men came back and pointed their guns at everyone here. They tied the whole crowd up with cords. Two of them talked about something, but I couldn't hear what they said. Tom pointed his gun at Pastor Troutman and told him he would be going with them. The pastor quietly walked over to them, not fighting or trying to get away or anything. That's when Billy snuck up behind Allen and knocked him out. They tied him up with us and they left with Pastor Troutman and Judy. That's where we are now."

"Are you sure they didn't hurt Judy or the pastor?" Jack's concern stemmed from the blows Judy had sustained. He thought she wouldn't be able to take much more pain without some possible permanent damage.

"I'm pretty sure. I know they didn't do anything while still inside the church. I'd bet they tied her up again."

"Thank-you for your help, Amy. We'll be there shortly, and I'll have someone drive you home. Try to relax and get some rest. I won't forget to call your parents."

Jack shut his cell phone and turned to talk to the officers assembled in the command post. "Amy Tuinstra has been found and is fine." A cheer erupted from the task force along with some tears of joy.

Jack waved his arms to calm everyone down and get them to focus again. "They took Judy Metcalf again, along with Pastor Troutman from the church. One of the three men was left behind after growing a conscience. He apparently tried to help Amy and Judy stay alive. Let's use that to get our hostages back and capture the other two men." He looked over at the men and women in the operation room. "Larry and Sarah, would you please drive down to the church and pick up Amy and take her home?" Both officers nodded and turned to leave after getting a copy of the directions from Jack.

"The rest of us need to be ready to move as soon as the van is located. Okay, let's keep this post open but also get to that church ASAP."

CHAPTER 77

William Benning drove slowly over the back roads as he held on to his last ounce of hope. He knew, even felt, Jimmy was close. His head swiveled back and forth as he watched for any sign of the wounded man.

Jimmy, who had taken shelter behind a large oak tree, saw the familiar car pass by. He rested for a few minutes, held his broken ribs, and took short breaths. The bleeding had clotted over but stung as sweat poured into the wounds.

William's brow furrowed with anxiety as he searched on the left and right. His hands were slick with sweat and his shirt soaked through with the realization of his impending death if he did not find Jimmy.

He wasn't being cautious as he drove. He honked the horn, shouted out the window, drove through the puddles from the recent storm. Every once in a while, he would yell out the window, "Jimmy, I know you're out here. I'm coming for you, Jimmy."

Jimmy kept low, hidden behind the tree. He glanced out just enough to see Benning slowly drive past again. He heard the yell, which had given him enough warning to find a place to hide.

He saw and heard when William turned into the gas station parking lot and got out of the car. It appeared that he walked directly toward the place where Jimmy hid, which wasn't more than a couple hundred yards from the back of the building.

Jimmy prayed quietly. "Please don't let him find me. If he does, he'll kill me. Please, hide me."

A drop of water hit his cheek then another and another. The heavens opened up with a downpour that spread across the region.

"This is awesome." Jimmy's spirit revived from the cloak of the rain. It also refreshed his body as he opened his mouth and drank. Thunder and lightning filled the sky above and drowned out all other noises in the woods.

William Benning turned and ran back to his car. He yelled over his shoulder, "I'll be back, Jimmy. You can count on it. As soon as the rain stops I'll be back. And when I find you I'm going to kill you. Do you hear me, Jimmy? I'm going to kill you." The car door slammed, and he drove off.

A look of relief came across Jimmy's face as he realized what had taken place right before his eyes. He had just witnessed a miracle. "Thank you, God, for hearing my prayer. I intend to keep my promise of turning my life around for you."

Jimmy tried to stand for the first time since the crash. He used the oak as a point of balance. Initially, the pain was intense and he got dizzy and thought he would pass out. He steadied himself and tried to slow his breathing down. It helped him stay upright. Pain coursed through his body like the feeling of being pummeled in a fight. Carefully, he put more weight on his legs until he felt like he could finally support himself.

He stood still and allowed his body to adjust from not being in an upright position in the past twenty-four hours. His equilibrium waned as his head swirled, and he stumbled when he tried to take his first steps. The steps were short as he shuffled and smarted, but he stood and walked forward. In the brush, to his right, he picked up a long, sturdy stick to use as a staff. He kept one hand on his ribs and the other on the staff-turned-crutch and slowly made his way to the telephone at the gas station. The sheets of rain fell harder and harder to the point he could not see anything in front of him.

As he hobbled, he wondered, "Why didn't Benning just wait for me at the gas station?" He contemplated this until he remembered he'd prayed to not be found. His prayer had been answered. "Maybe his eyes were blinded by the rain. And the lightning drove him back to his hideout." Jimmy smiled again and felt he was in much greater hands now. For the first time in his life, he felt comfort.

CHAPTER 78

"Mrs. June Stallings?" The voice came from the other side of the door, accompanied by knocking. "Mrs. Stallings, I'm Harry Nickols from the news team of WOZD-TV. I've been covering the story of the shooting and hostage situation from the Central Station since it began two days ago."

"I know who you are, Mr. Nickols."

"Yeah, I suppose you do," he replied with his head down, eyes cast on the floor. "I've been gathering information about those who were injured, which I know includes your husband. I want you to know how truly sorry I am for Peter."

June barely turned her head to look at Harry, who tried with all his soul to be compassionate and respectful to show her this wasn't an attempt to exploit a victim. He wanted to show this was a genuine attempt to bring attention to the pain that came to people who dealt with loved ones who had been hurt in crimes.

"Peter and I go back a few years." Harry chuckled slightly. "I remember the first time we met. I was covering a story about a minister who had been accused of embezzling thousands of dollars from his church. Peter told me my facts had better be straight or a lot of innocent people would get hurt. I admit I didn't listen to your husband because I wanted to get the story no matter what. I wanted to hang that pastor out to dry." Harry spoke as if he could see every detail happening again right before his eyes.

"The story aired during the evening news broadcast. The next day the minister was acquitted after he proved every cent that had come into the church went directly into the account it was designated to be in. I was sick to my stomach for three days afterward. But I learned from that experience. I learned I had to do more than just cover a story. I had to get the facts right. I had to get to the truth. Your husband taught me that, Mrs. Stallings. I've never forgotten that lesson."

"Mr. Nickols, why do you want to do a story on Peter? All he was doing was his job. He went to cover the news, just like you. What good can possibly come from airing a story about such violence?" Tears of sorrow and anger streamed down June Stallings' face. "I love my husband with all my heart, Mr. Nickols. But, as I sit here hour after agonizing hour, I lose a little more hope that there is really any good left in this world. I wonder how anything good can come out of this terrible, hateful crime to a man who did no wrong to anyone." June wiped the tears from her eyes and blew her nose.

"Do you know Peter has spent his entire life trying to help others? He sometimes gives up his weekends to help people who don't have as much in this world. He helps them fix up their homes, so that when the rain comes they won't be destroyed because of holes in the roof. That's what kind of man I fell in love with, Mr. Nickols." June turned back toward her husband as he lay on the bed still hooked up to life support machines. This time she let the tears fall without wiping them away.

"Mrs. Stallings, I'm sorry for coming here today. Perhaps we can talk at a later time after Peter gets back home." June didn't speak, didn't even look at Harry. She stared into the bandaged face of Peter and wondered what he might feel or think or understand, if anything at all.

She knew Harry Nickols had snooped around asking questions about what had happened to Peter and his current condition. Pastor Thompson told her he had shown up at the church asking questions there. Al Tuinstra also told her he had called the station trying to get information from the staff. Both men assured her no information had been shared and none would be unless it came straight from June.

She wondered what Peter would do in Harry's position. Peter always hated to meet with a family already torn apart by some tragedy only to ask them questions like "What are you feeling right now?" or "Can you tell us what happened?" Questions that only made the people feel worse than they already did. But for the sake of his job he would do it. June remembered how he would never go to or leave a family without saying a silent prayer for them.

"By the way, Mrs. Stallings." Harry's voice startled her, and she jumped slightly. "I went to the service at Eastside Baptist Church last night. I haven't been to church in quite a few years, well, other than to accuse that pastor of wrongdoing. I have to say the sermon touched my heart. Do you think Peter would mind if a rival reporter were to join him in worship?"

June gave a tight-lipped smile, "No, Harry, I don't think my husband or I would mind if you joined us for that. In fact, we would both be honored to have you with us."

"Great. I'll be praying for you and Peter. You should get some rest soon. It'll do you some good."

"Have you been talking to the doctors?" They both smiled as Harry left the room, headed back to his beat, looking for a story.

CHAPTER 79

"Our time grows even shorter, John Robertson. You must return to your physical body soon. It is also time for you to ask questions that are of the utmost importance." Pithel placed a strong hand on John's shoulder. "You must be aware that my Lord is patient with his creation. Yet he will allow you to make your own choice. He is a fair and loving God. He is also a jealous God, for he wishes to have you only for himself. Can you understand this, John Robertson?"

John nodded his head in understanding. "I've had a question I've thought about long before I met you, Pithel. It has plagued me and haunted me for such a long time I can't even remember a time when I didn't think about it. My pride kept me from searching out the truth. Imagine, me, a reporter whose job it is to find answers to tough questions, refusing to find what I'm looking for. Since I've been talking with you the question seems to have grown bigger and more urgent. You wouldn't know how that happens, would you?"

Pithel shrugged his massive shoulders and said, "I know the Almighty God can recall anything to your memory, even memories from the earliest days of your life. For him to bring a question to your memory I would not think to be very difficult. May I ask what might this question be, John Robertson?"

"I don't know quite how to ask it." He looked across the vast expanse of heaven then focused on the wall with the gates of pearl. "When you speak of Jesus, you speak as if he can love anyone. Can you tell me how that's possible when there are people who literally curse his name and hate him? Can Jesus really love people like that? If so, how? That's my question, Pithel."

"My friend, that is the greatest question you can ask, especially to one of his angels. It is one I answer with great joy." Pithel positioned himself to be able to look John in the face. "I must start at the beginning in order for you to fully understand how Jesus loves people, loves you. When God created man to walk the earth, he created him to praise him. As you and I know that doesn't happen very often. Man began to rebel against God almost from the beginning of the creation of the earth. They have continued rebelling more and more throughout the centuries."

Pithel stared back into history. "There was a time when God destroyed the earth with a flood because of man's terrible lifestyle. He kept one man, Noah, and his family safe, since they were the only righteous people on the face of the earth at the time. Soon after the flood, the earth began to be replenished with people; the same thing began to happen again. Humans did not want to follow after God. It was a sad time to be on the earth, John Robertson. It had been foretold that a Savior would come to save the world from their sins in the years to come. Do you know who that might be, John Robertson?"

"Yes, Pithel, that I know. It was Jesus."

"Yes. Come, journey with me."

John found himself in a field outside a city that looked familiar. "Is that Jerusalem?"

"Yes." The angel continued with the story. "Jesus came to earth in a most miraculous way, through a virgin birth. That has not and will not happen again, ever. Through his years on the earth Jesus performed many miracles, and it would take all of eternity to tell you every one of them. He healed the sick, gave sight to the blind, and hearing to the deaf. He also made the lame to walk, and fed five thousand people with only five small loaves of bread and two small fish. Those were just a few of his miracles. He also raised people from the dead." Pithel smiled as he looked over to John and asked, "Would you like me to continue with the list of miracles?"

John shook his head no.

Pithel became serious again, "Jesus loved being so close to his people, his creation. But there were also evil men who walked with him and tried to make trouble for those who chose to follow him. They tried hard to stop Jesus from doing the miracles, but each time they tried more people would follow Him."

They now stood inside a hall where they witnessed a man being beaten. "They finally decided they had to have Jesus killed. Those men brought him here." John immediately recognized the man being beaten. He saw the crown of thorns on his head and the soldiers hitting him. John's face wrenched in agony as the soldiers whipped him to the point of the flesh being torn off of his body. John was sure Jesus looked straight at him as he took the beating.

Pithel continued, "I tell you, John Robertson, this was the most difficult time in my existence. The entire army of heaven stood by, waiting for Jesus to call us. Each of us had our swords drawn ready to fight." Pithel clenched his fists, unable to speak. "He never called. He just took the pain."

Pithel touched John's shoulder as they left the hall.

"I'm glad we don't have to see that anymore." John's voice cracked.

They now stood on a hill just outside of the city. Crowds lined the streets as if a parade would be coming by shortly. Cheers erupted from some distance away, the sound carrying all the way to the top of the hill. Soon a band of soldiers marched up with a man who stumbled between them. "That is my Lord." Pithel pointed at the man in the middle. Another man struggled to carry a large cross walked next to Jesus.

"That can't be him. He looks nothing like the man we just saw."

John watched as the soldiers pounded nails into the hands and feet of Jesus. The cross was lifted and dropped into the hole that jarred the already broken body. John heard a moan.

"That, John Robertson, is the King of Kings hanging there. It was then that we, the angels, realized the men weren't taking his life. It was him giving his life to save his creation. He sacrificed himself for the sins of man." They stood silent as Jesus struggled to breathe. The crowd mocked him. John heard him say something about forgiving these people just before his head dropped with his final breath.

"Did he really just forgive these people for killing him?"

"That is the love Jesus has for his people, John Robertson."

"So what happened after he died?"

"His body was put into a tomb and sealed along with guards standing by. Three days later, he did what he had told people he would do. Do you know what that was, John Robertson?"

"You mean, the resurrection?"

"Exactly." Pithel slapped John on the back. "Now that was something to behold."

"But why did Jesus go through all of this, Pithel?"

"For you, John Robertson. Did he not make eye contact with you back in the judgment hall as he was being beaten?"

"You mean to tell me he actually was looking at me?"

"Yes, and then he died on that cross for you. It is his gift of eternal life he gives to you."

John's face went slack as he again saw Jesus look into his soul. His eyes didn't judge, didn't condemn, didn't accuse; he just looked at John with love.

CHAPTER 80

In the past two days, Harry Nickols had called Pastor Joseph Thompson at least a dozen times with questions about Christianity. The pastor asked him if his questions had anything to do with his story.

Harry could only laugh, "No, sir, I assure you these questions are genuine, sincere, and only for me. I need to know more about what you talked about at the service the other night."

Pastor Thompson let silence fill the phone line. This was a ploy he'd developed to see how serious people were.

"Come on, Pastor, you know that when a reporter gets on to something they have to get all the facts. That's just basic good journalism. And as a reporter, I have the responsibility to myself and to my readers to get my facts straight. Now, I know this isn't a story yet, but I still need, or should I say, I *want* the facts for myself. I'm a changed man Pastor Thompson."

"Yes, Harry, I can hear it in your voice that you have found the true meaning of life. You have found peace with God." Pastor Thompson's voice turned serious. "Harry, I must warn you; Satan is now going to come after you. He's not happy with your decision to follow Christ. I must advise you to pray, read the Bible, and find a study group where you learn about God and get the support you're going to need. And above all else, keep your eyes on God and not on man, not even on me. Man will fail you every time, Harry, but God- he will never fail you. Never."

"Yeah, I hear what you're saying. This morning I found myself going after a story I knew could have hurt a lot of people over a very small crime. I went to the scene and had actually started writing down all the information I needed. Then I looked over my shoulder and saw the mother of the young boy who had been arrested only moments before. I actually began to get emotional, pastor. Me, Harry Nickols, the toughest reporter on the beat, crying. I'll tell you this much; I'm ruined as a reporter." Although on the phone, Harry threw his arms in the air.

"Anyway, I went over to the mother and began to talk to her. I found myself not talking about the story but about how God knows about what she's been going through and that he loves her very much. At first she looked at me like I was crazy. She had this puzzled look on her face. But then she smiled at me and told me she needed to hear that today. I've never felt such joy in my whole life." He swallowed hard after getting a lump in his throat. "I think she's going to come to church this Sunday. Isn't that great?"

"That's wonderful, Harry. Listen, while you're working today, would you remember to pray for Peter, John, and Judy? The police just got a lead and Jack McDougal called, asking me to pray for them and the officers. He also told me- (and this is off the record Harry) –that Amy has been found safe. I pray that Judy is okay. Will you pray for them?"

"You don't have to ask me twice, Pastor. I'm already there. And I won't say a word about Amy until I hear from either you or hear it on the scanner."

CHAPTER 81

In the kingdom of heaven, prayers for Peter, John, and Judy bombarded the throne. The voice of the Holy Spirit also brought forward the petitions as saints prayed for those in desperate need of God's help. The music from the orchestra and choir never ceased to give praise and worship to the Almighty God. Angels circled above as the white-robed elders bowed their faces before the throne. On the throne, God accepted the praise offered to him as well as the prayers of his children on earth.

Suddenly, a large explosion of thunder rang out across the kingdom as the call went out to the army of angels. Throughout the universe, mighty warriors appeared outside the throne room. Over ten thousand stood at attention as others made their way from wherever they had been ministering. Each warrior's sword was drawn ready for any battle their Lord asked them to fight.

Historically, one warrior alone could easily wipe out an entire army on the earth. To have ten thousand of the Almighty's warriors assembled was a sight to behold. No one questioned what kind of battle would require the entire army of God. They already knew.

The door to the throne room opened, and an enormous angel stepped through the doorway. Although dressed similarly to the army before him, he stood larger than the host. He stepped up on a platform of solid gold and addressed the assembled mass. "My friends, the Almighty has called us to battle."

A battle cry erupted from the warriors. The sound was like the power of a mighty rushing waterfall. Their leader waved his arms to quiet them down. "Our King sends us to battle the forces of evil that, even as I speak, have launched a fierce attack on his saints and on heaven itself. We are to protect and deliver them safely out of the hands of Satan. Those we are to protect this day are Amy Tuinstra, Pastor Bob Troutman, and Judy Metcalf."

The warriors stood poised for the battle. Each leaned forward, clenching their sword.

"As you already know, a few moments ago Judy Metcalf accepted the love of Jesus. She is now a saint."

Cheers of victory rose from the warriors.

"Prepare for battle." The leader brought the legions of angels to attention. All swords were raised high in the air. They stood ready to fight for the cause of Christ and for the saints they have been called to protect.

Jareb and Pithel made their way forward. They climbed the steps of the platform and stood next to their leader. He turned to them and asked if they had anything to say to the army before the battle began. Pithel stood speechless as he looked at his fellow warriors before him, his friends. He shook his head. Jareb, however, nodded and stepped forward.

"My friends, I come before you urging you to be swift about the business the Lord has given us to do. These saints we have been assigned to encourage are anxious to see a victory over Satan this day. As for those refusing to bow their knee to the Almighty, they have made their choice. To those mortals who still have the opportunity to find Jesus the Christ as their Savior, have mercy."

Cheers from the army resounded throughout the Kingdom, as their swords continued to wave high in the air.

"Victory for the Almighty God." The angels roared as they repeated the words Jareb had just spoken to them. Jareb stepped back humbly and allowed the captain of the guard to call for the battle trumpet to sound.

One trumpet could be heard above the angels. The signal told them the time had come to fight. The sound continued as the whole host turned and flew away to meet the enemy. Pithel and Jareb stood together on the golden platform and prayed for a victory this day.

"May God give them strength," Pithel quietly said. Within the blink of an eye, the entire army had gone. Pithel turned to Jareb. "I will see you again very soon, my friend," Pithel said.

"Yes, and with a great victory for the love of God."

Before they left the heavenly realm, thunder summoned them to the throne room. They immediately turned without question, entered the vast hall, and bowed before their Master.

Pithel and Jareb joined the praises being raised and added their own adoration to their Master. "Bless you, Father God, Creator of all that is. You are the Almighty King of all the Ages. There is none above you. We gladly serve you with all of our hearts and with all the strength that comes from you. All praise to God."

As the music continued, thunder and lightning proceeded from the throne to inform Pithel and Jareb that their assignments were not yet complete. They were reminded Satan still worked and would not stop until he got a victory. The battle for the soul of John Robertson had only just begun. It would be a very difficult task to complete.

The thunder and lightning ended, and the angels stood, heads bowed toward the ground as they turned to leave. After they left the room, they turned to each other and offered blessings so that God would gain the victory in this battle.

"We must not fail the Lord." Jareb's passion spilled out of his soul as he pounded his fist into his hand. "We must do our utmost to secure the victory for our Master."

"I agree, my brother," Pithel replied. "Satan will not have the soul of John Robertson. We will become stronger as the saints continue to pray for him and for protection from the evil one." He bowed his head for a moment and then said, "I must get back to John Robertson's side. He is close to giving his life to Christ, and I do not wish for Satan to turn his heart away while I am here. Pray, Jareb, pray for his soul. Ask Peter Stallings to pray for the soul of John Robertson as well. Satan will concentrate his entire army on John Robertson since he has lost the battle for Judy Metcalf. Praise to God for that victory."

"I will pray, and I will also urge Peter to pray as well. God is with you." They shook hands before they left to complete their missions.

Pithel wanted to be on the front line against the demons and looked for any to stray too close to where he protected John Robertson. Jareb did not want to confront the enemy but still wanted a victory. Both, however, would fight for the souls of John Robertson and Peter Stallings.

CHAPTER 82

"Am I excited? I'm beyond excited. I'm ecstatic, amazed, and yet humbled." Peter danced around in celebration. "To be able to witness Judy accepting Christ, from the spiritual side no less, is so very incredible. I've never felt such jubilation in all of my life. I don't have the words to express how I feel."

Jareb had just returned from the rally. He filled Peter in about the entire host of angelic warriors and his meeting with the Almighty God.

"That had to be one amazing sight to see."

"Indeed it was, my friend. As amazing as seeing my fellow warriors banded together ready to fight, was watching your friend, Judy, become a new creation."

Peter contemplated being able to witness Judy accept Jesus while being held captive in the back of the van. With a smile on his face, tears of joy flowed down his cheeks.

Peter turned to the angel and asked, "Jareb, can we check on June and the hospital staff? With all the excitement, things must be going crazy."

The angel nodded and instantly they were at the hospital.

Staff ran in and out of the room, each on a mission. Pandemonium filled the ICU as every machine sounded alarms. No one could figure out what was going on.

"Check those lines again. Make sure they're all attached properly," Dr. Howard ordered a nearby nurse.

She checked them. "Everything is secure and working fine."

Dr. Howard finished getting the vital signs and listened to Peter's heart. He found nothing wrong. "This is so bizarre. In all my years, I've never had a patient have all the machines go haywire so often and not find anything wrong. It's truly amazing." He ran a hand through his hair and blew the air out of his lungs.

As soon as he finished the exam, all the machines went back to normal readings. The nurses hadn't touched anything in the room or given Peter any medication.

"I think we just witnessed a miracle," exclaimed the doctor.

———————◆———————

June sat in the corner of the room as Peter looked at her with bewilderment. Dark circles surrounded her eyes as the lack of sleep took its toll. Still, she tried her best to stand strong.

"Jareb, let's pray for June. She needs to get some rest. She's exhausted. And she's stubborn enough to not leave until she knows I'm going to be all right."

"I would be honored to pray with you."

They prayed for peace and rest to come to June Stallings while in his hospital room. As they prayed other angels who had other missions at the hospital joined in. When they completed their prayer, the group praised God for his mighty works and for his love. Peter looked back at June, who slumped in a chair in a deep sleep.

"Praise be to the great and glorious Almighty God." Peter proclaimed. "I love this prayer thing."

"Amen," came the unions reply from the angels.

After a few more moments of praise and worship, the angels made their way back to their posts. Peter and Jareb left for the next portion of their journey.

CHAPTER 83

William Benning had not yet given up his search for Jimmy Morten, especially knowing what was on the line for him if he failed. He searched the roads again as he drove up and down the highways, dirt roads, and two track paths made for the four-wheel drive vehicles. His Lincoln bounced around in all the ruts. He scolded himself for killing his two former employees too early, leaving him to search alone. Additionally, his nerves were shot as he could not find any trace whatsoever of Jimmy.

"Where can he possibly be? There's no way he should've survived that crash. He hit the tree head-on for heaven's sake," William muttered to himself as he searched. He thought of all kinds of crazy scenarios about where Jimmy might be. "Where are you, Re, god of the sun? Why have you deserted me? I need you to point me in the direction of Jimmy Morten. Show me the way to him, and I will give you anything you desire."

His Lincoln moved slowly, but he never caught a glimpse of Jimmy. Mile after mile, road after road, his search continued. William Benning's shoulders slumped and his chin fell to his chest as he finally came to the conclusion he would never find Jimmy. After two hours, he turned the automobile around and went back to the old house.

———◆———

Jimmy managed to make it to within a football field of the gas station. The staff he leaned on helped. His hands and knees throbbed and bled from the crash and the crawling. He managed to stay out of sight hidden in the woods. He had put some leaves and sticks in his shirt to act as camouflage.

When the rain stopped, the humidity level increased, which made it even more difficult to breathe. All the while he kept his eyes on the phone at the gas station. As he moved forward, he looked in all directions for the sound of William Benning's car approaching.

He never noticed the large figure beside him. The angel had appeared the moment he asked God for help. The more he prayed, the more strength and help he obtained from the angelic guard beside him. The camouflage he used wasn't too effective. With the help of Obed, the angel, however, the disguise had worked to perfection. William Benning had driven by him at least three times without once seeing him.

Jimmy stopped to rest against a boulder just fifty feet from the gas station. "One last burst of energy is all I need." He tried to push himself off the rock with the assistance of his staff. "I hope that telephone works. And I hope I can tell the police where I am." Exhaustion overtook him as he slumped back against the rock and slid to the ground. He shut his eyes and fell into a deep sleep.

As he slept, he dreamed about God talking to him. "Jimmy, I have a mission for you. I need you to serve me."

"But how can I serve you when I've been so terrible all my life?"

"You are a new creature now. You are no longer the same person you were a few hours ago. You have been given another opportunity to live and to serve me because you have accepted my Son, Jesus, into your life. I do not remember what you did before this time, Jimmy."

"You mean I'm a good person in your eyes? I didn't kill all those people earlier?"

"Yes, Jimmy, you are a good person in my eyes. You did commit crimes for which you will have to pay. But know this, you are now saved under the blood of Jesus Christ and you will live with me forever. Are you willing to serve me with the rest of your life, Jimmy Morten?"

"Yes, I'm willing to do whatever you ask me to do. I'll serve you for the rest of my life. I freely give my life to you."

"Then, Jimmy, the task I have for you is this: I need you to tell William Benning about me as you have found me. I need you to tell William that, he too, can find true life through the blood of Jesus Christ. The task I give to you is not easy. William Benning is a very hard man who will not be easily persuaded to believe what you have to say about me. I will give you the words to say to him and the power to overcome if you will trust in me."

Jimmy struggled to wrap his mind around the job God wanted him to do. Suddenly, he was surrounded by creatures who praised God. Music filled the air from an orchestra and choir.

Jimmy never considered himself to have any musical ability. In fact, he considered himself to be a terrible singer, but he felt compelled to join in. He lifted his voice and sang along with the angels.

"Glory to your name, oh Lord. Holy and Just. Worthy and Mighty. I lift my praise to you. I serve you because I love you so very much. . ." sang the choir.

He had no idea where the words came from but knew they felt right to be saying. For the first time in his life Jimmy had a sense of real peace, even knowing he would need to pay for his crimes, knowing it could mean life in prison or even the death penalty. Knowing this kind of peace allowed him to accept his fate in this life.

Being able to join in singing, to see those amazing creatures flying around, and to hear those men in the white robes praise to God gave Jimmy a warm feeling in his soul. He sensed he belonged and would be accepted here. It was the missing piece that filled the hole in his soul which had eluded him for most of his life.

He grew up in a home where his father would often come home drunk and would either beat up him or his mother. His mother always tried to be strong by putting her faith in God even when her husband wouldn't allow her to even go to church. Jimmy would find her sobbing somewhere in the small house, praying for God to help her find strength to get through it all.

He would try to comfort her by telling her that everything would be okay. She would force a smile through her tears and give her little Jimmy a hug and a kiss. Then she would thank God for giving her some more strength. Jimmy never understood why she said that until this very moment.

He finally understood that his comforting her gave her the needed strength. The realization of what he had accomplished with his mother caused Jimmy to thank God for being so gracious to his mother. His mother had died almost ten years ago from what the doctors said was "just too much stress for one person to handle." Today, he had been able to let go of his anger towards his dad for leaving and beating his mother and also his anger towards God for taking his mother away from him.

Jimmy woke up from his sleep refreshed yet still in pain. He felt ready to finish the task he had set out to do. He stood with the makeshift crutch and hobbled toward the gas station. One hand held the staff which was propped under his arm as he pulled himself forward one painful step at a time. The other hand held on to his rib cage.

CHAPTER 84

"What will really happen to those who refuse to believe in Jesus?" John asked. The question immediately brought a look of sorrow to the massive angel's eyes.

"There really is a hell, John Robertson, and it is truly going to be eternal death for those who will not accept the Savior's love. Let me tell you a story if you will allow me to."

"Please do," John said with a roll of his hand and a slight nod of his head.

"There was a rich man who had everything: fine food, fine clothing, and many people to share his wealth with. He was a very shrewd businessman in the trade market. He had made a name for himself throughout the region of Israel, between Jerusalem and Samaria. Yet he never gave God glory for all his wealth, not even one time.

"Outside the gate of his home, a beggar man sat, named Lazarus. Lazarus never had anything in the world. His parents abandoned him when he was young, and he learned to survive on his own. There were many days and nights he went hungry and cold, hoping the rich man might give him the crumbs from his table. Due to his exposure to the cold nights and the hot days, along with the rain, snow, and wind, he ended up with sores all over his body, which the dogs would come by and lick.

"Soon the time came for both the rich man and Lazarus to die. When they did, Lazarus was carried into paradise by my friend Jareb and me. When he arrived, he had comfort he never had in his life along with perfect peace and health. It was a wonderful beginning to his eternal life. Meanwhile, the rich man opened his eyes and found himself in torment from the fires of hell. It burned and tortured him, but his flesh did not burn off. From where he was he could see Lazarus off in the distance in comfort. He yelled to him asking him to dip his finger in water to cool his tongue because the flames were so very hot.

"Father Abraham, the father of Israel, sat by Lazarus when he arrived in paradise. He spoke to the rich man, telling him that when he was alive on earth he had everything while Lazarus had nothing. But now Lazarus had peace and comfort while the rich man had torment. Then the rich man asked to have Lazarus go tell his brothers about hell, but again Abraham spoke to him. He told him that his brothers had the prophets to tell them about hell and heaven and if they wouldn't hear them, they wouldn't believe Lazarus even if he came back from the dead."

John sat still, his face filled with shock. "Why would God, who is loving and merciful and gracious, allow someone to die and go to hell?"

"It is not my Master's desire for anyone to perish in the fires of hell. That is a choice not even the Almighty God can make. That choice is up to each person to decide. His invitation goes out to all to accept his Son as savior. Sadly there will be many who will perish. God still loves them very much, but he has set the law and he will follow the law to the letter. He must do that."

Pithel stared deep into John's eyes, "John Robertson, I can see that you are troubled upon hearing this story."

"Yeah, I guess I am," he replied.

"You know you do not have to spend eternity in the torments of hell. You can spend eternity in the peace and beauty and love of God. All you must do is accept him as your Savior."

Of all the stories Pithel had told, none had more impact than what he said next. "Know this, John Robertson, only you can ask him into your heart. I cannot do that for you, nor can anyone else. It is a decision each human must make for themselves. It is also a decision that can be made only while you live on earth. Once you die, the opportunity to accept his love dies, too. Do not delay, for time is not your friend. The Scriptures state, 'It is appointed to man to die once.' No one knows when that time will be.

"Remember your news broadcasts as an example, John Robertson. Do you remember all the different people you report as having passed away, from infants to the aged? Do you remember how we spoke about those innocent babies who are killed each day? They are now safe in the loving arms of Jesus. You can make sure you too are one of those."

Pithel ended with, "John Robertson, our time has come to an end. In moments you will be back in your physical body. You will then have the opportunity to make your choice of whether to accept or to refuse the love of Jesus which we have spoken about today."

CHAPTER 85

The van sped up once they reached a paved highway. Tom drove for the first time since the entire ordeal began two days earlier. Billy sat relieved, exhausted, with his arm broken. Tom spoke every once in a while, mainly to stay awake. Billy dozed in and out depending on which way the van veered. Eventually, he fell into a deep sleep. He snored loud enough to occasionally make Tom's skin crawl each time he hit the crescendo of his snore. Judy Metcalf and Pastor Troutman remained tied up in the back both wide awake, talking quietly.

"Pastor, what happens next? I mean, since I've accepted Jesus into my life, what am I supposed to do?" Judy asked.

"Well, Judy, the Bible states that the first thing you should to do is to be baptized. Do you know what that means; to be baptized?"

"Sort of, I guess," Judy wasn't comfortable not knowing the answer. "No, I don't know what that means."

"That's okay, not too many people know right away. I suppose that's a good reason to have us old preachers around." Pastor Troutman chuckled. "To be baptized means you are willing to show the world that you have accepted Christ as your Savior. It's a picture of what he did for you and that you believe and have accepted it for yourself. The picture is this: Jesus died on a cross, his death. Then Jesus was placed in a tomb, his burial. This was followed by Jesus being raised from the dead, his resurrection. Baptism is also an act of obedience to Christ, since he commanded that we be first saved then baptized."

"Okay, so I need to be baptized. I'll be glad to do that if we get out of here. But what if they kill us and we never get out of here and I can't get baptized?" Judy's voice filled with concern as she asked the pastor that question.

Tom had elbowed Billy awake as he listened to the conversation behind him. They listened to Judy's question and then the answer.

"Well, Judy, you don't need to worry. Let me share what Jesus did even while he hung on the cross." He glanced toward the front and saw the two men's heads craned to hear. "When Jesus died, he didn't die alone. Two other men were also condemned to die at the same time. I'm sure you have seen pictures of the crucifixion with Jesus hanging in the middle and men on both sides of him."

Judy nodded her head.

"Jesus had done nothing wrong other than to do miracles and love people. The two men were both hardened criminals who according to the law back then, deserved to die. Both men looked at Jesus. One man screamed and yelled for Jesus to rescue them from their crosses. He was actually just mocking and cursing him like everyone else. The man on the other side of Jesus yelled, too, only his words was different. He asked Jesus to remember him when he went into his kingdom. Do you know what Jesus did even while he was dying, Judy?"

Judy shook her head and said, "No, what did he do?" Tom and Billy leaned back as they waited to hear the answer.

"He turned to the man and said, 'Today you will be with me in paradise.' That to me is amazing. Even while dying, he forgave any who would ask, even the condemned man next to him. That man didn't have the opportunity to get baptized; he could only die with him. You see, salvation doesn't hinge on baptism. Baptism is an obedient act symbolizing you are a true follower of Christ. If we die right here in the back of this van, we are still going to be with Jesus forever because he has saved us."

Pastor Troutman had looked forward at the men up front. "I just pray that those two up there would also accept Christ. We should pray for them, Judy."

Judy didn't understand why but nodded her head and agreed with the pastor.

Tom hollered back, "We don't need no religion especially from an old time country preacher like you. I think it's time you both hush up for a while. No more talking or maybe you *will* die in the back of the van."

As Tom barked at their hostages, Billy laughed.

CHAPTER 86

Jareb told Peter, "There is one more thing you need to see before our time is over." Peter found himself back in the food court in the mall where Paul had been with his friends. It was getting late and Peter didn't understand what Paul was doing with these guys. Two other men, one tall and thin, the other a muscular man, approached Paul.

"Hey, kid, what's up?" The tall, darkly dressed man asked. "You looking for something, you know, to take your mind off things?"

Paul became nervous as he tried to get out of the man's way. "N-no I was just, I mean, I don't know. I have to go."

"What's the hurry, my man? We got plenty of time. We're just getting to know each other, aren't we? Come on, why don't you get to know me a little? You'll see that I'm a very nice person. I've got connections."

"Please let me go. I have to go visit my dad in the hospital."

"Yeah, right," the man said. "No, I think you're going to stay here and get acquainted with me for a while. Guys, come over here and get to know. . . I'm sorry, I didn't get your name."

"It's Paul," he replied as he trembled. "L-look I have to go. Can't we do this some other time?"

"I think now is as good time as any, don't you think? Have a seat right over there while I get some things ready, something to steady your nerves. I think you'll like this, Paul."

———◆———

"Jareb, please help me protect my son. He's so young and alone and vulnerable. I know I haven't always been around for him because of work, but I love him with all my heart. I'd never be able to forgive myself if anything happened to him. Please, I must pray for his protection."

Jareb nodded his head, "Yes Peter, pray. You must always pray." Jareb joined Peter in prayer for the protection of Paul. While they prayed, a mighty angelic warrior appeared behind Paul, ready to fight the forces of Satan should any attempt to attack.

As the mighty warrior stood ready, Jareb spoke to Peter, "The Father has given your son the protection he needs. Your son, however, must choose for himself what he will do in this battle. All the forces of heaven and hell combined cannot make any choices for any human. The choice your son makes tonight may determine the rest of his life's journey."

They stood and watched the scene with the angel next to Paul.

Jareb stated, "Please do not misunderstand, Peter. Your son has accepted Christ and that can never be taken away. He may still make the choice to not live his life for God. He would not be able to receive the rewards the Father has for those who have served him faithfully. We must pray that your son makes the right decision tonight."

Peter prayed passionately to God the Father for Paul to make the right choice.

As the tall, thin man turned to get his drugs ready, Paul made a quick dash across the food court and exited through a side door that led into an alley. Paul knew the back alleys from running there many times, but never to save his life. Panic began to fill his mind as he thought he heard a door crash open.

He stepped into the doorway of an old abandoned building halfway between the mall and home. He listened for footsteps. When he didn't hear anything, he crept out of the door and headed home.

The rest of the way he stayed close to the buildings to stay in the shadows. Ten minutes later, he fumbled with the house key but managed to open the door. He felt safe at home now that he had locked the door and turned off the lights.

Although no one appeared to have followed him, he didn't want to take any chances. He sat in the darkness, scared and shaking, and thought about his dad in the hospital dying while his mother sat next to him. He loved his parents but had never really felt close to them. He had always wanted to be independent and thought of as cool to his friends.

For Paul, however, independence had suddenly taken on a different meaning. He began to realize how much he relied on his parents, for everything from love and care, to food, clothing and shelter. In the quiet of the dark, empty house, Paul prayed to be forgiven of his selfishness and foolishness toward his parents.

He wasn't sure what his future held, but for now he felt content to be at home safe with his parents. He determined to follow the house rules even when he didn't agree with them. He also realized he had to share things like the incident at the mall tonight. "I promise not to shut you out of my life anymore."

As he sat, his heart slowed and he breathed normally again. His thoughts cleared and he relaxed. He found a sense of direction for his life that had not been there before. With the help of God and his parents, he would strive to keep these things he promised to himself.

Tentatively, he stood and went to his bedroom. Clothes were strewn about and some strange posters hung on the walls. He crawled into a pile of clothes and fell asleep.

CHAPTER 87

Knots formed in Jack's stomach as he crested the hill and saw the steeple in the little village called Wells Creek with the investigative team. He kept the hope alive of finding Judy soon and unharmed. He also prayed for the well-being of the others who had been held hostage.

The officers promptly arrested Allen, placing him in handcuffs and setting him in the back of the church guarded by two officers. Allen agreed to cooperate with Jack partly because his friends left him and, to some extent, because during the time he had spent with the small congregation he realized he had done wrong.

The officers interrogated Allen about his accomplices, where they were headed, what kinds of weapons they carried, and what their plans might be for the current hostages. They also asked him about who else might be involved or who they worked for. Allen told them everything he could remember.

While the officers questioned Allen, Jack talked to Amy about the state of Judy's and the pastor's health. "First, I want to make sure you're okay," Jack said. He knew he showed more concern for Judy than for Amy. He hoped Amy would understand. "Are you hurt at all? Did they hit or assault you or do anything to cause you any harm?"

Amy's mind swirled around the long question before she answered, "Like I said, I'm fine. Billy tried to hit me a couple of times, but never did. I'm sure it was my guardian angel protecting me. I would like to say that he," she pointed in Allen's direction, "did his best to protect us from the other two. I just thought you should know that."

"I'm very relieved to know you're not hurt, Amy. And I'll be sure to put what you told me about what Allen did in my report. Now if you could tell me what happened when Judy and the pastor were taken, I'd really appreciate it."

"Tom took Judy and Pastor Troutman out of the building while Billy tied us up and then hit Allen. All I know is both, Judy and the pastor were in good health when they left. They didn't hit them or anything, if that's what you're asking."

"I was about to ask."

"I'm sure Judy still has bumps and bruises from getting hit and all the rolling around in the back of the van. Oh, they did tie their hands behind their backs, but they walked out of the church on their own."

"Did they happen to say where they might be going, a direction, a name, a place, anything like that?" Jack raised a finger for every option as he asked the question.

"No, not that I can think of," Amy said. "Allen might know, though. They didn't talk about their plans too much. It almost sounded like they didn't have a plan. We only heard their names an hour or so before they left us beside the road. Their names are Allen, of course, Tom, and Billy. We never heard their last names."

Jack wrote down the names. Then he asked, "Were you able to see which way they went after they left the building?"

"No, I had my back to the door and couldn't see anything outside. Maybe some of the other people here who faced the door might have seen something." She looked at the people, but couldn't remember which ones had faced the door.

"Thanks, Amy," Jack said. He took out his cell phone. "Why don't you give your parents a call? I know they're worried, and I promised that as soon as we got here they would be notified. I would hate for them to think that I didn't keep my word."

Amy smiled as she accepted the phone and dialed her parents. Jack walked over to see if he could get some information from the other church members, allowing Amy to talk to her parents as privately as possible.

CHAPTER 88

Peter and Jareb talked about heaven and how beautiful and peaceful and perfect everything seemed to be.

"I'm on the outside and from here I can't think of any words to describe this place. There's no comparison to anything on earth. It would be like trying to put the Grand Canyon and the Alps together with the works of Michelangelo and the music of Beethoven all in one place. It would pale in comparison to this." Peter waved his arm as he spoke. "I really can't wait to see what's inside. Do you think I could get a peek?"

Jareb didn't answer the question. "It has truly been an honor to be with you these few moments of time. I trust you have found our God to be majestic, full of love and mercy. He wants you to serve him with all your heart and all your soul and all your might. Hold nothing back from the Lord, Peter, and he will bless you more than you can ever understand."

"Jareb, my friend, will I ever see you again before I come into the Kingdom?"

"The Almighty has not revealed that to me. But be of comfort, he will allow me to check on you every once in a while. And I am sure to see you in the very near future."

"You mean like a day being a thousand years, kind of in the future, right?"

"Yes, my brother."

Jareb prepared Peter to return to his physical body and resume his life on earth. The time for his departure from the wall of heaven had arrived. He spoke to Peter, not in a voice saddened by the loss of a friend, but for the sake of the departure. "It is time for you to return, Peter. We have completed our mission the Almighty God has brought you through."

Jareb looked into Peter's soul as he stated, "I have one final thought for you. The things you have seen and heard while here have been given to you to strengthen your faith with the Lord. It is his desire for you take this knowledge and use it for his purpose. Do not forget what Jesus spoke to his disciples while he walked the earth, 'Blessed are those who have not seen and yet they believe.' You have now had a glimpse of what heaven is like and you have felt the great love of God. Believe it and share it. Do not keep it for yourself, but give it away to those around you. And above all else, serve the Lord your God with gladness in your heart."

Jareb embraced Peter. "The Lord will be with you, my brother."

Jareb was gone.

———◆———

The white van turned down the long, two-track driveway that led to the old house where William Benning lived. Potholes, now mud holes, made the journey treacherous as the van bounced up and down over the narrow pathway.

"Isn't that Jimmy's pickup truck?" Billy pointed at the truck wrapped around the tree. "I wonder what happened to him."

"I don't know," Tom answered in a quiet tone with a trace of fear. "Something ain't right. Benning better have an explanation of what's going on or there just might be another accident."

"Poor Jimmy." Billy stared at the wrecked truck.

"Let's go find out what Benning's plan is. Then we can come back here and take a closer look at that pile of junk."

Tom maneuvered around the bed of the pickup truck, which stuck out in the road, in order to get to the house. Closer to the house, they recognized William Benning as he put a box into the back seat of his car. Tom drove the van right up behind the black luxury sedan to block it in.

"Time to find out what old Benning is up to," Tom said through clenched teeth. He pushed the door open and slammed it shut. The van rocked back and forth. Billy had to be gentler due to his broken arm.

———◆———

Pastor Troutman and Judy stayed quiet in the back as Tom and Billy walked up to the house. "I should be able to get loose soon, Pastor Troutman," Judy said, as the cord she had been working on began to slacken. "Then we'll find a way out of here."

"I'll keep an eye on our hosts."

Judy and the pastor heard voices yelling from inside the house. They couldn't make out the words, but it was clear neither side would give in. Judy worked feverishly to free herself from the cords.

Pastor Troutman worked on his own cords as he watched the back door of the house. He prayed for deliverance, strength, and a miracle.

———◆◆———

Inside the house, Benning argued, "You shouldn't have come here. That was the agreement. You were to complete your mission at the bus station. At that point, you should've gone into hiding for a month. It's been less than two days." His face softened for a moment as he continued. "You must go at once. It isn't safe for you to be here with me right now."

"Yeah, well you better get used to us being around, Benning, 'cause we ain't going nowhere." Tom's face reddened with anger. The veins in his neck tensed with each word he spoke. "Wherever you go, we go, too. So unless you explain what's going on here, we're going to become really close friends from here on in. Your choice."

"Okay, okay. Let's go into the parlor and sit down. I need to get some tea and then I'll tell you exactly what is going on with Anti-Pro." He directed them through the door and into the parlor. "This way, gentlemen."

CHAPTER 89

"My friend, our time has now come to an end," began Pithel. "You must return to your physical body. Your friend, Peter Stallings, is moments away from his return where he will be reunited with his family."

"Couldn't I just stay here with you? It's so incredible here. What would I have to do to be able to stay here, Pithel?"

"You have already been told what you must do, my friend." The mighty angel sighed as he stood in bright splendor. "The question you must ask is this: are you willing to take a step of faith and make a decision for your life? No one else makes the choice for you, John Robertson. Only you are capable of deciding where you will spend your eternity. It will either be here in the glorious realms of the Almighty God's heavenly kingdom or it will be in the dark torments of hell with Satan and all those who refuse the love of Jesus."

"I get it now, Pithel. I realize that I alone hold my eternal future in my hands." John thought about what he had just said. "That's really an awesome responsibility we as humans have. To be able to hold the power of life and death for all of eternity is incredible. To know even God cannot choose for us, but we ourselves must make the decision on our own." He turned to look Pithel square in the eyes with a new brightness in his own. "Well, except for some divine persuasion anyway."

Pithel bellowed with a laugh John had come to appreciate. It wasn't only laughter, but genuine joy coming from the heart of the warrior. The air grew serious as John spoke. "Pithel, I want to make the decision to give my life to Christ as soon as I'm back in that hospital room."

"That is wonderful news, brother," Pithel spoke with joy.

John realized that that was the first time Pithel had not called him by his full name. A smile crossed his lips and a mountain of joy flooded his soul as he realized he had already made the decision to follow Christ.

Pithel reached out and grabbed John Robertson's shoulders in his strong and powerful hands, but with a gentleness meant for an infant. "John

Robertson, I have genuinely had a wonderful time as we talked. Before you leave, I need to tell you one more thing. Give God your all. Hold nothing back from him. When you feel the world is destroying your soul, call to him and he will answer you. When all is going great in your life, praise him for his wonderful grace and mercy." Pithel wrapped his mighty arms around John and embraced him with brotherly love. "Good-bye my friend, my brother. I will see you soon, John Robertson."

"Good-bye, to you as well." John choked up with emotion. "Will I see again before I come to live here in heaven?"

"I do not know. Rest assured I will be as near as the Almighty allows me to be. He is very gracious and will most assuredly allow me to check on you every once in a while." He and John laughed one last time together, and then Pithel was gone.

CHAPTER 90

"Jack, come quick." An officer stuck his head in the door of the church and motioned for Jack to come outside.

"Excuse me," Jack said politely as he hurried out the door. The moment the door shut, Jack asked, "What is it? Has something happened?"

"I just got off the radio with dispatch. They told me Jimmy Morten called just a few miles from here. He has information about the bus station shootings."

"Did they send anybody over there yet?"

"Yeah, a deputy is heading there right now. I guess it's their jurisdiction. But we're cooperating, so it shouldn't be a problem. Do you want to go over there?"

"Yes, I do, Bill. Give me a second and I'll be ready to go." He turned back and stepped into the building and spoke to two officers. "Finish up and get him back to the station." They both nodded and turned to complete their interviews with the congregation. Jack closed the door of the car as Bill sped off toward the gas station.

Judy rubbed her wrists as soon as she freed them and then she helped the pastor. She frantically tore at the cords from his wrists with one eye glued to the back door of the house. As she loosened the cord, she thought about their escape route. A memory of when she and Jack had gone on a hike came to mind. She remembered his instructions on ways to keep as concealed from view as possible. "Stay low, go slow. Always watch your step and get into the tree line."

The cords fell from Pastor Troutman's wrists without much effort. "Okay, pastor, getting down the driveway will be the easy part, since it's a straight shot. From there, we'll just have to wing it."

"I'm ready whenever you are." The pastor had a determined look in his eye, one that said he would make it through this ordeal unscathed.

"Great. For now, keep an eye on the house in case they start coming out of here." Judy tried to remember the way out of where they were. She had only been able to get bits and pieces of directions from being tied up in the back of the van. The angle they sat in made it impossible to see over the dashboard in order to see where they had gone. She remembered them talking about a wrecked pickup truck. That would have to be their destination for now.

"Okay, pastor, we're going to quietly go out the side door. Head for those trees lining the driveway. We'll try to get back to where that pickup truck is wrecked. We'll figure out our next move after we get there."

She looked at Pastor Troutman and realized his age might prevent him from doing a lot of hard running, so she asked, "Do you think you can do this? It's going to get rough once we start running through the woods. And tougher once they realize we're gone."

Pastor Troutman nodded apprehensively, not giving Judy much faith. "Don't you worry about me," he snapped. "I may be old, but I can still do some running. I've been praying for the good Lord to give us strength. I believe my prayer will be answered. So let's get moving."

"Okay, but let me know if you need to rest," she said then added, "And I'll let you know if I need to stop." She reached for the side door handle, but stopped. "Open the door as quietly as you can, no squeaks. I'll be right back."

Judy ducked low as she made her way behind driver's seat. She raised her head just high enough as she looked for an object. With a sigh of relief, she slowly stretched her arm over the seat and grabbed the keys, still in the ignition.

The side door was open. Judy was impressed at not hearing any noise. She gave the pastor a 'thumbs up.'

As soon as she stepped out, Judy hurled the keys into the woods. She turned back to help the pastor, but he was gone. All she saw as she spun around was the bottom of his shoes as he had already made it to the treeline. She shook her head and smiled as she joined him a moment later.

They stayed low and moved slow between the thick trunks as they made the dangerous trek to the pickup. The distance between them and the men back at the house gave them some relief, but not enough to keep them from their destination. They moved toward the pickup truck down the driveway, being careful not to step on dry twigs or leaves. The rain from earlier in the day helped muffle the noise.

Like a cannon being fired, the back door of the house flew open and slammed into the back of the house. "Get down." Judy grabbed the back of Pastor Troutman's shirt and hauled him to the ground.

———◆———

William Benning stormed out of the house with a box in his arms. "You can stay here or leave. Your choice," he snapped.

Tom wasn't about to let Benning get away without a guarantee of him and Billy not being harmed. He wanted protection from Anti-Pro for their part back at the Central Station.

Benning shook his head and waved off Tom. That gesture only enraged Tom. Tom shouted, "Get back to the house, or I'll shoot you right now."

Benning ignored the command and walked toward the Lincoln. He slammed the trunk lid and went for the driver's door.

Tom fired. He barely missed William's head. Benning froze in his tracks.

———◆———

The pastor and Judy pressed themselves into the ground. Each thought the shot had been directed at them. Judy risked a glance over some foliage and saw Tom leap off the back steps and walk up to some man as he held the pistol out. "That must the one they called Benning," Judy whispered to the pastor. The pastor nodded.

They could hear Tom yell. "I'm not kidding Benning. Get back in the house right now or I'll kill you where you stand."

When Tom got closer to Benning, Judy tapped the pastor on the arm. "Time to move again." They eased deeper into the woods and stayed low. Sometimes they crawled in order to stay out of sight and not be spotted.

Pastor Troutman thought surely Judy could hear his heartbeat from both the exertion and fear. He said a brief prayer. "I'm sure I'll be praying quite a bit for the next little while," he thought.

———◆———

Behind the Lincoln, Benning lowered his head and sighed, "All right, all right, I'll go back in, but we must be gone in fifteen minutes. Do you understand? Fifteen minutes or we're all dead anyway. Believe me, it isn't me you should be worried about."

"What do you mean?" Billy asked. He moved right into William's face, and his hot, stale, breath made William turn his head as he gagged. "Just what do you mean we're all going to be dead in fifteen minutes?"

"And why shouldn't we be worried about you?" Tom added.

"Well, I'm relatively sure the police have heard from Jimmy. If that's the case, then he'll tell them where we are. So, within fifteen minutes, the police will swarm this place. We'll die trying to get away."

"They won't kill us," shouted Tom. "We've got hostages. We have some reporter woman and a holy man pastor. They won't risk shooting them so they won't shoot us either."

"May I suggest you bring them in here before the police get here and pin us in the house?" Benning's tone of voice told them he was still in charge.

"I suppose that's a good idea," Billy said. He made his way out the back door to get the hostages.

CHAPTER 91

Judy and Pastor Troutman cleared the first grove of trees and felt safer with that cushion blocking the view of the house. Both knew they had a long way to go before they were literally out of the woods.

"Pastor," Judy whispered loudly and pointed, "Let's go through here and then cut over to the main driveway. It'll keep us hidden a little longer. No one's coming after us so they don't know we're gone yet."

Pastor Troutman did his best to keep up with Judy. She ran like a scared rabbit going over and under trees and brush. He followed her through the thickest part of the trees. He ducked and dodged branches as they whipped back at him. Thorns grabbed at his pants and cut into his hands and legs. His lungs burned for air as they moved quicker and farther into the thick underbrush.

Judy cut around a fallen tree about twenty feet in front of Pastor Troutman and vanished from view for a moment. The pastor didn't see her reappear. She never did.

He hurried up to where he last saw her by the tree. He slid to a stop as he saw Judy had fallen to the ground and held her right ankle.

"Are you okay?"

"I don't know. I think it's just a sprain." She winced in pain as she rubbed the already swollen ankle. With her head she pointed and said, "Look over there."

The pastor saw two bodies sprawled in the woods. He nodded and sighed in recognition of the gruesome discovery. He then focused his attention on Judy and gently took hold of her ankle. Judy grimaced at the touch. It was twice its normal size. He feared the ankle might be broken. "We're going to have to make a splint," he said. He worked fast to find two sturdy branches which he placed on both sides of her ankle. With nothing to tie them with, he reached inside his pocket and took out his white, monogrammed handkerchief. He wrapped it tight around the leg and tied it in a knot. "It's not much, but it's all we've got," he said. "Do you think you can walk?"

He wasn't sure she heard had him when she gingerly stood up and tried to put some weight on the injury. She bit her lip as pain shot through her body. Somehow she managed to stay up. Her face turned ashen, and sweat dripped from her forehead as adrenalin pumped through her veins.

"Nothing's going to keep me here." Judy gritted with dogged determination. "Come on, pastor. We have some time to make up." They started out again, although much slower. Judy leaned on Pastor Troutman for support as he found strength to hold her up. Together they hobbled their way through the woods, Judy in pain as Pastor Troutman prayed.

CHAPTER 92

In Peter Stallings' hospital room, the alarms from the monitors went off once more.

"Not again," someone said. Nurses and doctors rushed in as before. Many thought he might have finally succumbed from his massive injury.

Deb Nolanski, back on duty, entered the room first. She stopped dead in her tracks. "How is this possible?"

The team of doctors and nurses stood in the doorway behind Deb. Shock and amazement was written on all their faces. No one could speak as eyes popped and mouths hung open.

In the corner of the room, June Stallings quietly stood to her feet and proclaimed, "This is a miracle from the Almighty God." She reached out to take her husband's hand as he reached out and took her hand. "Oh, Peter, I am so glad to see you."

He smiled the best he could as he looked into her deep brown eyes. He wanted to speak but the tube in his throat prevented him from doing so.

The doctors, who rushed to examine him, found it impossible to remain focused on their task at the sight of Peter not only awake but alert. They'd heard stories of people coming out of a coma seemingly in perfect health, but they never believed them to be true.

They found his heart-beat strong and normal. His lungs sounded healthy. Even his reflexes seemed normal. To their astonishment, he was in perfect health. Finally, Dr. Howard said, "This is one for the books. I can't find one thing wrong."

"It has to be a miracle. What else it could be?" asked Dr. Peterson. "Let's get that breathing tube out and check his head wound."

The nurses did as instructed. The entire staff stared at what they saw. No wound could be seen, just a small scar. The doctors and nurses scratched their heads. Some cried for joy as they stood with their mouths open. No one could believe any of this.

Finally Dr. Howard asked, "So, Mr. Stallings, did you have a near death experience? I mean the wound you sustained should have in, all actuality, killed you. Do you remember seeing any bright lights anywhere?"

Peter chuckled at the question. He answered with a voice weak from the tube and from not talking in several days. "No, Doctor, it wasn't a near death experience. I had a full life experience. I did see bright lights, however, and warm sunshine. I knew where I was the entire time. Would you like to know where I've been, doctor?"

"I most certainly would," Dr. Howard said as he pulled a chair over.

"Well, I'll be glad to tell you." Peter relived his time against the wall of heaven. "I met an angel named Jareb. He showed me things I thought I was doing right, when really I only pretended to do right."

He looked at June and squeezed her hand. Tears streamed down her cheeks and through her ear to ear smile.

"Oh June, things will be so much better now. I thought things had been good before, but now I know I was only playing church. It's time I gave my heart and soul to Christ."

The doctor didn't know what to say. He wanted to know what happened and Peter told him. "Hey, Doc," Peter spoke.

"Yes?"

"I need to go to John Robertson's room right away."

"I must recommend you stay in bed until you've fully recovered. We need to run tests to be sure you're well, physically and psychiatrically."

Peter huffed, "Do I look okay to you?" He turned to the assembled staff, who were still shocked, and said, "You just wait. There'll be another miracle before the day is done."

CHAPTER 93

Everything went by in a blur as Judy Metcalf and Pastor Troutman hobbled and stumbled through the woods. The pain in Judy's ankle increased as her adrenalin decreased. Pastor Troutman began to run out of steam.

"We have to fight through the pain and keep going, Pastor, or they'll find us."

They reached the wrecked pickup truck and took less than a second to see if someone might be inside. As they turned to continue on, they saw a trail. "Might as well follow it," Pastor Troutman said.

It was the same place William Benning had looked less than two hours ago. When Jimmy crawled through the woods, it hadn't been a trail, which is why Benning couldn't see it. To Judy and Pastor Troutman, the path stood out like a runway lined with lights. The narrow path shot straight forward and lead them away from the house.

"How're you doing?" Judy asked as they leaned against a tree for a moment. Her ankle throbbed with every beat of her heart.

Pastor Troutman bent at the waist with his hands on his knees as he sucked in air. He raised his right arm and gave Judy the "OK" sign with his thumb and index finger.

"We have to keep moving," she said. He nodded and eased his arm around her to take the weight off of her ankle.

———◆———

Tom held the gun on Benning as Billy went to get the hostages from the van. "You're not about to leave us here while you run off some place safe in your fancy car," Tom shouted. He wasn't a quiet person to begin with. Today he was louder than usual.

The telephone rang. Benning made a move to go to his desk to answer it. Tom held the gun right to his head. "I have to answer it, or they'll become

266

suspicious, which would make them send their people out here. We don't want them doing that." Tom hated the way Benning talked down to him, but also knew he was right about the call. He motioned with the pistol for him to answer the call.

Benning picked up the receiver, "Hello?"

Tom couldn't hear whoever spoke on the other end of the line.

"Yes, sir, they brought the hostages here." There was a pause as Benning listened. "No, one of the men is right next to me with his gun pointed at my head."

More silence.

Billy crashed through the door, eyes wide with panic. He tried to talk, but Tom stopped him with a nod at Benning on the phone. Billy, filled with nervous tension, bounced up and down.

"Yes, sir, I know what happens if we get caught. We're leaving here as soon as we clean up the loose ends with the hostages."

Billy tried to interrupt again. Tom shook his head to stop him.

Another long silence as Benning received the final instructions from the heads of Anti-Pro. "Yes, sir, I understand. Your orders will be carried out to the fullest." He replaced the receiver into the cradle.

As soon as he set the phone down, Billy exploded with his news, "They're gone, Tommy."

"What do you mean, 'gone'? They're not in the van?"

"No, they got loose and they're gone."

Tom's shoulders slumped as he let out a heavy sigh. He stared at the floor as he tried to think of a solution to their newest problem. The stress became unbearable. He stopped and pointed the gun at Benning and yelled, "Get out there and find them."

Benning, surprised by the demand, could only ask, "What?"

"You heard me. Get out there and find our hostages. You're the only one here who knows the woods, which means you're the only one who can find them. Now get moving or you know what I'll do."

"Oh, all right," Benning pouted. "But I'll have you know that I couldn't find Jimmy and I assure you I won't be able to find your hostages today. If you insist on finding them, however, I'll show where I think they might have gone."

They headed out the door and ventured back into the woods. Benning went right to the pickup. He had brought them right by the bodies of Bob and Elaine.

"What happened here?" Billy stood over the body of Elaine, whom he had met prior to the Central Station incident.

"Insubordination is not tolerated," Benning sneered.

"You worthless piece of garbage," Tom said through gritted teeth. "You'll get yours soon enough."

Benning dismissed the words with a wave of his hand. "I'm sure they went this way. As you can see there's no trail to follow."

CHAPTER 94

As Jack McDougal rode in the squad car to Jimmy Morten's location, he considered what life might be like without Judy. He wouldn't allow himself to believe she had been or would be killed. His years doing police work, however, told him otherwise. In almost every case he had investigated, especially where people had been abducted, more times than not, the victims were found…he would not allow himself to finish the thought.

He attempted to focus his attention on the scenery scrolling past the unmarked car, his mind swirling with thoughts and prayers. Their last conversation looped through his head. "How about I just have the hearse swing by the church on the way to my final resting place?" Jack asked himself questions like, "Was she being prophetic?" "Could I have done more?" "How could I have told her about Jesus in a better way?"

Jack's heart sank when he thought of all his years as a follower of Christ he couldn't persuade the one person he truly loved to even consider the possibility of accepting Jesus.

The only thing he knew to do at moments like this was to pray. He prayed for peace within his own soul.

The story of Jesus sleeping in the back of the boat while his disciples battled the storm came to his mind. He remembered the disciples woke Jesus up to ask him if he cared they were going to die. What Jesus said then made Jack think now. 'O ye of little faith,' Jesus had said and then said, 'Peace, be still.' Jack had always wondered why Jesus had said 'peace, be still' and not 'wind, be still'?

As he meditated on this, the answer came. Sometimes peace gets pretty rough. He remembered singing 'I've got peace like a river' in Sunday School which got him thinking about rivers. Rivers aren't always smooth and tranquil; they have rapids and falls along the way and sometimes they flood over their banks. Jack felt momentary relief as the Lord revealed the answer to his question. His life, like a river, was going to have places along the way that are filled with turmoil and strife and problems, but during these rough times Jesus would be there as his lifeboat.

Bill Owens, who drove the car, noticed when Jack took a deep breath and then sighed. Bill asked, "You all right, boss?"

Jack turned to look at Bill and told him, "I am now, thanks. How much farther?"

"I think we're less than five miles out."

CHAPTER 95

At the gas station, Jimmy stayed hidden behind the old rusted ice storage container on the north side of the building. There was a sliver of space between the machine and the building for him to be able to see down the road. After he made the phone call, time seemed to stand still. He was sure William Benning would find him long before the police got to him.

A county deputy was the first to arrive at the abandoned gas station. Deputy Kevin Mallory stepped out of the squad car and cautiously surveyed the area. Jimmy saw him and yelled out, "I'm over here behind the ice container."

Officer Mallory drew his service revolver. "Let me see your hands."

Jimmy tried to comply with the order, but failed. "I'm injured and can't move very fast. I'm not armed. Two days ago I was." He slowly crawled out from behind the ice container.

Deputy Mallory stepped over to Jimmy and put him in handcuffs. He then read Jimmy his rights and told him he shouldn't say anything else until his attorney was present.

Jimmy replied, "I know what my rights are, but I've done some terrible things I need to pay for. Since the shootings I've gone through even rougher times and I made some better decisions. No, sir, I don't think I'll wait for an attorney. I confess to the shootings at the bus station."

Just as he finished his confession, Bill Owens and Jack McDougal pulled into the gravel parking lot. Deputy Kevin Mallory informed Jack of how he found Jimmy and his confession to the shootings in Grand Rapids. Jack thanked the deputy and took over from that point.

Jack walked over to Jimmy Morten sitting next to the gas station wall. He said, "An ambulance is on the way for your medical treatment. You will then be transported back to Grand Rapids. While we're waiting, I need to ask you some questions about the shootings."

Jimmy nodded his head. "Anything you want, sir. I want to cooperate with you to the fullest. As I told the deputy, I realize now what I've done."

"Thanks, Jimmy. I'll be sure to put your cooperation in my report."

Jack pulled out his notepad before asking his questions. "Did you act alone or are there others involved?"

"There are others. I'm part of a group known as Anti-Pro. In fact, right through those woods over there," he directed Jack with a nod of his head, "is the man responsible for setting up everything I did. His name is William Benning. I don't know who he works for, but I know he's not the top man. You can get there by going around to the dirt road about a half a mile up the highway. It's a very narrow driveway, and you should see my wrecked pickup truck about halfway up the drive. Follow it up to the house. That's William Benning's house or command post."

Jack turned to Deputy Mallory, "Kevin, call that in to your boys and have them check it out."

"Yes, sir."

Jack turned back to Jimmy, "Is there anything else?"

"Yes, sir, there is," Jimmy stammered. "I don't exactly know how to tell you this, but, well, I think I had an angel watching out for me."

"What do you mean?"

"When I left the house I drove my pickup truck as fast as I dared go. I felt something horrible, like an evil presence, come over me. That's when I ran my truck into the tree."

Jimmy's face softened as he continued, "Somehow I managed to get out of the truck and crawl through the woods. I know my left leg is broken and a few ribs are too. When I got about halfway through the woods, Benning and his two assistants, Bob and Elaine, came after me. I don't know how they missed me, sir. They were literally right on top of me and should've killed me right there. But they couldn't see me. It's not like I could hide and I left an easy trail to follow. I mean, come on, I'm belly crawling through the woods."

"What happened next?"

"I remember praying. I told God I'd never prayed before, but if he'd protect me from these people I would start. That's when a strange feeling came over me, and I felt peace. A little while later all three came back out to look for me. Benning was angry because they couldn't find me. Then I heard a gunshot, a scream, and then another shot. After that it got very quiet for a moment. Then Benning started shouting, 'Come on out Jimmy, I won't hurt you. I need to talk to you.' The more he yelled the angrier he sounded. A minute later, he walked away."

Jimmy looked up at Jack, "I'm sure you'll find the bodies of Bob and Elaine in the woods near the truck."

Within twenty minutes the ambulance arrived to transport Jimmy to a hospital. Deputy Mallory agreed to escort the ambulance and remain with Jimmy during the process.

Jack motioned for Bill Owens to follow him into the woods. "We need to hurry before the sun goes down." They reached the edge of the woods where Jack tried to find the trail Jimmy had adamantly talked about. With all of his training, Jack couldn't find the path.

He turned to Bill. "You see any kind of path?"

"I can't say that I do, Jack. Are we in the right place?"

"I'm sure this is where he pointed," Jack snapped. He took a half step deeper into the tree line and froze. He thought he heard rustling in the brush. He whispered, "Did you hear that?"

"Maybe," Bill whispered back.

"Let's check it out."

Both men rested their hands on their revolvers, ready to draw and fire if necessary. Carefully they made their way into the woods. They stayed hidden behind the trees to not give anyone a drop on them. They moved methodically and deliberately, leapfrogging from tree to tree to cover each other. They made as little noise as possible.

The sound, somewhere in the woods, grew louder. A rhythm became evident with two distinct sets of sounds; a heavy step followed by a light step, almost a hop. Another noise sounded slower and heavier, but they kept pace with each other. Whoever or whatever came their way would have to come over a small incline before Jack and Bill would see them.

Jack and Bill used hand signals, telling each other what they were going to do. They would hold their ground until they crested the hill. They each drew their guns as they stood ready.

The two distinct sounds grew louder as they moved closer to the opening. Jack and Bill tensed up but remained steady. Guns trained on the top of the incline.

A heavy step and a light step followed by a slower, heavier step.

Suddenly a man's voice shattered the silence. "I know you're out here. I'm gonna find you." The voice carried through the trees far enough away to not be whoever neared the opening.

CHAPTER 96

Judy reached out and grabbed hold of a small tree with one hand. With the other, she reached back and pulled Pastor Troutman up next to her. Normally, such a climb wouldn't be a problem for either, but today with a broken ankle and an exhausted elderly man, it seemed impossible.

When the pastor got next to her, she then pushed him over the top of the incline.

Jack and Bill stood with their weapons trained on the old man but didn't fire or say anything yet. The man didn't appear to be a threat, especially in the condition he appeared to be in. The officers stayed in their positions behind the trees until both people came over the hill. They remained steadfast and vigilant as to what might come next.

Judy used her last ounce of strength to finish the climb. With one last burst of energy, she managed to throw herself over the top. She landed on Pastor Troutman's legs, who let out a soft groan. Neither moved any further, totally exhausted.

For an instant what Jack saw didn't register. He shook his head and blinked as he realized he looked down at the back of Judy's head. He put his gun into the holster as he called out, "Judy, you're alive."

"Jack? Jack is that you?" She thought she had become delusional.

"It's me," he said. He stayed focused knowing danger was still present and didn't allow his emotions to take over. "Bill, help me get these two out of here."

Bill hurried over, carefully picked up the older man, and set him behind a larger tree a few yards away. Jack stayed right behind him with Judy in tow.

"Do you know who's chasing you?" Jack asked Judy.

"The men from the bus station," Judy's voice was weak. "Some other man too."

"Okay. Judy, I need you to stay here while we go get them. Their party's over."

"We're not going anywhere. You just follow the path we were on, and it'll lead you right to them."

Jack stood up with a puzzled look, "What path?" He didn't wait for an explanation. He had three criminals to capture who he'd chased for the past two days.

The officers went back to their same positions at the top of the incline. The men's voices grew louder. Jack signaled to Bill with three fingers up followed by a fist which indicated they were approximately thirty yards away. Jack and Bill imitated the sound Judy and the pastor had made to lead the men to them.

It worked. Shushing noises could be heard, but they made plenty of noise with their feet. They closed in on the top of the hill. Billy reached the top first and ran past Jack and right to Officer Owens, who yanked him behind a tree and put his revolver on his forehead. He quickly handcuffed Billy and threw him on the ground.

Tom, who walked arrogantly, crested the hill. Jack waited for him to pass then apprehended him. Tom felt the barrel of Jack's pistol on the back of his head and immediately put his hands up.

Jack ordered, "Put down your gun and your hands behind your head slowly." He complied without a fight. Jack handcuffed him and set him behind another tree just as William Benning stepped over the top. Neither Jack nor Bill waited for him to pass. They stepped out from behind the trees with their guns trained on the rotund man. Benning's face flushed white as he fainted. He fell to the ground in a heap, where Jack cuffed him.

Moments later, after reviving Benning with a couple taps to the face, Bill led the trio out of the woods. Jack helped Judy and Pastor Troutman. Minutes later, they gathered at the small gas station where several law enforcement officers waited.

Officers read the men their rights before being placed in the back of separate cars for the trip back to the county jail in Grand Rapids. An ambulance was in route for Judy and Pastor Troutman.

"Jack," Judy called out. She felt stronger after she drank some water and ate some granola from one of the officers.

"Yes, Judy?"

"Would you mind if I went to church with you this Sunday?"

"Okay, where's Judy, and what have you done to her?" Jack teased.

"One more thing," she said. "Guess what I did while I was with Pastor Troutman?" She didn't give Jack a chance to answer. "I accepted Jesus into my heart. Surprise."

The news turned out to be the crack that broke the dam of Jack's emotions. He held Judy in his arms, oblivious to anything and anyone around them. Nearby, Pastor Troutman let out a few tears of his own. *"These are the moments I live for."*

The ambulance arrived on the scene. The EMTs worked to get Judy and the pastor the medical treatment they needed before they were ready for transport. Jack stood next to Judy as she was placed on the gurney and slid into the back of the ambulance.

"I promise I'll be at the hospital as soon as I can," Jack said.

"I'm holding you to that." Judy pulled him close for a final kiss before the doors closed.

The ambulance drove away carefully to avoid the ruts in the muddy road.

Jack couldn't get the smile to come off his face. He had reasons to celebrate. Judy had been found alive, with injuries, but nothing life threatening. Through the ordeal she had come to accept Christ as her savior. Amy Tuinstra had also survived being abducted. To top it all off, the shooter at the Central Station had turned himself in and the three men along with their leader had been captured.

CHAPTER 97

Near eight o'clock in the evening at St. John's Hospital, the nurses prepped Peter for his move out of the Intensive Care Unit. The entire staff continued to be stupefied and amazed by the miraculous recovery. They struggled to not only believe Peter had survived the gunshot wound but would live a normal life. Less than an hour from coming out the coma, he felt, as he put it, "Better than ever."

The word of Peter's recuperation traveled around the entire building, like a wild fire on dry grass. Nurses from all over the hospital came down to see the one dubbed The Miracle Man. They had to see for themselves how this man had gone from near death to a complete and full recovery. The visits were brief to allow Peter the privacy he needed as he talked with his wife.

"You're going to think I've gone crazy."

"You just try me." June's cheeks hurt from the permanent smile on her face.

Peter talked about his time next to the wall of heaven where he met the angel. He told her he realized he'd been playing church but not truly living the life. "Everything has changed, June. I'm giving all I have to Christ for the rest of my life."

He took her hand and held it tight as he looked deep into her eyes. "June, thank you for being my wife. I love you so much." As they embraced each other, the tears streaming down their cheeks ran together forming one tear.

"I love you too, Peter. It's good to have you back."

Peter suddenly pulled back and grabbed June by the arms. The quick move scared her. His brow furrowed as he said, "We have to get to Paul. He's been facing some tough situations and could end up in trouble. If we're not there for him, he could end up making the wrong choices."

He looked away into the corner of the room, "You know, June, I never realized how much pressure Paul is under. He's been hanging around some boys who aren't good for him, not because he likes them, but because they're there for him. I'm telling you right here and now that I'm going to be there for our son. I know you've been praying for him like I have, but I'm going to put my feet to my prayer. I'm going to trust God for his guidance on this."

June couldn't speak as she held on to Peter. She couldn't find the words, and her throat felt too restricted from her emotions to be able to talk. The Stallings' family would be a different household from this point on.

CHAPTER 98

Jimmy Morten had been transported to St. John's Hospital where the doctors treated his fractured leg, three broken ribs, some lacerations, and exposure to the elements. Two police officers handcuffed one of Jimmy's wrists to the side of the bed then went to stand guard outside the room. No one without proper identification and authorization would be allowed to enter the room.

Through all the turmoil and pain, however, Jimmy held up well. He had accepted responsibility for his actions. Even knowing what would happen as soon as he healed up, his spirits were high and his soul felt at peace. The media had been kept in the dark about the whereabouts of the shooter in order to protect him and to respect the victims.

The police would give a statement to the press after all the loose ends of the case were wrapped up, which included all the hostages and other victims being cared for. It was the primary responsibility of the police to make sure the prisoner was safe and taken care of medically. They were determined to let justice take its proper place in this case.

Jack McDougal made one promise to Judy Metcalf. WGRT would get an exclusive story, since many of the victims involved in the shootings and abductions came from the station. He would have to give a statement to the rest of the press corps assembled in the conference room of the hospital. The statement would be kept simple and to the point with just enough information to let them write their stories. The rest of the story would come from Judy, Peter, and John as they wrote their reports.

With the press conference completed, Jack made his way up to Judy's room. They talked about everything that had happened. Judy, who hours earlier had gone through such a terrible ordeal, seemed to have way too much energy. She talked a mile a minute without taking a breath. She had too much to tell.

"It was so scary." She grabbed his arm with a strong grip. "They kept chasing us through the woods. I was more worried about Pastor Troutman than for myself. I mean I might've been able to hold them off for a while, but he was looking so frail out there."

Jack finally held up his hands to stop her. "Judy, I really do want to hear all about what happened, but right now you really should get some rest."

"But, Jack, I'm so excited about what happened. I finally realized what you've been trying to tell me all this time. When I was in the back of that van talking with the pastor, I realized what I needed. That's when I asked Christ into my heart. Ever since, I've had this sense of strength and peace I've never felt before. I know I'm rambling on and on. It's just that I can't stop talking about it."

Jack laughed for the first time since the crime spree started. He leaned in close to her, giving her a gentle kiss. "Judy Metcalf, you really do amaze me. And that's why I love you so much."

"Jack?"

"Yes?"

"You never answered my question."

"Which one?"

"Will you take me to church with you this Sunday?"

"You know I will."

CHAPTER 99

"What's wrong, Peter?" June looked into the face of her husband's puzzled face.

"I have to go see John," he said as he threw the sheet off his legs. "Help me get out of the bed. I think I can walk on my own, but I'd love to have you with me. Something incredible is about to happen, and you have to see it to believe it."

"Are you sure you should be doing this?" She was concerned he would fall after being in the bed for so long.

"I'm sure. Please help me." She grabbed hold of his arm as he swung his legs off the bed. As soon as he unhooked the wires, alarms began to sound. The staff ran into the room, knowing for sure the miracle just ended.

Before they could get into the room, Peter and June strolled out arm in arm without a care in the world. They greeted the staff gathered in the hall. Peter said, "I have to get to John Robertson's room. Please don't try to stop me." The nurses, doctors and other staff made a path, while some followed along. Most mouths fell open still amazed at what they witnessed.

"Even Doubting Thomas believed eventually," June whispered in Peter's ear.

In the Intensive Care Unit at St. John's Hospital, Peter hung onto his wife's arm and walked into John's room. The full entourage of staff followed them. None of the staff knew what to expect but didn't want to miss whatever was about to happen. Although they had plenty of skepticism, after seeing two miracles in one day, within minutes they would see another miracle.

As they entered the room, a nurse had just replaced the IV bag. She also checked all the vital signs. She was engrossed in her work as she wrote the information in his chart. Finally looking up, she saw Peter and June in the room.

A smile pressed on her lips. "I've worked here for ten years and every one of the people here with injuries like yours have never left alive, let alone up and walk. It is so refreshing to see you're not only alive, but you are fully recovered. It's absolutely amazing."

Peter smiled humbly as he stood next to John's bed. More staff continued to cram into the room. As John remained in a coma, Peter took his hand and said a short, silent prayer. The nurse still talked and never noticed John's head slightly shaking from side to side. His right hand twitched as he moaned quietly. Peter noticed it, however, and he pointed for the nurse to see. He asked, "Would you like to see another miracle today?"

The machines that monitored his vitals changed their rhythm. The doctors and nurses noticed his heartbeat grew stronger as did his breathing. The entire staff stared in unbelief at John Robertson as his eyes blinked open. He looked like he wanted to speak, but the breathing tube prevented that.

Doctor Howard came over and gently removed the tube. He stood astonished as John breathed on his own.

"It's good to see you again, Peter," John said in a weak voice. "Are you as well as you look?"

"I am, John. It's good to see you too." Peter's face shone with a bright smile. "I feel like I'm supposed to be here, but not just to show the staff how you've been healed. Perhaps you could tell me the reason I'm supposed to be here right now."

"I believe I can tell you." He pointed to the chairs and suggested Peter and his wife sit down. "I really don't know how long this will take." Peter and June sat in the chairs next to the bed and waited.

Other doctors walked in and saw John Robertson sitting up and talking. They scratched their heads and threw their hands in the air. One of the doctors was overheard saying, "Why did I even bother going to medical school?"

"I told you there would be another miracle today." Peter couldn't help himself with the *"I told you so"* comment.

After a twenty minute examination the doctors left the room, baffled. Some of the staff passed it off as something to do with the star alignment. Others didn't know what to think. Only a few believed a miracle had taken place at St. John's Hospital.

After they all filed out, Peter and June moved the chairs to the bedside and waited for John to tell them why they were here. John took a drink of water and a deep breath before he spoke.

In his heart, Peter knew what was about to take place. He remembered the story of Jesus walking on the road to Jericho when a blind man shouted for Jesus to have mercy on him. The crowd tried to keep the man quiet but he shouted even louder, "Jesus, Son of David, have mercy on me." Jesus stopped and asked that the man be brought to him. The people who stood close by the blind man led him to Jesus and put him directly in front of him. Jesus then asked, "What would you like me to do for you?"

The blind man replied, "I want to receive my sight."

Jesus, then, simply said, "Go your way; your faith has made you whole." Immediately the blind man received his sight.

Peter brought his attention back to John, who said, "Peter, I would like to accept Christ into my life. Would you pray with me?"

"I would be honored to pray with you, my brother."

John's emotions overtook him, but he managed a smile at being called brother by Peter. It sounded just like Pithel before he came back to the hospital bed. Joy overwhelmed him as he closed his eyes.

John asked God to forgive him and asked Jesus into his heart. The prayer was simple, but heartfelt. It also gave John a new life.

When he said "Amen," Peter swore he heard a choir singing in celebration. John's eyes filled with tears of joy and relief. June dabbed at her eyes as she smiled at yet another miracle at the hospital.

Doctor Howard returned a short time later. He asked John about his near death experience. He got the same answer Peter had given him earlier.

"I just don't know how that's possible," he mumbled as he walked out of the room.

Two of the nurses came into the room after everyone else had left. Deb, the head nurse, asked tentatively, "We have to know: did you really see angels?"

John smiled as he answered, "Ladies, let me tell you about angels." He proceeded to tell them the entire story while Peter added bits and pieces along the way. Both Deb and Rebecca left the room with the promise to return to find out more.

Peter told John he thought he had heard music when he finished praying. He asked John if he heard it.

"I heard it," John said. "It's the same music I heard while talking with Pithel. That's the angel who talked with me."

"So that's celebration music for when someone gives their life to Christ," Peter said. He smiled and hugged June.

A woman slipped into the room unnoticed as the three celebrated the new birth of John Robertson. The woman's face had striking features with bright eyes and a button nose but also looked worn down from what life had brought her.

John finally looked up and saw her by the door. A puzzled look crossed his face as he saw something about her he recognized. He couldn't place where he knew her from. "Do I know you from somewhere?"

The woman walked slowly over to the foot of the bed where she stopped and said, "We grew up together."

John's mouth dropped open as the recognition of who she was hit him. He couldn't believe who he was seeing. "Jennifer," he whispered. "How long has it been since I last saw you? Fifteen, twenty years? How on earth did you find me?"

"Well, it's kind of a strange story," she stated.

"Trust me, nothing you say will sound strange today."

"This morning, I left my lunch on the kitchen counter. I never do that. I hurried home to eat. As soon as I sat at the table, the doorbell rang. It scared me a little." She moved around from the foot of the bed as she continued, "When I looked out the window, I saw this huge man on the doorstep looking directly at me. He was dressed nicely and looked gentle enough, so against my better judgment, I opened the door. When I did he said a brother John Robertson was at St. John's Hospital who wished to see me."

"Pithel," was all John could say.

"You're the only John Robertson I've ever known. Anyway, I called my supervisor and told her I needed to come to the hospital. And here I am." She put her arms around his neck and embraced him. "Oh, John, I've missed you for such a long time. I thought I would never see you again, other than on TV."

Peter and June enjoyed the moment as the two renewed their friendship. June leaned over and said, "How many more miracles will there be today?" She grabbed Peter's hand as she said, "Let's give these two some alone time. I want some of that with you anyway."

Peter gave John's hand one last squeeze as he headed for the door. John turned back to Jennifer.

"Tell me," John said quizzically, "the man who came to your door, did he by chance laugh?"

"As a matter of fact, he did laugh. It was a loud and boisterous laugh. I would have been annoyed by it if he wasn't being so polite to me."

"I suppose he didn't tell you his name, did he?"

"No. But he did say you would be able to figure it out, seeing how you are a reporter." Jennifer looked at John, who seemed to have gone to another place. "Do you know him?"

"I think it's safe to say we've met," John quipped. "I'm afraid that if I told you who he was, you might leave and not come back. You'd think I'm some kind of a lunatic," John said while his finger drew circles around his temple.

"You would be surprised at what I might believe today, John."

"Hey, that's my line." John took her hand because he wanted to hold it and because he didn't want her to leave. "Remember I warned you."

"I'm ready," she said.

John took a deep breath as he said, "The man who came to your door, Jennifer, was an angel." He scrunched up his face as he waited for her reaction. When she didn't roll her eyes or try to pull her hand away, he continued.

He told her the entire story from being shot to having just received Christ into his life moments before she arrived.

"I'm so happy for you, John," Jennifer said. "After all these years, you've finally come to know Christ. Only I feel ashamed that I haven't stayed in touch with God like I should've been doing. I just started going to church again and reading my Bible. I've messed up my life too."

"Well," John exclaimed, "maybe we can learn about God together. I know I'm going to need someone to tutor me. How about you and I get together with Peter and his wife after we get out of here?"

"I would like that very much, John. I would really like that."

CHAPTER 100

Amy Tuinstra gave her statement to the police officer. Her parents came into the hospital room, faces filled with joy and relief as they hugged and kissed Amy. They were grateful to God for bringing their daughter home.

Amy gave her parents an overview of the whole story. Then she told them the strangest yet the best part she went through. "You know what sticks out the most in my mind? It was that they would always hit Judy, but they couldn't seem to touch me. They tried, but they just couldn't harm me."

She quickly added, if only for her own peace of mind, "Not that I wanted Judy to get hurt. For some reason they wouldn't, or couldn't, put their hands on me. They tied me up, but they didn't hit me."

"What do you mean?" her dad asked.

"Well, they tied us to trees in the middle of nowhere. Then one of them hit Judy and knocked her out again. When he tried to hit me, he missed. Instead he hit the tree and broke his arm. The way he hit the tree was like he had been redirected. I say that because I know God protected me."

She continued to analyze what had happened. "They could've taken anyone from the bus station, but God chose to let them take me. I think it's because I'm protected by his almighty hand. He wouldn't allow anything to happen to me. To someone else in the bus station though, they might not have been given the same protection. It's difficult to say this, but I thank God I was able to go through this."

A doctor walked into the room and said, "Well, Amy, it looks like everything checked out great. There's no reason for you to stay here any longer. If anything were to change for you, feel free to either call or come on back in. For now, you're free to go home."

St. John's Hospital had celebrations all over the place, from the ER to the ICU. People cried, praised, laughed, and healed. Some did all at the same time.

———————◆◆———————

Two days later the theme music for the evening news played. "Good evening. Welcome to WGRT news. I'm your anchor, John Robertson…"

EPILOGUE

The celebration continued throughout the realms of the heavenly kingdom. The angels joined with the choirs as the orchestras played. All the saints in the kingdom praised God for the great and awesome display of his love to mankind.

The celebration was interrupted by none other than Satan, who ranted and raved outside the gate once again. "Why doesn't he allow me to enter? Tell him to let me into the Kingdom at once."

The guards stood fast with spears crossed. Satan knew better than to try to break through. Even with his power, he would be no match for these two guards who now had the power of God with them while they stood guard.

"Why does he always make me wait out here? He knows I must speak with him. I have urgent business with your Master and must not be detained any longer. Now, let me in this instant."

The more he carried on, the more child-like he became. He didn't get his way and now he threw a tantrum, thinking that would get him before the throne quicker. But Satan still waited.

Finally, a messenger came to the gate and spoke with the guards. They lifted their spears and allowed Satan to enter. He moved with a very arrogant and indignant attitude as he made his way to the throne room of the Almighty God.

In the throne room, Pithel and Jareb bowed, along with the twenty-four elders, and gave praise and worship to God, who created them and allowed them to do his bidding. The large beasts flew around, "Holy, holy, holy, Lord God Almighty, who was, and is, and is to come."

Thunder sounded from the throne. Pithel and Jareb stood up with their heads still bowed as their Master spoke to them. They were given rewards for the mission accomplished with a victory for God. As they received their rewards, they placed them at the feet of Jesus. Jesus placed one hand on each of the angels and praised them for a job well done.

Satan burst through the doors, anger on his face as he marched to the front of the room. He pointed a finger at the two angels and shouted, "How dare you take my souls. Those were my souls you have given to God and I want them back."

Loud thunder crashed that stopped Satan's tirade.

Pithel turned to Satan and, spoke as a warrior, but with a touch of meekness, "Those souls you refer to made their choice of their own free will. They chose the Almighty God and the love of Jesus. You have lost them, Lucifer. They now belong to Jesus."

Satan glared at Pithel with narrowed eyes and vowed to curse him. He paced back and forth thinking about his next move. He knew violence in the throne room wouldn't be tolerated. He was also positive God wouldn't allow any curse to exist in his presence.

He stopped and stood directly before the throne. Those worshiping continue even when Satan raised a finger and drew in a quick breath as if ready to speak, but shook his head and turned away. Finally, after a brief thought, he let out an evil scream, "I will be victorious next time. I vow to take your precious souls with me to the pits of hell." He turned and stormed out of the room.

The music played on with their melodious strains of praise without missing a beat. The beasts flew through the throne room, their voices raised in worship. The elders bowed their heads as they cast their crowns before the Almighty God.

Pithel and Jareb bowed their heads as they had been given leave from the throne room. As they walked out of the Creator's presence and the doors began to shut, they heard thunder call out another warrior to step forward for a mission. The two angels stood in the hall and embraced as brothers, "To the Glory of the Most High God." They then parted and went their separate ways.

Pithel contemplated his mission as he flew quietly outside of the walls. "The Lord won a great victory today."

He sat on the hillside where he had met John Robertson. "The saints must remain vigilant and strong, always watching, always praying. They must keep their faith in God. I pray for those who do not know the love of God to not delay in making a decision."

Pithel saw one of his fellow warriors leave the heavenly realm. "Another battle begins now."

The End

CPSIA information can be obtained at www.ICGtesting.com
Printed in the USA
LVOW11s0426220915

455185LV00001B/78/P